EVERYTHING
YOU
HAVE

Kate Ruby is a pseudonym for an award-winning TV drama producer and screenwriter. Her previous novel, *Tell Me Your Lies*, was a Richard and Judy Book Club pick in 2022 and is now in development for TV with a major US network after a fierce bidding war for the rights. *Everything You Have* is already under option for the screen. Kate balances her writing career alongside her work as an executive producer, with recent credits including *The Girl Before* for the BBC and HBO and *The Flatshare* for Paramount Plus.

KATE RUBY

EVERYTHING YOU HAVE

SIMON &
SCHUSTER

London · New York · Sydney · Toronto · New Delhi

First published in Great Britain by Simon & Schuster UK Ltd, 2024

1 3 5 7 9 10 8 6 4 2

Simon & Schuster UK Ltd
1st Floor
222 Gray's Inn Road
London WC1X 8HB

Simon & Schuster: Celebrating 100 Years of Publishing in 2024

Simon & Schuster Australia, Sydney
Simon & Schuster India, New Delhi

www.simonandschuster.co.uk
www.simonandschuster.com.au
www.simonandschuster.co.in

A CIP catalogue record for this book
is available from the British Library

Paperback ISBN: 978-1-3985-0028-0
eBook ISBN: 978-1-3985-0029-7
Audio ISBN: 978-1-3985-2878-9

Typeset in Sabon by M Rules

Printed and Bound in the UK using 100% Renewable
Electricity at CPI Group (UK) Ltd

MIX
Paper | Supporting
responsible forestry
FSC® C171272

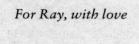

For Ray, with love

The howl emanating from somewhere deep in the undergrowth sounds like someone being brutally murdered. I startle as my gloved hand jiggles the lock, the key on the other side rattling against the doorframe, the sound loud in my ears. An amorous fox, I've identified the cry now, but the shock is enough to momentarily break me out of my trance. To make me realise how foolhardy it is for me to be here, in the dark of the night, trying to inveigle my way into the house. But the problem is, I've come too far. I've burnt my life to ashes, and the only way to salvage anything from the wreckage is by proving that someone else lit the match.

A minute later, I've finally succeeded, forcing the key from the lock with the paper clip I've found in my handbag. It tinkles as it hits the tiled floor, every sound magnified to my straining ears. I take a gulp of air, try my best to squat on the ground next to the cat flap, the tight dome of my pregnant belly agonizingly squashed between my knees and chin. Losing my balance, I roll backwards and land on the cold ground, my hand cradling my precious bump. If I FaceTimed Steve now, showed him the depths I've sunk to, could we laugh together? Would it prove to him how sincerely I want to make up for what I've done?

No, I think, pushing myself awkwardly back up onto my heels. It would simply confirm to him that his wife is a delusional sociopath, and his decision to walk away from me – from us – was the only one he could make. The sole way to convince him I'm not who he thinks I am is with cold, hard facts. With the evidence I'm convinced I'll find in her bedroom if I can only manage to get inside.

I use my own keys for the next part, sliding them along the rim of the cat flap, working my way past the magnet that's meant to keep it firmly shut against feline invaders. The manufacturers clearly didn't give enough thought to forty-something women with a taste for vengeance. Before long I've made it through, the twin rings on my left hand, which I stubbornly refuse to take off, scraping against the plastic door as my fingers scrabble on the cold floor, grasping desperately for that key.

Finally my palm is wrapped around it, the metal spikes cutting into my flesh. I struggle upwards, lean against the wall to try to catch my breath. I push the key into the lock, holding it still for a final second. This is my last chance to turn back, to stay a professional woman with a chaotic personal life, instead of a crazy person in danger of being sent to prison.

I startle as a siren's wail cuts through the quiet. The lights inside are still off, but the houses are packed tight on this terrace, plenty of windows overlooking the tiny square of garden. There's no guaranteeing a neighbour hasn't called the police on me by now. I turn the key to the right, vowing to myself that I'll be quick. I left the sane version of Sasha behind too many weeks ago to snatch it back now. This person, the one I barely recognize, is the only one who has any hope of rescuing me now.

It's time to see if I can win.

ONE YEAR EARLIER

JENNA

Cheese. A sweaty, shiny lump poked out from under the fridge like a fungal toenail. Jenna forced herself to look away before the girl – Penelope, a name she couldn't quite believe was for real – could follow her eyeline. The last thing she needed was for her potential new flatmate to catch her judging her hygiene standards.

'It's gorgeous!' she sang, looking around the dingy kitchen, wincing at the sound of Stoke-on-Trent pushing out of her vowels. She wanted to sound like she belonged here, like she'd be able to blend into North London as well as any wild animal released into a new habitat.

'Thanks!' said Penelope, as proud as a queen in her castle. 'We really love it.'

She said 'thanks' like it started with an F, as though she'd wandered here from Albert Square, but Jenna was savvy enough to know that she was posh – properly posh – from the weird flowery dress that was more like a kimono hanging from her lean body, the way her skinny limbs dangled out of it and swung confidently through the air when she made a point, her black curls shaking out past her shoulders. Her entitlement was baked in.

'It's so cosy,' said Jenna, keeping her enthusiasm as high as she could pitch it. 'A proper home.'

This time it was as if Penelope heard another note, suddenly seeing the dirty kitchen through a stranger's eyes. There were a few wine glasses abandoned on the kitchen table, red wine still puddled in a couple of them, and an ashtray with some butts that didn't look legal. 'We were at school together so sometimes it gets a bit like a sixth-form common room,' she said, whipping up the ashtray and emptying the contents into an overflowing swing bin.

Jenna couldn't think too hard about how mucky it all was. Archway was only a twenty-minute Tube ride from Bright, whereas the other two places she'd seen that day would mean journeys nearly as long as the coach ride from Stoke. And they'd both been total shitholes. She shifted her weight in the new, pinching black pumps she'd splashed out on instead of a train ticket. She *had* to get this job, *had* to get this room. The list of reasons why was too long, too scary, for her to count, even in her head. She doubled down.

'But that's so great!' she said. 'Living with your best mates!' She pushed away a stab of dread about trying to join a tight-knit gang with a kimono for a uniform – it had been bad enough when her mum had forced her to go to Brownies. Penelope was wiping a mangy sponge over the table now, her left boob nudging out from the soft cotton, no bra in sight. 'What's the landlord like?'

Penelope looked down at the table, a blush creeping up. 'It's actually my aunt's. She's moved to Normandy, let me take it on for her. She's a bit crazy.' She made a gurning face, red-lipsticked mouth twisting upwards, eyes rolling, like the two of them were in on the joke. 'That's why the rent's a bit mates rates.'

Jenna swallowed. Did she honestly think that £650 a month was some kind of favour? The room was like a budget airline landing strip, a single bed squashed against a damp wall. If she got the job at Bright she could just about make it work if she lived on boiled rice and never went out, but it was hardly a bargain. Still, she thought, as she had no friends in London anyway, that wouldn't necessarily be a problem.

'Got a few crazy relatives of my own that I've left in the attic,' Jenna replied, grinning back at Penelope, feeling a little aftershock at her own words. The statement was truer than the other girl needed to know for now. 'It's really generous of you, passing on the love.'

'Thanks,' said Penelope, glowing with pleasure. She paused. 'We've got a couple of people coming round later for viewings. Well, four actually. Just so you know. Full disclosure and all that.'

Jenna felt a hot starburst of anger. Why did everything in her life have to be such a battle?

'They won't be me though, will they?' she said, holding Penelope's gaze.

Penelope giggled nervously. 'What's the job you're inter-viewing for, anyway?' she asked.

'Creative assistant at a branding agency. The boss is …' Jenna felt like she knew Sasha Fulton's Ocado order by now, the amount of research she'd done. 'She's a legend in that world.'

Although maybe Ocado was too downmarket for her. Maybe there were other, more glamorous grocery options in Highgate, where she lived. It wasn't far from here, but it was also a million miles away – grand homes built from grey stone, dumped as wide as Monopoly houses on tree-lined streets. It had been a risky detour, going up there before this viewing, but she reckoned it would pay off.

'Right,' said Penelope, blank-faced. 'Isn't branding just the same thing as advertising?'

'Definitely not,' Jenna said, her self-control finally deserting her, the words sharper than she intended. 'It's *way* more subtle. Everything you buy, every club or bar you think you're choosing to go to – it's been branded. It's been made to seem a certain way so you connect to it. Like you're a better person because you chose it.'

She was starting to worry that she was losing her grip on this situation, accidentally sounding like the kind of flatmate that'd hypnotize you and then feed your remains down the waste disposal.

'Sounds interesting,' said Penelope, in a bored drawl that suggested the absolute opposite. 'I'm an actress.'

Jenna was quiet, trying to summon up the right response, before Penelope raced on, 'And between jobs I work in the Whole Cup on Junction Road. It's full of creatives. It's a real . . . hub.'

'That's amazing!' said Jenna, noticing the way her affirmation visibly flooded Penelope with relief. Her silence had obviously made her insecure about her joke of a job.

She took another look around the kitchen. The oven was crusted with a thin brown film, a lone baked bean taking centre stage between the four rings. She looked back to Penelope, knowing she couldn't afford to get the ick.

'I should've mentioned, about the job; it's actually my second interview. I think it's more of a . . .' – she made air quotes, a dickish gesture she'd never made before – 'formality. So, I'm pretty much all set if you'll have me. It's . . .' She paused, as if searching for words of sufficient depth. 'Whoever gets to live here is really lucky.'

'Thanks!' said Penelope. 'And good luck for today,' she added, earnestly. 'I really want you to get it.'

Jenna felt a tingle of triumph run through her body:

somehow she already knew she had, even though there was no evidence for it. The room too. After everything she'd done to get this far, including a few things she couldn't risk thinking too hard about, she couldn't afford to fail. She took a final look around the kitchen, imagined her Diet Cokes already nestled in the fridge, her mug on the draining board.

She scooped up her bag, preparing to leave, tossing her hair the exact same way Penelope did. 'Thanks. I really appreciate it,' she said.

SASHA

Sometimes I look back now and wonder whether, if that Tuesday morning had started better, my whole life would be entirely different. I lever myself backwards on the hard sofa and wrap my palms around my round belly. Of course, I wouldn't wish away this pulsing life inside me, but trapped inside this crappy rented flat, my due date rapidly approaching, it's hard not to blame that idiotic earlier version of myself for the bin fire of my perfect life. Of course, it wasn't actually perfect, but the fact it looked that way in a certain light almost made it so.

Jack was the first person I saw that day. Shoulders flung back, one arm draped over the back of his chair as he eyeballed his phone, master of the kitchen – he barely acknowledged my presence. I didn't have time to try to force some manners out of him; I was rushing, as usual, traversing the large, beautiful kitchen to stick a pellet in the Nespresso machine and trying to work out if a butter-smeared frozen pitta bread counted as healthy. I stuck one in the chrome Dualit toaster that sat proudly on the oak kitchen island, then turned to scrabble around in the fridge. The nutritionist my fertility doctor had sent me to as a last resort went on endlessly about how food was 'Mother Nature's Medicine', and her toneless drone had become a radio frequency all its own inside my anxiety-ridden brain.

As the pitta noisily popped up and Jack didn't even flinch, I started to feel guilty. I was some version of parent to him, after all. He needed rehabilitation.

'Shouldn't you think about . . .' His brown eyes turned upwards to meet mine, a slow, deliberate roll. 'You've got German today, haven't you?'

'No. I mean, yeah. But Mr Griffiths is off.'

'Right.'

His eyes returned to his phone, and I stood there, my coffee cup suddenly too hot in my hand. I'd been halfway to the table, but now I backed away, let the coffee splash down into the deep white sink, rendering it a crime scene. A little bit spat up at me, soaking into the cuff of my green silk shirt. I grabbed a J-cloth, but only made it worse.

'I thought I'd just work here this morning,' added Jack innocently.

Work looked suspiciously like TikTok from where I was hovering.

'Right. Well, your dad's already left.'

'Obvs.'

Four whole syllables was clearly way too much effort to expend on your stepmother.

'So don't forget to double lock.'

'You've got it, Sasha,' he said, a lazy smile playing across his face now he'd got his way.

I grabbed my bag and slammed out of the house, the sticky heat immediately making me wish I'd remembered my baseball cap. Should I call Steve, ask him if he thought his pride and joy was heading for a life of aimless drifting? No – I didn't have fifteen sweaty minutes spare to stand outside the Tube, listening to his frustration erupting down the line. Jack would be fine, his easy charm and paid-for social confidence would ensure that. Besides, thanks to his rank indifference to me, I didn't particularly care either way, at least not today.

That realization made it unexpectedly hard to breathe, my heart suddenly shrink-wrapped inside my chest. Because what if this was it? By now, I'd cursed enough periods and peed pointlessly on enough sticks to know that there were no guarantees that this wasn't my only shot at parenthood – the two surly, shaggy-haired teenagers who often made me feel like a lodger whose rent was so low she couldn't risk asking for an extra slice of toast at breakfast. And of course Steve cared, but it felt like a semi-detached kind of sympathy, a card sent in lieu of attending the funeral. He was a parent twice over, the job almost done. I couldn't help suspecting that if his forty-three-year-old wife decided to give up her demented quest to hold her own baby in her arms there'd be an element of relief, even if he'd never be cruel enough to admit it to me.

I'd involuntarily stopped on the pavement, frustrated commuters reduced to weaving around me. I couldn't risk this much self-examination – in order to keep going, I had to stay intact. I reminded myself I had interviews that day, a process I enjoyed. I liked the way people offered themselves up to me, the chance to hold their stories about themselves against the light and see if they rang true.

JENNA

Bright's offices were near Old Street, although none of the lunchtime crowd clogging up the streets looked remotely old. For the over-fifties, age was nothing but a number, their hair dyed and cropped close to their heads, all big glasses, equally big trainers and 'statement jewellery'. Jenna's nerves began to ripple through her again, her interview get-up suddenly seeming like an unexploded bomb – she could've saved the money on her stupid black pumps and worn trainers instead, and the black Zara shift dress was starting to look more suitable for a funeral. The funeral of her career – what if Sasha Fulton thought she was so off brand for the branding world that she sent her packing the second she set eyes on her?

Soon Jenna was sitting in Bright's reception, taking tiny sips of the sparkling water the receptionist – her black-rimmed eyes surfing Jenna's shitty outfit – had handed over when she arrived, telling her casually that Sasha was 'running a few behind'. She weighed the green glass bottle in her hand, not allowing herself to take a proper swig – she couldn't afford to need a toilet break at a critical moment. She examined her surroundings instead: bare lightbulbs illuminating a stripped pine floor, a sofa shaped like a lower case 'b', a pink neon 'Bright' sign shining above the reception desk. It was more like how she imagined a Michelin-starred restaurant would look than an office; a million miles away from the grey cages where she'd temped in the university holidays.

As the minutes ticked by, anxiety tightened around her throat like a noose. What if the candidate before her was so extraordinary – Double First from Oxford, boarding-school polish and the biggest, whitest trainers on the block – that she'd already lost her chance? Or what if the fact that she'd asked to be scheduled after lunch, so she didn't have to pay for a night's stay in London with money she blatantly didn't possess, meant that she'd never have that money? Just as her paranoia was reaching fever pitch, she noticed that the receptionist was trying to get her attention.

'They're ready for you!' she hissed, from behind the desk.

'Sorry . . .' said Jenna, flustered, jumping to her feet. As she did so, she realized that Sasha Fulton had already glided into view from behind the frosted glass partition that kept mere mortals out of Bright's inner sanctum. She was taller than Jenna had imagined from her photos, wearing a green silk shirt with a complicated knot that tied around the waist of her skirt, emphasizing her stick-thin silhouette. The kind of boy that Jenna had been dreading to see was trotting behind her, a wiry character with dark hair that stuck up in clumps as if he was too posh to brush it. Sasha fixed him with a warm gaze that made Jenna's stomach turn over.

'Thanks so much for coming in, Jay. Can we get hold of you if you're halfway up the Himalayas?'

'Hey, that's the magic of 5G!' he laughed, sticking out his hand, the sleeve of his white shirt webbed with creases. Sasha laughed too as she took it, simultaneously turning to survey the sofa. By now, the smile Jenna was trying so desperately to keep fixed on her face felt more like a knife cut.

'It's Gemma, isn't it?' said Sasha.

Jenna didn't bother to correct her, just nodded mutely.

'Follow me,' she said, turning on her heels.

SASHA

'*Me in a nutshell*' – that was the first thing that was written underneath his name, like his whole glorious personhood couldn't possibly be represented by the dry facts on his CV. The nutshell contained the news that, although he'd been christened Jeffrey, he'd like me to call him Jay because 'it annoys my mum', and that as a child he'd loved dinosaurs so much he'd wanted to be a palaeontologist. Co-ordinating my meetings and booking my flights would be no *Jurassic Park* fantasy, but at first he parried my questions deftly.

'I know it sounds super creepy, but I love the idea of making your life easier,' he said, smiling disarmingly, and making me wonder if my first assessment had been a bit harsh. 'I know how much I'll learn from you, just by osmosis.'

Don't get me wrong, it wasn't like I wanted some kind of admin slave who I could hurl staplers at if my coffee wasn't quite frothy enough. But nor did I want an assistant like the last one, Clemmy, who'd left me shivering on the tarmac in Stockholm at the end of a work trip, my return flight set for the following week. We both knew it was because she'd booked it on a comedown – she'd networked her way into oblivion at an awards do that I'd gifted her my ticket to attend, too hormonal and teetotal to face it myself – but her 'apology' landed more like a slap. 'It's awful, I know, but I guess it's because you're not challenging me enough,' she'd said, blue eyes watery with self-pitying tears, conveniently omitting the fact she'd only been hired for the job two months earlier. 'I'm on autopilot, Sasha, and I dunno . . . planes crash when they don't get fuel.'

She'd left soon after – a 'mate from uni' was starting a 'premium sushi delivery service' and offering her shares, and her input was so vital and urgent that she couldn't even work her notice. So now, sitting across the desk from this parade of eager beavers, my eyes were narrowed and my claws were sharpened, ready to pounce on the slightest whiff of entitlement. It was all internal of course: on the outside my head was cocked at an unthreatening angle, a wisp of hair softly trailing down the side of my face. I gave Jay/Jeffrey a gentle smile as I set my trap.

'So, Jay, let's turn it around. What do you need from a manager to perform at your best?'

His brows – big furry beetles that topped his wide, freckly face – knotted together as if they were mating. He was scrambling for an answer, but nothing was coming just yet. It wasn't cruel, throwing curveballs like this one. It was the responsible thing to do – now I'd know exactly who he really was.

'I just really need the freedom to express myself,' he stuttered eventually. 'I'm a highly creative person, that's why I thrived so much in Footlights.' A little reminder of his Oxbridge credentials, clearly never far from his consciousness. 'I want the chance to prove that to you.'

As I looked at him, my smile now more of a smirk, it was almost as if he melted, as if he became Jack for a split second. Jack, who could barely stand to rip his eyes from his phone to contemplate me, his far-from-wicked stepmother. These entitled boy-children were like Russian dolls, countless versions that came in different sizes, all told they were special enough to deserve the spoils without any discernible effort. Jay's fate was sealed, even if he didn't realize it yet.

As he ran on, regaling me with tales of his intrepid travels on his year off, as if they hinted at some kind of *Robinson Crusoe*-esque sense of derring-do instead of parents with a permanently open wallet, I glanced down at the next CV. No dreaming spires for this one, and no time spent pretending to help orphans in far-flung corners of the globe. All she had under her belt was an average degree from an average university and a few unglamorous temp jobs. It was her cover letter that had impressed me initially – it had felt honest and heartfelt, and the fact that she'd mentioned specific campaigns that had forged my reputation in the industry didn't do her any harm either. I pushed my chair back as I stood up, my smile never leaving my face as I made it clear Jay's time in the sun was over. Maybe Jenna Hall was the one destined to shine.

Shine was only one word of many for what Jenna Hall would turn out to do.

* * *

Her nervousness was palpable. As she sat down, she wrapped thin fingers around her pale, bare elbows, goosebumps puckering her skin. Every bit of her seemed to be hiding; her face was sharp-featured and pretty, but it was obscured by her dark bob as her gaze skimmed the floor. Yet when she found the confidence to look up, her brown eyes had an intelligence to them – a watchfulness – that made me want to know more about her.

'Would you rather something else to drink?' I said, nodding at the mini bottle of San Pellegrino she'd abandoned on the coffee table. 'I can get someone to make you a cup of tea?'

She finally unlatched her hands. 'I'm fine, honestly,' she said, shoulders dropping from around her ears. 'Thanks a lot for seeing me.'

Anxiety combined with a Midlands accent meant that each of her sentences ticked upwards at the end.

'Thanks for coming!' I said, still trying to put her at ease. 'Did you travel down from Stoke today?'

'No, I slept on a friend's sofa last night,' she said.

'So, you know people down here?' I asked, then heard the words reverberate inside my head. How smug I must seem, perched behind my glass desk in my £200 shirt, no label to tell her it was part of a midnight grief binge on Net-a-Porter. I rushed on, saving her from answering my patronizing question. 'Anyway, what made you apply? What is it that makes you want to work in branding?'

She considered the question for a second. 'I suppose I like the idea that you're telling millions of people a story.'

'Right,' I said, then deliberately paused. Interviews are a storytelling exercise too – my questions are the chapter headings, then I let the person across from me fill in the blank pages. More often than not, they haven't got control of their own narrative, so I was hungry to know where Jenna was going with this.

'So, you have to make people feel something, don't you?' she said, warming to her theme. 'Even if it's a bottle of beer, they need to feel like it's speaking just to them.'

'Yes, triggering emotion is a big part of what we do,' I replied, deliberately neutral.

'Or the opposite – you're making them feel like they're part of the cool gang. Telling them they've made it to the next tier,' she continued, cheeks flushed. 'You're leading people, and if you're doing your job well, they don't even know it.'

It was accurate, what she said. Precociously clever, even. Far more so than any of the other answers I'd received to the question that day.

She took a breath, then carried on.

'But what I love is that now, the way the world is, it only works if you're a force for good. People want companies to be ethical, and branding can help underline that.' She smiled at me. 'I want to be a force for good, otherwise what's the point?'

'At work, or generally?' I asked.

'Generally!' she said. 'And the fact is, I know f—' She blushed. 'Pardon my language. I know nothing right now. There's no reason for you to give me this job. But what I do know is that you are a legend in this business. And even if I'm making your coffee and dropping off your dry cleaning for the next five years, I'll learn so much from you, it'll be worth every minute.'

'Dry cleaning,' I said, teasing her. 'Now there's an ethical minefield. Much more on brand to handwash.'

'I'd do it, honestly. If you wanted me to. Sorry – I know I'm not being very cool.'

She wasn't. Her eyes were as bright as fairy lights, her angular face stained red by her outpouring of enthusiasm. What she didn't know was that I liked it. She felt authentic, which was a word we used far too glibly in my business, throwing it out in pitches like it was a fancy ice-cream topping. It seemed to me in that moment that Jenna understood the dark side of the industry but wanted to plant herself in the light. And surely that was the perfect combination?

'So, if this works out, how would you feel about moving to London?' I asked her. 'It's not a big starting salary, I'm afraid.'

It embarrassed me a bit, truth be told, what we paid new starters. But it wasn't me who set the rates, so I didn't waste too much time fretting about something that I told myself – conveniently – I couldn't change. Besides, Martin and Bridget, the company's founders, were all about the bottom line in every area of the business. They certainly never let me forget my brutal yearly financial targets.

'I'm ready to leave Stoke,' she said, all the energy draining from her suddenly, like a child's party balloon sucked dry of helium by pick-up time. 'It's now or never.'

'Stoke's not that bad!' I said, seized by a strange desire to cheer her up. 'I actually lived there for a couple of years. My mum taught English at Keele Uni.'

I took a quick glance down at her CV, reminding myself that she'd been to Staffordshire University, just up the road from Keele. My mum would've said 'university' in a way that made inverted commas appear in the sky, but I wasn't judging Jenna for it.

'Wow, weird,' she said. 'I bet you never worked at the Pizza Express though?'

It was a segue that gave me an opening to have her talk me through every twist and turn of her CV – all the car show-rooms and insurance companies she'd temped at that would have made the other candidates I'd seen that day quake in their boots.

'I know how lame this must all sound,' she said, petering out, but I shook my head.

'Not at all,' I said. 'It sounds like you're a grafter.'

I could tell from her expression – the way her mouth involun-tarily twisted, revealing a blob of pink lip gloss on her slightly wonky teeth – that she didn't really believe me, but I was being sincere. Despite my heinously expensive shirt and my smooth vowels, I didn't come from money myself.

Soon it was time to wrap up, my next willing victim lined up all too quickly. Jenna's nerves resurfaced as she stood up to leave, smoothing the wrinkles out of her 'business casual' shift dress. She stuck out a slightly clammy hand.

'Thanks for your time.' She looked down at the scratchy hessian rug that covered the polished wooden floor. 'I know this job's a total long shot, and there's no reason you'd give it to me, but I still really appreciated the chance to just . . . be here, I guess. Talking to you.' She turned her gaze upwards on the last few words, looked straight at me.

'I enjoyed it too,' I said. I had. It was weird. 'And I shouldn't really say this – HR will chop my head off – but you're my favourite candidate so far. Don't rule out the big move.'

Jenna beamed and I felt an egotistical burst of pride – this was how much working for me could mean to someone. 'That's amazing!' she said, then dimmed a little. 'Sorry – um . . .' She hesitated, and I smiled encouragement, even though I could see Lorna from HR bearing down on us officiously, a shiny-looking girl with big gold hoops in her ears trotting behind her. 'I lost my mum last year,' Jenna added, the words tumbling out of her. 'I shouldn't even say that, should I, but . . . fresh start, all those clichés. I'm going to cross everything.'

'You do that,' I said quickly, out of Lorna's earshot, giving Jenna a smile that was more of a secret handshake. We both knew the deal was sealed.

JENNA

Jenna's fingers hovered over the return ticket on the screen of her phone, filling her with an insane urge to send it to trash and stay put. The commuters rushing past her didn't feel hostile anymore; instead they felt like they were sweeping her along with them, making her part of their pack. The £2 glass bottle of water she'd been forced to buy didn't even feel like a rip-off, it felt like an exclusive secret she'd had whispered in her ear. Perhaps she'd just ring Penelope and throw herself on her mercy, ask if she could sleep on the sofa – the way she'd pretended she had with her imaginary friend – until the first pay cheque came rolling in. Why had she even blurted out that lie? Was it because she knew that Sasha would never hire her unless she somehow convinced her that she had enough of a foothold in this shiny, slippery world to not be a liability?

That shaming thought made the fizzy excitement immediately start to drain away. She knew that she'd made a connection with Sasha; she'd seen it in her eyes. At first her nerves had made an idiot of her – she'd felt like she had too much to lose – but she'd got through that. In fact, she felt like her vulnerability had worked in her favour. The problem was, it wasn't just down to Sasha. There were obviously bigger, scarier people at Bright, like that wasp-chewing HR bitch who'd shooed her out. She couldn't start celebrating just yet.

Jenna squeezed herself onto a packed, smelly Tube heading for the bus station. She wanted to escape the sweaty armpits and tinny music from other people's headphones, but every stop increased her sense of dread. It took her closer to a home that wasn't home anymore. The reasons for that weren't simple, however effectively she'd managed to weave them into a narrative that had made tears well up in Sasha's blue eyes.

The train juddered to a stop at Victoria, Londoners swarming off it to start sunny evenings, the stresses of the day already in the rear-view mirror. Jenna knew her commute was going to be way longer, way harder, and she steeled herself. Perhaps she needed this. The sweltering bus journey would be character-building.

The reminder she needed that she couldn't afford to lose.

SASHA

Maddi shook the little dish of salted almonds at me, cocked her head.

'One more?' she said, a smile playing around her lips. 'One for the road?'

'It's such a stupid expression, isn't it?' I said, playing for time. It was nice here, no question, but my failure to hotfoot it home was a crime I was going to pay a high price for. I pushed the thought away, sank backwards into the velvet bucket chair I was sitting in, let myself enjoy the ease of being with someone who really knew me and still seemed to unequivocally like me. 'Do you think that's what they did, back in the day? Swigged another whisky and then swerved off down the dual carriageway?'

She knew what I was doing. Signalling the waiter across the crowded bar, she efficiently ordered two more glasses of Chablis before I could drag the decision out any further. Friends since Freshers' Week, we decoded each other's subtext with ease.

'Maddi ...' I whined, without conviction, as the waiter walked away.

'Sorry,' she said, not sorry at all. Maddi had a mixture of warmth and authority that I'd always envied, knowing how far it took her in every area of life. By day, she ran her own architecture practice, persuading clients to part with millions to fulfil her vision for their perfect home. By night, she was married to her university boyfriend Richard, with two perfectly timed children now close to adulthood as well as an adorable seven-year-old afterthought.

'This is definitely my last drink,' I insisted.

'Okay, but how long has it been since we did this? Between getting the twins through their exams, and you ...' She stopped, the realities of our two lives crashing into each other and mangling inside her head. She weighed her words. 'How are you feeling? I don't want to be constantly asking you, but I don't want you to think I don't care.'

'I would never think you didn't care,' I said, letting my hand briefly cover hers across the mirrored table. We'd always loved this place – a bar with a feeling of vintage luxury buried deep in Soho – from the days when it had been an unaffordable treat on our graduate salaries, to now, when it was time that we were poor for, rather than money. 'I've taken a few cycles off, to let my body ...' My throat closed up, and I paused. It was hard sometimes to feel that me and my body were friends, which was a very particular kind of loneliness. Last year's miscarriage – the hope the pregnancy had given me, followed by the aching grief – had made it feel even more like a trickster I had to regard with wariness. 'And then I'm going to go again. Maybe even next month.'

'Right,' said Maddi carefully. It was almost as if she was the one who was pregnant; pregnant with the stats I knew she would have done a deep dive into, because understanding my problems was one of the myriad ways she showed me that she loved me. She always wanted to make my struggles her struggles, so she would surely have already felt the pain of all the cold, doom-laden facts the internet had to offer about fertility after forty. I preferred to surf the message boards – the miracle stories they contained, the anonymous, hapless dreamers I found solace swapping tips with.

'I'm switching doctors, actually. I'm going to this guy in West London who gets amazing results with people who've had no success elsewhere. Not everyone loves his methods, but at this stage I'd rather take a big swing.'

'Okay,' she said, as if she could only manage single-word answers now. She was experiencing whatever the complete opposite of a poker face was, worry and disapproval etched deep into it.

Our drinks arrived, and I took a big gulp, as if it was the 1940s and I was preparing to drive through the night to Aberdeen. I thought about making the joke out loud, but there was no point – it was as if all the ease and fun had suddenly drained away.

'Tell me about you!' I said, with the empty zeal of a children's TV presenter. 'How's Richard? How are the girls? Are you expecting straight-A triumph?'

Maddi took the bait, her pretty face lighting up at the mention of her beloved twins, immediately launching into a blow-by-blow account of their final term. I was watching her more than I was listening to her, enjoying the feeling of the dam bursting, the ease between us flowing back in. For me, there was something ageless about her face – her dark skin still smooth and soft, the lines around her brown eyes light pencil strokes rather than deep folds – but let's face it, I had a lot invested in denying the passage of time for both of us. Maddi was Indian, her parents strict Hindus, her not so much. Her choosing Pete had initially been as much of a shock to them as my choice of a man had been to my mum, Steve being closer to her age than to mine. Even now I wasn't sure she was over it, but we weren't close enough for me to lose much sleep about it.

'They're amazing,' I interjected, when she finally seemed to have run out of words. 'Particularly Willow.'

'Obviously,' she grinned.

Willow was my godchild, at least my first. Since then, I'd somehow managed to acquire another six, plus two stepkids, and no children that didn't require a prefix. I extinguished an unattractive stab of jealousy at the glow Maddi was still exuding; even if her offspring sometimes drove her mad, she never had to question whether she loved them, whether she was invested in their future, whereas I often felt like I was faking it.

I took a wary downwards glance at my watch, which Maddi spotted immediately. I really needed to go home, but my bum seemed welded to the velvet.

'Oh, come on, let's have one more,' she said. It was a surprise to see that my glass was empty, but the truth was, the room was becoming very slightly soft focus. An unfortunate side effect of eighteen months of semi-abstinence was that I'd become a shocking lightweight.

'I'll share one with you,' I said. 'My final offer.'

Maddi rolled her eyes, ordering two glasses as I ducked down into my handbag for my phone.

Hi darling, I wrote, then paused for inspiration. *The interviews overran so I was late to meet Maddi.*

The best lies contain a grain of truth – at least I thought so, back then. And the interviews *had* run over, my strange communion with Jenna leaving me twenty minutes behind schedule, the other candidates a homogenous mass of bores and boasters. Once we'd finished, Lorna had huffed with silent judgement, refusing to contact Jenna and give her the good news. Apparently we had to 'audit' the decision in the morning and check for 'unconscious bias'. It was giving me a little thrill, the knowledge that I was about to change Jenna's life, so perhaps the delay wasn't such a bad thing. Now I had extra time to savour the anticipation.

I looked back down at my phone, my stomach lurching with a mixture of guilt and the effect of the white wine that was sloshing around inside it with nothing but salty almonds to soak it up. *I'll be home in no time xx*, I added, even though coming up with the self-justification had already cost me two precious minutes. I shoved the phone deep into the recesses of my handbag before the shifting dots of a return text could spike my shame.

'Cheers!' said Maddi, as I surfaced from under the table. 'Here's to third time lucky.'

* * *

Steve and I have argued so many times recently about whether or not I invested enough in being a stepmother that it's hard for me to swear that my more positive 'memories' aren't a bunch of snapshots that I took from a very flattering angle. These days, I only see him at our weekly couple's counselling sessions, which he's using to try to effect a 'loving divorce' and I'm using as a last-ditch attempt to win him back. Ruth, our long-suffering therapist, talks a lot about our 'subjective narratives' as her gaze darts between the two of us, Steve rigor mortis stiff at the opposite end of the sofa from me. The room itself is soft and chintzy, a snug haven in the basement of her Holland Park home; sometimes I fantasize about the two of us making it into the middle of that sofa, our hands intertwining, knuckles gently grazing my ever-expanding bump. Or is it our bump? Even the simplest fact evades capture right now.

It's true that on this particular night I was ... not exactly drunk, but not exactly stone-cold sober either. And yes, I was trying to hide it, but wasn't that the responsible thing to do, the parental thing to do, under the circumstances? Fourteen-year-old Georgie tracked my every move from beneath her thick, marshmallow-streaked fringe from the moment I tripped into the kitchen. It was exhausting, knowing instinctively that they'd prefer to have their dad all to themselves.

'Hello, gang,' I said breezily, forcing myself not to sway. 'Sorry I'm late.'

They were all sat around the island, pizza boxes open in front of them, the greasy lids thrown backwards. I couldn't help noticing that while Steve and Jack had already devoured theirs, Georgie had only nibbled the centre of her margherita, the crusts stacked up high like debris. It gave me a familiar twinge of worry that her horrible faux-hippy private school had her on a one-way train to an eating disorder with all its impossible unspoken rules, through which she haplessly blundered her way every day. The irony was that I also lived under the edicts of a set of unspoken rules: every time I mentioned my fear to Steve, it was his face, not his words, that told me I'd overstepped the mark. My prickly, hurting stepdaughter had no idea just how much empathy I had for her.

I pecked the side of Steve's mouth, dodging both the disapproval of his offspring and the acrid taste of pepperoni in the process.

'The San Aqua pitch went on forever,' I said, 'and I couldn't cancel on Maddi. It felt like a million years since I'd seen her.'

Steve got up, crossed to the oven where he'd kept my pizza warm. 'They expect too much of you,' he huffed. 'Neuroscience has proved that long hours are completely counter-productive. Einstein used to go sailing in the afternoons.' He pulled the pizza out of the top-of-the-range oven paid for by his generous trust fund. 'Sailing!'

Steve loved neuroscience. His work as a screenwriter – I use that term in the loosest sense – gave him plenty of time to explore it. My workaholic tendencies, born out of many years spent scrabbling to build the life I wanted single-handed, drove him nuts.

'Can I have a plate?' I asked, as he carried on riffing on this familiar theme.

'Yes, m'lady,' he said, doffing an imaginary cap, ruffling his thinning blonde hair in the process. I heard a quiet, mean snigger from Georgie at the implication I was a princess, but I chose to ignore it, smiling at him instead of turning around. He smiled back, his eyes twinkling with affection, and I felt an unexpected surge of love. Lust, too – the age gap between us, the weather-beaten quality of his skin and the deep grooves beneath his eyes had never put me off. I liked his towering height, the way his angular body had to fold in on itself like origami to reach down and kiss me. I liked the way his blue eyes tracked my every move, like I was the most mesmerizing flash of light. And the things that sometimes infuriated me about him – his uncompromising moral certainty, his stubbornness – were also the things that made me feel safe. He wasn't constantly anticipating disaster the way I did, forward planning to avoid being caught out.

I turned back to the kids. 'So, what are we watching?' I asked.

It was 'family movie night' as Steve had optimistically dubbed it, and a fight about whether to watch a sassy gang of women rob a casino or the latest *Fast & Furious* movie immediately erupted. We were both sat at the island by now, and I let my fingers trawl the skin on the inside of Steve's wrist, subtly communicating my amorous intentions. Two hours of men screaming abuse and flipping ridiculous cars or women proving they were just as badass as the boys was no longer high on my wish list for a Friday night. More fool me – he barely registered my touch, too absorbed in refereeing the escalating battle. It made him feel needed, I could tell; with teenagers, these scraps of emotional engagement felt like declarations of love.

I subtly slid my phone out of my bag, even though no devices at the table was one of Steve's red lines for 'family movie night' (the neuroscience was watertight on the matter). I opened Instagram, my fingers lightly tapping out Jenna's name without me having consciously told them to do it.

I maybe should've asked myself why it was so easy. She was the first Jenna Hall to come up, her account wide open for anyone to nose through, and nose I did, putting her posts together to make one big picture, like they were a fiendish jigsaw puzzle that only I was clever enough to complete.

There was a picture of her in a mortarboard outside a grim municipal building, her grin as wide as the sky, her degree certificate thrust towards the camera, 'I did it' written beneath. She obviously fought for her wins. I felt an illogical stab of pride, like the space–time continuum had warped and her achievements were already something that allowed me to bask in the reflected glow. Next there was a shot of her surrounded by a gaggle of girls on a night out, all tight dresses and tumbling hair extensions. They grinned and pouted on a dark street like their lives depended on it, but Jenna's face was set. She stared straight at the camera like it was her clear gaze capturing the image, not the lens that was turned on her. 'Friday I'm In Love' said the caption, although her expression gave no hint of it.

'Sasha,' said Steve, my name an admonishment in his mouth.

'Sorry!' I said brightly, pushing my phone back into my bag and smiling an apology.

Instagram was still open as it slid inside, Jenna's photos bright and seductive, the last image the one that gripped hold of me most tightly. It was a picture of a woman in a flimsy summer dress, taken from behind, her face turned away from the camera as she looked at the view. I peered more closely at the photo. Was she looking out over Manhattan from a tall building that was part of the tourist trail – the Empire State Building or the Statue of Liberty perhaps? It seemed odd that she was turned away, looking at the horizon, instead of capturing the moment with an excited grin. The caption was a single word: 'Mama'. Had Jenna taken it, a bucket-list trip, her mum too ravaged by illness to want her face caught on camera?

I stared at it for a brief second, aware of Steve's eyes on me. I was prying, it was inappropriate. Why did I even care?

JENNA

It was a stupid mistake, trying to save a day's rent by kicking the morning off at 5am, but when the HR woman had told Jenna quite how mean the salary really was, she'd known her new life was going to demand serious sacrifice. She'd nearly protested to Sasha when she'd called straight after with congratulations, but the excitement in her new boss's tone had stopped any rogue words spewing out. For so many reasons, she couldn't afford to lose this before it had even begun. The trick was to make herself indispensable, and then start pushing for the kind of wage that would allow for a real life.

Stoke-on-Trent was still blanketed in darkness when Jenna got up, no other signs of life in the flat just yet. There was a cereal bar left out on the Formica kitchen counter, a card propped up next to it. A spray of green glitter erupted from the envelope as she opened it, a fat fairy waving a wand that drew *Good Luck* in the clouds. Jenna decoded Paul's squiggly, left-handed scrawl. 'You don't need it, you'll smash it,' he'd written, 'but we're all gonna miss you.' She almost ripped it up and left the pieces scattered on the table, but it was better her anger stayed hidden for now. She shut the front door behind her with quiet determination, shoving her keys through the letterbox and enjoying the satisfying thud that they made as they landed on the hard floor.

The train belched its way towards London, her huge ruck-sack in danger of blotting out the sunrise that filtered through the window. She scrabbled around inside it for her make-up, applying mascara in the cramped toilet, the wand waving through the air like a sooty sword, foundation going on too thick. And then, almost too soon, she'd arrived. Euston Station was an explosion of people, all of them rushing to be some-where, anywhere. As Jenna humped her possessions across the concourse to left luggage, she felt like a trashy tortoise, her whole life a dead weight on her back. But when she got to Bright, devoid by now of anything but a printed cotton shop-per swung casually over her shoulder, her mood immediately started to lift. She was here. She'd been chosen. Today she'd have to hang around for the snotty HR lady to beckon her through, but soon she'd be sweeping past the bare lightbulb that hung over the reception desk like it was second nature.

* * *

Sasha didn't appear until ten-thirty, almost an hour after Jenna had finished having her credentials checked and been released into the office. The wait had felt interminable, anxiety gnawing in her belly as she tried to look like she was googling something vital and important so she wouldn't appear a slacker to the nosy gazes that tracked her movements. Jenna added up all Sasha's component parts the second she walked in – the long, mushroom-coloured silk dress that skimmed her body, gathered loosely at the waist by a drawstring, would've looked like a potato sack on someone less elegant; the apologetic smile she gave was perfectly judged, genuine but not costing her any authority. She had it all under control.

'Jenna, hi!' she sang. She handed her a tiny cardboard cup with a line drawing of a squirrel stamped on the side. 'Sorry to keep you waiting. First-day treat.'

Jenna took a big, appreciative gulp and nearly choked. This was no Starbucks froth-up – it tasted rich, exclusive.

'Thanks,' she spluttered, but Sasha was still talking.

'Bit of a selfish one really,' she continued, sipping her own coffee. 'It's a latte from the place downstairs, one and a half shots. Kind of annoying, but it's the only way I can drink them.'

She airily dropped her bag – a huge vanilla-coloured leather sack with scraped gold buckles – onto her desk, a phone ringing inside it. 'Oh, and mine's with oat milk.'

Jenna bit the soft flesh of her cheek inside her mouth, controlling rising stress. Sasha was going to require a manual, she could tell that already. She'd need to get her hands on it fast.

'Although seriously, whoever milked an oat – what am I like?' Sasha continued, looking directly at Jenna as she spoke. Her smile was so twinkly, so piss-taking of herself, that it was hard not to like her. Jenna needed to make sure she didn't fall for it.

'Tastes amazing,' she replied, grinning back. 'So you're definitely getting something right.'

'I'm glad you approve!' said Sasha, cocking her head towards an empty meeting room as she extracted her phone and dumped the call with only the briefest glance at the screen. 'Come on through. Let's get this party started.'

Jenna pushed her chair back, risking a glance at the two juniors who sat within the same cage of desks, with whom she'd only exchanged the briefest of hellos so far. The boy – ginger hair surfing his chin, glasses more like goggles – had been watching her exchange with Sasha like it was the Wimbledon final and he was courtside. The girl – shaved head, annoyingly beautiful heart-shaped face – had a look in her eyes that was harder to read. Was it contempt? Was it envy? Jenna would have to wait to find out.

* * *

The meeting room had the uniform cool of every nook and cranny at Bright. A table that looked like a slab of wood from a recently chopped down tree sat in the central space, a pendulum light hanging low over it. Jenna perched at the edge of one of the deep chairs covered in thick green velvet that sat on either side of the murdered oak, trying to look like she belonged there. Sasha was bent low, spreading out sheets of cream paper, her blonde waves skimming the pages. Did she create that magic with tongs, wondered Jenna, automatically fingering her own short brown mop, which now felt coarse to the touch. Or was that why she was late – did she spend every Monday morning in the hairdresser's chair, paying a fortune for someone to help her 'be Sasha'?

Sasha looked up. 'I want you to take a look at these,' she said, in a sober tone. 'They're Bright's code of ethics – what we expect from ourselves and from our employees. Martin and Bridget, our founders, take them very seriously. It's the foundation of how we all operate here.'

Jenna stared down at the pages, hoping she was imagining the blush that seemed to be boiling her cheeks. She couldn't be sure that her interview didn't mean she'd already violated Number Three: *Always be truthful with your colleagues, even if the consequences scare you.* Then there was Number Five: *Teamwork and co-operation are at the heart of what we do. There is no such thing as healthy competition!* The look on the face of the bald beauty made her suspect otherwise. How seriously was she meant to take these?

'Do any of these worry you, Jenna?' asked Sasha, before she'd even finished reading.

Jenna kept her eyes trained downwards for a second more, buying herself time. Number Eight burned her eyes: *Do your best, but don't let perfectionism be the enemy of genius.*

She pointed at it. 'What does that even mean?' she asked. 'That it doesn't matter if I fu—, if I screw up?'

Sasha laughed her warm, throaty laugh. 'You just fell straight down the hole!' she said, leaving Jenna struggling not to feel like the punchline to a joke she was too dumb to even grasp. Sasha seemed to sense her discomfort, her voice gentler as she continued. 'Perfectionism is really just another word for shame, and that makes it toxic. We all try our best, and we all inevitably make mistakes. To be free enough to be creative, we have to accept that.'

Jenna couldn't figure out the correct response to that.

'Hey, earth to Jenna?' said Sasha lightly. 'I know it's a lot to take on, but I really think you've got this.'

Bright was starting to feel more like a cult than a workplace. 'I'm just, like . . . taking them in,' she said. 'New start and all that.'

'It *is* a new start,' said Sasha. 'That's what you wanted, right?'

'Yes,' said Jenna, a bit too fervently.

'So, practicalities-wise . . .' Jenna opened her notebook, determined to start the journey to becoming indispensable right then and there. 'Of course, there's going to be the boring assistant bits – travel booking, diary management, blah blah blah – but I'm also going to pull you into the campaigns I'm overseeing. It moves fast – we're pitching for new business, working with existing clients. You'll work like a dog, but you'll learn all the tricks too.' Sasha was already starting to gather up the papers, her gaze sliding towards the messages that were flashing up on the screen of her phone. 'Sorry, bad analogy. You get what I mean though.'

Within seconds, her boss was out the door, only a lingering waft of her bittersweet rose perfume and the list of Bright edicts left in her wake.

* * *

'If I was a car, I'd be a ... I'd be a ... Bentley!' shouted Ginger, his eyes closed, his hands waving wildly in the air. Jenna had found out that he was called Fergus – she'd definitely never met a Fergus, so it was hard to forget – and he was a creative exec. He looked like he could either be fourteen or forty, with his crumpled linen pinstriped blazer and his stupid glasses.

'Interesting comp,' said Sasha, her face hard to read. Did she genuinely think he was smart, or was she just keeping the brainstorm moving? 'Can you get it on the board, Jenna?'

Jenna was wasting so much time reading the room that she was forgetting she was meant to be writing the room. She scribbled furiously on the whiteboard as Donovan, the team's art director, piped up.

'So that makes me think sleek. Classic.'

Donovan was definitely in his forties, shock waves of grey running through his cropped hair. He was Black, dressed in the kind of understated navy suit that even Jenna's untrained eye could tell must have cost the earth, the open-necked shirt beneath it exposing smooth flesh.

'Yes ...' said Sasha, pausing to think. Jenna scanned her other five staff, watching how they quivered as they waited for her to pronounce. How did Sasha pull it off? She was friendly, but she never let them forget for a second that she was the puppet mistress here. Did it take conscious effort, or was it as easy as breathing for her? 'But guys, we all know the pitfalls of classic. Repeat after me ...'

Everyone laughed, starting to talk all at once. Jenna grabbed for the words, desperately trying to scribble them down. *Bland. Boring. No vision.*

'No, it's *no visibility*,' squawked the bald eagle, who'd turned out to be called Chloe.

'Yeah, right, sorry,' stuttered Jenna, crossing the stupid, wrong word out. Suddenly it felt like everyone was staring at her, picking her apart the same way she had them, clocking the too-tight black skirt she was wearing, more car showroom than boardroom. Her hand shook as she wrote the correct phrase, the worst nicknames they could give her screaming in her ears. Her breath was jamming in her throat now, panic rising. She had to stop getting derailed by the fear of failing at this, the thought of what she had to lose. Sasha's dulcet tones cut through the painful internal monologue.

'Don't apologize, Jenna,' she said, throwing her a secret smile that had to be a callback to Number Eight. '"No vision" is an excellent addition, so let's not cross it out.'

As Chloe's jade-green eyes narrowed in annoyance, Jenna exhaled a breath she didn't know she'd been holding.

'There are a lot of whisky brands in the market,' continued Sasha. 'And "classic" is the way so many of them sell themselves. Jack Daniels. Tallister. So we need a vision for this that goes beyond classic. Sure, the clients have bought a hundred-year-old Scottish distillery, but let's not get lazy. Think about what Absolut did when they blew up the whole vodka market.'

The chatter started up again, but Sasha didn't choose to engage this time.

'I want us to break for today,' she said. 'Reflect on what we've talked about before we come up with an action plan to present to the client. Don't forget, this is still competitive. We need to think about the whole 360 degrees of the campaign. How will it land for social media, brand ambassadors, events? No one's drinking whisky at Wimbledon, so where do we go?'

'Book festivals,' piped up Fergus. He'd definitely been alive since 1956.

'Maybe,' said a doubtful Sasha. 'And what if we treat it as

more disruptive? What does that look like?' She turned to me. 'Do you ever drink whisky, Jenna?'

Now everyone really was looking at her, six expectant faces waiting for her to speak. Jenna froze.

'Sometimes I have a JD and Diet when I'm out,' she said, before she could wash the Midlands vowels out of her response. A couple of lips curled in amusement, but not Sasha's.

'Right!' she said, delighted to have her point proven. 'I say whisky, and you're using a brand name. JD have got their part of the market sewn up, from Texas to Stoke-on-Trent. So, we've got our work cut out, gang. Go forth and ponder.' She was still talking as the team gathered up their notebooks and phones.

'You too, Jenna – you might just turn out to be our secret weapon.'

* * *

By seven, the adrenaline had drained out of Jenna, the dawn start and relentless pace taking their toll. The contract that Lorna had officiously walked her through said she finished at 6.30, but the office was still full of people, hunched over computers or perched on each other's desks, swilling from the reusable branded water bottles Bright handed out as standard issue. They were made from rice husks, apparently.

Jenna was googling the Taiwanese whisky market, the latest stop on her world tour, when Sasha laid a gentle hand on her shoulder.

'Jenna?' she said, looking down at her, face serious. Jenna's heartbeat was like a piston. Could it all be over already? 'I'm going to remind you about seven.'

Jenna's thoughts were scrambled. The contract definitely said it was six thirty.

'Number Seven!' added Sasha, with that teasing warmth that was powerful and disarming all at once.

'I'm sorry, I don't remember what it . . .'

'I'm going to give them to you to take home and read in peace, without my eyes on you. Number Seven is: *We respect the need to rest as well as to work. A good work/life balance is the cornerstone of our continued success.*' Sasha gestured to the rest of the floor. 'I know they're all still there, hammering away, but it's your first day, and you're knackered. Go home.' She flung out her manicured fingers. 'Shoo, seriously.'

'Really?' asked Jenna. 'Are you sure?'

She didn't like the idea of slinking out the door before Chloe did, but it seemed like she didn't have a choice. Besides, Sasha was pulling on a stylish cream mac, clearly preparing to leave herself. She waved a goodbye to her friend Anna, a hot mess of an art director who'd given Jenna one of the most genuine welcomes of anyone at Bright. It had been in marked contrast to her high-and-mighty assistant Scarlett, who'd somehow conned Jenna into doing a lunch run for both of their bosses like she was the scummiest scullery maid in *Downton Abbey*.

'Of course – start enjoying yourself. Have some fun!' Jenna detected a note of sadness in the way Sasha said 'fun', stored the knowledge away. 'There'll be days when you'll need to be here till midnight, but the rest of the time there's no need to feel like a dead man walking just to prove yourself to me. Besides, your friend must be so excited you're finally here.'

Her friend. The closest thing she had to a non-imaginary friend in London was Penelope, with her endless 'friendly' emails about the bank-breaking security deposit – Jenna would have to get it out on her credit card on the way back to Archway. According to Lorna, the HR robot, it would be a full two weeks until her first pay cheque would land in her account.

'She is!' said Jenna quickly. 'We're actually going to the pub tonight. The Falcon Tavern – she's getting there early so we can get seats outside.'

Where were the words even coming from? The Falcon Tavern was a posh pub she'd passed as she'd raced the surprisingly short distance that separated the leafy calm of Sasha's neighbourhood and the grimy sprawl of Penelope's. Even at warp speed she'd known she wouldn't be able to afford so much as a tonic water in that place. And it wasn't as though Sasha, with her inevitably chic home and the husband Jenna knew existed from the large rock on her left hand, would want to know about her new assistant's tiny little life, the real or the fantasy version. Jenna, by contrast, wanted to know everything. *Needed* to know everything. She wasn't yet sure if the husband came with a matching set of kids, although she'd overheard Sasha talking about a teenage girl today when Fergus had been going on and on about how 'vital' it was for another of their campaigns to 'reach into the heart of Gen Z'.

'Oh wow, that's down the road from me,' said Sasha, obliviously enjoying the 'coincidence'. 'Me and my husband love that pub.' She belted her mac up tightly, even though the weather was far too hot to make a coat advisable. 'I won't be in until at least eleven tomorrow, so don't bother coming in at the crack of dawn to impress me.'

'Is there a meeting I forgot to put in the diary?' asked Jenna, on guard. 'I didn't see anything in there.'

'No, you didn't miss anything,' replied Sasha abruptly, her expression clouding. She picked up her handbag. 'It's just a . . . it's just a thing I have to do. I'll be in as soon as I can.'

Whatever the 'thing' was, she was clearly dreading it.

'So, I'll have an latte on your desk for eleven, if you're not here before.' Jenna smiled directly at Sasha, mimicking her teasing lilt. 'One and a half shots of lush oat goodness.'

It worked. Sasha beamed at her. 'That would be perfect, Jenna,' she said. 'I'm starting to wonder what I ever did without you.'

'Well, now you don't ever need to wonder,' said Jenna, at the exact moment that Sasha turned away and cut across the crowded office.

Jenna watched her retreating back – her thin shoulders, the way she effortlessly balanced on the stilts of her open-toed high heels. She looked unbreakable. Untouchable.

Only time would tell if that were true.

SASHA

Jenna's second day at Bright was destined to begin without me. I woke up later than normal to the sight of a rumpled bed, Steve's side vacant. I wasted too long smoothing the covers until they were just so, then padded downstairs to the kitchen, the heat of the July day giving the house a sticky closeness. He'd abandoned the silver jug from his ridiculous Ferrari of a coffee machine on the counter, the leftover milk in it already starting to curdle. Irritation thrummed inside me as I rinsed the jug out in the sink, but I refused to let it bloom. I needed us to be on the same team today.

The French windows were flung open, and I stepped through them, the flagstones hot against my bare feet.

'Steve?'

He was further down the long garden, sat on his haunches examining the big growbag of tomatoes that was set up on a wooden bench. He turned towards me, smiling in a way that looked guarded to my paranoid eyes. I walked over to him, laying my palm between his shoulder blades.

'So, are they thriving?' I asked.

'The tiger toms are in the lead,' he said, reaching into the bag to hold one up for me. 'I'm not sure if the poor old piccolos are even going to survive. 'Taste one for me, will you? Give me your verdict.'

The idea of eating a sharp little fruit before I'd even brushed my teeth was in no way appealing, but I took it from him anyway. Steve was an obsessive, each craze or passion absolute until he moved on to the next thing.

'Mmm, I'm not sure they're going to win best in show,' I said, swallowing down the slimy little lump. I looked down at him, keeping my voice deliberately light as I continued. 'We ought to get a bit of a move on.'

'I know,' he said, the stress he was tamping down audible to my sensitive ears. He unfolded himself, smiling down at me with infinite kindness. 'How are you holding up?'

I flashed a grateful smile back at him. 'Let's just see what he's got to say.'

* * *

Dr Rindell's offices were a clammy Tube ride away, right on the opposite side of the city. He was a very West London sort of a doctor – prohibitively expensive, with a waiting list a mile long that you could only cajole your way onto via a referral from a previous patient. The whisper was that some of his methods were so cutting edge, so controversial, that he had to trust in the discretion of the people he took on. It appealed to me, the idea that he might be my secret weapon, but I knew for Steve it would likely flag up my scary desperation. I'd deliberately spared him the details of the hoops I'd jumped through to get us this appointment. It was pathetic really, the way I was still trying to underplay how much I wanted this.

We were squashed up so close on the Tube that there was no room for any meaningful conversation about what this day really meant to us. Besides, by this point, I'd developed a kind of Stepford-wife positivity about the whole process that left no room for nuance. For the sake of my sanity, I had to believe that something would eventually work if I only tried hard enough.

It was a principle that had reaped dividends in other areas of my life, and I wasn't prepared to sacrifice the arrogance of that conviction just yet.

My anxiety began to kick in once we were in the hushed waiting room, an earthenware goblet of Ayurvedic tea placed in my hands, scorching my palms as I obediently sipped. The taste of it, the fact that coffee was clearly akin to anthrax around here, immediately reminded me that a part of me was broken, that I was here to be fixed. I darted a glance at Steve, marvelling at how he was both sat alongside me and miles away.

The hands of the clock ticked past the time of our appointment and kept right on moving. Steve stayed obliviously buried in his Kindle, but after almost half an hour I started to get twitchy. I had back-to-back meetings the rest of the day, including the usual routine with Bridget and Martin to go through my projected earnings for this quarter. I couldn't turn up flustered and rushed – should I text Jenna and have her boot a couple of less important things out of my diary? *Hold the oat latte for now, I'm running late!* I wrote. *Hopefully see you by 11.* Now my fingers ground to a halt. Should I add a kiss? Yes – she'd looked like a rabbit in the headlights when I'd made her speak in the creative brainstorm yesterday; she needed to know I wasn't scary. I pressed send, warmed by my own warmth, then looked back at the clock.

It was a whole forty-five minutes now – maybe that was just the vibe here, everyone else too rich and bohemian to have a schedule. I snuck a glance at the other patients around us, realizing with a stab of sadness that up to now I'd been averting my eyes from their pregnant bellies. They looked so young and fertile to my jaded eyes, but I shot the thought down as soon as it arose. They were probably here because they'd struggled too, and they were living, breathing evidence that Dr Rindell knew his onions.

'Sasha Hamilton-Edwards?'

For once, I'd used my married name. Steve had really wanted me to take it wholesale, despite both the professional impossibility and the slightly galling fact that I was the second Mrs H-E. Using it here felt like a way of giving him an easy win, and I could see by the expression on his face that it was music to his ears.

As I got up, I finally looked directly at one of the pregnant girls, shooting her a smile. Her partner was with her, almost surgically attached, and the pair of them beamed back at me as if their happiness was so abundant they desperately needed places to dump it.

'Congrats,' I whispered as we followed the receptionist to the consulting room, a disobedient lump rising up in my throat.

* * *

Dr Rindell stood as we entered, extending a tanned hand from his cufflinked white shirt. He was small and compact, handsome in a slightly too-smooth way that made me wonder if he availed himself of the cosmetic treatments I knew this clinic also offered. His dark, bright eyes swept across me as if he was making a split-second calculation, getting the measure of me before we began. Once he'd finished his appraisal, he shook hands with Steve.

'Thanks for agreeing to see us,' I stuttered, my voice sounding high and reedy in my ears, as we sat down in the smart upholstered chairs in front of his desk.

'No need to thank me – it's always a privilege to be sought out,' he said, as if all I'd had to do was politely enquire, all the obstacles I'd navigated to get us into this room mere figments of my imagination.

'I've heard . . .' I looked at Steve, perceiving a deep weariness in his expression. '*We've* heard, from so many people, that you're the best in the business!'

If Steve was weary, it wasn't wholly surprising, even though it filled me with a lonely kind of fury. When we'd met, me already thirty-seven, I'd been careful not to mention babies. I wasn't stupid; he was a single father of two children who were still hurting from a cut-throat divorce. The last thing he'd want was to feel duty-bound to add another sibling into the mix, and I learned quickly that he was nothing if not honourable. By the time it had got serious enough for me to have an engagement ring on my finger, I was thirty-nine. He was generous enough to agree we should try, but I couldn't help thinking, in my darker moments, that a part of him hoped that at my age it wouldn't come to pass.

Dr Rindell made a self-deprecating little gesture with his hands. 'I like to help where I can,' he said, then reached for a sheaf of notes. My heart dropped, my palms moist. 'You two have been on quite a journey, haven't you?'

I nodded, not trusting myself to speak. Steve reached for my hand, the gentle pressure of his touch slowing my racing pulse a little. 'We have,' he agreed.

The doctor smiled at me. 'I appreciate this is hard,' he said kindly. 'Do you mind if we go through it?'

'Of course not,' I said.

'So, you did three rounds of IVF, one with IXY?'

'Yes,' we chimed. 'And that last one worked,' I added, the words chasing after each other too quickly. 'Worked' was obviously a highly subjective term, considering I wasn't holding a baby in my arms, but the fact that I'd briefly conceived was a piece of positive evidence I desperately clung onto. She – I'd always believed she was a she – had slipped away before the

momentous twelve-week mark, too early for anyone beyond
those very, very close to me to even acknowledge that she had
existed. But I liked to think, in my relentless search for the
positive, that she'd come partly to give me the bravery to keep
going.

'So we *can* conceive,' I added. 'That's why we're determined
to keep trying until we manage it again. I'm sure there's more
I could do to ensure I make it to full term, and . . .' I ground to
a halt, stymied by Rindell's unreadable expression.

'Sasha . . .' he began. 'I can call you Sasha, can't I?' I nodded
mutely. 'You do understand how much fertility tapers for
women after forty-two, I'm sure.'

'Obviously,' I said, humiliation making me unattractively
sharp.

'So what your body could achieve a year ago is not necessarily a road map for what it can achieve now. And looking at
your FSH levels—' I hated all these cold anachronisms doctors
trotted out; he was meant to be the wizard in this field, the one
with the magic wand who vanquished all doom '—I can see
why the previous clinic were resistant to putting you through
more treatment.'

'Yes, I know all that,' I said, the words tumbling out of me.
'But isn't it my decision? Some people can't stand it, the injections and the horrible procedures, but for me – for us – it's a
price worth paying.' Was I imagining it, or did Steve's hand feel
stiff in mine? 'Of course it is, if it works.'

Rindell moved to speak, but I was on a roll now. I was a
professional pitcher, looking to close.

'And you're the guy, aren't you? The guy who makes it work
against the odds! I know people question your methods sometimes . . .' I saw his jaw clench, his body retracting as I breached
the code of silence. But it was true – I'd heard he coaxed eggs

out of hiding using doses of drugs that other doctors wouldn't countenance. 'But I love that about you – that you don't give up on women.'

He watched me silently, the compassion in his gaze making my skin crawl. I wasn't stupid – I knew what it heralded. My gaze darted to Steve, a loving kind of pity painted across his face by now. For a split second I wanted to punch him.

'Sasha, I don't think I can use your eggs to get you pregnant. Not with these stats. But . . .'

Tears had started to roll down my cheeks, and he wordlessly pushed a silver tissue box across his desk towards me. 'That doesn't have to be the end of the journey.'

When I spoke, I knew I sounded petulant. A child who wanted the chocolate, not the apple she'd been offered instead.

'I don't want to adopt or foster or anything else. I've already got stepchildren.'

I saw the light in Steve's eyes dim at the tone I spat it out in, but I only felt a brief spasm of guilt – I didn't have the emotional capacity right then to let his wounded feelings derail me.

'Have the two of you ever discussed the idea of egg donation?' said Dr Rindell, refusing to be deterred.

I shook my head, unable to even look at him. I hadn't allowed myself to think about anything beyond my own baby. That was the idea, wasn't it? To hold on to an idea so tightly that it couldn't help but manifest? It was certainly what the self-help books I'd come of age with had preached with an almost religious fervour. He paused, waited until I was forced to look up.

'I understand what I've told you today wasn't what you were hoping to hear.' I hated how patronizing these doctors were, the sugar-coated power they wielded over me. 'But I would urge you both to give it some thought. I've had many, many patients who've found it to be an incredibly rewarding choice, once they'd adjusted to a different route to parenthood.'

'I told you . . .' I started, then forced myself to sound less hostile. Is there anything the world despises more than a 'nasty woman'? 'I want *my* baby, not a stranger's. I want her . . .' I was stumbling now, my fully formed fantasy shamefully spilling out of my mouth. 'It – to be a part of me.'

I thought of my father. I barely remembered him; in fact, the memories I did have were probably fraudulent, fragments of photographs that my hungry imagination had somehow animated. My fifth birthday, him holding me firmly between his knees as I lunged towards the cake to blow out the candles. The three of us, our brief family unit, feeding ducks in the park, me so small my mittens had strings that peeked out of my coat sleeves. He'd drowned when I was six, the circumstances kept deliberately hazy. My mum had felt that suicide was too big a burden to put on a child, a choice I intellectually understood, but which hadn't eased my sense of foolish humiliation when I finally found out the truth as a teenager. A baby, *my* baby, would be a tiny fragment of him, my magical thinking stretching into the past as well as into the future.

'There's no pressure to make an immediate decision,' said Dr Rindell. 'Why don't you go away and give it some thought?'

Steve squeezed my hand again, looking into my tear-stained face with a love that I felt too mortified and angry to appreciate. Instead, I searched his gaze for any disloyal hint of relief.

He turned back to Dr Rindell. 'I think my wife's right. I can't see us ever pursuing that route.'

I felt myself flinch – it was something about the way he spoke for my body – but I forced myself not to react. It was important I kept Dr Rindell on side – he needed to see how strong I was, how resilient. Perhaps with time I could convince him I was hardy enough for more treatment, however slim my odds. I didn't want him thinking this was goodbye.

'We really appreciate you making space for us,' I said. 'We'll be in touch.' I abruptly pushed my chair back; the squeal it made against the parquet floor was like a scream.

Steve jumped up in tandem, reaching across the desk for the doctor's hand. 'Yes, thank you for seeing us,' he said, shaking it firmly, man to man. Another surge of fury spurted up inside of me; this was an uncomfortable half hour that they'd both ultimately recover from, but me? I didn't have that luxury. Fertility was nothing more than another bastion of male privilege and, as with all the other varieties, they didn't even have the good grace to notice.

Perhaps it was as early as that first appointment that the rot set in, the determination to wage my personal battle at any cost. I knew better than to let my bloody-minded determination show; instead, I smiled wanly and held tight to my husband's hand as I offered a demure and grateful goodbye.

JENNA

Jenna didn't yet have a key that first night, so she rang the doorbell, waiting awkwardly in the sweltering evening heat. The house sat on a long Victorian terrace, which curved off the gridlocked, fume-choked stew of the Holloway Road. You could see immediately that the street was pulling in two different directions, some of the houses smartly painted with a single brass number, others a mess of individual doorbells and overflowing bins. Although there was only one number on Penelope's door, its green paint was peeling off and the bins gave off a fruity stench that started to turn Jenna's stomach as the minutes ticked past. Perhaps they'd forgotten she was moving in.

Finally, Penelope appeared, her long, dark hair coiled on top of her head, her cheeks brick red. She was wearing a stained stripy apron over a white T-shirt.

'Jenna!' she exclaimed, giving her two little pecks, one on each cheek. 'Welcome to Casa Penelope. I've made a spaghetti puttanesca. You hungry?'

Jenna dropped her rucksack in the chaotic hallway, shoes and delivery boxes littering the space.

'Yeah, I am, actually,' she said, allowing herself a feeling of relief. Maybe this could be home, rather than a place to crash.

She had no idea what it was Penelope was offering, but she was grateful. It sounded way better than the crushed salt-and-vinegar crisps at the bottom of her discarded rucksack.

'Then follow me,' sang her new housemate, strutting back towards the kitchen.

Unlike on her first visit, the messy kitchen was full of people, all of them crammed around the wooden dining table that ran along the side of the room. Penelope bypassed the table, crossing instead to the oven where her sauce was bubbling on the hob, leaving Jenna marooned in the space. She stood there awkwardly as her new landlady pointed at the gaggle, throwing out a stream of names and professions which Jenna did her best to absorb, all while trying to look engaged and smiley enough to ensure that her new housemates wouldn't hate her on sight.

Soon Penelope was whacking down plates that were piled high with pasta, motioning to Jenna to sit down at the opposite end of the table from her. Jenna sank into her seat and took a big bite of her dinner, partly to avoid having to try to break into the quick-fire conversation. Penelope's sauce was delicious, salty and interesting, and Jenna wondered if she could just fade into the background, but it was not to be.

'So, what actually is *branding*?'

The question was posed by Claudia, a trainee barrister with a fierce peroxide crop and a thousand-mile stare. Her tone of voice made it sound like a closing courtroom argument for precisely why Jenna was a complete moron.

Jenna's mouth was full of slippery tails of spaghetti, and she struggled to swallow as she scrabbled for a response. 'It's . . . it's all about how you make consumers feel about what they're buying.' Watching Claudia's mean little mouth pucker into a patronizing smirk at this pointless profession, she forced herself to stay chipper. 'Like you do in court, I bet. You have to make the jury fall for your amazing, persuasive argument. Same thing.'

Claudia's expression visibly softened at that. It didn't matter who it was – in Jenna's experience, flattery would get you absolutely anywhere. Now Laura, a chubby primary school teacher whose doting eyes followed Penelope around the dirty kitchen like she couldn't believe she was living with the coolest girl in the Upper Sixth, started prattling on.

'Jeez, I wish I could make my Year Twos feel whatever I wanted them to feel!' she said, performatively twirling a large clump of Queen Penelope's pasta onto her fork and beaming gratitude in her idol's direction. 'Maybe I could make them feel like they DON'T need to pee in their pants when I'm reading them *Each Peach Pear Plum*. This morning I had to get an actual mop from the store cupboard because . . .'

So began a fascinating anecdote about six-year-olds' wee wee. After a few plot twists involving disinfectant wipes and clean underwear, Jenna found her eyes roving the kitchen, barely registering when her last new housemate asked her a question.

'So, what's Stoke-on-Trent actually like?' said Sanjay, cocking his head in a way that told her he was actually going to listen to her answer. Far warmer than the others, he was a playwright; a claim he underlined by wearing the right costume: mud-coloured cords firmly tucked into leather boots and a knitted vest with a checked shirt underneath.

'Um . . .' The question made Jenna's body – her whole being – clench tight. She forced herself to breathe. 'Pretty fucking dull!' she said, barking out a laugh. 'I'd much rather be living the dream with you guys in Archway.'

Their plates were clean by now, and she was mercifully spared any more questions about where she'd come from.

Penelope stood up and clapped her hands together, neon nail art flying through the air. 'So, *Settlers of Catan*?'

Everyone started babbling away, excited, while Jenna tried to arrange her face into a shape that implied she knew what they were talking about.

'Are you up for it, Jenna?' asked Sanjay.

'Settling in Cape Town?' she said, making everyone burst out laughing.

'*Settlers of Catan*!' cried Penelope, leaving Jenna none the wiser. 'It's a board game.'

'I only got into it when I moved in here, but it's really fun,' said Sanjay kindly. That he was trying to offset her humiliation was actually worse than being laughed at. 'You've got to play. Everyone has their own settlement on an island.'

'Riiight,' said Jenna, struggling to keep the scorn out of her voice. What kind of grown adults were still playing board games?

'Pleeeease!' said Penelope, darting a pitying look at Sanjay that she caught. *Great*. Now she would have to play their stupid game, even though she was planning to be in the office by eight thirty and it was already past eleven.

'Sounds amazing!' she said, teeth gritted, and Penelope gave a little cheer, filling up her glass in celebration, the bottle wobbling in her pissed-up grip. Jenna swiped her hand over her own glass before too much sloshed in.

'I shouldn't,' she mock-giggled, doing her best to look disappointed. 'Tomorrow's only day two.'

None of them had noticed that her half glass had stayed that way for the whole evening, and she wasn't about to draw attention to it. Although it was drunks who couldn't be trusted, in her experience it was moderation that made people suspicious.

'You're so good, Jenna!' said Penelope, squeezing her arm

and starting to stack the plates while they waited for Laura to find the board.

Jenna joined her, scooping up mismatched cutlery and grabbing the remaining plates. Penelope took the pile from her hands and dumped it in the sink along with her own, immediately turning her back on the assorted dishes as though a washing-up fairy was booked for midnight. She smiled at Jenna.

'You enjoying the wine?' she asked.

'Yeah, I am,' said Jenna. She forced a gulp and smiled, feeling petty for her spurt of rage about the game. Penelope had done nothing but try to make her welcome. 'Thanks for feeding me, and . . . making me feel at home.'

'No probs!' said the other girl. 'I'm a bit too pissed now, but tomorrow I'll tell you all about the kitty and stuff.'

Jenna looked around for any sign of a pet – all she could see was a scratched-up cat flap with some masking tape sticking it shut. 'The kitty?'

'Yeah,' replied Penelope, the drunkenness rolling off her, suddenly all business. 'We have a household kitty we all pay into. We mostly use it for food and wine. Bog roll if we don't nick it from the pub.' She patted Jenna's arm, slipping away towards the others. 'Don't worry about it now, I'll be giving you the full rundown.'

Jenna's stomach lurched. She felt hoodwinked – she'd worked so hard to figure out where every penny of her tiny salary would go, and now there was an extra tax just for living here. She could hardly back out now, not when she'd eaten their food and pretended to drink their wine. More fool her for thinking she was part of the family.

Making that mistake once had been stupid, but twice was criminal. She lifted up the plates and tipped the remains of her red wine into the sink, standing stock-still as she watched it swirl and twist its way down the plughole.

* * *

The next morning, Sasha was even later than she'd said she'd be. Jenna grew increasingly anxious as the minutes ticked by and the oat latte she'd promised her – paid for out of her own pocket – went stone cold. Three whole quid's worth of sucking up, gone for nothing. The text her new boss had sent, and the kiss she'd dropped in at the end of it, were an unexpected bonus, but when Sasha did arrive, that warmth seemed to have gone as cold as the coffee. Ghostly pale, she flung her beige mac over the back of her chair and sank down into it, barely making eye contact. Jenna crossed to her desk and hovered uselessly, cup in hand.

'Oat latte, as promised!' she said, forcing an upbeat tone to remind Sasha it was their thing. 'I could just put it in the microwave?'

Sasha barely raised her eyes. 'I'm fine for now, thanks Jenna,' she muttered. 'I just need to get through some emails. I think you should go and ask the rest of the team what help they need for the presentation.'

Jenna looked across the floor towards the packed meeting room, feeling like she'd been asked by her commanding officer to cross enemy lines. All she wanted to do was stay here and quell her paranoia that Sasha's black mood was down to something she'd done.

'Okay,' she said. 'If you're sure you don't need me.'

Sasha flashed her the briefest of smiles, then turned her body towards her computer, leaving Jenna with nowhere to go but over the top. She played for time, printing out multiple copies of the research and diligently stapling them, but then she had no choice but to head over to the conference room. She tried to slip in noiselessly, but the door clunked heavily behind her. Everybody stopped what they were doing and turned to stare. Swallowing hard, she held out a sheaf of printing.

'I've been doing some extra research,' she started. No one responded. 'In case . . . in case it's useful to you guys.'

'Thanks, Gemma,' said a boy who looked barely older than her, breaking the silence.

He'd been there yesterday, but he hadn't been one of the shouters so she'd barely clocked him. Nothing about him shouted, in fact: he wore a plain, black T-shirt that wasn't plastered with some Seventies band who should've been left in the graveyard of Smooth FM; his brown hair was just brown hair, with no peroxide streaks or any kind of stupid hat perched on top of it. And his voice sounded authentically London, not like the accent her new flatmates dipped in and out of before returning to Downton once they'd downed a few drinks.

'It's Jenna,' she said, before she could catch herself.

He gave a little salute. 'Jenna. Got it,' he said kindly. 'I'm Pete. Come and sit down.'

'Yes, join us,' said Chloe. She paused, her head cocked, her palms pressed together as if in prayer. 'We've got a policy of instant feedback here at Bright. I don't know if Sasha told you that?'

'No,' said Jenna, immediately on red alert. She glanced out across the office – Sasha looked marooned out there on the empty floor, her gaze constantly drifting off into space.

'It's so we can all course-correct as we go,' said Chloe bossily. 'It stops any workplace gossip too, which is strictly against Bright's company values.'

Jenna's heart was already plummeting: where was this going?

'The word "guys" is problematic for us,' Chloe continued. 'It's gendered, even if it's not intended that way.' She was on a roll now, leaning forward across the table for her teaching moment. 'And there's so many alternatives these days.' She grinned as she casually threw out a few. 'Peeps. Folks. Y'all. There's no need to make anyone uncomfortable anymore.'

Jenna's cheeks were on fire; all she could do was stare down at the shiny, polished table as though there was a message scraped into it. Some alternative ethics, perhaps. The irony wasn't lost on her; she knew that everyone around the table would be witnessing how much she shrunk as Chloe's words landed. She forced her head to jerk upwards as if it was pulled by an invisible string.

'Wow,' she said. 'Guess we're not in Stoke anymore, Toto!' Scattered laughter emanated from the group, and Jenna knew it wasn't directed at her. Something delicious flickered in Chloe's cat-like green eyes, like she wasn't sure where she stood. Jenna capitalized on the shift in mood, her smile humble now. 'Got it. Thank you, Chloe.'

Chloe embraced the switch. 'Thank *you*, Jenna!' she said, her elfin face one big self-satisfied grin. 'Onwards!'

Pete's eyes darted to Chloe, and back to Jenna, in a way that told her he respected her left hook. 'So, let's have a butcher's at the research you did,' he said, reaching across the table to hand around her print-outs.

* * *

Sasha's mood didn't improve as the day went on. At lunchtime, she mutely handed Jenna her credit card, which bore an intriguing alternative surname, sending her out to buy sushi from a specific place that was tucked away in the nearby backstreets. Jenna considered asking her to cover the latte, but the words stuck in her throat at the sight of Sasha's closed-off face, and besides, spare change was something only broke people possessed. When she found the place, it turned out it wasn't one of the usual takeout chains, but a proper restaurant, with a bill and a wait time to match. Though when she finally handed over the spoils, Sasha only poked at the food with a single chopstick like it was a specimen in a lab, and then, after suffering a couple of bites, abandoned it on the far side of her large desk. She didn't exactly ask Jenna to clear it away, but it was clearly what she expected. Jenna scooped the plastic tray up and took it off to the kitchen, unable to resist trying a couple of the delicious-looking rolls. She'd probably have stayed there till the tray was empty, ignoring the reek of coffee grounds and microwaved soup, if Fergus hadn't bumbled in to make himself a 'chai latte'. Instead, she swiftly scraped the remains into the food recycling, hoping she didn't look like a greedy little pig hanging around a trough.

Sasha was standing up waiting for her when she reappeared, cocking her head towards a meeting room. Jenna quickened her pace, excitement and fear duking it out. This could be very bad, or it could mean that Sasha was going to confide what was wrong.

'Jenna . . .' Once inside, Sasha ground to a halt, as though her next words would cost her dearly. 'I'm having a tough day,' she said at last, her face visibly crumpling. 'I'm meant to be meeting Bridget and Martin later on to talk numbers and update them on where we are with the pitch prep . . .'

Her voice cracked, and Jenna instinctively reached out a hand, lightly touching hers.

'Hey, sit down,' she said, and, to her surprise, Sasha obeyed, her legs buckling like a colt's, her fragile body landing on the uncomfortable grey sofa. Jenna dropped down too, onto a chair that sat at an L-shaped angle to her boss's. She immediately regretted it – Sasha stiffened at the proximity, her voice steadier and more professional when she continued.

'I wondered if you could speak to their creative assistant,

move the meeting. I think if it's assistant to assistant, it'll be more discreet. They'll probably be grateful to get the time back in their diaries.'

'Course I will,' said Jenna quickly. 'What do you want me to say?'

Sasha looked momentarily helpless. 'I don't know. Can you just make something up?'

That she could definitely do. 'Yeah, no problem.'

'Thank you,' Sasha said, her voice full of gratitude. 'I promise it's not . . . I'm not normally like this. I won't be putting you in compromising situations every single day.'

'I'm your assistant, I'm here for whatever you need,' said Jenna. 'Going undercover is my jam.' Ugh, she'd gone too far. But no, Sasha actually laughed, a ray of sunlight shining through thick cloud. 'Can I do anything else – get you a cup of tea?'

Sasha stood, her poise returned. 'The best thing you can do for me is speak to Pete and let me know it's sorted,' she said. 'Thank you, Jenna.'

* * *

Martin and Bridget's lair was on the next level up. It occupied the whole floor, an attic space with a skylight, the ceiling so low in places you had to duck. Pete was tucked under the eaves, bent over an iPad as he tried to ignore the incessant yapping of a grubby white Yorkshire terrier who raced back and forth across the space like he was in a relay race with an invisible rival. An older woman sat nearer the founders' glass-walled office, her desk larger than Pete's and so clean it looked like a military operation; a carafe of water and a pen pot sat on opposite sides, like a pair of soldiers standing guard. She looked up as Jenna came in, fixing her with a cold stare.

'You're Sasha's new girl, aren't you?' she said. She scowled down at the dog. 'Buster, be quiet!'

Jenna snuck a glance through the plate glass behind her, the first time she'd set eyes on the power couple who ran Bright. They'd founded it in the 1980s, which surely meant they weren't far off their eighties themselves, but you'd never have known it to look at them. Parked opposite each other at two beautiful wooden desks, their faces were alive with the impassioned debate they looked to be having. Bridget's ash blonde hair fell neatly around the shoulders of a monochrome column of a dress, no grey to be seen, while Martin's close-cropped hair made his baldness seem like a choice. Even through a window, they were formidable.

'Yes,' Jenna said, gesturing quickly to Pete. 'I just came to talk to—'

Luckily, Pete read her body language and jumped out of his seat. 'Tell you what, let's walk and talk,' he said, grinning at her. 'I need to pick up some print-outs from graphics.'

He hustled Jenna back through the door she'd just come through, pulling out a packet of cigarettes as soon as they reached the landing.

'Nasty habit,' he said. 'Do you have it too?'

'I'll watch you,' she replied, non-committal. Of course she didn't smoke; it was a smelly, dangerous waste of money. But she hadn't decided how much of a rule-breaker this Jenna – Bright Jenna – should appear to be.

Pete turned around, pushing open a hatch in the wall that she hadn't even seen. 'Come on,' he said, stepping out onto a thin strip of roof.

She followed him out, vertigo overwhelming her as soon as her feet landed on the ground. The truth was, everything felt like vertigo these days, elation and terror so tightly plaited together that she didn't know which thread to believe in. She risked taking a proper look at the London skyline: the dome of St Paul's rising out of the mass of grand stone buildings, the brand-new office blocks that stood alongside, either heinous or beautiful, depending on which way you looked at them. For Jenna it was definitely the latter – she admired their nerve, the way they insisted on their right to take up space.

Pete was already lighting up. 'Okay, so maybe I was wrong about you being a smoker,' he said. 'But here's my second crazy guess of the day. Sasha doesn't want to meet Bridget and Martin, does she?'

Jenna needed to operate at speed. 'She's just working really hard to get under all those ideas that were being thrown around yesterday.' Pete was tracking her expression closely. 'She wants to make sure she's . . . synthesized them properly.'

'*Synthesized* them?' His eyes twinkled with amusement. 'They just want to hear she's got some fucking great idea for a brand ambassador and a slogan to hang the campaign on.'

'Exactly,' Jenna said. 'And that needs an extra day.'

'I saw her face when she came in,' he said softly. 'And then she just sat there like a lemon. She'd never stay out of a meeting when we're this close to a pitch. There's something up, isn't there?'

Jenna didn't reply, the hot sun making a trickle of sweat slither down her chest and pool in her bra. She decided to take another risk.

'You're the one pulling the strings, aren't you? So how about you create a clash in the diary? If they think they had to cancel on her, they won't mind, I bet.'

Pete gave her an admiring smirk. 'You're no fool, are you?'

'Hope not.' She smiled back, hoping his comment was tacit agreement. 'I owe you one.'

'Yeah, you do,' he said, taking a sharp puff on his cigarette.

''Cos I'm telling you, Jenna, in this place, we need to have each other's backs.'

'What should I be looking out for?' she asked, but this time it was Pete's turn to stay silent. He shook his head, took one last drag of his cigarette and ground the butt into dust under the heel of a biker boot. Then he eased back through the hatch, his wiry body poking halfway out as he extended a hand. 'Coming?' he said.

* * *

Sasha flushed with relief when Jenna told her what she'd done. 'I'm sure you broke at least three of Bright's company values with that bit of subterfuge, but who's counting?'

'Not me!' said Jenna, trying to control her triumph at achieving the win. It was only day two and Sasha was already treating Bright's company culture like a shared joke between the two of them. But the camaraderie didn't last long. Her boss soon retreated back to her desk, where she hid behind her monitor and pretended to work for the rest of the afternoon. Jenna observed how her fingers kept freezing on her keyboard, her gaze faraway. She must've been counting the minutes, because as soon as five o'clock came, she sprang out of her seat, threading her arms into her faithful trench coat. She bent down over Jenna, leaning in close so she could speak quietly.

'I have to leave,' Sasha said. 'I ordered a cab, and it's arrived way quicker than I expected. Could you shut my computer down for me? I've got a couple of PowerPoints up that need saving to the server. It's open still – the password's off.'

'Sure.'

'I'll see you in the morning.' She stopped, holding Jenna's gaze. 'Thanks for today.' Her voice had a tremor in it again.

'Look after yourself, Sasha,' Jenna said, matching the low intimacy of her boss's tone.

She waited a couple of minutes after Sasha had left, her heart a drumbeat in her chest. Then she crossed to Sasha's chair, her spine straightening and her shoulders stretching out like wings as she settled in. The documents on the screen were boring, visual decks she'd already seen, but the flashing banner at the bottom was anything but. She snuck a furtive look across the floor: Fergus was laser-focused on his own monitor, while Chloe was laughing so loudly on a Zoom call that she sounded more like a sea lion honking for fish, no bosses around to shame her into wearing headphones and talking quietly. The coast was clear.

> **To: SashaH82**
> **From: Maddisamson**
> How'd it go today darling? Thinking of you xx

> **To: Maddisamson**
> **From: SashaH82**
> Writing this from the loo because I can't face anyone seeing me – tells you all you need to know xxx

> **To: SashaH82**
> **From: Maddisamson**
> Darling, I'm so sorry if it was bad news.
> Do you want me to call? xxx

> **To: Maddisamson**
> **From: SashaH82**
> Rindell won't treat me. And if he won't treat me, then NO DOCTOR will treat me. I can't get my head round it – it's like I'm having an out of body experience. Steve tried to be kind, but I can't

help thinking he's a bit relieved. And now I've
got to go home and eat dinner with his living,
breathing kids who I swear think I'm Cruella De
Vil just because I exist. I'm sure Georgie's being
bullied and I genuinely want to help her, but it
seems like I can't even be a proper stepmother,
let alone an actual mother. I feel this stupid sense
of shame about all of it, and then I feel ashamed
of being ashamed. Ugh, FML. Thanks for being
the best friend I could ask for – just knowing
you're there means so much to me, S xxx

To: SashaH82
From: Maddisamson
I'm so gutted for you, Sasha. But
don't give up hope . . .

Jenna didn't even notice Lorna's approach until the last
moment, her eyes too busy sucking up the messages like they
were state secrets. Their gazes met above the monitor: Jenna
twisted her face into a new shape – humble and diligent –
before giving Lorna a shy smile. Meanwhile her right hand
stabbed at the keyboard, forcing the screen to fade to black.

'Hi, Jenna, how's day two?' said Lorna. 'Have you taken
over from Sasha already?' She tittered at her own joke.

Jenna tried to make her smile look natural. 'Not at all.
Sasha's just at a meeting – somewhere else.'

Lorna gave her a puzzled look, as if Jenna might be slightly
simple. 'I wasn't asking where Sasha *was*, just checking in on
you. Bright treating you well so far?'

'Yeah, no. It's great,' said Jenna, stumbling over her words.
'I love Bright.'

Chloe was looking over now, her Zoom call abandoned; Jenna's discomfort was obviously far more entertaining.

'Good to hear,' said Lorna, in a clipped voice. 'Well, if you need anything, you know where my office is. It's good for us to keep checking in while you're still in your first three months.'

It was a not-so-subtle nod to her probation period.

'I really appreciate that, Lorna,' Jenna said, keeping her grateful smile fixed firmly in place.

Once Lorna had finally fucked off, Jenna tore a scrap of paper from a little pad on Sasha's desk. It was from a hotel in Italy, the name embossed in swirly writing. *Dr Rindell*, she scrawled quickly, before she could forget – now she'd be able to google him when she got home. She went back over the messages in her head, adding *Georgie* under Dr Rindell's name. Chloe was still staring at her, and Jenna quickly pushed her chair back, heading back to her own desk.

It wasn't just the content of the messages that pinballed around her brain on the way home, it was also the flavour they'd had. The last one, which she'd only had time to skim, was a response from this Maddi person, a slush-fest about how she felt just the same way about Sasha, how much she meant to her. Did Jenna have anyone who felt that way about her?

The thought deflated her, the adrenaline of the whole operation draining away, replaced by something more acidic.

SASHA

I let myself get a black cab home, watching the meter tick upwards as we idled in the rush-hour mayhem of King's Cross. I didn't care – I was grateful for this tiny bubble of the day when I didn't have to put on a brave face.

Steve wrapped his arms around me the second I got through the door, and I let myself lean into him, accepting every morsel of his strength. I sobbed into his chest, not caring that my nose was running and my mascara was painting black streaks across his T-shirt.

'Do you want a gin and tonic?' he asked, after he'd given me a good few minutes.

'No reason not to now, is there?' I replied. 'Maybe I'll go the whole hog and smoke some crack.'

He led me down to the kitchen, pouring us both a stiff one.

'Was it awful being in the office?' he said, as he put the cool tumbler into my hand.

I nodded ruefully.

'Told you not to go,' he said, and I smiled but didn't reply. It was hard to explain to him that if I opened the door to cosseting myself that way, evil spirits could start to blow in. For all the smiles and the kisses on emails that Bridget and Martin doled out, there was always an iron fist clenched tight inside the velvet glove. Jenna – clever little Jenna – had proven herself ten times over by delivering me from their scrutiny today.

'Are the kids upstairs?' I asked.

'Yes,' he replied, and then added the killer afterthought. 'You should probably go and wash your face.'

I fought a sudden surge of rage. *I should probably go and wash my face.* Even inside the walls of my home I needed to be pretty and acceptable, pain conveniently wiped away the way I wiped bad ideas off the whiteboard at work. Was that all my dreams of motherhood were? Delusions to be cleaned up and replaced by something more palatable? More realistic?

I looked over to the kitchen counter. He'd made some fancy chicken salad, the dressing sitting next to it in a little glass jug. He was trying to look after me. He was trying to look after all of us.

'I'm going to get changed,' I said, forcing myself to appreciate the gesture. He was my husband after all, and it had been far from a given I'd ever have one of those. 'I'll be down in twenty minutes.'

* * *

It turned out I needed forty. By the time I came back down – face dutifully washed, mascara reapplied – dinner was already on the table, the three of them in full flow.

'I don't know why you don't get it, Dad!' exclaimed Georgie, her round cheeks red with frustration.

Steve chuckled in a way that I knew was going to infuriate her even more. '*I* don't get why your generation don't believe in healthy debate. Why is it illegal to have a different opinion from you?'

'So, you're denying fossil fuels are killing the planet?'

'No ...' protested Steve. 'I'm just saying it's unrealistic to pretend that they can be obliterated from a functioning economy overnight.'

Now Jack jumped in over him. 'He just doesn't care 'cos he's old. He's had his fun, he's had his kids – he got to have us when no one gave a shit about this stuff.'

I slipped into my seat, trying not to let Jack's emphatic past tense puncture me. The idea of a tiny, mewling sibling was probably too gross for them to even contemplate. No one seemed to feel the need to greet me, although Steve did at least slide a hand – weather-beaten from a summer spent tending his beloved tomatoes – over mine.

'Your generation think you invented activism, but it's bullshit,' he told them, enjoying himself now. 'Me and your mum marched against everything. Nuclear weapons, Section 28 . . .'

Silence shimmered between them for a second, all three of them thinking about Jasmine. She'd left Steve for one of their university friends when the kids were six and eight, disappearing to France to set up a 'retreat centre' soon after, a place Steve was bitterly convinced was no more than a commune for swingers. Jack and Georgie sometimes saw her in the school holidays, but they could barely remember her being a day-to-day presence in their lives. When I butted up against the parts of them that were armoured up, hard to love, I could hardly blame them for it.

Georgie shook herself free from her memories, returned to the task at hand. 'I just think we should ban private cars. And plastic.'

Steve cocked his head. 'I'm curious. Do you think Ubers run on thin air or on carrots?'

I saw her mouth tremble as she decided whether to indulge his teasing or hate on him. She craved his approval, underneath all the bravado.

'For fuck's sake, Dad!' she yelled. 'You're a total dinosaur.'

I felt a sudden surge of purpose. She was taking out her pain about her mum on him, even if he was too close to see it. Perhaps I could be more than a stepmonster, for once.

'Don't speak to me like that.'

Before Steve's anger could bed in, I piped up.

'We're doing a campaign for a big airline at work,' I said to Georgie, bravely withstanding the withering gaze I got back. 'Of course, they use fossil fuels, but I really think they're trying to make a difference with all the new technology they've introduced to try and get to net zero. I should show you the research, see what you think. It's your generation they want to reach, prove that it's more than greenwashing.'

How glib I was back then, how easily I shapeshifted, always finding a 'third way' through any moral conundrum that made it possible for me to work for whatever client I won.

'I can answer that for you right now,' snapped Georgie.

'Read it. See what you think,' I said, keeping my tone light. Just a cool stepmum, finding fresh ways to connect. 'We pay people your age or a bit older to come and talk to us,' I continued. 'Your generation are the future, Georgie.'

Annoyance and relief were duking it out for Steve. He was always wanting us to be closer, but directly undermining him probably wasn't his preferred route.

'Yeah, well, I might just do that,' she said, surprising me. Then – a rare event – she smiled. 'You lot need educating.'

'Then school us,' I said, smiling back as I picked up the wine glass that Steve had filled for me and taking a large gulp. It wasn't quite a crack pipe, but it had the desired effect.

* * *

Mascara, caked from multiple applications, finally slid from my eyelashes as I apologized to Steve later that night. We were standing in the en suite, me holding a cotton pad between my fingers and trying not to look at the fine lines that cross-hatched the skin around my eyes. They said too much about my biology, demanded a reality check that I emphatically didn't want.

'I wasn't trying to take her side,' I said, watching his face in the mirror. He was brushing his teeth with his state-of-the-art toothbrush, painstakingly sliding the slim head around his molars. 'I just think she's struggling. It's not worth matching her rage with more rage. It's petrol on a bonfire.'

'Ssh,' said Steve. 'Petrol's a swear word in this house.' Our reflections gave each other a sly smirk and I leaned into him. 'Thanks for trying,' he said. 'It means a lot to me.'

'Of course,' I said, turning my body to face forwards and leaning back into his chest.

'It makes me know, with every fibre of my being, that we'll be okay,' he continued, his lips moving against my ear. 'At least we've made a decision now. We can start moving on with our lives, as a family.'

Did he feel my body stiffening, or was he too oblivious? 'We haven't even properly talked about it yet,' I said.

Steve looked down at me. 'No, but ... what you said to Dr Rindell – you were pretty definite, Sasha.' He paused. 'Fierce!'

Was he trying to turn my pain into some kind of sexy compliment? I gripped the cold enamel of the sink, my breath jammed in my windpipe.

'And I'm not even allowed, what, twenty-four hours to think about that decision?'

Steve stepped backwards, palms turned upwards in supplication, as if he was asking God to send down instructions for how to deal with an emotional woman. 'I'm sorry if I've got it wrong, Sasha. I was trying to be supportive of your choice. You said you didn't ... that you didn't want a stranger's baby.'

That's when I crumpled, my body buckling onto the toilet seat. I wasn't ready. I could only digest this meal in very small portions.

'But maybe it wouldn't feel like a stranger's baby,' I said, rallying, the words surprising me almost as much as they did him. 'It would be your baby,' I continued, 'and I'd carry it. So, it would be my baby too.'

It's not my best quality, my determination to win an argument at any cost.

Steve's shocked face looked like a slab of granite. 'But Sasha, I just don't know if I want, if I could . . .'

I stood up and crossed to the mirror, determinedly scrubbing at my left eye with the sticky pad of cotton wool. I'd found a semblance of inner steel again. It was a relief. 'I don't want us to just dismiss the possibility,' I said, my naked, stubborn face staring back at me. Goading me on.

'Okay,' he replied, the two syllables landing as heavy as lead.

I can see it now, the humanity of his response, just as I can see the humanity of my plea. The irony is that the hateful sessions we have with Ruth are giving me the exact degree of self-knowledge that I needed back then – in that hallowed time before I burnt my life to ashes. But without the ability to time-travel, those insights offer me no discernible route to winning my husband back. To him I'm still a liar, a fraud, his love for me no more than a confidence trick I somehow played on him.

'Thank you,' I said, dropping the grimy black pad into the recesses of the pedal bin and letting the lid slam shut with a satisfying thud.

JENNA

All Jenna wanted to do when she got home was perform a deep dive on the mysterious Dr Rindell, but unluckily for her, Penelope had other plans for her evening. As she headed to the kitchen for a quick glass of water to wash away the sweaty commute, her housemate-slash-landlady appeared from nowhere, pulling an open bottle of white wine from the fridge door.

'Who needs water when God invented Sauvignon Blanc?!' she sang, looking at Jenna standing hunched over the sink and wiggling the bottle in her direction.

If she said no, she'd seem like she was being moody about the famous kitty. If she said yes, she'd be proving its worth. But by now it was too late to say anything – Penelope was already pouring two glasses out.

'Just a drop for me,' Jenna said, glugging from a pint glass of water. She needed to get ahead of this. 'We should talk about the kitty, shouldn't we?'

'Oh, yeah,' said Penelope, faux casual. 'Good plan. Let's get the boring stuff out of the way.'

Soon they were sitting at the scratched kitchen table, Penelope ticking off items on her long, elegant fingers.

'So, we do a big Tesco order once a month for all the house

stuff: loo roll, basics like pasta and rice, booze . . .' She stumbled briefly. 'Cleaning products'.

Jenna looked at the black grime that was ground into the table's wooden grooves. Penelope's family had obviously been eating puttanesca off this table since Margaret Thatcher was PM. They'd probably voted for her too, even though Penelope would never admit it.

Jenna cocked her head. 'Yeah, so, do you have a rota for cleaning?'

Penelope looked blank. 'No, we just do it like – as and when.'

As and never. 'Right,' Jenna said, forcing her tone to stay neutral.

'By the way,' continued Penelope, 'thanks for washing up last night.'

Someone had to, thought Jenna. She couldn't have left those plates festering in the sink, mould colonies mushrooming in the summer heat.

'No probs,' she said.

'So.' Penelope was all business again. 'In total it's eighty quid a month, and if there's any left over after three months, we use it for treats.'

'Eighty quid?' said Jenna, unable to keep the panic out of her voice. With the £650 rent, the sky-high bills and her travel costs, she was going to be trying to hoover up Sasha's leftovers every single day.

Penelope's expression grew cold. She took a long pull from her wine glass, carefully placing it back on the table. 'Do say if that's a problem,' she said, in a tone that implied the absolute opposite. 'Like with everything, I try my hardest to make it mates rates. We all save in the long run.'

Save on what, Jenna wanted to scream. It all depended on

where your baseline was; that Sauvignon Blanc didn't cost a fiver, that was for sure. She took a tiny sip – to her taste buds, it was pure bitterness. It did a job though – it gave her a way to swallow down her feelings. The stakes were too high to risk the alternative.

When she spoke, she'd honeyed her words. 'No, that's fine.' She paused, gritted her teeth. 'Thanks for making it so easy for all of us.'

Penelope's glow came flooding back immediately. 'You're welcome,' she said. 'And thank YOU for being the newest recruit to the gang!'

'And what *are* the treats?' asked Jenna. 'Just so I can start getting excited.'

'Oh, you know . . .' replied Penelope, giving a naughty grin. 'A gram of coke here and there, a bottle of bubbles for a birth-day party. I prefer cash for those.'

So, she'd be subsidizing them living the lives of 1980s gang-sters? This was getting worse and worse. Jenna pushed back her chair and stood up, stretching her mouth into a smile like it was an elastic band.

'Can't wait for the parties!' she said, already walking out. She reached into the fridge as she passed and poured more Sauvignon Blanc into her glass until it reached the very brim. When she got to her room, shutting the door firmly behind her, she leant out of the tiny window and let the wine rain down onto Penelope's scrubby garden. The foxes who howled and shagged below her at night could have the first party of the summer.

* * *

Jenna couldn't waste any more time fuming about Penelope's domestic dictatorship – she had work to do. She sat on the narrow bed and shoved her pillows up against the wall, her creaky old laptop balanced on her knees, settling in as best she could.

It only took a few keystrokes for her to find him. Dr Rindell's website was slick, discreet. There was a portrait shot of him looking serious in his green scrubs, his dark eyes staring intensely into the camera like it had asked him a question that he was only prepared to answer via telepathy. His consulting rooms were somewhere in Notting Hill, a place that still sounded made up to Jenna, nothing more than a backdrop to a cheesy rom-com that she'd once hate-watched while scrolling Instagram.

Dr Rindell boldly promised 'unprecedented results' using methods that were 'at the forefront of reproductive technology'. It wasn't all science, though – he really knew how to pull on the heartstrings to drum up business. It was 'a privilege to help my clients finally achieve the dreams of parenthood others have denied them,' he said, although clearly he didn't think he could help Sasha live the dream.

Jenna shut the laptop for a minute, delighted with her newfound knowledge. Sasha's life wasn't the picture-perfect fantasy it had first appeared. She was vulnerable. Jenna looked down at the scrap of headed notepaper from the Italian hotel her boss had holidayed at, finding the other name she'd scribbled down. *Georgie.* She recalled that Sasha's lunchtime credit card had a different name on it, a complicated double-barrelled one. *Hamilton-Edwards.*

Instagram delivered immediately. Georgie Hamilton-Edwards thought meat was murder and that you should TAX THE RICH, at least according to her favourite T-shirt. That said, she also liked skiing in Verbier and attended a school that, judging by its Harry Potter vibes, definitely wouldn't have let the likes of teenage Jenna into its hallowed halls. In short, she was mixed up. Probably in desperate need of a friend.

Two hours later, after switching her attention back to the research Sasha had *actually* given her to do, Jenna snapped off the bare overhead light. The cracks and crevices in Sasha's life were already starting to open up, and it was only day two. Jenna was drawing a map of her life, marking out territory. And soon she'd have perfected her plan of attack.

SASHA

By the next morning I'd acquired a fake kind of peppiness – it was a Band-Aid over an open wound, but for now it would have to suffice. Bright was an unforgiving place, and so too was the inside of my head. Steve was wary of me, my handbrake turns too much for him to keep up with. I pretended not to notice, instead continuing my quest to beat an invisible gang of opponents for the crown of Stepmother of the Year.

'Bye, darlings,' I trilled, as I prepared to leave the house. Steve was intentionally busying himself with his ridiculous coffee machine, so I swerved him in favour of Georgie, risking putting my bare arms around her shoulders. She was a solid mass, hunched over the table, unenthusiastically nibbling a dry slice of sourdough toast. Jack slouched opposite, ploughing into a bacon sandwich, mayonnaise smearing his newly stubbly chin.

'I haven't forgotten our conversation last night,' I told Georgie conspiratorially. 'I'm going to look into how I can get you involved when I'm in the office.'

She looked up, hopeful. 'Would you pay me?' she asked.

Steve rolled his eyes, and I faltered.

'You'd be an influencer,' I said, deflating at the sight of her scowl. The new phase of our relationship I was trying to will

into being would be hard-won. And my God, I needed a win.
'Probably,' I added.

I'd pay her myself if I had to.

'Then I'm in,' she said, grinning with transactional glee.

'So, we've got a plan!' I said.

* * *

Jenna was already in the office when I arrived, the only assistant
to be seen. Scarlett tended to stroll in at ten, unapologetically
slurping coffee or making a loud call. I felt a little starburst of
smugness about my wise – some would say counter-intuitive –
decision to hire her.

'Hey, Sasha!' she said, a warm grin on her face. 'Do you need
a coffee? I've been pulling together that inspiration board for
the brand ambassador you asked me for.'

'I'm all good,' I said, coming to a halt behind her chair so I
could look at the screen. I was craving caffeine, but I was also
too nosy to wait a second longer to see what she'd done with
the first big task I'd set her. It would be either a win or a fail
for both of us.

The first page was a bulleted wish list – how we wanted the
whisky brand to land.

- Heritage with a twist. Plays on the remote, beautiful
  Scottish location of the distillery. Appealing to millennials
  and old-school connoisseurs too.
- Exportable Britishness. Never parochial – reaches a
  global consumer base.
- Exclusive – high quality, limited quantity. Priced that way!
- Prestige product, for those 'in the know'. Brand
  ambassador to bring out that emotional response in the
  consumer.

She must've been absorbing information like a sponge in those meetings, even if she'd looked like a rabbit caught in the headlights of an oncoming truck.

'This is great, Jenna!' I told her, and I saw her flush with pleasure. 'You're really grasping what we're trying to do with it.'

'Thanks,' she said, cheeks aflame. She looked up at me from her seat, nervously twisting some strands of hair around her index finger. I couldn't help but find it gratifying, how unashamed she was about wanting my approval, the contrast with Georgie not lost on me. 'Let me show you the images now.'

She clicked through, the next board filling the screen, a sea of faces jigsawed together. I could see some of the celebrities I'd suggested – a couple of sexy, forty-something Scottish actors with Oscar nominations and complicated private lives that gave them roguish charm – but she'd gone way further than that in her thinking. There was a grime star in there, a precocious female novelist with a debut that had stopped people in their tracks with its sexual boldness, a performance poet from Brixton who'd been netting awards left, right and centre.

'Mmm, interesting . . . I mean, obviously the names I gave you were only a jumping-off point.'

Jenna swivelled her gaze upwards to look at me, hearing something off-key in my compliment. I heard it too, sharp and unexpected. Was it a strange kind of shame I was feeling? The fear that my original list had breached 'never parochial' without me even having the smarts to notice?

'I want to unpack your thinking with some of these,' I continued smoothly. 'How do you think they relate to the product?' I checked myself – it wasn't like I was on a mission to destroy her confidence. 'I mean, they're emerging cultural icons for sure, but how do they evoke the brand values we're pursuing?'

Jenna's hair spiralled loose from her finger, her blush rising again, but for different reasons now.

'I just didn't want us to pick someone . . .' Her eyes found one of my Scottish actor suggestions, looking out at us from the screen with crinkly-eyed mischief. Or was it just white male entitlement – I couldn't tell anymore. 'I didn't think you'd want it to feel too . . .'

She'd hung herself, and she knew it, but I wasn't planning to execute her. I cut across her before she was forced to say more.

'We definitely want the choice to feel fresh,' I said, making sure my smile stayed in place. 'But it needs to feel coherent too. It has to be someone who feels like such a great fit that we can use them across a wide range of platforms and promotions. A hotel they lend their name to, say. Or hosting an influencer dinner in the Highlands. I'm not sure all of these guys quite do that for us. Or am I wrong?'

Jenna closed the file as my interminable speech finally ended. 'N-no. I get what you mean.' It was hardly like she could disagree with me. She tried for a sheepish smile. 'I'm getting waaay ahead of myself, aren't I?'

I risked a light squeeze of her hunched shoulder. 'Not at all,' I said. 'I love how much you're throwing yourself in. Don't think I haven't noticed you working round the clock, even though I thought we agreed it was against the rules . . .'

I was aiming for jokey, but she stayed earnest.

'I don't mind, honestly. I want to get my head around it. You've given me such an amazing opportunity.'

'Not at all,' I said, starting to back away. 'I'm lucky to have found you.'

I was exiting the office by now; I'd get my own coffee for once.

* * *

The lifts at Bright were mirrored, and I looked myself in the eye as the one I was in descended to the ground floor. That exchange had rattled me. I was a natural mentor, wasn't I? A person who raised up younger women, carving out a path for them that had never been carved for me?

Yet there was an uncomfortable familiarity about the fixed grin Jenna had given me as she'd apologized for overstepping. It was the smile you gave when you had to appease the person with the power. I used to give that same fixed grin back in the bad old days when a middle-aged male client, sometimes even a boss, complimented my outfit in a tone of voice designed to tell me that what he was really thinking about was how it would feel to peel it off. It was tragic really, the way it had alienated me from the senior women; they'd all seemed so regal and fierce back then, even though they were probably just forty-somethings like I was now. I'd watched them silently observing, probably despairing internally of power dynamics they knew were too dangerous, too primal, to risk calling out. It had felt like we were left to fight among ourselves for the scraps, while the men had carte blanche to carry on netting the spoils.

The lechery still made my skin crawl, and I pushed away the memories as soon as the lift doors pinged open. Obviously, I wasn't like that, and I'd double down on the praise and encouragement I offered Jenna as soon as I got back. I walked briskly to Squirrel, nabbed a double shot latte, then decided to take a circuitous route back to the office. What I really needed to be thinking about was everything else. There was a tiny grassy square nestled between the crush of buildings, the green bleached yellow and arid by the unusually hot summer. I ground to a halt beside it and perched on a bench.

This new wondering of mine, whether I could feel like a

mother even without the baby being made of my own matter –
it was more than a strategy, wasn't it? More than a cheap trick
to try to dodge the wave of devastation that was threatening to
crash over me as soon as I let the truth of Dr Rindell's words
settle? *Yes*, I told myself firmly, even though I was clearly the
last person I could trust.

I sat in the sun for a few minutes, trying to let the warm
glow lull me into a state of calm, before reluctantly figuring
it was time to return to the office. I stood up, dusted myself
down practically and metaphorically, and decided to go back
past Squirrel as my first noble deed of the day. An extra latte
later, with a couple of their delicious brownies added to my
order for good measure, I re-entered the office. I'd just have
to hope Jenna was the only Bright employee under twenty-five
who didn't claim to be gluten intolerant.

She didn't – in fact, she was delighted. She took a gulp of
her coffee and then began to apologize again, but this time I
cut across her.

'Honestly, Jenna, I love your initiative. *I'm* sorry if it didn't
sound that way. You know I've been a bit frazzled this week.'
It was convenient, the way I was able to blame the threat I'd
felt – quick and animal – on something else.

'Are you okay now, Sasha?' she said softly.

'Yes, yes I'm fine,' I replied hurriedly. I couldn't risk her
knocking against the livid bruise. 'But it means I haven't taken
you through all the other campaigns we're working across.'

'Like what?'

'Maple. We've been working on their rebranding for the last
few months.'

'The airline?' she said, a tinge of wariness in her voice.

'I know, I know,' I said, smiling a rueful apology. 'My
stepdaughter's already given me climate emergency grief

this morning. But their CEO is passionate about them being part of the solution, so it's a positive if we help them gain market share over the less responsible fuckers. And it's a huge campaign for us – it'll make a big difference to our year-end numbers.'

'How are they part of the solution?' asked Jenna, cocking her head inquisitively so that her blunt fringe swished to the side. Unlike Georgie, she was asking a genuine question.

'Their technological innovation is way out in front of their competitors. They're actually converting industrial emissions into fuel, and the planes are much greener too – the whole fleet's being replaced with lighter models. They've made all of their goody bags sustainable, looked at the supply chain for the catering. And we've designed this new visual branding for them.'

I crossed to my computer to pull it up.

Jenna took another sip of her coffee, following me to my desk. 'But Georgie thought it was just spin?'

I looked up from my keyboard, startled by the sound of Georgie's name coming from her mouth – had I mentioned her in passing? I must have. Jenna clearly missed nothing.

'Yeah, basically,' I said. She gave a mischievous grin like she instinctively understood my stepmotherly frustration, and I couldn't help smiling back, even though it wasn't wholly appropriate. I busied myself with pulling up the visuals, the cartoonish green maple leaf we'd designed to use across all the branding, more like something from a cool Netflix animation than a dreary airline.

'Wow, that really pops,' said Jenna. 'And obviously it's better they're doing something rather than nothing, right?'

'Exactly!' I said, gratified. 'Which is what I want Georgie to understand. The real world isn't about impossible perfection.

You're much better off with a compromise you can pull off than some holy ideal you can never achieve. It's like a basic life lesson.'

Jenna nodded solemnly, as though she was acknowledging my wisdom. 'So, have you got a plan to convince her?' she said.

'I want to bring her into the Next Generation group we run,' I told her. 'Elevate.'

'What, the under-twenties thing?' she said.

'Yeah. This is probably the first time in your life you've been too old for something, right?'

She laughed. 'I'll survive.'

The Elevate project scooped up young people who combined big ambitions with challenging backgrounds, giving them the kind of connections and exposure that could make all the difference to them forging a career in the industry. The flip side? We got direct access to what kinds of campaigns and messages struck a chord, and also – this part was far more important than we let on – which ones struck them as tone-deaf. My privately educated stepdaughter was far from the target profile, but I figured stretching the rules this one time wouldn't do any harm.

Jenna called over from her monitor. 'I just looked it up,' she said. 'The next meeting's happening in a couple of weeks.'

'Great!' I said.

Did she hear the anxiety in my shrill squeak? The idea of Georgie's sullen presence in the heart of my working life suddenly seemed less appealing now that it was a real possibility. Jenna looked as if she was weighing up whether to speak.

'Spit it out,' I said.

'Only if you wanted, obviously, but I could come too? Looks like you've got a clash in your diary, so then if you needed to leave early, I could stay with her. I want to get across everything about this place anyway.' She grinned. 'Sorry, does that sound like I've drunk way too much of the Kool-Aid?'

'No, not at all,' I said, beaming. She could bathe in the Kool-Aid for all I cared – she really was the answer to my prayers. She'd be the perfect buffer: young enough to make Bright feel like it wasn't the evil empire, but not so relentlessly woke that she'd make me look like a capitalist pig. 'I would actually *love* that.' I paused, contemplating the way she peeked up from behind her desk, like a flower growing and blossoming in new terrain. 'You're exactly the kind of person I want her to aspire to be.'

I'm living, breathing proof that you should be careful what you wish for.

JENNA

Jenna looked at herself critically in the narrow mirror that hung in the hallway outside her bedroom. It was Tuesday, and she was trying even harder than ever to make her wardrobe transform into something it wasn't. She'd rolled up her jeans in an attempt to make them look Parisian and chic, but they weren't designed for that and now they were pretty much cutting off the blood supply to her ankles. She'd put on one of her two white shirts over the top, tucking just the left side in, but now it looked more like 'no uniform' day at secondary school than Lily-Rose Depp strolling down the Champs-Élysées.

The door of the master bedroom swung open, Penelope yawning and stretching in her animal-print pyjamas. It was infuriating – she looked more chic straight from bed, with cheetahs pawing their way across her tits, than Jenna did after forty-five minutes of frantic self-styling. Sunlight streamed through the big bay windows that ringed Penelope's room, bathing her in a glow that made her look unreasonably beautiful.

'Morning, chicken,' she said, wiping sleep from her eyes. 'How did you sleep?'

Jenna had been up until it was too scary to look at the time, combing through all the presentations and creative briefs that

Bright had prepared for Maple. She knew she had the sallow face to prove it, but she decided to style it out. 'That bed's so comfy,' she said. 'I was out like a light.'

'So glad you like it!' said an oblivious Penelope. Even if Jenna had switched the light off at a normal hour, the bed's ancient mattress had springs that worked their way into her back like a medieval torture instrument. 'That room's a bit snug, but I like to think it's cosy. It was a junk room when I was a kid, but I used to go and sleep in there on a lilo when I stayed with Auntie Alice, 'cos it meant I was closer to the foxes.' Penelope gave a dimply smile at the thought of her adorable younger self. Then her expression hardened. 'You won't forget that cash for the kitty will you, Jenna? I've already put the Sainsbury's order in for Sunday, so it'll be coming out of my account any day now.'

Jenna had been trying and failing to force herself to go to the cashpoint for a few days. She struck her forehead with her palm like it was down to stupidity, not fear.

'Sorry, work's been mental. I'll get the cash out right now, so I don't forget.' She looked at her phone, lying by her feet. 'Shit, I should go. Today's a big one.'

'Don't worry, I know you'll smash it,' sang Penelope, heading for the bathroom. She'd be as oblivious to the circle of grime that ringed the sink as she was to the dark circles that ringed Jenna's exhausted eyes.

* * *

Jenna ground to a halt next to the cash dispenser, commuters jostling her as they headed for the dark mouth of the Tube. It swallowed her card whole, and she steeled herself before tapping in her PIN. Here it came – the verdict. Jenna was many things, but she wasn't stupid. She knew the kitty on top of the rent and everything else was unmanageable, but somehow she'd kidded herself that she'd be taxed less or paid more than she'd calculated. The proximity to her overdraft this soon after Bright's first miserly payment was terrifying. She had to steady herself against the wall as she keyed in the amount she'd need to keep Penelope at bay, her stomach lurching. 'Beggars can't be choosers' was a phrase of her mother's that had echoed through her childhood, cutting like a knife. Uttered to all the kids in her family, it had still always felt like it was intended to pierce her heart alone. Jenna looked out at the grimy chaos of Junction Road, lorries barrelling past, the air thick with fumes and panic. This life she'd embarked on was meant to right so many wrongs. She couldn't admit defeat so soon.

She yanked the notes out of the machine's thin, mean slit and shoved them into her purse. As she turned towards the Tube, she caught sight of the pub, the fabled Falcon, standing proud on the opposite corner. She always peered through the windows when she walked past it, wondering if she'd spot Sasha in there, smooching her mysterious husband on one of their date nights. She'd had no luck on that score, but what she had spotted was a tacked-up sign advertising for staff.

Now she looked down at her open purse, at the handful of bills that would be exiting it almost immediately. She didn't have much of a choice.

* * *

Sasha was already in the office when Jenna arrived, a bag of nerves even from ten paces. She was twisting her long blonde hair around her fingers as she sat at her desk, taking gulps from her Bright-branded bottle.

'Georgie didn't come in with you, then?' Jenna asked, dumping her cotton shopper on her desk.

'Well remembered,' said Sasha, smiling ruefully. 'But Christ, no. That'd mean getting out of bed before eight.' She stood up, crossing to the printer, then paused, her bottom lip caught between her teeth. 'Not that she's not a nice girl. She is. Most of the time.'

It had been gradual but significant, the way the intimacy had been creeping up on them over the last few weeks.

'Course I remember,' Jenna laughed. 'I'm the one who's babysitting for you.'

A little flash of pain crossed Sasha's face, wiped away before it could be spotted by anyone less attuned than Jenna. The mere word 'baby' seemed to trigger her boss, and judging by the mysterious appointment that had appeared in her diary for a couple of weeks' time, she hadn't given up on her dream. Jenna had deliberately tried scheduling a couple of things on top of it to see what Sasha would do: each time she'd snapped that it couldn't be moved, then looked down at her desk, trying to cover her distress.

Jenna kept prattling on before things could get awkward. 'I stayed up revising all the stats last night,' she said as she switched on her monitor. 'She'll be booking a round-the-world airline ticket by the time I've finished blinding her with science.'

'Listen, if you can get her to raise a smile, that'll be enough for me.'

Sasha was ordering the papers she'd pulled off the printer, briskly stapling them. She paused, her head on one side, studying Jenna.

'Jenna, your shirt ... It's coming out of your jeans on the left. Might just want to ...' She mimed tucking it back in, like Jenna hadn't spent a full half hour trying to perfect the way it would tumble casually over her hip.

Jenna looked away, face burning, shovelling the fabric back into her too-tight waistband. Turning back around, she fixed a peppy smile in place. 'Thanks for telling me.'

'Of course,' Sasha said breezily, laying the papers on Jenna's desk. She herself was wearing a slim-cut magenta linen suit, which might've made someone else look like a children's party entertainer. Instead, she was willowy and elegant, a foxglove swaying in a summer garden. 'We girls have to stick together, don't we?'

* * *

At 10.20, Jenna got a call from reception announcing Georgie's arrival. She swivelled around to ask Sasha if she should go and collect her, feeling a spurt of satisfaction at how flustered such a simple question made her boss.

'No, no, I'll go,' Sasha said, nervously slurping more water. 'It's just . . .'

Jenna threw her a conspiratorial smile. 'Annoying that she's late?'

'Yes!' agreed Sasha fervently. 'I was going to take her for coffee, walk her round the office, and now we'll have to go straight into that stupid meeting.' She shook her head. 'It's not stupid, obviously. It's important.'

She stood up abruptly, her water bottle clenched tightly in her hand like it was a favourite toy.

'Maybe she was nervous?' said Jenna, looking up at her from her desk. 'I dunno . . .' She paused. 'You're the boss here. You're pretty powerful.'

Sasha's shoulders dropped. 'That's a big maybe,' she said, smiling despite herself. 'Why don't you come with me? We need to go downstairs now anyway.'

There were a couple of people sitting on the long sofa; luckily only one of them was a sulky teenager, which meant the fact that Jenna already knew exactly what Georgie looked like wasn't obvious. She looked smaller and shyer than she did on Instagram, where she often shot for outraged fierceness. A pink streak ran through her dark hair; in person, it gave her more the vibe of a colour-blind badger than the punk rebel look she was surely going for. Her oversized green sweatshirt made her look stocky and square, its sleeves pulled down over bitten fingernails. Baggy, wide-legged jeans tented over battered purple Converse. She couldn't have looked less like Sasha's daughter if she'd tried. And in fact, she probably had.

'Hi, darling!' said Sasha, her voice so tinny and fake that Jenna almost felt sorry for them both. 'Did you get held up? We probably need to go straight into the meeting – I was hoping we could get a coffee first, but . . .'

'I can go,' Jenna offered quickly, sticking out a friendly hand. 'I'm Jenna, your m—, Sasha's creative assistant.'

Georgie looked at Sasha accusingly. 'You have an assistant? Bit . . .' She paused, casting around for something sufficiently damning. 'Buckingham Palace, isn't it? Have you got a footman too?'

Sasha's response seemed to get stuck in her throat, giving Jenna time to jump in.

'Doesn't feel anything like that,' she said. 'I've only been here a few weeks, but I'm having the best time. I can't believe how much I'm learning.'

Sasha threw her a grateful smile – Jenna had already figured out her boss was pathetically addicted to praise. 'I started as an assistant,' she agreed. 'It's how you learn. I don't think you'll necessarily start as a CEO. I mean, I could be wrong about that, but . . .'

Sasha tilted her head towards the lift, giving a teasing smile to Georgie, who quickly stood up to follow, grabbing the scrappy vinyl rucksack that lay at her feet.

'I'll get those coffees,' said Jenna. 'I'll be quick. Oat latte for you, Sasha; flat white for me – just need your order now, Georgie?'

'Double macchiato, yeah?' Georgie replied, barely looking back, her private-school education trilling out of her vowels. Giving orders didn't seem to be quite such a hardship for her either.

* * *

Jenna half ran, half walked back from Squirrel, the three coffees wobbling in the cardboard tray. She didn't want to miss a thing. The meeting was being held in the bowels of the building, and she dashed down the looping stairs, too impatient to wait for the lift. She shouldered her way through the double doors, then ground to a halt.

It was like Batman's lair in there, a whole other world within Bright that she hadn't even known existed. Workstations were scattered around the room higgledy-piggledy, an army of late teens hunched over laptops like they owned the place. The modern art that Bright prided itself on decorated the walls down here too, but it was even more ugly and abstract than it was upstairs, even harder for Jenna to find the beauty that someone smarter than her would surely just 'get'. Interspersed with the artworks were screens flashing up questions that were either pretentious or profound depending on your state of mind – '*Who would you be if today was the last day of your life?*' demanded one. Jenna was momentarily hypnotized, the question almost sickening, but then it melted away. WELCOME TO BRIGHT'S NEXT GEN CREATIVES appeared in its place. LET'S FORCE A BETTER FUTURE. It was followed by a rush of images – riots and fires and melting ice caps, all sped up like fate on steroids.

Jenna pushed forwards through the gaggles of people searching for seats, her eyes scanning the room for Sasha and Georgie. There was a semicircle of stools at the front of the room, fringing a low stage, and she spotted the two of them sitting near the end. Pete and Chloe were on the same row, a couple of other senior team members dotted nearby. She crossed to them and handed each their coffee, noticing how Georgie's hand trembled as she took it from her. Jenna took note: it tied in with a quote the younger girl had posted on Instagram late at night the Wednesday before – '*Some Days I Need Permission to Just Suck*'. When she'd gone back on Georgie's feed early the next morning, it had been deleted, as though shame had beaten honesty in the battle for her public persona.

As Jenna took a seat, Chloe bounded up onto the stage.

'Hi, gang!' she said, speaking into an oversized mike that was completely unnecessary for the size of the room. 'We're so excited to have you here. Like the sign says,' she pointed dramatically at the flashing screens all around them, 'You. Are. The future!'

The room suddenly erupted with noisy whooping and clapping like they were in some kind of cult. 'Let's look at how YOU are helping shape the creation of our campaign for Locker Room,' Chloe went on. Locker Room was a bog-standard sports chain – trainers and running gear – but now Bright was on a mission to sprinkle on the fairy dust.

'You said they were just another greedy retailer, ripping you off when you bought their stuff,' said Chloe, relishing the febrile energy. 'You talked, they listened. Now they're refurbishing basketball courts and sports facilities in deprived areas, right across the UK!'

More cheering.

'And it doesn't stop there. They're supporting local teams at a grassroots level by gifting training gear. And may I say,' she pointed to the screens again, 'the capsule collections that some of you budding designers helped to devise are right up my alley!'

A selection of images strobed across the screens, outfits so dizzyingly cool that Jenna couldn't imagine anyone would risk staining them with their sweat. Once the montage was over, Chloe invited a couple of the group up on stage to introduce a promo they'd made, zigzagging across the country to ask teens in urban areas what made them feel like organized sport was something they'd want to be part of.

'Could you imagine making something like that?' Jenna heard Sasha whisper to Georgie, but all she got back was a sullen headshake. The moody pout made Sasha recoil, but Jenna caught something in the girl's expression that her boss was missing. Georgie was more intimidated than angry; this was yet another tribe that didn't want her – didn't see her – and what she really craved was to be seen. Jenna felt a secret smile cross her face – she could deliver that, no problem.

She leaned across Georgie's solid body to get Sasha's attention. 'You're up next, you start presenting as soon as the clients get here,' she hissed, handing her the cue cards she'd prepared.

'Thanks, Jenna,' Sasha whispered back, grabbing them and making to stand.

Just then, the door at the back of the room opened wide, a giant tooth of light biting into the darkness. A man stepped through, illuminated like he was the second coming. But it wasn't just the light – it was the way he entered the space like he owned it, no anxiety about disturbing the flow of proceedings. Jenna looked back at her boss, aware she hadn't yet crossed the room to the podium.

Sasha was frozen where she stood, staring at the figure in the doorway, her face a mask of shock.

SASHA

The Maple top brass had mentioned a few times that they were negotiating with a 'heavyweight' who they wanted to bring in to head up their in-house marketing operation, but it had just been peripheral noise. I'd been working as hard as ever, but often on autopilot, obsessive thoughts about whether or not I still had a shot at motherhood consuming my every waking moment. Now that background noise had become relentless static, horror freezing me in place as I stared at the man striding into the room like he owned it. How was it that I was standing in front of the person who had chewed up my twenties and spat them out? Not that anyone my own age would have much sympathy for my wilful self-harm – it was only Jenna's generation who might be outraged on my behalf.

I gripped the index cards tight in my shaking hands as I approached the podium. Christ, everything about me was so analogue, including my eggs and my chequered dating history. Jenna smiled at me from the front row, nodding discreetly to the laptop, and I started up the roster of slides that I'd worked on with the team. As my finger hit the space bar, I risked darting a glance at Fred. His compact body wasn't the muscular wedge it had been in his forties, his outline softer. That thick, dark hair I'd buried my fingers in, wishing I didn't have to lose him again and again to his real life, was streaked with silver. Some things had diminished, but also nothing had. His dark green eyes still looked like they could see something that no one else was smart enough to detect. He still radiated that unshakeable confidence about his place in the world that had hypnotized me back then.

'The climate crisis is worse than anyone could ever have predicted,' I said, forcing my voice to stay steady. 'And it's your generation who are paying for it.'

The sight of him had left me so raw that the images of species nearing extinction and raging forest fires nearly took me to the edge. Did I really want to bring a child into this carnage? Still, I kept my nerve and found my focus as the slides rolled through.

'That's why we all need to come together to find solutions that can transform the way we live our lives. Learn to walk lightly on the only home any of us will ever have.'

I'd been keeping my gaze trained anywhere but on Fred, but now I had to direct my words towards him. He had to feel my grown-up stature and charisma – this account was way too important for Bright to lose. He was watching me with that intensity that used to make me feel like I'd won some incredible prize. Now all it did was chill me.

'Maple are passionate about transforming the aviation industry, so it can be part of the solution, not just part of the problem,' I continued, laying out the company's race to reach net zero via all their technological innovation. I couldn't help feeling bitter. Fred had always been the problem, never the solution, but it had taken me years to see it. We'd worked together here, him second-in-command to Bridget and Martin in the distant days when I was their assistant. At first, I'd thought he was avuncular, but in fact he was more like a vulture. He consumed my heart until it was nothing but dead meat, letting me believe we were living out a love story.

Pushing my feelings aside, I realized I'd reached the fun part of the presentation: the sustainable treats you'd find in Maple's goody bags; their delicious, locally sourced in-flight meals. I flicked through images of their new branding – lush trees and, yes, maple leaves – that spoke to a greener future. I talked about 'brand ambassadors' – people inside and outside the business, possibly including the teens who sat in front of me – who would spread the word about what they were trying to achieve. And then I finally stopped talking, my mouth dry and arid. My sweaty hands clutched at the podium: I was all too aware that it was only the first leg of the race that I'd run so far. I looked out at the baby faces in front of me, trying to assess how the message had landed. Georgie looked as sulky as ever, but hopefully she was no barometer.

The signs seemed good. 'Those planes are sick!' said a skinny boy in the front row who was a part of the directing cohort. 'I'll be an ambassador right now if you're gonna fly me business to New York. Yes, please!'

Everyone laughed, a swell of noisy feedback filling the room. I risked another look at Georgie – she was peering around the packed space, absorbing the way the group sparked off each other. Maybe she was starting to think it was something she might want to be a part of.

'So, you can connect with what Maple are trying to do?' I asked, quelling the cacophony of voices. 'You feel like they're doing something different from the herd?'

As shouts of agreement rose up from the crowd, my eye caught Fred's. I regretted it immediately. It turned out I hadn't forgotten that smile of his – the way it conveyed interest without giving off any real warmth, like an electric fire that was purely decorative.

I stayed focused on the kids. 'And what is it that makes you feel like they're really trying to make a difference? That it's authentic, more than just greenwashing bullshit?'

'They're not murdering animals,' yelled one girl from the back.

'They're putting cash into better technology, not just using their dirty old planes till they wear out,' shouted another.

I let the answers roll in, trusting that Fred couldn't help but be impressed. At least I'd got this bit right – Bright's branding was connecting with the age group every industry was dying to seduce, and he was seeing the live show. But then, a familiar whine of complaint from the front row put my self-satisfaction to bed.

'I'm not being funny, but fossil fuels are still fossil fuels. They're not at net zero now, are they?'

Heat rose up my body. Why had I taken the risk of bringing her here?

'Putting those pretty pictures of leaves on the outside of a machine that's killing the planet doesn't make it any better.'

Now she was leaping to her feet: I had to get a handle on this, and fast.

Georgie turned her body towards the packed room. 'Have you guys forgotten it's a climate emergency? It's a fucking EMERGENCY!'

There were a few seconds of silence, a tiny reprieve in which I hoped that I could smooth the comment away as part of a healthy debate and eyeball her back into her seat. I could see Jenna laying a hand on Georgie's arm, subtly pulling her downwards. But then the room erupted into thunderous applause, shouts and catcalls of agreement ricocheting around the space.

'I hear what you're saying . . .' I started, trying to keep my professional mask intact while glaring at her in such a way that she'd know she'd be grounded until her fiftieth birthday if she didn't shut it down. 'But the reality is that we need a functioning global economy. Travel is part of that. So, isn't there an argument for prioritizing the most environmentally responsible solutions available to us right now?'

Fred's eyes were tracking me, inscrutable, as if this was some kind of spectator sport.

'Those are the kind of bullshit excuses your generation uses to shut us down,' Georgie yelled. It was almost funny: when it was Steve who was in the firing line, I told him to go easy on her, counselled sympathy and understanding. Now it was me taking the bullets, I was pure bloodlust. 'But it's time you paid the bill – we're not going to let you get away with it anymore.'

I kept my voice deliberately calm, hoping it was only me who could hear how it shook. 'Thank you for sharing your thoughts. We're here to hear a range of opinions, so perhaps you could *sit down* and let someone else speak.'

I held her gaze for a second, my eyes flashing steel, and she started to lower herself. There were other eager hands waving in the air, the ordeal nearly over. But then she suddenly jack-knifed back up, her fist raised like she was some kind of freedom fighter, rather than a private school kid who loved Deliverooing herself vegan doughnuts.

'This is how they silence us!' she shouted. 'We have to say no to their bullshit!'

Now the room exploded into chaos again, the order I'd started to impose immediately evaporating. I was filled with a surge of gratitude when Chloe sprang to her feet, joining me at the front and raising her voice over the noise.

'We're pretty much out of time for today anyway. Thank you for a . . .' Chloe gave a little shimmy of her shoulders, her bare brown arms slicing through the muggy tension. She was the kind of annoying person who could flirt with a flight of stairs, but right now I was grateful for her ability to shift the mood. 'Lively debate – little bit extra!' She grinned at me as she said it, and I forced myself to mirror her expression.

'Yes, thank you everyone,' I said. 'There's a lot here for us and our colleagues at Maple to digest as we move forward with the campaign.'

As Chloe wound things up, I hopped down from the stage and headed for the exit, willing my heart to slow. I could barely look at Georgie, but as I cut across the room, Jenna caught up with me.

'You handled that SO well,' she whispered. 'You were a fucking badass.'

Maybe it hadn't been as bad as it had felt from up there. 'We'll talk upstairs,' I muttered back.

I hadn't been planning to be secretive about bringing my stepdaughter to Elevate, but I'd rapidly revised my strategy. Now I'd have to find an appropriate way to pull Jenna into the subterfuge.

'Sasha.'

The deep voice sent my heart rate skyrocketing again. It had been too much to hope for, that I'd be able to slip away with just a polite wave across the room.

I ground to a halt and forced myself to smile. 'Hey, Fred. Little bit of theatre for you there!'

Playing it for laughs was a risk, but it seemed to pay off. 'You know me, Sasha,' he said, a smirk playing across his craggy face. 'I like to keep it raw.'

I was grateful that he didn't think the whole thing had been a shitshow, but the quid pro quo was that he was now making my skin crawl. I unconsciously looked down at his left hand, forcing down a sickening wave of revulsion. Yes, he was still married. This was just standard operating procedure for him.

'So, you'll be at the full pitch later in the month?' I managed.

'Yeah, course I will,' he said, raking his fingers through his hair as though he was revelling in how thick it still was. 'I'm running the show now.'

'Great.' I awkwardly gestured to the door. 'So, I'd better get on with it. Bye, Fred.'

And then I was out of there, Jenna bringing up the rear.

At that moment, I wondered: could my life get any more impossible?

Yes, it could. And it would.

JENNA

Jenna stayed close to Sasha as they left the dark basement room, careful not to speak too soon. Her boss's eyes were trained straight ahead, her thin finger hitting the lift button as if she was detonating a bomb. She'd been humiliated, and it was better if Jenna didn't push on the bruise in case Sasha offloaded on her. There'd been something off in the exchange with the Maple exec too, an awkwardness that seemed to be about more than Georgie's public display. Sasha had been self-conscious and aloof all at once, a mangled version of herself that Jenna had never seen before.

She calculated that it was better if Sasha broke the silence, and by the time they'd reached the first floor she was off, spittle erupting from her mouth as rage overtook her. 'What the fuck did she think she was she doing?' she growled, hands balled into fists.

Jenna shook her head in solidarity as the lift reached their floor and the doors opened. 'My mum would've given me a slap if I'd made a scene like that.'

'If I strangled her with my bare hands, it would only be fair that I walked free,' hissed Sasha, stalking across the floor. Her face clouded as she flung herself down in her chair. 'No, scrub that from the record. She's a child – I guess I need to do better as well.'

Jenna felt a pulse of excitement run through her, a gambler's dangerous high. The words were out of her mouth before she could pull them back.

'Look, I may be way out of line saying this, but the way I see it, she looks up to you.'

Sasha spun her chair towards Jenna, eyes wide in disbelief. 'Looks up to me? I'm sorry, Jenna, but are you serious? She just made me look like a fucking idiot in front of a whole room full of people.'

Jenna doubled down. 'Trust me, she does. You're just the last person who'll ever notice!' Sasha's face was still a mask of doubt, but Jenna ploughed on. 'That whole room was lapping up what you were telling them. They were leaning right in. And she was basking in it – she'd just never tell you.'

Jenna wasn't sure she'd ever used the word 'basking' before, but she liked the way it sounded coming out of her mouth – it added a lick of colour to her narrative.

'Do you really think that?' asked Sasha, the compliment creeping up on her and taking hold like a blush. Sometimes she was too easy a mark. 'Most of the time she . . .' She checked herself, swinging from left to right in her chair like the motion soothed her. 'She's not always the easiest at home. And why would she do what she just did if she had even a dirty little pocket of admiration for me?'

Jenna paused for a second, playing for time. 'Maybe she's scared,' she suggested. 'Maybe she's scared of how much she wants your approval, so it makes her run the other way, make a twat of herself.'

'You're very perceptive, aren't you?' Sasha said, the gratitude that shone from her eyes giving Jenna a little jolt of genuine warmth, which she quickly froze into oblivion. 'Maybe you're the Georgie whisperer. I most certainly am not.'

'I might be talking shit, but I reckon I'm on to something,' said Jenna, as earnestly as she could. 'And if you bring her to another one of those meetings, I promise I'll try and get her to be a bit less Wednesday Addams.'

Sasha laughed, turning back towards her computer. 'Not sure I can face it quite yet, but I might lose my mind and take you up on it.' She paused, looking around the still-empty floor. 'Let's not mention to anyone who she is, okay? You're the one who put her on the list for Elevate, not me, and it's all a bit chaotic, I think . . . who actually comes.'

She was staring intently at her screen now, trying to throw the statement away.

'Sure,' said Jenna, mirroring her fake cool. 'Your secret's safe with me.'

Shared secrets were exactly the kind of currency that Jenna needed.

* * *

Sasha was in back-to-back meetings the rest of the day, so Jenna slipping away early for one of her own went unnoticed.

Unsurprisingly, her interview at the Falcon was nothing like the one she'd had at Bright. She'd made sure that first encounter with Sasha had felt like a date between two people who really wanted the relationship to end up meaning something. This was more like a sweaty shag in the toilet cubicle of a club at kicking-out time.

The Falcon's bar manager looked ancient and baby-faced all at once, his bald head and pink cheeks steamy with perspiration, his dark eyes haunted and lined in a way that suggested every single shift was stress on a stick. Jenna ultimately decided he was mid-thirties, suppressing a shudder at the thought of being stuck in a dead-end job like this when forty was within touching distance. There was 'no fucker left to hire since

Brex-shit,' Neil told her, and at this point he'd hire 'pretty much anyone'.

'No offence!' she chirped, cocking her head in a way that forced him to make eye contact. Up until that point, his gaze had been roving around the bar like a bucking horse, searching for the next crisis he'd have to gallop in and fix. When it occasionally reached her, it seemed to hit her legs – exposed in a pair of oversized cotton shorts that she'd hoped were very Bright – before it met her eyes.

The bar was kind of skanky, but in that London way that came full circle and ended up being stylish for some indefinable reason that you could never hope to bottle. The maroon leather on the chairs was ripped and dirty, the wobbly old wooden tables coated in grime. The mirrors that covered the walls were speckled and dingy, but in a way that allowed the low lighting to bounce and reflect, giving the whole room a hypnotic kind of glow. The wine came in little beakers that looked more suited to giving a toddler orange squash in, but that also served to remind Jenna that she was a long way from All Bar One. As far as she could see, the clientele all seemed to either be wearing stretchy Lycra, like they'd popped in for a pint on the way back from training for a marathon, or the kind of floral tea dresses that should've made them look like total nannas, but instead made them appear impossibly chic. It seemed as though every single one of them owned a shaggy dog with an impeccable, Insta-ready blow-dry that lay obediently across their feet.

Jenna suppressed a sigh. It was hard to imagine ever feeling like she really belonged in this city. She pushed the thought away before it could take root – that was a secondary goal, and her primary mission was going better than she ever could have hoped.

'Yeah, right, no offence,' agreed Neil, turning back to her

crumpled CV with an apologetic grimace. 'Her' CV might be pushing it. She'd made some skilful subtractions and additions before it reached Neil's sweaty grip. According to the piece of paper in his hand she didn't have a full-time job, for one thing – she couldn't have him thinking she wouldn't be available for the random shifts he'd want to believe he could throw at her. And she'd apparently worked in one of the only Michelin-starred restaurants in striking distance of Stoke, conveniently long since closed. She'd seen the pretentious foodie flourishes on the menu that was scrawled on a blackboard next to the bar; the handful of shifts she'd done at Pizza Express during her A-levels were not going to cut it here.

'Your CV looks great!' he said, after a lightning-fast skim, and Jenna allowed herself to breathe out. 'We love what Francis King did in the nose-to-tail movement. Teaching people how tasty offal can be, using every scrap of the carcass.'

Jenna froze, but before the awkwardness could calcify, Neil's plump face broke into another smirk.

'Don't worry, I know his reputation. Bit of a cock, even though he's also a bit of a genius, right?'

Jenna gave a stiff nod.

'Yeah, very clever,' said Neil. 'Don't commit yourself verbally. Walls have ears!'

'You took the words right out of my mouth,' she replied quickly.

'Must've been while you were kissing me?' Neil replied, quick as a flash, then blushed. 'It's a song. Guess Meatloaf's before your time. Ignore me.'

Jenna left a gap in the conversation, careful not to take the edge off his awkwardness. Sasha often did that when people banged on too long in a meeting, subtly reminding them exactly who was in charge. The last thing Jenna wanted was Neil feeling emboldened enough to lay a clammy paw on her arse when she was juggling plates and juggling lives, desperately trying to get back to her real job.

'Why have meatloaf when you can have rump steak?' she said eventually, gesturing at the night's menu on the board.

'Exactly!' he replied, relieved she'd given him an escape hatch. 'Anyway, the job's yours if you want it.'

Jenna forced her voice into an upward lilt. 'Oh wow, amazing!' she said. 'I love everything about this place already.'

She knew it was ridiculous, but she couldn't help feeling that the basset hound at the next table was looking up at her with contempt as the disingenuous bullshit left her mouth. She stared back into its rheumy eyes, its long ears skimming the dirty floor, then lifted her gaze to its owner, a small woman with a gigantic laptop and the kind of thick-framed black glasses that looked like picture frames. Jenna's sense of superiority was short-lived; the fact was, you had to be very successful to wear accessories that stupid. Maybe the woman was a friend of Sasha's. Maybe they met here for drunken dinners, swapping stories about what professional ballers they both were.

She felt another intoxicating rush of fear and excitement. It was dangerous to be here, but the thrill of being inside another part of Sasha's life made the peril worth it. If Sasha came in, she'd just have to hide. Spy on her from a whole new vantage point.

And besides, danger had never put Jenna off anything before.

SASHA

These days, my feet are like a couple of fat little piglets, only able to live out their sweaty, swollen lives inside a pair of size eight men's trainers. I have to lean backwards on the sofa to ease the ugly things off, each minor indignity of pregnancy feeling like a punishment from the gods for all of the sins that got me here. I don't know how a flat as poky as this can echo with silence, but this evening the quiet feels deafening.

I still can't help thinking that the events of that Elevate meeting were pivotal. If it wasn't for what went down there, I might still be snuggled on the luxuriously wide velvet sofa of my marital home, bickering with my exasperating husband about the latest must-see war documentary he insists on streaming. Instead I'm bickering with myself about whether half a glass of cold Pinot Grigio is reprehensible or just about acceptable while I'm suffering this strange version of solitary confinement.

Georgie was too cunning for me. By the time I got the chance to start ranting to Steve about how she'd humiliated me in front of not just my colleagues, but also my client (I stumbled a bit on the last word), she'd already pleaded her case to him. I'd started my diatribe as I stepped through the door, hurling the pair of elegant open-toed high heels I took for granted across the hallway.

'Sasha, Sasha ...' he said, giving my bare arm a strange kind of pat. 'Just come downstairs and have a drink. We'll talk about it. It's just crossed wires—'

'Crossed wires?' I interrupted, in a barely contained shriek. I stomped down the stairs after him, snarling at his retreating back. 'It wasn't crossed fucking wires. It was ... it was a hit job.'

I didn't like the deliberate way he swung open the fridge door, his head pushing inside like there was some kind of mystery as to where the white wine was. He was playing for time. He poured me a generous glass, gave me a smile that was meant to be conciliatory but just came off as patronizing.

'She was terrified you'd feel like this.'

'Sorry?' I said, slamming the glass down on the marble counter, the wine almost splashing over the brim. 'Are you taking her side?'

'She called me straight after in a real state. Told me what happened.' Steve turned towards me, his palms face up like he was pleading for reason. 'You know what she's like – she's passionate about her beliefs. She thought you'd invited her there to share her honest feedback on the work, but she knew as soon as she started talking that you were angry with her.'

I gave an unattractive snort through my nostrils. 'Bullshit. She knew exactly what she was doing. It was an attack. She wanted to make me look like an incompetent idiot.'

Steve's hands dropped now, the metre of space between us suddenly feeling more like a mile. 'My daughter isn't a vindictive person,' he said, his words deliberate .

My heart plummeted, landing somewhere close to the floor. The parenting exam never ends if 'step' is the prefix. Not unless you choose to spoil your paper and walk out of the hall.

'I know she isn't,' I said, the robotic agreement I knew he

needed to hear almost choking me. He'd defend either of his kids to the ends of the earth; sometimes, when I tried to hold on to the wisp of a memory of my own father, I envied them. I'd been robbed of the chance to feel that primal, reflexive love from him.

'But if she'd been actively trying to humiliate you, that would've been vindictive,' he said evenly, taking a slow pull from his glass.

There was something quite deadly about the way Steve argued, lawyerly and precise. I'd have preferred a screaming match, truths hurled like Molotov cocktails, rage given a chance to burn itself out.

'So, okay, maybe it was just incredibly immature.' I stumbled, my fingers nervously playing with the stem of my glass. 'She obviously knows she embarrassed me.'

Steve shook his head emphatically. 'No, no – she said how brilliantly you ran the whole thing. Sounds like the suits were eating out of your hand.'

A prickly heat buzzed under my skin as I guiltily pushed the thought of Fred away. 'I wouldn't say that,' I muttered, taking a hungry gulp of wine.

I crossed to him then, the yawning chasm between us suddenly too hard to bear, full of secrets that I'd left for dead, abandoned in the empty space. He opened his arms immediately, folded me in. 'Try to let it go, Sasha,' he said, resting his chin on the top of my head. 'If anyone knows how infuriating she can be, it's me. But I really think, in a funny kind of way, she was trying to impress you.' He swung my body backwards, directing a twinkly smile at me. 'When you stop to think about it, it's actually progress.'

It struck me, the way his words echoed Jenna's. That couldn't be a coincidence, could it? Maybe I was being too hard on Georgie. Either way, the last thing I needed was for the two of us to become alienated. Our next appointment with Dr Rindell was fast approaching, and I needed to get Steve onside.

'So, what do you fancy – Deliveroo or my terrible cooking?'

He held my gaze, that goofy adoration of his fully restored. 'Deliveroo obviously, but there is literally nothing that's terrible about you.'

If only that were true. I shake off the memory, shifting my heavy bulk on the sofa, wishing cosmic timelines could operate in two directions, rather than just relentlessly pushing us forwards into an uncertain future. If they did, I'd have some home truths to share with that skinny, skittish version of myself. I slump backwards against the cushions again. Everything, including my grasp of astrophysics, feels hopeless tonight.

* * *

After dinner I decided I needed to capitalize on our difficult conversation. Georgie was – purely coincidentally, according to Steve – staying over with her friend Alice, and Jack emerged only briefly from his room to snuffle around the fridge for supplies to take back into it. While Steve and I were rinsing out the containers from the vegetable korma we'd had delivered – as if diligently recycling made up for the blatant wastefulness of ordering in – I started my stealthy persuasion.

'So, you remember we're seeing Dr Rindell on the fifteenth?' I said, my head bowed over the recycling bin, as though it were a casual, throwaway comment.

It was hard not to be crushed by the metallic chill of his reply. 'Less than two weeks?'

'Yes.' I straightened up, keeping my own voice deliberately pleasant. 'So, we've got more than enough time to talk about it.' I grabbed a couple more plastic trays and sloshed water over them, specks of rice peppering the stainless-steel sink. 'And we can always cancel.' I turned to him now, my eyes beseeching him not to fell me again. 'But we did agree we were going to really think about it.'

Steve's face softened and twisted, his love for me fighting his instinct for preserving the status quo. 'I know we did . . .'

I almost articulated the 'but' for him – it floated above us like a helium balloon – but instead I drove the conversation forward.

'I think it'll be easier for me, the Georgie stuff – all of it – if we have our own child.' I'd been working on this next line – I hoped it would reach his soft heart. 'Perhaps I put too much pressure on the relationships with her and Jack because that's all I've got. And perhaps a baby that's a part of all of us will glue us all together. Finally make us feel like a real family. That's surely part of the reason we went through the IVF?'

It had taken time to convince him of that too – to stop re-lying on 'fate' like he'd counselled when we'd kept failing to conceive naturally – but I'd succeeded.

He crossed to where I stood at the sink, putting an arm around my shoulders. 'But you know that biologically . . .'

I batted his words away with my hand. It was too painful to go there, forward momentum more important than risking a look back at the dreams I'd already had to abandon. 'No, I've thought about it now, and it would be *my* baby. *I'd* carry her. *I'd* be her mum.'

Steve was quiet again. 'Do you really not feel like we're a proper family, Sasha?'

Now it was my turn to choose not to fell him. He had his own impossible fantasies; they just happened to be different from mine. Was finding love later in life always like this? More wisdom, more kindness, but too many scars and bruises to ever have that smooth, unblemished radiance that young love achieves so effortlessly?

'I do and I don't,' I said, carefully. 'Like, I do when we're all squashed up on the sofa watching a movie, but . . . I'm not their mum. In fact, I'm a constant reminder that their mum isn't here for them. And that's really hard, for them and for me.'

Steve's shoulders slumped at that, but then he rallied.

'I'm sorry if I don't always appreciate how hard it is,' he said. 'And I know how much you want this. It's just difficult to get my head around – all the nappies, and the sleepless nights. It's a lifetime ago for me.' He finally smiled. 'But I guess maybe love would conquer all . . .'

'Exactly!' I said, quick as a flash. 'We're biologically pro-grammed to love our children. It's science.'

'Oh, it's science is it?' he said, kissing the tip of my nose.

'It is,' I said, kissing his mouth in return. I knew more talk-ing could only weaken my cause, but I added, 'Just do the next appointment with him. Then we can decide.'

* * *

When I brushed my teeth that night, I looked myself squarely in the eye, trying to kid myself that I'd achieved some kind of divine alchemy. I'd turned the gritty dirt of the day into my own kind of spun gold. To believe it, I had to pretend I hadn't seen the way Steve had initially crumpled as he contemplated the ten-day stay of execution. I also had to bury the wolfish look of assessment on Fred's face when he'd told me he was in charge of my professional destiny. And reframe the unbridled anger Georgie had displayed in that meeting room, not a trace of admiration to be found. The fact was, the dirt was still there – all I'd done was gold plate it.

And everyone knows that gold plating starts to tarnish and erode as soon as it's put under any kind of pressure.

JENNA

Some days Jenna found herself struggling to stay in character as an admiring and indispensable apprentice. No matter how hard she tried, the exhaustion of working a second job was starting to take its toll, the long game harder to play as a result. And Sasha's habit of begging her for 'Gen Z insight' and then blatantly ignoring it was one of the danger zones.

Take the Trellicker Whisky campaign. Despite all of her carefully curated suggestions, some craggy old bastard who'd apparently been big in gangster movies during a phase of the Nineties called 'Cool Britannia' (obviously no one told them back then that anything or anyone claiming to be cool never is) had been lined up as the new face of the brand. Callum McBride was being paid the best part of a million pounds to shoot a promo in which he'd cross land and sea to get to the remote distillery the whisky came from. It was a kind of James Bond vibe, some sort of twisted consolation prize for the fact he'd been tipped for the role at least twice and never got it. That had been a while ago – now he was two divorces down, with a newborn baby on the way with an embarrassingly young TV co-star, so the Trellicker money was probably a lifeline for him. Jenna stared at his sandy face on her computer screen as she adjusted some of the visual inspiration boards for the upcoming shoot per Sasha's scrawled notes. He gazed into the camera with a moody kind of certainty, his palm massaging his stubbly cheek, his piercing blue eyes ringed by deep folds that advertised his thirty years of partying. Jenna childishly scowled back at him. Would it always be faces like this – white, male and glazed with misplaced self-belief – that would be crowned as some kind of tin-pot royalty?

Suddenly Sasha was at her shoulder. 'Doesn't he look great?' she said, virtually fluttering her eyelashes at the screen. 'I still can't quite believe we persuaded him to do it.' She was leaning over Jenna, so close that she could smell her perfume. It was an obscure, expensive French brand that came in a fat glass bottle which Sasha kept in the top drawer of her desk. Jenna had sprayed a tiny spritz of it on her wrists the other night when she was the last one in the office, though it had been wasted on the sweaty punters in the Falcon.

'Maybe he needs the cash,' she replied. 'Doesn't look like he's done any films for a while.'

The words dropped out of her before her tired brain could catch them. Last night she hadn't got back from the pub until after midnight, and she'd had to get back up at six to wrangle the statistics for the Maple campaign into some kind of order, her alarm a relentless siren that sounded like the police racing to a murder, to ensure she didn't sleep through it.

A flicker of annoyance crossed Sasha's face as she straightened up. 'TV's where it's at now, Jenna,' she said. 'The budgets are off the scale.'

'I know,' Jenna said apologetically. 'It's just – new baby and all that . . .'

Sasha caught her bottom lip between her teeth, her eyes clouding. Bingo – more evidence that the mysterious 'appointment' in the diary next week was another round in the ring with Dr Rindell. Sasha didn't like to lose a fight – she must be trying to force him to treat her.

Her boss gave her a tight smile. 'I think he just really responded to the auspices of the brand.'

'Yeah, no, of course.' Jenna had worked out that Sasha started talking like a walking dictionary when she was pissed off – she needed to row back fast. She swiftly switched documents on her screen. 'I've also collated all the focus group feedback on the Maple ideas so we've got it organized by demographic. I know you've got that meeting with their top team on Wednesday.'

'Wednesday?' snapped Sasha, heading back towards her own desk. 'I thought it was next week?'

'Originally, but then Bridget and Martin asked to move it up.' Jenna attempted a reassuring smile. 'Don't worry, we're well prepped going by the timeline. There's already a visual package, statistics you can use . . .'

Sasha's voice rose an octave. 'I know, but . . .'

Trellicker was definitely her happy place; anything related to Maple made her jumpy and skittish. Was it just the memory of Georgie's humiliating performance, or something more? Jenna was still picking over her odd interaction with that fossil of an exec when they'd left the Elevate meeting.

She risked a joke. 'I'm guessing you won't be inviting Georgie this time?'

Luckily, Sasha laughed. 'Yes, I think I'm going to take a rain check on that.'

Jenna paused, enjoying the feeling of Sasha's focus on her.

'What? You can say it, Jenna.'

'I dunno. I honestly still think it was a fucked-up attempt to impress you. Prove she was enough of a grown-up to speak up in your important meeting.' Should she risk the blatant lie that was forming? 'I mean, she basically said that to me.'

'*Really*?' said Sasha, suddenly eager. 'It's funny, you and my husband are singing from the same hymn sheet. She told him she was just trying to understand what my job actually involves.'

'Yeah, but she's never going to understand that – you're Sasha Fulton!'

'Stop . . .' said Sasha, batting a hand.

'But you know, if she wants to get a handle on what starting out in the media business is like, start thinking about what her career might look like in the future, I could go for a coffee with her. Try and make what happened more of a positive?'

Something complicated flitted across Sasha's face. 'I . . . Are you sure?' She paused, obviously wrestling with how appropriate it was, neatly scrubbing the fact that she'd already asked Jenna to lie to the rest of Bright about Georgie's identity. 'I really need to find ways for us to be closer. It's . . . there's a lot going on.' She gave a staccato laugh. 'Sorry, too much information.'

The irony was almost too delicious.

Jenna aimed a reassuring grin at her boss. 'Course I'm sure.'

'And it'd be good for her,' said Sasha. Jenna knew these manoeuvres all too well by now – the fancy footwork Sasha would dance to make sure something self-serving looked like a good deed. 'I think you could be an excellent role model.'

'Really?'

'Yeah, you're a grafter. You know what it takes. Not everyone your age does. I don't want to use the word "entitled", but . . .' Sasha gave a self-deprecating giggle. 'But I just did.'

Jenna controlled a hot surge of rage. Georgie was entitled for sure: the skiing holidays and wall-to-wall Apple products littering her Insta were testament to that. But Sasha's little laugh spread further and wider than just her stepdaughter – it was directed at all of the generations beneath hers. Jenna could still feel the ache at the base of her spine from being on her feet until midnight, the dull throb in her feet, the ringing in her ears from Neil's barked commands. Those sacrifices were just to get by; when Sasha was her age, working her arse off in one cushy career job, she was probably only five years away from her first mortgage. Hers had been a sacrifice with a guaranteed payoff.

'Let's fix it up,' she said, trying not to sound too eager. Too hungry.

* * *

Later that night, Jenna was counting out four twenties, trying to make sure she didn't accidentally slam them down on the kitchen counter. It was the second instalment of the kitty, and it felt no less infuriating than the first.

'Thanks, lovely!' said Penelope, greedily grabbing the notes the second they'd all landed. She fanned herself with them theatrically. 'I'll make sure I invest them *wisely*.'

Jenna forced herself to smile. That was six hours of pint-pulling and table-wiping that Penelope was treating like a prop in her one-woman show.

'Do you get like, shower gel with it?' Jenna had made the mistake of leaving her minty green Source in the bathroom, only to find that a day later the volume had plummeted and Laura smelt suspiciously like a toothpaste factory at breakfast. 'Or is it just toilet paper?'

'And wine!' said Penelope, flinging open the door of the fridge and blithely ignoring the question. 'Don't forget the wine, Jenna.'

She shook an open bottle of white in Jenna's direction, smiled an invitation.

'You know I don't really drink that much,' said Jenna, keeping her tone as neutral as she could.

'Yeah, we noticed, but this New Zealand Sauvignon Blanc was on special when I did the Sainsbury's order. My dad tipped me off about it. Seriously, you need to get involved!'

'I'm all right, honestly.'

The two girls eyed each other for a moment.

'Shower gel's not on our list,' said Penelope eventually. 'I think everyone likes their own brands, but I guess we could put it to a vote.' She adjusted her expression, looking almost pained now. 'I really like to try and keep my beauty products as clean as I can. For me *and* for the planet. But I know I can't expect everyone to subsidize my personal choices . . .'

Jenna had to hand it to her, she was wily as fuck. 'Don't worry, it's fine.' She crossed to the sink and filled a tall glass tumbler with tap water. 'I'm just still trying to get my head round the . . . the *nuances* of the kitty.'

Sasha really was rubbing off on her; now she also sounded like the Fulton dictionary when she was pissed off.

'It's pretty simple really,' said Penelope, giving her a patronizing smile. 'But just ask me anything as it comes up.' She leant her long body against the counter, taking a slug of her wine. 'Oh God, let's stop wanging on about the boring practical stuff. Tell me how it's going at the Falcon! I love those guys . . .'

Penelope's barista job at the Humble Bean was only a few doors further up Junction Road from the pub.

'It's brutal,' Jenna said, voice clipped.

'I hear you, sister!' said Penelope, eyes wide. 'Hospitality's knackering, isn't it?'

But you only have one real job, Jenna wanted to scream. *And no one ever starts a fight because they've had too many double macchiatos.*

'Sure is!' she replied. 'And how are the auditions going?' It wasn't like she didn't know – if Penelope had had a sniff of acting work outside the special kind she did in her kitchen, she'd definitely have forced the whole house into mounting some kind of victory parade.

The other girl's smile slid pleasingly southward. 'Bit slow,' she said lightly. 'But my agent says it's always this way in summer.'

'Yeah, I'm sure that's right,' said Jenna. 'Although we're casting all the background artists for the Trellicker Whisky campaign we're doing right now.'

Penelope gave a tinny laugh. 'Don't think I'm quite at the stage of becoming an extra.'

The kitchen door creaked open, Sanjay appearing in the gap.

'Evening, campers!' he said, giving a cheery salute, fully oblivious to the tension. He steadied himself on the edge of the table. 'Oops, might've had a couple.'

It was impossible not to like Sanjay. 'Hi and bye,' Jenna said, making sure it sounded friendly. 'I've gotta . . .' She gestured upstairs. As she swung open the kitchen door, Penelope called after her.

'Meant to say, someone called Paul rang. On the landline! My aunt refuses to get rid of it, but . . .'

By now Penelope's words were nothing but static, Jenna's heartbeat so loud in her ears that it drowned out everything around her. She hurried upstairs, hoping that Penelope would forget about it after she'd slugged some more of her favourite wine.

She'd been a fool to think walking away from the people who claimed to love her would ever be that easy.

SASHA

Is there a snapshot, a moment you could freeze for posterity, in every first date that goes the distance? A fleeting moment that perfectly encapsulates the relationship that's being birthed? When I was internet dating, I'd only ever commit myself to a single glass of wine, always ensuring I dropped into the conversation early that I had a presentation the next day, a plane to catch – fill in the blanks. I'd met far too many sociopaths who'd somehow faked normality in their profile to take any risks. If the man in question was a pleasant surprise, I'd let myself find out more on a second date. There were very few second dates. I see now that Fred's betrayal had wrapped barbed wire around my heart.

Thank God Steve gamed the system. As soon as the first sip of wine had slid its way down my tight throat, I let him know it was a one-glass scenario. His face – his handsome, scrunched-paper face – was a picture of disappointment. He'd never done this before, he said. It was his kids who had forced him online. His last first date had been eighteen years earlier, and he'd made us a dinner reservation, just like he had back then.

There was something about the lack of guile combined with the abundance of effort that broke me. I told him I'd somehow

find a way to write my imaginary pitch at the crack of dawn
and let him order a bottle.

I trusted him.

He should never have trusted me.

* * *

Dr Rindell seemed genuinely delighted to see us again when
we returned to his office. His smile was broad, his handshake
firm. He steered us into his expensive leather chairs, taking his
own seat behind the imposing desk.

'I didn't think I'd see you again,' he said, his sharp gaze
trained on me. 'I appreciate that it was a very difficult conversation for you both.'

'For sure,' I said, trying and failing not to sound brittle.

Dr Rindell steepled his fingers, taking a wary pause. 'So, I
assume if you're here, you've been discussing the alternative
routes to parenthood that I laid out?'

I couldn't help myself, the words spraying out of me. 'We
have, but . . .' Steve's hand was on my arm now. 'I read these
stories about people who give up, decide to adopt or travel the
world, and it just happens for them. Like, well, like a miracle.'

The set of the doctor's face told me exactly what he thought
about the potential for my body producing any kind of miracle.

'Yes, it does happen sometimes, even with challenging numbers like yours. But if you really want to be parents, I wouldn't
be staking your hopes on a miracle. And as I said last time, I'm
not comfortable putting you through more invasive treatment.'

Steve squeezed my hand. 'We appreciate your honesty,'
he said.

One of us did, but it wasn't me.

I steadied my voice, refused to let the humiliation bloom
inside me. 'We do. And we've been talking seriously about the
egg donation route.'

'Just talking,' said Steve, quick as a flash. 'No decisions have been made.'

'We really took on board what you said,' I told the doctor, hoping my smile conveyed a humble admiration for his wisdom. 'And we're excited to hear in more detail about what a pregnancy with egg donation would look like. So we can—' I turned to Steve, directed a demure smile at him '—talk more and make that decision as a couple.'

Rindell paused, observing the tableau we made. I could tell he was no fool. After that brief interlude, he launched into his spiel; the process we'd go through of choosing a donor egg, the fertilization with Steve's sperm, the implantation into my body and the successful pregnancy that would hopefully result. I'd googled the whole thing obsessively of course, then gone back onto the message boards and clinic websites, looking for a different set of success stories from my previous quarry. People who couldn't believe they'd agonized so long, who were adamant that a baby who was conceived this way felt no less your beloved child than any other would.

'Very helpful,' nodded Steve, once we'd heard the doctor out. I eyed his profile. My husband was so unfailingly polite that it was hard to detect whether the information was melting his defences or building them even higher. I lobbed a few more questions, trying to create more of a runway, hoping it would allow his feelings to take off. The statistics in themselves had to be working on him, the numbers nothing like the doom-laden digits we'd been given for another round of IVF.

'I know it's not what you dreamt of,' Rindell said when we'd discussed it from every angle. 'But as I said last time, the patients I've had who have gone down this path are very positive about it.'

'I can appreciate that now I've had a few weeks to sit with it,'

I said. 'And I'm excited there's still a way for me to be a mother.' I squeezed Steve's hand again, aware of how it sounded. 'No, what do they call it – a tummy mummy? Obviously, I'm already a stepmum.'

'I'm pleased to hear that, Sasha,' said Dr Rindell, his eyes subtly pulling towards the small digital clock on his desk. It was silly, the hurt I felt at that subtle reminder that my fight for motherhood was just a tiny part of his business plan. 'How about you, Steve? What are your thoughts?'

Steve gave a brief smile. 'It's all certainly very interesting.'

My heart clenched tight with dangerous hope. Was he coming around, or just trying to convince me – or himself – that he'd given it his best shot?

'Good, good,' said Dr Rindell, springing to his feet. 'Well, I look forward to hearing from you once you've made a decision.'

I fought to keep my face neutral, to avoid conveying the fact that, as far as I was concerned, we already had.

JENNA

Jenna had never actually sat down in Squirrel. It was only ever a pit stop for Sasha's oat lattes, as well as the additional order her boss often gifted her as a thank you. Sasha had an old-fashioned fondness for cash, frequently thrusting tenners in Jenna's direction. 'Come on,' she'd say, 'let me scoff one of those million-calorie pain au chocolats vicariously,' as if the fact that Jenna's shape was rounder than Sasha's pencil of a body meant the calories didn't matter. Last week she'd had her revenge, pocketing the £6.50 her coffee and pastry would've cost and telling Sasha they were so delicious she'd devoured them on the way back to the office. But it was more than spite; even with the night shifts at the Falcon, the cost of London was breaking her bank balance every single month.

Walking past the snaking lunchtime queue, Jenna scanned the long trestle tables at the back for any sign of Georgie. Nothing – maybe she wouldn't even bother to turn up. She joined the end of the line, controlling her disappointment. This whole arrangement had been so perfect – maybe too perfect. But ten minutes later, as she finally approached the counter, Georgie appeared at her elbow.

Jenna fixed a smile on her face. 'Perfect timing!' she trilled. 'Do you know what you want? I'm going to have the burrata and prosciutto focaccia.' It appeared her transformation into a total London wanker was well under way.

Georgie wrinkled her nose, light bouncing off the silver ring that pierced it. 'I'm vegan,' she declared. 'You know animal researchers have worked out pigs can think like a six-year-old?'

Jenna swallowed. 'Okay, so . . . something without a face.'

Georgie turned to the girl behind the counter, who was by now struggling to control her impatience. 'It's not just about meat – dairy's just as bad. What do you have that's plant based?'

One puy lentil soup later, the warm focaccia now feeling like a war crime in Jenna's hand, the two of them squeezed themselves onto one of the narrow wooden benches that ran down the long tables. Silence reigned.

'So, what do you want to ask me about Bright?' Jenna asked, taking a guilty bite from the focaccia.

Georgie gave her a dismissive sneer. 'I don't *want* to ask you anything. I only said I'd do this to shut my dad up about upsetting Sasha at her meeting.'

Jenna wasn't going to rise to it. She gave the younger girl a teasing grin. 'Come on, I bet there's something you're dying to know!'

Georgie was skewered, grinning back despite herself. 'Okay. What does Sasha, like, *do* all day?'

Jenna considered the question. The truth was that Sasha worked incredibly hard, wrangling her team, her capricious bosses and her demanding corporate clients without breaking a sweat. Sometimes Jenna's agenda almost got derailed by a sneaky admiration. Almost, but not quite.

'She works her arse off,' she said truthfully, ignoring the snark in Georgie's question.

'I didn't say she didn't,' Georgie shot back, locking her arms across the Extinction Rebellion hoodie she was wearing.

Jenna angled her next shot more carefully. 'You know what, I actually reckon you'd be really good at Sasha's job,' she said, watching how Georgie's body language unlocked at the compliment. Of course it did – every single one of her Instagram posts was a desperate howl for affirmation. 'It's all about getting ideas across and judging by the Maple meeting you're really good at that!'

'Do you think so?' Georgie said, then reined in her pleasure. 'Yeah, well, I had to say what I did. People need to wake up.'

'I know,' said Jenna, taking a sip of her açaí smoothie. 'Sasha just expresses stuff in a different way from you.'

She wasn't here to undermine her boss, not today. Patience would prove to be a virtue.

'It's not the same thing,' protested Georgie. 'What she does – she's selling her soul for corporate cash. You know that, right? If I were you, I'd get the fuck out while I still HAD a soul.'

Jenna stifled a sigh. The concept of rent, of council tax and Tube fares and 'kitties' was obviously an alien one for Little Miss Pocket Money.

'Yeah, but we work for lots of different companies. We run pro bono campaigns for charities too, plus Elevate's an outreach programme.' She forced herself to laugh. 'It's not all petrol and palm oil, I promise.'

Georgie had a creepy, intense stare. 'How old are you?' she demanded.

'Twenty-three.'

'So, you're not that much older than me.'

'No,' said Jenna. 'And it's not like I don't give a shit about things. But I want to learn. I want to be part of the cultural conversation.' Jenna paused, choosing her next words carefully. 'I want to make a difference from the inside.'

A slow smile spread across Georgie's face, the words catching fire inside of her.

'What, so you're like a spy? You're . . .' Her eyes lit up with the pure romance of it. 'You're an agent for change.'

'Yeah,' said Jenna, watching the girl closely. 'I'm an agent for change.' She finally took a bite from her sandwich. The cheese was cold and congealed by now, greasy and unappetizing on the swallow. She stood up, wanting to give Georgie a minute to herself. 'Do you fancy some dessert? They do an amazing beetroot brownie.'

'As long as it's plant based,' Georgie called imperiously to Jenna's retreating back. 'Make ABSOLUTELY sure they don't use any butter.'

* * *

A full hour had passed, the lunchtime crowd long since dispersed. Jenna had texted Sasha under the table to check it was okay to take such a long break and had received a string of party-time emojis in return. The brownie, which looked like a cowpat, seemed to have sweetened Georgie up. With a little sly coaching from Jenna, she was splurging about every aspect of her life. The time she'd skipped school to join an Extinction Rebellion barricade, her best friends, the 'sleepovers' they had that involved no sleep and a lot of booze pilfered from their oblivious parents' wine fridges.

It was sad really, knowing what Jenna did about her. The stories might be true, but she was pretty sure Georgie hadn't been a part of them, beyond maybe eavesdropping on the real participants in the school changing rooms.

'You can't tell Sasha any of this, okay?' Georgie said, when she finally paused for breath.

'Course I won't,' Jenna told her. 'You don't need your mum and dad knowing all your deepest, darkest secrets.'

'Sasha's not my mum,' corrected Georgie. Her hands, dirty nails like black crescent moons, twisted the napkin she was holding into a thin rope.

'No, I know, but . . .' Jenna took a risk. 'Who *is* your mum?' Georgie's face registered something complicated.

'She lives in France,' she muttered.

'I'm sorry.'

'Yeah, but . . . she lives by the sea. It's fucking stunning,' she went on, in a louder voice, as if daring Jenna to say something else.

Jenna wasn't fooled; the way Georgie spoke was as if her beloved dog had been killed, but she was trying to comfort herself with the thought that at least she no longer had to walk him. A flash of absolute clarity hit her, if only for a second. She knew all too well that that kind of grief – the complicated kind, which can't be summed up neatly by 'In Deepest Sympathy' cards – didn't gently fade away of its own accord. It was more feral, more vicious. It was just a case of whether it turned inwards or outwards. She deliberately looked away from Georgie's face, training her gaze on the relentless London traffic that streamed off Old Street roundabout. She couldn't risk starting to feel sorry for her.

'Not much sea in London,' she said, keeping her tone light. 'Have you always lived here?'

'Yeah,' said Georgie. 'Dad and me and Jack stayed in the house when Mum left.' Her tone shifted too. 'And then Sasha moved in.'

She might as well have said it – the cuckoo in the nest. And the last thing she was going to want – the thing she probably most dreaded – was that cuckoo having a chick. Sasha's perfect life was way more fragile than it first seemed, once you got close enough to spot the cracks.

The thought of her boss made her look at the time on her phone – she really did need to get back now. However much Sasha wanted her on this peacekeeping mission, she'd also want her to get her mile-long to-do list finished by the end of the day. Sasha was pretty oblivious to what was actually possible, demonstrated by the fact she'd signed off on a salary that was so hard to live on a London rat would most likely turn his furry nose up at it. Jenna was grateful for the way her momentary sadness calcified into something harder at the thought. This was the kind of fuel she needed.

'I didn't see much of my mum growing up either,' she said. Georgie looked at her with that strange intensity she had, not bothering to reply. 'It's tough, isn't it? You can't help but miss them.'

Her tone conveyed too much, but luckily Georgie was too self-absorbed to hear anything untoward.

'It's okay,' she said, though the set of her face gave her away.

'Can I try a corner of your brownie?' asked Jenna, intentionally lightening the mood. She felt sure the intimacy of the moment would stay hanging in the ether, doing its work. 'It looks so yum.'

Georgie shoved the mess of it across the table. 'Yeah, the beetroot makes it really sticky and nice.'

Just as Jenna had suspected, it was grim, possibly worse than a cowpat. She forced herself to swallow. 'Amazing! Who needs butter?'

'Right?!' said Georgie, lighting back up.

Jenna picked up her bag from the floor and grabbed her coat from where it had fallen off the bench. It was time to close this deal. 'Well, I could chat to you all day, but I've got to get back.'

'Yeah, no. I've got loads to do too,' said Georgie, the words coming too fast to convince. It was half term; Jenna reckoned she'd spend the afternoon lying comatose on her bed, lost in an online world that was almost as scary as the real one.

'I'm so glad Sasha suggested this,' said Jenna, lightly touching her arm. 'Though I feel like I didn't give you any proper *careers advice*.' She made a face as she said it, so Georgie would feel they were both in on the joke. 'We should do it again,' she added lightly. 'Or you could come back to Elevate.'

'Yeah, okay,' Georgie said, with a shy smile. 'Maybe I will. See how you deal with those bloodsuckers.' She gave a little fist pump, like she was staging her own tiny revolution. 'Don't forget, you've got to keep fighting from the inside.'

'Too right,' said Jenna, pulling the dark-green vinyl raincoat on. She'd bought it from the charity shop on Junction Road, hoping one of those effortlessly cool dog mummies from the pub had ditched it when they'd loaded up on the best the new season had to offer. She was pretty sure it worked on her – she'd seen Sasha admiring it when she'd left for lunch. 'Like I said, I'm an agent for change.'

She stopped long enough to put her number into Georgie's phone, then set off back to the office, rain bouncing off her hood and streaming down her face. By the time she got back, there was already a message. *Thanks for the brownie, and the life advice! See ya soon, G xx.*

Game on.

SASHA

I was a bundle of nerves when Jenna got back from lunch. I stood there with bated breath, waiting for her to unwrap herself from her shockingly awful anorak and tell me if it had gone well. I was experiencing a strange kind of emotional vertigo from the fact that in this particular moment it was my assistant who was the boss of me. Or maybe it wasn't vertigo – maybe it was more of a premonition.

'So, how was it?' I said, trying and failing to sound nonchalant. I grabbed my phone from my desk, pretending to be distracted by an important text.

Jenna dropped her wet coat onto the back of her chair, droplets of rain dripping onto the polished wooden floor. 'It was ...' She paused, an unreadable expression on her face. 'She's complicated, isn't she?'

'She's had a tough time,' I said, which was true.

I waited for her to add something, hope draining away like water down a sluice. It was pathetic; I'd kidded myself that this was a good and noble plan – a way to help Georgie be more grown-up – when all the time it was me who needed to grow up. Who'd have guessed how desperate I was to hear an impartial observer tell me that my stepdaughter actually liked me?

'She's really lucky she's got you.' Jenna perched on her seat, affording herself another interminable pause. 'And I think she knows that. Underneath at least.'

'Really?' I said, pathetically hopeful. 'What did she actually say to you that made you think that?'

Donovan was heading towards me, a sheaf of print-outs in his hand. It was the worst possible time for a meeting, but I'd promised we'd go over the latest mock-ups for the Maple campaign.

'A few things . . .' said Jenna.

I grabbed my iPad, stood up. What came out of my mouth next was impulsive. It was too gross to vomit out my neediness between the hushed, oatmeal walls of the office – it was a place where I was duty-bound to exude calm authority. I needed to move this undercover.

'Tell you what, I could take you for a quick glass of wine after work and debrief properly?' I forced myself to sound more professional. Normalize it. 'I always like to do a proper check-in with my assistants when we're getting towards three months anyway, and I find it tends to work much better if we do it as an offsite. I've been meaning to find us a time.'

An *offsite*? Now it sounded like I was spewing a management textbook.

'Sounds great!' Jenna said, her face instantly lighting up. It *was* good management, I told myself. Her delighted expression was proof of that.

'Sounds like a plan,' I said over my shoulder, disappearing into the conference room before I could embarrass myself even more.

* * *

'So, what do you fancy?'

Jenna's eyes were roving the room, her body rigid in the tall swivel chair set next to the bar. Why had I ever thought that this was a good plan? Deia, a big, buzzy tapas bar close to the office, had felt like the most relaxed place I could take her, but now we were here, neither of us were even remotely relaxed. I was just doing a marginally better job of faking it.

'Um, white wine?' she said hesitantly. 'Or are you meant to have like, sangria, here?'

I aimed a smile in her direction that I hoped wasn't patronizing and signalled for the barman.

'Can we have a couple of white Riojas, please?' I asked.

'Large or small?' he twinkled. He was closer to Jenna's age than mine, but he was protecting his tip by making sure I didn't feel it. His thick, dark hair was slicked back, his Spanish accent lilting and musical. I took a sideways glance at Jenna to see if his appeal was working on her, but her face was more watchful than charmed. 'Silly question,' he added. 'Large?'

'You guessed it!' I said, inwardly cursing. Apart from the fact that I was trying to keep my drinking to a minimum, I wasn't sure how long we could both endure this terrible idea of mine. That said, calling for small measures felt like too much of a slap in the face. God, this was starting to feel like one of my dreadful post-Fred, pre-Steve internet dates. I never knew which kind was worse, the socially inept ones who left long, awkward silences or the ones who never stopped talking, spraying spit as they ranted about what psychos their ex-wives were. No wonder meeting Steve had made me feel like I'd finally shut the door on my feelings for Fred. The memory made me shudder – the next Maple meeting was far too close for comfort.

'Coming right up,' the barman said, throwing me a grin as he headed for the big fridge behind him.

'Can we have some salted almonds too?' I called after him. Then I swivelled towards Jenna on my chair, resting my left elbow on the marble bar. 'I'm so glad you were free for us to do this,' I lied.

'Yeah, me too,' she said. It reappeared then, that gratitude I'd seen in her face when I'd first suggested it. Perhaps I was the one who needed to relax.

'And I want you to know that you're doing a brilliant job.' She looked down at the bar, awkward. 'Don't be embarrassed,' I said. 'Hey, Jenna, look at me. You can own it. You've earned it!'

Her gaze slowly peeled upwards. 'So, you definitely want to keep me?' she said, looking at me intently.

I paused for a second, but not because I was questioning my decision. No, it was more that I was blindsided by how soaked with emotion those seven words seemed to be.

'Yes, yes of course I do,' I said, keeping my tone breezy. I felt a rush of guilt – I'd obviously terrified her, with all my talk of an 'offsite' and the approaching three-month deadline. 'This drink is really just to say thank you, and to see if there's anything you want to raise with me.'

The barman reappeared before she could reply, setting down our condensation-coated glasses with a flourish. They looked like a pair of buckets to my Dry August eyes, but I put my fertility woes to one side and took a generous swallow. My shoulders immediately started to drop, my whole body loosening.

'Thank you,' I said to him, grabbing with my free hand a few of the nuts he'd also brought us. I raised my glass, and Jenna copied me. 'Cheers!' I said, observing the tiny sip she took and feeling slightly ashamed of my lairy swigging. That was the problem with enforced restraint – when I took the reins off, I always set off at a gallop. 'To a bright Bright future!'

She laughed, visibly relaxing. 'I see what you did there!' She paused, taking another small sip. 'Georgie's won SO big getting you as a stepmum.'

Here it was – the conversation I'd been angling for. But now the moment had arrived, I was scared to run with it.

'I'm not sure about that,' I said quietly. It wasn't false modesty. 'And whatever you said earlier, I don't think she believes it for a single minute.'

'No, she does,' said Jenna, impassioned. Now I felt my own cheeks heat up, which was ridiculous. She didn't miss it. 'You've earned it, Sasha,' she said, giving me a cheeky side-eye.

'Shut up,' I said, laughing as I lightly whacked her wrist. Then I pulled back my hand like my fingers were burnt, shocked by the fact that I'd touched her. The booze had obviously gone to my head – I sternly reminded myself I wasn't propping up this bar with Maddi.

Jenna didn't seem to mind. 'She's just hurting,' she said softly, her fingers working up and down the stem of her wine glass. She held my gaze, almost as if we were on some strange kind of date. 'She told me about her mum.'

The moment was broken – it was pathetic how a part of me bristled. It felt like Georgie didn't even bother confiding what her favourite pizza topping was to me. 'What did she say?' I asked stiffly.

Jenna obviously sensed the twist in my mood. 'I mean, she was fronting it out,' she added quickly. 'She barely knows me.' She plunged her fingers into the nuts, nibbling on them, salt clinging to the gluey pastel lip gloss she always wore. I waited, time seeming to stretch thin. 'She feels rejected, you know?' She turned towards me as she said it, her eyes full of emotion that didn't seem merited. 'It's gutting for her. To be dumped by your own mum.'

How stupid I was – she'd lost her mum too. Of course, Georgie's loss – so different in shape, but modelled from the same pain – had touched her. I searched for the right words. I wasn't very good at this kind of thing, but nor did I want to be an emotional vampire, sucking her dry while I got her drunk.

'I'm sorry if it was hard for you to hear that, with what you've . . .' But before I could finish the thought, she was running on, that flash of emotion wiped clean from her face.

'You just need to keep going, Sasha,' she said, her voice decisive now. 'Wear her down.' Her smile was naughty as she took a longer pull from her glass. 'Kill her with kindness.'

I looked around the bar, louder and fuller now. 'Instead of just killing her?' I said, making sure I laughed as I said it, taking the sting away. It did sting though, how hard-fought every version of parenting seemed to be. I stared down at my now near-empty glass. Despite everything I'd just said to myself, I was tempted to shoot for a refill.

Jenna must've seen me looking guiltily at the barman, who was deep in conversation with a couple further up the bar about the relative merits of two reds. 'Go on, Sasha, you can have another one.'

Was it weird or comforting, the way she seemed to always be three seconds ahead of what I was thinking?

'Only if you have one too,' I said, ignoring the fact that her glass had only lost a couple of centimetres off the top.

'Promise I will after this one,' she said, signalling for him before I had a chance to pretend I was still wavering. He beamed at us, gestured that he'd be a couple of minutes. I watched Jenna, trying to detect whether his smile stirred anything in her. I was hungry for some psychic insights of my own.

'He's flirting with you,' I said, even though I wasn't sure it was specific. He seemed to be a man who flirted with air.

'Do you reckon?' she said, sounding almost weary.

Even now – with Steve likely stirring a mushroom risotto to the strains of Radio 4 and thinking fond thoughts about my arrival home – I hadn't wholly turned off my capacity for mutual attraction. Maybe the notion of it, if not the reality, was the air that I still liked to breathe every now and then. 'He's kind of hot,' I said, simultaneously averting my eyes so I didn't seem like some old lech. 'Do you not think so?'

'Don't really see people that way,' she said, her face blank as she looked at his craggy profile. 'It's about the whole person, isn't it? Not like – their meat suit.'

I knew I should stop, but somehow I couldn't. 'So, what kind of . . . of person—' this was a minefield '—do you tend to like?' I took another mouthful of wine, grateful for the wet slide down my dry throat. 'I mean, obviously you don't have to answer that.'

Her mouth flipped upwards, her expression amused. 'I can answer it, Sasha.'

She sat and thought for a second while I cursed what a mess I was making of this clumsy attempt at intimacy. Of course, I should have shut it down – demanded the bill, not another drink – but instead I found myself leaning forward, eager for the next morsel she might throw me.

'Yeah, it is about the whole person, the connection between us.' She splayed her fingers across her heart as she said it. 'I need to really feel it.' Intensity melted back into cheekiness. 'And I can tell you wanna know what I mean by "person". You're right, I'm not just talking about boys.'

'I mean, great!' I said, way too quickly. 'Good for you.'

Now I was veering into 'try hard mum' territory, which was probably even worse. I certainly had form for failing at this one.

The barman swept towards us, smiling an apology. 'Sorry, ladies,' he said. 'Same again? Something to soak up the drinks, maybe?'

'Just a small one,' I said, Jenna's reply layering over mine.

'Can we get something else to eat?' she was asking, looking down at the empty bowl of almonds.

I ordered us some padron peppers and manchego, telling myself it was a good thing I was offsetting the booze. Hopefully Steve wouldn't be too offended when I only picked at the dinner he'd have lovingly prepared for us, and it was nice for me to have the chance to treat Jenna to something, considering how paltry her pay was.

'How did you meet Steve?' asked Jenna, as if she'd read my mind.

I lied airily, as I so often did. 'Just through friends.' It was pathetic, six years on, that I still thought Bumble was something to be ashamed of.

'Cringe!' laughed Jenna. 'At least with an app you know you're both up for it.'

Obviously, cringes were generational. 'Have you started using them since you moved here?' I asked. 'Or is there someone at home?'

Her face darkened, her hand shooting out for her glass in a way I hadn't seen before.

'I don't need to be going home anytime soon,' she said.

Was this more evidence of the rawness of her grief? Perhaps, but the energy that was crackling from her felt more like fury than it did sadness. Before I'd managed to summon up the right words, the food was appearing in front of us. I picked up a thick triangle of cheese, guilty about how grateful I was for the distraction.

'Steve's going to kill me for spoiling my appetite,' I said, dipping it into the quince jelly that was smeared on the side of the plate. 'But manchego's too delicious to resist.'

Jenna picked up a slice more cautiously. 'Is it like, jam?' she asked.

'Sort of,' I said, stuffing a second piece into my mouth.

'What's he like?' she asked lightly, nibbling on the cheese and ignoring the jelly.

'Steve?' I said. 'He's lovely.'

'What's he really like, though?' she said, her free hand – either consciously or unconsciously – moving back across her heart. She was wearing a tight black shirt in a synthetic fabric, a beige bra visible through the gaping slits between the buttons. It was hard sometimes not to rip the clothes off her back, swap them for a whole new set of items that would actually flatter her. The kind that might allow her to glide through Bright with an ease that so far was proving elusive, partly thanks to the sneers – too subtle for me to discipline – that the likes of Scarlett constantly threw her way. I thought about the bulging tote bag of clothes that was languishing under my desk, destined for the designer resale shop around the corner. The moody woman who owned it inevitably gave me pennies against the pounds I'd spent on them first time around. Could I do a good deed and gift Jenna the things that would fit? After tonight, it felt like it might not be an overstep.

Somehow, nothing was feeling like an overstep by now, including her question. And anyway, it was kind of fun to answer it. 'He's a sweetie,' I said. 'He's incredibly kind. He's a real cheerleader for me and the kids. He knows everything about everything, he's so well informed. He's incredibly loyal. Loving to his bones. He's not like . . .'

'Like the others?' she said quietly, studying my face.

My body clenched at the acuity of that.

'Sorry,' she laughed. 'Being nosy now.' She looked down at the marble bar, almost bashful. 'It's just really nice, hanging out. It's not like I've got a fucking army of friends here. So, sorry . . .'

'Don't apologize!' I said, squeezing her arm. It *was* nice, gratifying even, how much me carving out this time obviously meant to her. 'I've been the one asking the nosy questions. *I'm* sorry.'

She shifted in her seat. 'It matters a lot, you caring about me,' she said, the words catching in her throat.

'I do,' I said, allowing that tinge of maternal affection I felt for her to live and breathe. 'And I know you've been through a lot.'

She didn't speak, her eyes trained downwards again. I watched as a couple of tears splashed onto the marble. I took a breath in, instinctively reaching over to put an arm around her shoulders.

'I'm sorry . . .' she gulped. 'Sorry to be such a dick.'

'You're not a dick,' I said, my head bent close to hers. 'It's so unfair, losing a parent young.'

'I just . . .' She turned her head to look at me. 'I just miss her. You only get one mum. She'll never get to see what I . . . what I become.'

I paused a second.

'Do you have any siblings?' I asked gently. 'Is your dad around to support you?'

She gave an angry shake of her head. 'Nope. It was just me and her.'

I sat with the bleakness of that, watching how her face shut down as she said it, as if the pain was too much to feel.

'I don't often tell people this,' I said eventually. 'But I lost my dad when I was still little. And I'm an only child too.' Jenna looked up, eyes tracking my face as if she was testing my sincerity. 'Maybe . . . maybe that's why we get on so well.'

She held my eyes for a second longer, then leaned back, wiping her face, and shook out her shoulders.

'Urgh, thank you,' she said, then took a generous swig from

her wine glass, meeting my gaze again with a watery smile.
'You're the best, Sasha.'

'No, you're the best,' I said, relieved that I'd redeemed
myself, made her feel better. I wasn't always great at the emotional stuff, something my long-suffering husband could be
quick to point out.

Jenna looked at down at her phone, anxiety streaking across
her face. 'I'm so sorry, I need to go,' she said.

'Listen, you don't need to be burning the midnight oil for
me . . .'

'No, I really have to go,' she said, quickly sliding off the
stool. 'I've got a second date.'

'Oh, right,' I said, signalling for the bill. 'Have fun with . . .
with them.'

She smirked at my awkwardness in a way that felt sweet
instead of sour, then grabbed her coat from the back of the
chair. I ordered her a cab on the Bright account, standing on
the pavement after I'd waved her off until all I could see were
its tail lights illuminating the darkness.

After that I decided to walk a few blocks before I got my
own cab, trying to compute the evening we'd just shared. Was
it wrong that for the most part I'd actually enjoyed it, including
the transgressive moments of intimacy? *No*, I told myself. It was
just a testament to the fact that I wasn't a slave to hierarchy.
We'd been two human beings enjoying a human connection,
and how could that be anything but good?

JENNA

The bar was somewhere behind King's Cross, a loud basement that required a smudgy black stamp on the back of your hand to gain entry. Her drinks with Sasha had made her half an hour late, but there was no way she could've cut that precious meeting short. But now, the air-punch triumph she should've felt had been destroyed by her failure of self-control. She mechanically shot her hand out for the stamp, her heart pounding in her chest as she scanned the crowded bar for Louis. It wasn't excitement about this second date that was making her heart beat faster – it was something much less magical. Panic? Shame? She didn't have a label for it, but she knew she urgently needed to purge it from her system.

Louis was sitting at the bar with a half-drunk pint, one trainer-clad foot snaked around the empty stool next to him. It pulled up the hem of his trousers, exposing a sock with a colourful cobra snaking around his ankle. Ugh – he was probably the kind of person whose mum sent him jiffy bag 'care packages' in case he got homesick. Some tea bags and a packet of plasters, his favourite childhood sweets.

'Sorry I'm late,' said Jenna, the cold twang of her tone in no way reflecting the sentiment.

'That's ... that's okay,' said Louis. He whipped his face

swiftly to the left, as if he was urgently searching for the barman, but as Jenna scanned his profile she could see that it was more an attempt to conceal the reflexive hurt that painted his features.

'My boss wanted to take me out for dinner,' she continued, still enjoying the accolade despite where the evening had ended. 'So, it wasn't like I could say no to her.'

Louis turned back towards her, leaning in for a kiss and pitching his voice low, a callback to the intimacy of the weekend they'd just spent together. '*You're* going to be the boss soon, I can feel it.'

As his face loomed forward, Jenna felt like she was being smothered. The chestnut curls she'd enjoyed tightly wrapping around her fingers now seemed more like the head of a mop. His dark eyes no longer looked like molten chocolate; instead they felt like the wet gaze of an ancient cocker spaniel.

It wasn't surprising her change in mood was giving poor Louis whiplash. After a night out in a club, they'd spent a straight twelve hours in his bed, but it hadn't just been about sex. They'd talked until the birds started chirping, then eaten breakfast there, soft boiled eggs and soldiers he'd made for them both. In another life it might've felt like the start of something, but not in this one. Now she let their lips make the briefest contact, grateful when a harassed girl leaned over the bar to take their order.

'I'll just have a lime and soda,' she said, turning to Louis. 'Do you want another pint?'

'Yeah, sure,' he replied, face falling like the scaffolding had been taken down. 'You sure you don't want a proper drink?'

He pulled out his phone to pay, as stubbornly chivalrous as he'd been in bed, but she waved his offer away.

'I'll get these,' she said. Even though every penny counted, the cost of allowing him to treat her would be too high for both of them. 'And no, I already had two glasses with my boss.'

It was those two drinks that had made her forget the rules. At the thought of it, Jenna almost doubled over on her bar stool, felled by a sudden explosion of shame. The tears that had leaked out of her eyes and splashed onto the poncy bar, the confidences she'd spilled. Sasha, the last person she could afford to expose herself to, had seen her naked. It was no wonder that the last person who *had* seen her naked was paying the price for it.

When the drinks arrived, Louis made another valiant effort to jump start their night.

'I really enjoyed Saturday,' he said, dark eyes burning with sincerity as he looked into hers. 'I fucking hate dating apps, but it was worth it to meet you.'

After they'd matched, they'd messaged back and forth all of last week, Jenna thinking of funny things to tell him as she rushed between shifts at the Falcon and long days at the office. It had been nice to have someone to take the piss out of Penelope with, even if he'd never met her, and she'd heard all about his heinous boss at the law firm where he was a trainee. It was no wonder if had all felt so natural when they'd finally met, Louis waiting outside the door of the Falcon when she'd finished her shift so he could whisk her away, Prince Charming with an Uber for a carriage.

'Do you?' said Jenna lightly. 'I quite like them. All of the different people you get to meet.'

He'd ticked 'monogamy' on his profile, hers said 'prefer not to say'. Now she'd well and truly said it, his crestfallen face making it clear he'd heard her. Their evening would be over soon, they both knew it.

It was as if a part of her floated above the two of them – a better, nicer Jenna who haunted this version. That part wanted to tell Louis that she was equally confused by the way the door on her heart swung open and shut, suddenly locking itself tight against people she'd once liked or even professed to love.

This Jenna – the earthbound one – didn't have time to be that soft. Not on him, and not, more crucially, on herself. She couldn't lose focus.

This Jenna had a plan to execute.

SASHA

Speeding is definitely a vice I have, and driving to Reading that September day, I could feel my foot pushing down too hard on the accelerator, shitty dance music blasting through the speakers. If Steve had been in the car we'd have had to listen to something meaningful, like a seminal David Bowie album in its entirety, but I was heading to my mum's alone, driving his car but liberated from his good taste. I was still driving too fast when I swung off the main road into my mum's driveway, scrabbling to turn down the loud music that was puncturing the quiet as I braked. It obviously roused her, as she was soon hurrying out of the front door, her pleasure at seeing me written across her face.

'Hello, sweetie, let me get a proper look at you,' she said as I climbed out of the car. She hugged me close, her tanned, creased hands swiftly mapping my body. 'I feel like you're skin and bones.'

It was true that stress – the still-unresolved decision about treatment, the ghostly shadow Fred was casting over my working life – meant I was running on nervous energy. But I wasn't going to admit it.

'You just think that because you're my mum,' I said, hugging her back.

She started up the drive towards the small red-brick house, gravel crunching under her green Crocs. 'We need to get some lunch in you. There's far too much food – I was covering myself in case you changed your mind about bringing Steve and the kids.'

I gave an impromptu snort, which I quickly turned into a cough. The idea that Georgie and Jack would willingly drive to Reading for the afternoon to eat falafels in my mum's postage-stamp garden was pure fantasy. The suggestion was almost humiliating in its absurdity, but the truth was, my mum probably thought it was plausible because I did such a good job of selling her my perfect life. It existed alongside the perfect whisky and the perfect airline I was currently peddling elsewhere. We loved each other deeply, but we'd never had that instinctive closeness some mothers and daughters fostered so effortlessly. Perhaps it would be different for me, I thought, even though daring to imagine it felt dangerous when I still had so far to go.

'You know what it's like with teenagers,' I said airily. 'We haven't got a hope of keeping up with their social schedules.'

That too was largely fantasy. Georgie spent far too much time holed up in her room staring at her phone or watching Netflix with her noise-cancelling (parent-cancelling?) headphones jammed on her head. If it hadn't been the case, I might've been less keen to encourage her newfound association with Jenna. I could see it was blurring professional boundaries, but Jenna swore she didn't mind, and Georgie lit up at the mere mention of her. Jenna had convinced me to let her take her to another Elevate meeting, swearing to me afterwards that she'd been good as gold. I'd been deeply reluctant, but I guess I was looking for ways to paper over the cracks – to believe Steve's narrative about what our family was, and in turn persuade him to believe in my more radical reframing of what it could be.

'Don't worry, I remember . . .' said Mum, with a hint of acid. 'Come and say hi to Siobhan. She's in the garden.'

We made our way through their ramshackle little house, stuffed with piles of books and broadsheets and posters for obscure foreign films. The comfy chaos had driven me mad when I'd lived with her – the barbs she'd directed at my teenage self were probably justified – but now that we weren't spiky housemates, the familiarity was comforting.

'Hello, stranger,' said Siobhan, taking off her gardening gloves and running a hand through her neat grey pixie cut before giving me a brisk squeeze of greeting.

The two of them had been together twenty years now, an easy companionship that had ended a long period of single life for my mum. The boyfriends she'd had after my dad's death had never lasted more than a year or two, but a girlfriend turned out to suit her perfectly. Lasting love had found us both late, but for very different reasons.

* * *

Mum had never really understood my work – both the nuts and bolts of branding itself and my passion for it. Right then, I was trying to describe the intricacies of the Trellicker Whisky campaign, while the two of them looked at me like I was speaking Mandarin. Siobhan was busying herself with serving up a green salad from a big wooden bowl they'd brought back from one of their many intrepid trips.

'We're going to use this beautiful, remote island for the shoot next week. Jim, the photographer we got, normally shoots Oscar portraits for *Vanity Fair*. Stuff like that. It's a really major campaign for me.'

'And tell me what this Colin man's been in again?' said

Mum, taking a swig of her white wine, her distracted gaze darting to the oven where a quiche was baking. 'I'm sure I must've heard of him.'

I couldn't be bothered to tell her, yet again, that Callum's name was Callum. I was starting to feel silly, my work so frivolous in comparison to educating the next generation of thinkers. I swiftly changed the subject.

'It's been a great one to train up my new assistant on,' I said. 'She's from Stoke, Mum. I think it's partly why I hired her.'

'Stoke!' said Mum. She turned to Siobhan. 'Do you remember I did two years at Keele, teaching this Feminism in Modernist Literature course, just before I moved to Brunel and met you? Sasha had to be dragged out of London, kicking and screaming.' She turned back to me. 'Surprised it didn't make you run a mile when she told you.'

'It was the sixth form!' I protested, the old outrage building up in my chest, so many years later. 'I had to leave all my friends behind in London.'

'It was character building!' said Mum, with an exasperating smile. She looked back to Siobhan. 'I taught some wonderful young women there. It's a campus, so it was much more friendly with them all living onsite.' She turned back to me. 'Did your assistant go there?'

'All those whiny cows with their poetry books and their shitty boyfriends, sitting round the kitchen table spilling their guts,' I snarked. It was me being acidic now, old hurts flaring up. I used to sit on the outskirts moodily flicking through *Just Seventeen*, wondering how her students found it so much easier to connect with my mother than I did. One of those frequent visitors even stayed on the sofa bed for a few days, the two of them talking intensely late into the night, the kitchen door firmly closed in my face. They all treated her like some kind of wise guru, while our only interactions seemed to be screaming matches about whether or not I was old enough to take the last train back from London.

'Come on, now!' said Mum, not unaware of where my spikiness was coming from.

'And yeah, she did,' I said, already embarrassed by my petulance. 'I don't think she could afford to leave home.' I felt a wave of affection for Jenna – her lack of entitlement, her uncomplaining determination to get ahead in life. 'And then she lost her mum and decided to make the big move to London.'

'That poor girl!' said Mum, her face slack with sympathy even though she'd only discovered Jenna's existence thirty seconds ago. 'How did she lose her?'

'I don't actually know,' I said, spearing a lettuce leaf. 'I'm her boss, I haven't wanted to pry too much.' I smiled to myself, thinking of the easy camaraderie we'd found since that impromptu night spent drinking wine in Deia. Since then, the vibe between us had felt way more like a partnership than a hierarchy. 'We've got pretty close now though. I feel like I can probably ask her about it.'

Siobhan gave me a warm smile. 'I'm sure you're a terrific boss, Sasha,' she said, crossing to the oven to retrieve the quiche. Internally, I smugly agreed with her.

'Do you want a little top-up with the main course?' asked Mum, swinging the wine bottle towards my glass. I instinctively placed my palm over it and Mum raised her eyebrows. 'Are you trying again?' she asked quietly.

I swallowed. She knew some of the story – the two IVF attempts, the heartbreak of the miscarriage – but what she didn't know was that I'd been told conventional treatment was no longer viable. The path we were looking at now, Steve was gradually edging closer to agreement with, but it still felt too personal to articulate.

'Don't forget I'm driving,' I said lightly. 'And yes, we might be.' I turned to Siobhan, swallowing down the lump in my throat. 'That quiche smells amazing.'

* * *

Mum and I stood by my car, the newfound chill of a September evening making me pull my coat tight around my body. It was a visceral reminder that time was passing, that decisions needed to be made.

'Thanks for driving all the way up here,' she said, her arms encircling my body all over again. 'I know how busy you are.'

'No, Mum, I . . .' I hugged her back. 'It's important. I really wanted to see you.'

Mum paused a moment. 'I'm sorry if . . . I heard what you said at lunch. I know it was hard, all those girls sucking up my time and attention.'

'I didn't mean to be so shitty about it,' I said. 'You meant a lot to them. I bet you changed some lives along the way.'

Mum got a faraway look in her eye, a memory she didn't choose to share. 'Some of them were so . . . so lost. I got too involved sometimes. I hope I'm a lot more detached with my students now.'

I grinned at her. 'Yeah, you're sixty-seven. You've got no fucks left to give.'

She smiled back. 'I don't like that expression, Sasha. But I hope you know I have a lot of fucks to give for you. And it *was* hard for you, I see that now. It wasn't like you had a father around who you could lean on instead.'

My heart balled up tight in my chest, a sense of panic coming with it. I couldn't risk going there. 'No,' I said, one syllable all I could manage.

'He'd have been very proud of you,' said Mum gently. 'Even if he wasn't well enough to stick around to see it.'

My eyes were brimming now. I needed to go. 'Thanks, Mum,' I replied, clicking the space-age key that was buried in my pocket. The car made an ostentatious growl to tell me it was ready for action.

'Please let me be here for you with the IVF if you decide to do it,' she continued. She touched my cheek lightly with her fingertips. 'I want to do better now.'

I looked into her face – so loving, so lined with life experience – and longed to confide what path to motherhood I was now hoping to take. But something stopped me

'Thanks,' I said. 'I will.'

'And . . .' She looked almost guilty, wrestling with what it was she was trying to say. 'It's not everything, Sasha. Don't get me wrong, having you is the biggest joy of my existence, but you can have a very happy life without . . .' She stopped short of saying the word out loud. 'Academic research confirms it.'

I forced my face to stay neutral. How many times had I heard this now, almost always from well-meaning mothers who didn't have to feel the pain I experienced every day?

'I'll keep you posted,' I said, swinging the car door open.

* * *

Looking back, I can see it's no coincidence that this particular night was when the decision was definitively made. Steve and I stayed up so late that dawn streaked our bedroom window, his doubts gradually worn away by the force of my persuasion. It wasn't so different from the successful round of IVF that we'd longed for, I told him. No one needed to know how we'd done it, not at first. The fact we'd been encouraged by Dr Rindell to choose an egg donor who was as close a physical match to me as possible would hopefully make that easier. From his children's point of view, they'd be meeting their half-sibling, and for the baby, it would be too early to know anything more complicated than the fact they had two parents who loved them. We could tell them when they were old enough to understand. And with each of us related to the new being who had arrived in our lives, we'd finally be a bona fide family, an equality of love created that we hadn't yet experienced.

'Okay, Sasha,' said Steve, kissing me wearily in the wee small hours. 'I know how much this means to you.' He looked ruefully at his watch as he prepared to sleep, his regular Sunday morning tennis game nothing more than a fantasy by now.

'It's the next chapter for us all,' I said, sinking back against the pillows, wilfully ignoring how much was missing from the words he'd plucked out to finally give me his agreement.

What was in it for me, to look between the cracks?

JENNA

It was October now, the night before the Bright team were due to present the full creative package to Maple, and Sasha was a human stress ball. Jenna watched her profile as she leaned heavily over her desk to stare at her screen, her face pale and pinched in the light it radiated. It was weird, she'd coordinated the whole Trellicker Whisky campaign without breaking a sweat, hiring a new A-list director a week before the remote Scottish shoot when the first one disappeared and dropped them in it. This was just a bunch of visuals being shown to a gang of executives in the boardroom upstairs, and she was acting as though she was on death row.

Sasha's head jerked upwards. 'Can you come and have another look at these?'

Jenna's heart sank. This was meant to be Sasha signing the visuals off, not looking for more creative input. They urgently needed sending to the art department to be printed in high resolution for the presentation – Scarlett was sulkily waiting it out at the other end of the office in anticipation. Although keeping Scarlett waiting was kind of a bonus. That morning Bridget and Martin's beloved French bulldog Buster had had an explosive attack of diarrhoea in a meeting room and Scarlett had immediately exited, waving an airy hand towards the kitchen so Jenna could equip herself for the clean-up. Sasha might've protected her from the disgusting job, but she'd been off at one of her mysterious 'appointments', so as the 'junior assistant', Jenna had been left on her knees with a bucket of soapy water, trying to ensure the green rug wasn't left with brown stripes. At lunchtime Scarlett had patronizingly congratulated her on an 'ace job'.

'I'm sorry if it's a pain to stay,' Sasha added when Jenna didn't move quickly enough, a hint of steel in her voice. 'But Fred Williamson's expecting a lot from this. Have you got somewhere you need to be?'

Jenna hurried over, trying not to look at the clock. She had a shift at the Falcon, a big birthday party booked in the function room. According to Neil it would be 'all hands on deck' – so far, that was as far as his hands had got, but Jenna was constantly on guard.

'It's not a pain,' said Jenna, hurrying over. 'We've got to get this absolutely perfect.'

What would be worse – missing the shift altogether or turning up late? She could try faking something non-specific and yet gross and female-sounding enough to embarrass Neil into silence, but then she'd lose the cash for the shift. Outrageously late was harder to spin – she'd have to try to get Sasha out of this neurotic funk of hers as fast as possible.

'Yes, we do,' agreed Sasha, eyes still nervously scanning the screen. She pointed at it. 'Read it out loud for us, will you?'

The script was written across the white background in a retro courier font, like it had come steaming out of a hot typewriter in the 1950s. Jenna tried to make the words sound as profound as the typeface implied. '*When they go low, we soar higher.*'

Sasha shut her eyes, standing stock-still. 'Say it again.'

Finally, on the fourth go, Sasha's eyes sprang open.

'Do you like it, Jenna?' she demanded.

There was no right answer here – Sasha clearly had cold feet, despite the weeks the team had spent finding a phrase that could wrap up Maple's new environmental commitments whilst still sounding aspirational and joyful. If Jenna gave it the thumbs-up she'd sound like a fool, but if she poured cold water on it, they might be here all night. She made a split-second calculation. A newer assistant had been fired off Donovan's desk only last week; however warm and friendly Sasha had been since their night out, Bright was no safe space. And she couldn't risk the whole house of cards she'd built falling down.

'I did like it,' she ventured. 'But yeah, you're right, maybe there *is* something missing from it?'

'Yes!' agreed Sasha. 'You're so instinctive at this stuff, Jenna.' She traced the words with an elegant finger. 'Perhaps it's too confrontational. Like we're negging on the competition.'

'Maybe,' agreed Jenna, her mind racing. 'Just need to go to the t— . . . loo.'

Sasha waved an airy hand, not even bothering to turn around. 'Off you go. Sometimes I get my best ideas when I'm doing something else. My husband says neuroscience can explain it, but I've got no idea what he's talking about.'

Safely out of sight, Jenna sank down onto the closed toilet seat and reluctantly called the pub, praying she'd get some random barman. No such luck – instead it was Neil who picked up, the start of the evening rush a threatening hum in the background. All she could do was try to drown him in a flood of words.

'I'm so, sooo sorry!' she said, after explaining that she'd had to go back to Stoke for a 'family emergency'. 'The train's just been stopped here for half an hour, between stations. We're not even at Rugby. I think you should just get someone to cover.'

'Oh, should I?' snarled Neil. 'So you know, do you, a bunch of staff who are just hanging around at home on a Thursday evening, waiting for my call?'

Jenna looked up at the bathroom's ugly strip lighting, her heart pounding in her chest. 'I'm taking this really seriously, Neil. I hate letting you down.'

'Well maybe you should have thought about that when you casually booked yourself a mini-break with a sliver of fucking time to get here. I'm not sure about this, Jenna . . . about you. I've got a business to run here.'

Jenna's teeth were grinding now – the threat of losing the job was within touching distance. She wouldn't survive another month in London without it.

'Neil,' she said, forcing the kind of authority into her tone that she saw Sasha employ when she needed to bring the team to heel. 'I didn't want to have to say this but . . .' She created a pause, just the right length to build tension. 'My mum is seriously ill.' Her throat was thick now, the lie too close to the truth to let her stay mechanical. 'I had to risk my commitment to someone today. I'm sorry it had to be you.'

The words didn't sound remotely like her own. It was uncanny, the way she'd learnt to cloak herself in Sasha's skin.

Neil paused, his voice halting and uncertain when it came. 'Sorry to hear that, Jenna.'

'But if I get into Euston soon enough, I'll come in, I swear to you.'

'I'm sorry for what you're going through,' he said, bullishness returning, 'but I need to know you're committed. If your life's too complicated for this job, you'll need to move on.'

'Sorry again,' said Jenna, swiftly hanging up and taking a few expensive seconds to let her heart rate return to a normal pace.

She drew back the lock and pushed open the door. There – painting on her lipstick with painstaking care, as if her face was a work of art – stood Scarlett. She dramatically widened her eyes in the reflection, before spinning around.

'I'm so sorry about your mum!' she said. 'I couldn't help overhearing.'

Untrue – she could've fucked off out of the toilets as soon as she'd heard where the conversation was going.

'I don't want to talk about it,' said Jenna harshly, forcing her voice not to crack with the unexpected wave of grief.

Scarlett's green eyes imperceptibly narrowed, reminding Jenna that she was dangerous – their contracts specifically banned two-timing Bright with another employer. It wasn't a problem for someone like Scarlett: her flat was most likely bought outright by the Bank of Mum and Dad. She could afford to be judgemental about what Jenna had to do to survive.

'But thanks,' Jenna added more softly, crossing to the sink to wash her hands even though she hadn't peed. 'I appreciate the support.' Then she dashed back to her desk, Sasha's face a mask of annoyance when she got there.

'There you are!' she snapped. 'Were you gassing with Scarlett? I've just told her she can go home, we're not ready. She'll just have to come in at the crack of dawn, same as us.'

'Sorry,' said Jenna, for what felt like the hundredth time that hour, scrabbling internally for a way to soothe Sasha. 'But I think your husband might have a point . . .'

'Tell me,' said Sasha, skittishly clicking and unclicking the metal ballpoint pen that was clutched tightly in her left hand.

'Well, like when Michelle Obama used that phrase, *When they go low, we go high,* some people said it was a bit superior, didn't they? So maybe you're right. Maybe we need to sound like we're more of a friend to the consumer. We're all in the same boat, trying to do the right thing and save the planet together.'

It was hard to know in retrospect whether breaking the deadlock by unpicking the entire emotional thrust of the campaign was the smartest or the stupidest move she could've made.

Sasha swiftly became consumed by what the 'underlying moral implication' was for every combination of words that they came up with, scrawling obsessively on the whiteboard they'd wheeled out of the conference room until it looked like a leftover prop from *A Beautiful Mind*. She Deliverooed them a dinner of katsu without even asking Jenna if she was in for the long haul, oblivious to the way her eyes tracked the progress of the clock above their heads as she imagined Neil's rage mounting with every minute that ticked by. As 8.30 approached, she decided to make another desperate bid for freedom.

'I think we've got it, right there,' said Jenna, circling one of the earliest slogans they'd come up with that night. *Let Maple Fly You Higher* it said, with a series of shoutlines designed to run underneath that would unpack the airline's environmental commitments. The image would be one of a uniformed air steward pouring champagne into the glass of a cashmere-clad, biracial customer, cocooned in her luxurious business-class seat. 'It sounds inclusive, but it still has that aspirational vibe to it. You're taking the higher ground AND you're higher status. Win-win, right?'

As Jenna watched Sasha staring silently at the board, pondering the phrase like it had been written on a stone tablet, she had a sudden wave of existential exhaustion. Most days she enjoyed the job, even if her reasons for doing it were way more complicated than her CV gave away. But right now it felt like a deal with the devil. Spin glowed up to look like moral choices.

'I think you might be right,' said Sasha, a grin slowly

spreading across her face. 'We start them off with that sexy thrill of first-class travel and then appeal to their guilty conscience as they track down the page. Chocolate first, granola second.'

'Exactly!'

'It'll be great if it pushes up air traffic for them,' continued Sasha, tapping the screen. 'The projections they're trying to reach since they floated on the stock market are off the scale. This campaign's going to be critical.'

'Yeah, but . . .' Jenna almost didn't know where the words were coming from. Perhaps the exhausted parts of her had banded together and were staging a protest. 'Overall the trend's for people flying less, isn't it? Lockdown proved you didn't have to. It's the way it has to go in the end.'

Sasha turned away from studying the screen to look at her, the smile she gave not quite reaching her eyes. 'I mean yes, obviously. But also – we want this campaign to work. So, not right now for Maple.' She wagged a finger, giving an exaggerated smirk to signal she was joking. 'Jenna, tell me the truth, has my stepdaughter already recruited you for her cult?'

Jenna forced herself to laugh, even though it nearly choked her. Sasha's generation had had it so fucking easy, and they still couldn't quite wean themselves off the sugar rush. At her age it had all been starter mortgages and guilt-free foreign holidays for them. No wonder all their environmental concerns or sad eyes about the 'housing crisis' felt like crocodile tears. None of them could be bothered to let this shit get too real.

She was sailing dangerously close to the wind now; she needed to rein it in. 'You're okay, you don't need to deprogramme me just yet!' she said.

She was having brunch with Georgie the following week, a whole new kind of interaction. If there was any recruitment to be done, she planned to be the one doing it.

'Well, that's a relief,' said Sasha, blue eyes like slate. She sank back in her chair, making to turn off her computer. 'I think we're done for tonight.' When she smiled over at Jenna, the warmth had seeped back in. 'Thank you – I really appreciate you putting in the hours. This campaign's . . .' She looked away for a second, something close to dread on her face. 'It's key to the fourth-quarter numbers. I can't screw it up.'

If it was dread Jenna was picking up on, it didn't feel like it was just about the numbers. Either way, she didn't have time to investigate Sasha's emotions. She took a slurp from the kombucha that had come with their katsu and stood up from her own chair. 'No worries. It's exciting. You listening to me. Letting me contribute.'

Sasha's face predictably lit up at that.

'You're welcome!' She was pushing her phone and her iPad into her big handbag now. 'I've always loved what I do,' she added. 'Doing something creative – helping to shape culture – it's a real privilege.' She paused, the bag packed. 'We're very lucky.'

The last sentence landed heavily, like a coded warning. She hadn't enjoyed Jenna questioning her ethics, that much was clear. Jenna grabbed her coat from the rack, but before she could put it on, she noticed how Sasha's eyes were tracking up and down her body. It wasn't like Neil's creepy eye-fucking, but it was still weird.

'Hang on,' her boss said, then darted down to her desk drawers, pulling out a bulging cotton shopping bag.

She extracted a shirt, holding it up by the shoulders. Jenna adjusted her face, trying to look surprised by the contents, even though she'd had a sneaky look in the drawers a few days ago when she'd been the last person to leave the office. At the time she'd wondered if it was a stash of dry cleaning Sasha was too embarrassed to ask her to drop off.

'You liked this shirt when I wore it to the staff drinks the other week, didn't you?'

Jenna couldn't help but like all of Sasha's amazing wardrobe – she wore her outfits, they never wore her. Jenna couldn't imagine ever having that confidence herself – most days it felt like her tiny, cheap wardrobe was laughing its arse off at her.

'Yeah, it looked amazing on you.'

It was grey silk, a sliver of fabric running down both sides of the neck that Sasha had tied in a loose bow. It was grown-up and sexy all at once.

'I just don't wear it that much,' said Sasha. 'I've got a lot of stuff that just doesn't get much of an outing. I've promised Steve I'll Marie Kondo the fuck out of our cupboards so his shirts aren't permanently homeless.'

'Okay,' said Jenna uncertainly.

'Would you . . .' Sasha took an awkward step forward, the bag held out in front of her like an offering. 'I was going to sell it all, but I'm lazy, and I won't get much for it anyway. Why don't you take it? See if there's anything you like in there.'

Jenna froze.

'Honestly, just take it. I think the shirt would look really nice on you, maybe over a pair of jeans. There's a couple of dresses in there too, and that sparkly navy sweatshirt with the puffy sleeves.'

Jenna unconsciously looked down, scanning her solid body and finding it wanting. Some days she'd kidded herself that her H&M jeans looked like Chloe's or Scarlett's, but on those days she'd clearly been a fucking idiot. Here, held out in her boss's hand, was all the proof she'd ever need.

'Oh wow, that's so kind of you,' she said, hoping humiliation wasn't making the words sound spiky.

No chance of that – Sasha's smile was one of pure relief,

which made Jenna feel even more wretched. Was she really that much of a ragbag embarrassment to her? The silent, deadly rules that London ran on would never speak themselves out loud to a girl like her.

'You'll look amazing in that stuff!' Sasha said, hand on her hip. It was gross how pleased with herself she was. 'We could go for a cheeky glass of wine to toast a job well done?'

Jenna could barely make eye contact. Even if she hadn't had to somehow teleport herself to her other job, she couldn't have stood it.

'Um, I'm actually going to the Falcon. I'm really late.' She didn't want to antagonize her again. 'Which is fine, but—'

'Oh God, Jenna, I'm so sorry,' said Sasha, as if she hadn't made it crystal clear that Jenna was chained to her desk until she decided the working day was over. 'Let me order you an Uber. Bright definitely owes you one tonight.'

So, it was Bright's fault now, the two of them just a pair of downtrodden colleagues at the mercy of their horrible bosses.

'You meeting your friend from uni again?' Sasha asked, as she busied herself with her phone. 'Or are you hanging out there with your flatmates these days?'

'I'm seeing Cara, my mate from Staffordshire,' said Jenna. Her imaginary friend who suddenly had a name. And she was most definitely imaginary – no one from Stoke had ever been christened Cara.

Sasha laughed. 'You'd better watch out for me and Steve if you hang out there at weekends. No one wants their boss catching them doing shots on a Friday night, do they?'

The gap between fantasy and reality was enough to make Jenna cry, and the risk of seeing Sasha at the Falcon no longer felt like an exciting high-stakes gamble.

She might need to cash in her chips sooner than she'd planned.

SASHA

We'd had a late night on the eve of the presentation, one of those adrenaline-fuelled creative marathons that reminded me of my fledgling days in the industry. I'd kept Jenna right at the heart of it, hoping she'd appreciate the insight into how close to the wire the thrust of a big campaign could go. Truth be told, she'd seemed a bit sulky about it by the time we'd left, but it wasn't like I hadn't tried to sweeten the pill.

I was congratulating myself on that fact as I stepped out of the lifts, juggling two Squirrel lattes in my gloved hands. The bag of outfits I'd gifted her, fancy labels on every single one, was an expensive kind of thank you, plus the steaming cup of coffee I was holding was an extra treat. I wasn't unaware of how pitiful her salary was, how little wiggle room it gave her for clothes that flattered her figure or lunches that didn't get tipped out of an old yoghurt pot. I couldn't really understand how she afforded all those nights out at the Falcon, with its six-quid 'house wine' and overpriced pork scratchings.

It would come good for her, I knew that – I would personally ensure she got the opportunities she deserved. I was proud of how I was mentoring her, listening to her ideas and giving her a public voice in a way I'd never had at her stage of the game. My bosses had only cared about how handy I was with a cafetière or, on the worst days, how my carefully chosen dresses skimmed my taut, twenty-something body.

Ugh – Fred. I took a gulp of coffee, as if caffeine was a well-known antidote to anxiety. I was on the office floor by now, where I could see Jenna's head bent low over her desk. No sign of Scarlett meanwhile, despite my telling her she was needed here early. Alongside the irritation, I felt a familiar flash of smugness at my excellent choice of assistant. Anna should've paid heed to my warnings when she'd hired Scarlett.

'Morning, gang,' I called out.

The other members of the team were ranging around, nervous energy pulsing through the office. Anna had laid out huge, glossy print-outs of the new images and was poring over them with Chloe, while Fergus was having an intense phone conversation in one of the meeting rooms, his straggly ginger hair tenting over his big round glasses. Jenna looked up and smiled at the sound of my voice, a point of calm in a storm. I smiled back, trying not to look too delighted that she was wearing the silky Theory shirt I'd strategically placed at the top of the bag.

'Morning, boss,' she said, standing up as I held out her coffee to her. 'Oh my God, thanks for this!'

She'd never called me 'boss' before, and the sound of it gave me a little jolt, but I didn't waste any time trying to decode it. I was too busy taking in how different she looked, a previously loose pair of my black cords snugly encasing her bottom half, creating a lovely balance with the trapeze shape of the shirt.

'You look lovely!' I said, making an internal decision that I'd let her sit in on the presentation that afternoon. Bridget sometimes developed strange vendettas against assistants – 'I'm just allergic,' she'd say airily, like it was a medical condition – then gradually found a way to get them excluded or permanently disappeared over the weeks that followed. Now I'd given Jenna some camouflage, it felt safe to take her further into the belly of the beast. None of this logic seemed remotely illogical back then – I wasn't so much a boiling frog as one that had long since been dissolved into a tasty soup by the sustained heat. God, I was a fool.

Jenna paused a second. 'Yeah, don't tell anyone,' she stage-whispered, 'but I think I've got a fairy godmother.'

I laughed as I headed off in search of a copy of the new print-outs, a warm feeling spreading through my upper chest. 'Glad they're working out for you,' I called back to her. 'Now let's take another look at those shoutlines we came up with in the cold light of day.'

* * *

I liked to have boards when I gave a presentation, not just a series of fleeting images on a screen. It made the ideas feel tactile and tangible all at once – serious enough to be committed to physical form. I hoped it made my campaigns feel classic and considered, rather than marking me out as some kind of analogue dinosaur. Right now, standing at the wooden easel that had been set up in the boardroom, a captive audience that included Martin and Bridget sitting in front of me, I wasn't so sure.

Of course I'd lost faith in myself. Fred was in the front row of seats, strategically occupying a place on the left-hand end rather than front and centre. He leaned backwards in his chair, limbs loose, reminding everyone he could take up all the space he wanted. His black jeans and striped T-shirt should've looked too young, too casual, but instead they contributed to the weird ageless quality he'd always possessed. It was like nothing could touch him – mortality was for mere mortals in Fred Williamson's life bible. I let my left hand fall casually across my body, secretly investing my wedding and engagement bands with magical powers that would ward off evil.

Martin and Bridget strode to the front of the room, perfectly in step, as always. They were either hopelessly codependent or a sinewy masterclass in branding – I'd spent the best part of twenty years trying to work out which.

'Right, lovely Maple people,' said Bridget. 'We're so grateful you've entrusted us with such an exciting – such an *important* – campaign.'

Martin nodded in silent, sanctimonious agreement, and then took up the baton.

'It's *so* important that we knew we had to put our best woman on it.' He turned his attention towards me, and I tried to arrange my face into an expression of ironic humility. 'Sasha's been leading the team to try and find that sweet spot between covetable luxury and the shared environmental responsibility we all feel so deeply committed to. Let's see how they've done, shall we?'

My gaze met Fred's for one unfortunate second, and I tried to insulate myself from a cascade of memories – there were too many occasions when I'd stared into those blue eyes and wholly lost myself there. The sadness I'd been so stubbornly refusing to feel suddenly gripped me. There had to still be time – time to make up for what I'd lost by submitting myself to that particular emotional wilderness for so long. He gave an almost imperceptible smile, one that seemed to ask what this me – the Sasha who was a woman, not a girl who was faking it – had to offer him. My eyes flicked to Jenna, squashed in at the back, overwhelmingly grateful that the passage of time meant that her currency would never be measured in the terms mine once was.

I nodded to Pete, Martin and Bridget's creative assistant, and he efficiently turned the first board over for me.

'We wanted to start by defining how consumers feel about Maple right now,' I said, making sure my tone was firm and assured. 'What's their instinctive, emotional response to the brand?' I pointed to the column on the right of the board, opposite the current Maple logo on the left. 'And these are some of the words they used.'

I started to throw out the carefully curated selection – I wanted to make Fred and his team feel good about their place in the market, but also know that there was plenty of room for improvement if they got fully on board with our ideas. I needed to bring this account home, even more so knowing that I would likely be disappearing off for my geriatric maternity leave in the coming months. Bridget was old-school about these things – I got the feeling that in the corporate jungle of the Eighties, you had to park your baby in your briefcase and never miss a step.

'The words they're choosing – heritage, reliable, trustworthy, upmarket – they're all good things to have associated with your brand.' I paused for effect, avoided focusing on anyone specific. 'But let's look at some of the phrases they associate with your main competitors and see how you feel about the contrast.'

Pete's hand seamlessly slid across with the next board.

'Virgin Atlantic – people identify them as fun. Disruptive. Anarchic. Hedonistic. They'll take you on trips to locations you aspire to: Miami, LA, New York.' I paused again. 'You fly to all these destinations too, but your commitment to those routes isn't triggering the same sensations and associations with consumers.'

Fred gave me a lazy, wolfish smile from the front row. 'But you're here to wave your magic wand, right, Sasha?'

There was something in his tone, in his honeyed vowels, that felt like a siren going off. I darted a look at Martin and

Bridget, their faces neutral. I was clearly being paranoid; after all, if they knew we had any kind of history, surely they never would've made me lead on this campaign?

'We're certainly going to try,' I told him, in the tone of a headmistress threatening a week's detention.

I took them through a couple more rival brands, trying my best to stir up a feeling of jealous inadequacy, before diving headfirst into our ideas about how to reposition Maple to carve out market share and a new era of traveller loyalty. I started with the arresting new visuals – all bright greens and stylish fonts – before diving into the ethical sell.

'None of your competitors are putting their commitment to being part of the environmental solution front and centre,' I told them. 'With your commitment to net zero by 2029 – the new fleet of planes, the technological advances you've made with fuelling them responsibly – you can afford to start shouting.'

I snuck a look at Jenna, remembering the hurt I'd felt last night when she'd undermined the entire campaign after we'd finally landed on a slogan that worked. Her negativity had meant there'd been no air punch moment – it had killed the camaraderie between us stone dead. Still, I sprinkled a flavour of her moral questioning over the wrap-up of this first section.

'Of course, flying is a complex decision, but when we decide we need to do it, we want it to be done in the most responsible way possible. You're not a faceless corporation, you're a friend and ally to the people you fly. You share their hopes and aspirations for a greener future. Let's make this the start of a whole new era for Maple and for their customers.'

Fred turned to a couple of his colleagues on the front row, expression inscrutable, then nodded his appreciation.

'Yeah, I like it,' he said, smiling that self-satisfied smile. 'So come on then, let's see the full visual package.'

Pete slid the next board onto the easel.

'The big reveal!' I said, reaching out a hand to touch it, hoping they couldn't detect the subtle quiver of my fingers. I took them through it – the way the new vivid green would define their visual identity and cut through a crowded market, the new kind of traveller we wanted to depict enjoying their business class, and finally, the slogan we'd crafted to bring all the elements together.

'*Let Maple Fly You Higher.*' My eyes crept to Fred's face as I said it – what a cruel twist of fate it was that I was still looking for his validation. 'We think the double meaning won't be lost on business travellers. Maple's going to offer you the most exclusive business-class experience. It's aspirational and luxurious. But it's also—' I gave a warm smile to Jenna, silently acknowledging her contribution '—with you on your journey to taking the higher ground. To doing better. To being part of the solution, not part of the problem. The emotion grabs you first, and then the facts nail why it matters in the text that runs below.'

I took a step away, turned myself towards the Maple crew.

'So, we'd love to know what your gut reaction is to these initial ideas.'

The two junior execs huddled around Fred like he was a fire and they needed to keep warm, their voices low and urgent. After what seemed like roughly a century, they broke apart.

'Great work, guys,' said Fred, the words too flat and neutral to let me breathe out just yet. 'Love the visual overhaul, love the direction of travel.' He laughed at his own joke, then paused, looking off into space. 'I guess I'm thinking back to that meeting you let me sit in on. The one with all those kids you promised me were the future, making me feel like I'd got here on my free bus pass.'

My stomach cratered as a ripple of nervous laughter spread through the Bright team.

'I'm thinking about that girl who wouldn't shut up.' He twisted round to take in the rest of the room, a disarming grin spread across his face. 'Pink streak in her hair, shit-ton of attitude. And I mean, good for her. All power to her. I doubt she's flying business just yet, but if she *is* the future, we need to start impressing her right now.'

My mouth was too dry for me to speak, my gaze locking with Jenna's for a fleeting second.

'Totally,' I croaked. It was impossible not to feel that Fred, with his big-cat energy, wasn't enjoying my discomfort. 'But obviously the brief was to start with the visual branding and the business-class offering, because that's where so much of the revenue sits. If we're moving forward together, we'll be deep in the weeds with all classes of travel, modifying the language in a targeted way.'

'Yeah, Sasha, I get what the route was that got us here,' he said, voice silky. 'I guess I'm asking if I can pay extra for a quick detour.'

He laughed, swivelled his gaze to Martin and Bridget, who tittered along obediently, their faces tight with tension. I needed to bring this home.

'I think we need to create an interim stage before we commit,' he continued. 'Go through the same process with economy, premium economy.' He winced for comic effect. 'Oof, it's an ugly word, isn't it? Wonder if we just tell the truth and call it cattle class?'

Bridget gave me a staccato nod, panic in her eyes. The truth was, Bright's annual earnings were running at least ten per cent below what we'd been hitting by the fourth quarter of the previous year, despite us projecting to the board that we'd deliver aggressive growth. The multi-million-pound Maple account was critical for making up the shortfall – I couldn't be personally responsible for it disappearing in a puff of smoke. I was senior, expensive. Old. It wasn't such a ludicrous idea that I would disappear with it, particularly if a baby kept me out of sight and out of mind for too long.

I was gabbling now. 'Of course. We can throw ourselves into that initial stage of the broader creative immediately. I can—'

Fred cut across me, his hand swiping through the air. 'No, no. I wanna use what Bright's got. It's not like every agency's got that demographic trapped in the basement, ready to feed back. I want to do the broader presentation TO them. Get that cockatoo girl back – I want to hear from our toughest critics. No sugar-coating. This campaign's going to define us through a whole new era.' He half stood up in his seat, looked around the room. 'We have to get this right!'

My breath hitched in my windpipe, trapping any sensible comeback. I did a split-second calculation. Hardly anyone here knew who Georgie was, and certainly not Bridget and Martin. Chloe ran Elevate, so she might've spotted her there on her repeat visits, but I could surely just disappear her from the records, never to be seen again? But this was way bigger than the Georgie problem. We needed the guaranteed business to come through now, not in some hypothetical future.

'The good news is, we've got Gen Z brilliantly represented in the core creative team,' I said. 'My lovely assistant today, Pete,' I made a theatrical little gesture towards him, still sitting by the easel, and he gave an awkward thumbs-up, 'and my creative assistant, Jenna,' I added, pointing to her at the back of the room. 'There's a bunch more who aren't here in the room today . . .'

Fred's eyes narrowed, his thin lips twisting into a tight knot.

I knew way too much about him – the way his moods could switch like a freak weather event. That faux friendliness of yore was swiftly leaving the building. 'Yeah, but that's not what I'm asking you to provide me.'

All I can say in my defence is that in that moment I was truly desperate. 'Jenna,' I said. 'Do you want to come up here and talk about how you helped mould the slogan? You reacted quite strongly against the phrasing we first came up with, didn't you? I feel like you found it quite triggering.'

That ubiquitous word – it felt like in the modern workplace, it got thrown around like confetti. Sometimes it felt like these days, you could be triggered by a swivel chair and need a week off. That said, looking at Jenna now, it felt like I'd genuinely triggered her with the mere use of the word. She was folded down in her chair, shrinking away from all the bodies that were craning their necks to get a look at her.

Her eyes flashed panic. 'I don't . . .'

'Come on up!' I said, cheesily beckoning her forwards like we were on a Saturday night show. I pushed away any guilt about her obvious discomfort. This was the perfect opportunity for her to show what she could do in front of the top brass, exactly the process I'd been trying to kick off by bringing her into this high-profile meeting.

She awkwardly shuffled across the room until she was standing next to me, her right hand jammed deep in the pocket of her (or were they still my?) cords.

'So, Jenna,' I said, smiling performatively, 'talk us through that first shoutline we had, and why you felt it needed to change.' I threw Fred a self-deprecating smile, trying to wipe away the remnants of his scowl. 'Let me tell you, I didn't appreciate it at eight pm last night.'

His frown disappeared, swiftly replaced by that sleazy

half-grin he kept sending my way. Heat prickled my cheeks, and I took an inelegant slurp from my water glass.

'I think it was *When They Go Low, We Soar Higher*,' said Jenna haltingly.

Chloe, sat in the centre of the second row, stared at her, laser-beaming pure hatred. My stomach clenched – I hadn't had time to fully think through the politics of my genius move. It was Chloe's phrase first of all – she'd given forth in one of the first meetings about what a culture-defining leader Michelle Obama was, how the phrase had 'entered the collective lexicon' and would resonate with consumers 'on a subconscious level they can't even trace to source'. Now I was standing up here with my mini-me, dismantling her whole ethos in front of the client. I'd need to make sure Jenna wasn't the one who paid the price for it when Chloe got her alone.

'So, what was it that you bumped on, Jenna?' I asked. 'How did you persuade me we needed to pivot?'

'Just sounds a bit snotty, doesn't it?' said Jenna, her long Stoke vowels suddenly seeming to bounce off the walls and amplify themselves to a deafening volume. 'Up its own arse.' Seeing Bridget's nose wrinkle at the unfamiliar sound triggered a rush of protectiveness towards my unpolished assistant. Besides, even if Bridget found the words distasteful, they'd be sending a useful signal to Maple, telling them we were more than just an echo chamber of privilege. 'Like, it comes from Michelle Obama, right?'

'I think so,' I said, all innocence.

'It's a cop-out though, isn't it?' she said, her voice rising. 'It's a luxury, just taking yourself higher. The people who are making a real difference in the world are fighting for what they believe in.' All I'd needed her to do was demonstrate that we'd altered the language, not go into a full-scale environmental rant in front of an airline. The point was made now – a fact I tried to communicate with a look – but she wouldn't stop. 'People like Extinction Rebellion. They actually get their hands dirty, they don't back down and make compromises.'

'What I *heard* you say at the time,' I said smoothly, 'was that the tone of the phrase sounded morally superior. Distancing for the consumer.' I opened myself to the room. 'No fun!' I declared, in the most fun way I could muster. 'Which was an incredibly useful insight for me to have.'

I stared directly at Jenna for the last line, my eyes flashing her a warning.

'Kind of . . .' she said, face sullen.

I cut across her before she could dig us a bigger hole.

'So, the two of us burnt the midnight oil, ordered a Deliveroo, and took it to here!' I said, spinning my body back towards the easel. '*Let Maple Fly You Higher*. It's inclusive. It's got a sense of shared moral purpose – your customers want and need to fly, but they also want to do their bit. The emotional response we trigger with the shoutline is swiftly met by all the cold, hard facts running below, detailing your frankly incredible commitment to being part of net zero. No other airline holds a candle to you there.'

I gave Jenna a warm, appreciative smile that I hoped would bring us back in line.

'It's a subtle tweak that we believe makes a big difference. And I wouldn't have got there without Jenna – without her unique Gen Z perspective, and also our ability as senior creatives to hear it. That kind of cross-generational teamwork is in our DNA here at Bright.' I looked at Jenna. 'Your generation are at the heart of the work we create. And all of our work *must* come from the heart.'

I waited for her to speak, to role-play our chemistry for the room. It was a wait that felt eternal. 'Yeah, I'm learning so much here,' she finally said.

'And I'm learning from you!' I riffed back, catching Fred's eye. 'Because at Bright we know that it takes a village.'

Jenna stood there, rigid and silent. The nerves were obviously getting to her, plus some justified embarrassment about veering so wildly off script. I needed to let her off the hook.

'Thanks so much for coming up here and sharing something about the part you played,' I said, gesturing to her that she could go back to her seat.

I hated the sense of relief I felt at watching her disappear back into the tight crush, but it was hard to suppress my anger at how close she'd come to derailing the whole presentation. Perhaps anyone as new to the game as her could lose the creative thread under that kind of pressure? I certainly didn't want to shame her the way I'd have been shamed back in the day if I'd delivered that kind of performance. There was a smattering of applause, a tiny nod of approval from Bridget, and then another sticky silence.

'Yeah, very impressive,' said Fred, once he'd let the quiet last long enough to unsettle us all. He turned around, twinkled at Jenna. 'I knew your boss when she was still learning to sell ice to the Eskimos. You'll go far with her.'

I kept my face neutral, waited to see where he was going.

'Thing is, Sasha . . .' he continued, combative and flirtatious all at once. 'You just proved my point.'

He was waiting for a reply. 'How so?' I asked lightly.

'We need their voices. She told you something you needed to hear, so why not ask more of them what they think?' He turned up his palms in a gesture of helplessness. 'I know, I'm the dickhead Johnny Come Lately who arrived after this campaign had been commissioned. But the Maple board brought me over to be a disruptor, and it's patently fucking obvious we have to reach the whole consumer base, not just the one per cent they asked you to snare. Future-proof ourselves.' He pointed at Jenna, like a medieval king singling out a peasant. 'You could smell what was wrong, couldn't you?'

Jenna gave a shrug, wisely not risking more.

'So could the girl with the pink hair.' Fred paused, shifted tone. 'Let's get moving on a bigger, broader campaign. I know it's a pain in the arse for you that it's not guaranteed just yet – I might even have another firm pitch too. But if you win it, I'll commit us to five years, pump the budget right up.' He grinned at me. 'As Sasha might remember from back in the day, I'm someone who loves taking the big swings.'

He stood up, stepping close to me so that he could face the whole room. I instinctively lurched backwards, nearly toppling the easel.

'I dunno, I feel like we could do something really special here, guys.' Nodding once at the assembled crowd, he headed for the door, beckoning for us to follow. 'So, let's go and raise a glass to that.'

If only he'd known how lucky he was to be spared Chloe's favourite lecture on the evils of gendered greetings.

* * *

The Pol Roger champagne we'd ordered, intending it to be popped in joyful celebration, tasted sour and medicinal in my dry mouth. I wasn't meant to be drinking – the treatment would hopefully be starting before too long – but I also wasn't meant to be subjecting myself to undue stress. It was an un-squareable circle, I thought, downing half a glass.

Fred had manoeuvred himself into the centre of the room by now, and was holding his glass aloft and bossily tapping it with a teaspoon. The fact that he was so unbearable should have been comforting – a bullet dodged – but instead it tasted just as sour as the champagne. I forced a rictus grin onto my face and prepared to toast him.

'This is already a great campaign,' he began. 'And it's going to get even better. Even bigger. Even smarter.'

I snuck a look at Bridget, standing close by, and noted that her smile looked just as painted on as mine. With good reason: if he really thought that, why was he implying we'd be in some kind of creative death match with another agency?

'I'm anticipating a bright future for Maple and Bright – see what I did there?!' Fred's gaze landed on me, and I gripped the stem of my glass so tightly I feared it might shatter and slice into my flesh. 'And it's an unexpected pleasure to have Sasha at the helm. You know, I was her boss, back in the day. I wouldn't go as far as saying she was my protégé, but I marked enough of her homework to know she'd go far.'

'Thanks, Fred,' I said, as listless as Jenna had been during the presentation. She was over in the corner with Pete, her eyes trained on me. I was still angry, but seeing that obvious admiration mollified me somewhat. Of course she'd been nervous, trying to match my years of experience up there in front of everyone.

'So, charge your glasses,' said Fred. 'Onwards, team Maple-Bright!'

Our feeble cheer made us sound like a bleating herd of sheep headed for the abattoir. The truth was, it was hard to fake collective excitement when all we could see were our Christmas bonuses sliding downwards towards a fat zero. Knowing how mercurial Fred was, I knew we urgently needed to rally. I took a firm step forward into the circle.

'Exciting times!' I said, gesturing to him. 'And I want to thank you, Fred.' I gave a small shrug, acknowledging what he'd failed to deliver us. 'No, seriously. Thank you for giving us permission to really challenge ourselves creatively.' I looked around at the team, silently forcing them to follow my lead. They got it, stepping closer and bringing some much-needed energy, Jenna crossing the room to stand beside me for the next toast. 'It's a privilege. I promise you, we won't let you down.'

Fred gave a smug nod, unable to resist the compliments. 'I know you won't, Sasha,' he said softly. 'You never did back then.'

Our eyes met for a brief second, my cheeks flushing so fast that I had to look away. I gave him a tight little smile, excusing myself for an unnecessary bathroom break.

Jenna's eyes flicked between us as we spoke, and I could feel them tracking me as I abruptly left the room. How attuned she was, I thought, using the reminder to dampen my anger about her performance earlier. How caring.

How blind I was. The only thing Jenna cared about was Jenna herself.

JENNA

Tonic torrented out of the squat glass bottle, fizzing and popping over the ice and erupting over the rim of the glass as Jenna splashed it out from too great a height. She needed to rein in how much she let her inner world explode into the outer world, seething frustration like a 24/7 fireworks display.

'Sorry about that,' she said, watching how the girl she was serving nervously licked the rogue tonic off her hand as it splashed her. She was nervous all round; Jenna took a sneaky peek at the man she was buying the drinks for, currently running a hand through his thick, red hair as he surveyed the pub like he owned it, not even bothering to check if she needed help at the busy bar. 'That'll be sixteen pounds fifty.'

'Sixteen pounds fifty?' said the girl, incredulous. She recovered herself. 'I mean, sorry . . . it's just . . .'

Jenna threw her a sympathetic smile. 'A double gin and tonic's seven quid, and then the pistachios are two pounds fifty.'

The girl's date had bought a bottle of Chablis first, a cool £45. Now it seemed it was her turn; Jenna reckoned it was only a first or second date, and that the girl was trying to prove that she was a good feminist who paid her own way, even if it meant she had to eat cold noodles for lunch into eternity. Or maybe that was just Jenna herself.

'Maybe I'll dump the nuts,' the girl said. 'Is that all right?' she added apologetically.

It was a ball-ache – they'd have to be poured back into the large mason jar that sat on the shelf while the impatient Friday night customers behind her huffed and puffed, but Jenna didn't want to make her feel any worse.

'Course,' she said, holding out the card machine. 'They're like a million calories anyway.'

'You star!' said the girl gratefully, grabbing the slippery glasses and scuttling back towards the worn velvet sofa her date was manspreading across.

Jenna wasn't feeling like much of a star; instead, she felt distinctly earthbound. First, she'd nearly lost her second job, bawled out by a sweaty, red-faced Neil when she'd arrived late for her shift the night before the Maple presentation; he'd given her an official warning thanks to Sasha's last-minute creative meltdown. Then she'd dragged herself out of bed the next day, dressed head to toe in the uniform Sasha had foisted on her, only to be humiliated in front of a whole room of VIPs. She knew her anger and hurt in that moment had made her veer too far off script, but Sasha shouldn't have expected her to be a ventriloquist's dummy.

She'd discovered in their chilly debrief that she'd 'conveyed her message wrong', a strange kind of double-speak that Jenna was still struggling to decode. Apparently, it wasn't that she was forbidden from expressing her own opinion, free speech of course being a cornerstone of creativity at Bright; it was that she needed to express it in a way that 'pulled in the same direction as the overall strategy'. Basically, she'd fucked up, helping to convince that moody man-child from Maple that the campaign was worse than useless until they'd proved to him that they were speaking to her entire generation, including the ones who'd rather paddle a leaky dinghy to Kathmandu than increase their carbon footprint one iota.

The fact was, if anyone had got under his skin it was Georgie, but it was easier for Sasha to take the whole mess out on her assistant. Her stepdaughter was too dangerous, particularly now that Chloe had painstakingly tracked her down to make sure she'd be visible in the next Maple meeting, as well as part of all the prep leading up to it.

'Jenna!' Neil was looming over her and clicking his fingers in her face like they were about to dance a tango.

'Sorry ...' Jenna switched back into worker-bee mode, grinning at the bearded man closest to her at the bar, who was straining for her attention.

'I'll take over here,' said Neil, sweating stress. 'Get your head back in the game. I need you to go and cover the restaurant side.'

Burning-hot plates and Friday-night expectations – Jenna didn't relish the prospect, but at least the tips were better over there. She spent the next hour or so concentrating fiercely on doing the best she possibly could, pushing Bright out of her head. She had to stop failing at each job because of the relentless pressure of the other one. Happy customers and generous tips were soon rolling her way as she doggedly ploughed on towards closing time.

When she first saw them – three heads bent over their menus on table thirteen – she convinced herself she was imagining it. North London gastro pubs were surely full of hoodie-wearing, entitled teenagers anticipating a £20 truffled mushroom burger. But when she looked again and saw the glint of Georgie's nose ring and the Nirvana tour dates running down her back, she knew this was no hallucination. Would Sasha be joining them? Why had she ever thought this would be a fun game of chicken?

She froze, then looked around frantically for Marc, who was covering the other section. He was running to the pass, grabbing plates for a party of six – there was no way he was adding another table to his roster to do her a favour. Now Steve – because it must surely be Steve – was looking up and around, his long, stringy neck giving him the vibe of a nosy ostrich. There was no dodging this.

'Hi!' she said, sailing up to the table. 'Sorry for the wait.' She and Georgie were locking eyes by now – Jenna gave the girl her best Sasha death glare to silently entreat her to stay schtum. Georgie's mouth levered open, then snapped shut just as quickly. 'Have you had a chance to take a look at the menu?'

Steve smiled up at her, wiping condensation from his tortoiseshell-framed glasses with the sleeve of his blue chambray shirt. 'We have, and I'm afraid we've got a couple of questions for you,' he said, with an air of cheerful concentration.

Wow. She'd obviously suspected he was older than Sasha, what with the ex-wife and the teenage kids, but somehow she'd imagined him as a salt-and-pepper George-Clooney-alike. The real Steve felt like he came from a whole other generation; she could see he might be considered handsome by some, but surely not to a woman as fit and youthful as Sasha? If they did have a baby together, people would probably think he was its granddad.

'Fire away,' she said, deliberately averting her eyes from Georgie. Jack, her brother, held himself completely differently from her, sitting backwards in his chair, chest wide, fingers idly tapping on his phone, exuding a confidence that Georgie could never hope to score.

'The cavolo nero – is it organic?' Steve gave her a rueful grin. 'Sorry to be a North London cliché. It's just that it's a magnet for pesticides if not.'

'I dunno,' said Jenna. 'I don't think so, but I can check with the chef. See if there's anything else that is, otherwise?'

Steve swivelled his head so he could get a good look at the busy, noisy room. 'Don't worry, I don't want to add to your Friday-night woes,' he said kindly. 'I'll have a salad with the steak, medium rare. Kids?'

Jack butted in immediately, before Georgie could draw breath. As Jenna scribbled the order, her eyes were still surfing Steve, a realization gradually dawning. Sasha's uncharacteristic edginess over the Maple account didn't feel like a coincidence – Fred was kind of Steve's dark, evil twin. Where Steve's focused attention was considerate sweetness, Fred's felt like a nasty breed of control. While Steve had craggy good looks, Fred was hanging on way too tight to youth. The way Fred spoke to Sasha – the little hints of flirtation; Jenna was starting to think that what was between them was more personal than she'd realized. Maybe the two of them had history. It would certainly explain why Sasha became such a full-scale bitch whenever he set foot in the building.

'And G—' Jenna stopped herself, her eureka moment almost making her careless. 'And you, what would you like?'

Georgie giggled, her cheeks flushed with the thrill of the situation. 'I'm actually vegan?' she said, cocking her head. 'Do you have any recommendations for me?' She twisted around to scowl at the rest of the table. 'Feel free to change your orders, by the way. You don't actually need any animals to die for your dinner.'

'Georgie . . .' said Steve, laying a gentle hand over hers. She stayed scowling, but she didn't push it off.

'Apparently the mushroom stroganoff's amazing,' said Jenna smoothly, refusing to play ball. Next she zeroed in on the empty seat next to Steve. 'Er, will anyone else be joining you tonight?'

'No,' he said, and her heart began to slow to something approaching a normal pace. 'We've given my wife the night off. She's probably got her feet up watching some terrible dating show on Netflix.' It was hard not to be touched by the way his face automatically lit up at the mention of Sasha. 'So that's it for us.'

'Great!' she replied, slightly too enthusiastically. 'I'll put all this through for you then.'

She backed away as fast as she could, grateful now for the frenetic pace of the evening – it didn't afford her much time to brood on how she was going to persuade Georgie to keep quiet about her second job. She didn't know how Sasha thought she was surviving on the pittance that Bright paid her, but she was equally aware that her boss finding out how she'd squared the circle would be a complete professional disaster. Blissful ignorance was Sasha's jam.

Jenna turned out to be just as good at serving the rest of Sasha's family as she was at serving Sasha herself. 'Absolutely delicious,' beamed Steve when she whisked away his plate, a sliver of fat all that remained of his huge sirloin steak. She watched Jack greedily gulp down the whole crème caramel she brought him without offering anyone a bite. Meanwhile, she delivered Georgie enough secret, conspiratorial smiles to ensure that she wouldn't feel moved to blurt out who Jenna was to the rest of the table.

'A cash tip's better for you, isn't it?' said Steve once the meal was over, lightly tapping the PIN number for his gold Amex into the card machine. When he palmed her thirty pounds, well above what was due to her, it was impossible not to like him. He did it so modestly, so discreetly, nothing like Sasha presenting her with her cast-off outfits like it was Children in Need.

'Wow, thank you,' she said.

'No, thank *you*,' he replied, contemplating his teenagers with an intensity to which they were both oblivious. Jack was already glued to TikTok, the screen of his phone kept just out of his dad's eyeline, and Georgie was rummaging in her vinyl rucksack for her lip balm. Steve turned to Jenna with a crooked smile. 'You made tonight a real pleasure.' His voice dropped as he looked back at his kids, like he was confessing a secret. 'It's so important that we find ways to spend real time together.'

The words pierced Jenna, despite herself. She'd never had a parent feel that way about her. No, worse than that – that chance had been stolen from her. She looked again at the empty chair that Sasha could so easily have been sitting in, a familiar rage stirring inside. At least she was here to witness something she'd not known for sure before. These three were a unit of their own, Sasha an optional extra. And how much could Steve really want yet another optional extra when he had so much love for the original model of his family?

Jenna smoothed her face into a cheery mask, waving a conspiratorial goodbye to Georgie and pushing the cash Steve had given her deep into her jeans pocket. It certainly wasn't going in the communal tip jar.

Who even cared about snooping on emails now, when she'd picked up so many clues to Sasha's life in a single night?

Soon she'd have all the ammunition she needed.

SASHA

The two halves of my life had started to feel like a pair of jigsaw puzzle pieces that refused to fit together, however hard I squashed one against the other. It was the week after that horrific Maple meeting, the pressure on to come up with a whole new campaign and snatch victory from the jaws of defeat. The team were anxious and irritable, the stakes too high and the disappointment too big to birth creative brilliance. And meanwhile, a whole other potential birth was consuming my every waking moment.

Steve and I were fully committed to the treatment now. We'd finally agreed on a donor, having combed through profile after profile in the clinic's database. The mother was a similar height and build to me, with blonde hair and blue eyes just like mine. Unlike me, though, her eggs didn't fall into the geriatric category. I already felt an overwhelming sense of gratitude to her for having felt moved to help a woman like me for nothing more than a nominal fee. Steve had 'made his contribution' – the doctors loved their discreet euphemisms for a teenage boy's favourite sport – and four embryos had been created in the lab. Before long I would be starting the brutal hormone injections that would run up to the implantation.

On this particular day, I was juggling a pitch on a new

account – a US eyewear company who wanted to get into the UK luxury market – with an urgent update on Maple's economy class branding from the visual team. Jenna had somehow scheduled things so I only had ten minutes between them to scoff a Pret sandwich, my afternoon appointment with Dr Rindell meaning I'd have to leave straight after the internal meeting.

It was yet another reminder that we were out of sync. It was like the Maple pitch – or rather Fred Williamson – was a deadly pesticide, poisoning anything in its path. I needed to restore health. Over my brief lunch break I pulled Jenna into a meeting room, trying to stay authoritative while spraying crumbs from my cheese and ham baguette.

'The diary just doesn't work today.' I paused, confounded by the blank mask that looked back at me from across the oak table. Who had body-snatched my loyal and witty wingwoman? 'I know it sounds weird, but the trick to being a good assistant is thinking as if you're your boss.'

'Okay.'

I couldn't help but exhale with frustration. Was this all because I'd given her the mildest dressing down of all time after her disastrous performance last week? My twenty-something self would have been savaged and left for dead by Martin and Bridget, but instead I'd used phrases like 'better synergy' and 'staying connected'. I'd hoped she wasn't a textbook snowflake like Scarlett, who'd recently put her menstrual cycle into Anna's calendar via some cute little moon emojis so that Anna would have due warning of when she might need a 'duvet day'. Maybe I'd been wrong about that.

'Jenna, if this is about last week, I had a responsibility to give you honest feedback. You somehow managed to help make Fr— . . . Maple, feel like we had a full-scale Gen Z crisis on our hands by going on about Extinction Rebellion. Something that now has to be solved before we can win the account outright. You knew how much we needed to bring this home.'

She paused a second, her body folding in on itself, unreadable to me. I sat and waited, oddly nervous. I couldn't take any more eruptions in my life, not right then. When she looked up, her eyes were almost pleading.

'I was trying to help! I *was* trying to think like I was you. Of course I don't believe no one should ever fly again, but I thought you invited me up there so they could hear what the holdouts in the market they're after actually think.' She smiled weakly. 'The Georgies.' Taking a deep breath, she managed to stutter out the rest. 'I'm sorry I fucked it up so badly. I haven't been able to sleep, thinking you might fire me.'

She looked so vulnerable right then that it was hard to keep up the righteous indignation. It didn't sound anything like what she'd said to me the week before when I'd first confronted her – or how it had felt in the conference room – but maybe she'd had time to reflect. And the truth was, I wanted my ally back. My mini-me. She was serving herself up to me on a plate and I gobbled her up.

'I'm sorry I dragged you up there unexpectedly. It was a lot to ask of you.' I doubled down, looking her straight in the eye. 'The fact I did is a testament to how much I rate you, Jenna.'

Her grateful smile was all the reward I needed, any lingering resentment swept away. 'I won't role-play without warning you in future. And I promise I'll keep Georgie under control too.'

I shuddered at that. I really did need us to be a tag team so Georgie didn't go off script. 'You've got your brunch at the weekend, right? She's super excited about it.'

Jenna nodded. 'I won't let you down,' she said, all earnest sincerity.

I scooped my phone and sandwich wrapper off the table, time short before the next meeting.

'Give it here,' said Jenna, motioning for the greasy cardboard.

'Oh no, you don't have to do that,' I said, already feeling my fingers loosening.

'You don't have time to go to the kitchen, let alone separate it all out. And I don't want my boss getting bawled out by Lorna.'

We rolled our eyes at each other, camaraderie restored as we thought about the notice Lorna had left pinned to the kitchen cupboards on Monday morning, a plea written from the kitchen itself demanding we all kept it cleaner and paid more heed to the recycling bins.

'Bawled out by "the kitchen", surely?' I said over my shoulder, sandwich wrapper now abandoned on the table.

'Yeah, he's a right grinch!' said Jenna, scrunching it up with a smile and following me out.

* * *

My chat with Jenna turned out to be the sweet spot in my day. Trying and failing to manage the squabbling art team was nowhere near as rewarding, and I landed in front of Dr Rindell frazzled and irritable. I was a few minutes late, Steve already sat in a chair before the large desk. Rindell barely looked up, his head bent over our notes. When he did, I immediately knew his mood was even worse than my own.

'You still haven't completed a single counselling session,' he said snappishly.

Before the treatment could start in earnest – the hormone injections I'd be plunging into my belly until I looked like a swollen blue pin cushion, and then, all being well, the embryo transfer – we needed to have at least one session. If my cycle played ball, we were only a fortnight away from being able to begin, hence his visible frustration that we hadn't yet fulfilled that requirement.

'We've discussed this more than once,' he added. 'It's protocol here – many clinics ask for multiple sessions. How have you not done it already?'

I pulled a discreet face at Steve, who pulled one back – both of us were a bit intimidated by the good doctor. He was a 'move fast and break things' kind of a guy, which was why I'd chosen him. It certainly wasn't for his bedside manner.

I jumped in. 'I think it's just that we're both so busy. Work's been a shitshow for me, and it just hasn't happened. We're decided anyway, so do we even need—'

Steve cut straight across me, something he never usually did. 'I'm sorry,' he said sincerely. 'It's an admirable policy, and you're right, you have raised it before. We've got no excuse.' He looked at me as he said it, a little bit accusatory. This spoke to one of those 'greatest hits' arguments that characterize any long-term relationship. 'We'll maybe try and do a couple of sessions, in fact.'

'Hang on,' I snapped, feeling my cheeks flush. 'Therapy's not ... it's just not my thing. I know you like a bit of navel-gazing sometimes, but it's not how I choose to deal with stuff. One session's fine.'

'Not my thing' was an understatement. I'd had a period of bleakness at university, eventually dragging myself to the doctor on campus. All I'd wanted was to try a course of anti-depressants to see if they took the edge off, but they'd insisted on counselling as a first step. The one thing I remembered from the single session I'd attended was how frozen it had made me feel – more alone, not less. The therapist's gentle questioning about the loss of my dad hadn't made me break open, it had made me disappear.

'Navel-gazing?' said Steve, his characteristic calm rupturing before my eyes. He'd undergone a period of psychoanalysis a couple of years earlier, creeping out of the house at six every single weekday morning to talk about himself, in a way that only someone without a full-time job could manage. I'm not sure if it was my 'gentle' mockery or the nine o'clock bedtime it had required, near-celibacy an unappealing side effect, that had finally made him stop. I'd been mightily relieved, either way.

Dr Rindell's eyes darted between us, absorbing the dynamic. I sensed the jeopardy, acted accordingly.

'Sorry,' I said, reaching for Steve's hand. 'I was joking! And yes . . .' I turned back to Dr Rindell with a compliant smile on my face. 'We hear you. If it's clinic protocol, we'll get ourselves straight onto the couch.'

'Look, all I care about is getting you pregnant,' said Rindell, with an air of weary annoyance that made me feel slightly vindicated. He didn't seem like a man who'd signed up for the cult of relentless self-examination, and he was a health professional. 'But we need to have the boxes ticked. Those embryos are ready and waiting.'

My breath knotted tight in my throat, my eyes damp. It felt so close now, this whole new version of us. Of me – a mother. An ocean of events would be consigned to the past, no need to topple backwards and drown there.

'That's such an amazing thought,' I said.

We'd opted to have the embryos created and frozen in advance, partly to accommodate how hush-hush we were keeping the treatment. If work became impossible, and I had to delay last minute, we could be flexible. And if the first cycle didn't succeed, as it hadn't with my own eggs, we'd be ready to go again quickly.

'How exciting,' said Steve, no corresponding emotion cracking his words in two.

I noticed his hands in his lap, his long fingers splayed over his corduroy-covered knees. I hadn't even noticed how our hold had uncoupled itself over the passing minutes.

The anxiety was shouting for my attention by now, but all I did was stick my fingers in my ears.

JENNA

The Humble Cup wasn't a particularly humble place, even without Penelope queening it up behind the counter. It was a Saturday morning, and the crowd wasn't so different from the Falcon, except now they were jostling for flat whites instead of gross, stinky natural wines. Georgie had insisted on buying the coffees, and now she was coming back from the counter with two steaming drinks in her hands. She sat them down with a flourish.

'Real cups, not disposable,' she said smugly. 'I had to tell them that the compostable ones are a fucking con. I ordered us both the avocado on toast.'

Jenna took a greedy gulp of her latte – she'd forgotten to add on an extra five minutes' waiting time to allow for Georgie's ranting window. 'Good on you,' she said, the hot coffee burning a passage down her throat.

Georgie's eyes widened, a sentence forming that was clearly hard for her to get out. 'I just wanted to say, I'm sorry . . .' she started awkwardly, before pivoting back to anger, her safe place. 'I cannot *believe* Sasha pays you such shit you have to do a second job. It's meant to be all—' she waved her hands in the air theatrically '—creative, but it's just fucking corporate capitalism, isn't it?'

Jenna knew how close to the wind she'd sailed the last few

weeks, first letting her anger spill out in the Maple presentation and then making stupid mistakes because her second job was leaving her so exhausted. But now things were back on an even keel, her reach into Sasha's life was deepening by the day. The last thing she needed was Georgie's self-important outrage blowing everything up.

'It's really tough, getting a start in a creative industry,' she said. 'Hundreds of people applied for my job. Sasha gave me a chance.'

'Yeah, but you should be able to eat!' said Georgie, consciously or unconsciously pushing the biscotti that had come with their coffees across the sticky table, as if Jenna was Oliver Twist, come to life in twenty-first-century Archway. She couldn't take much more of this.

'Look, I'm making it work,' she told Georgie. 'I'm glad we're mates—' the girl lit up at that statement, as Jenna had known she would '—so I know I can trust you not to tell Sasha. It was funny, wasn't it, pretending we didn't know each other?'

Georgie gave a conspiratorial smirk at the thought, but she was still like a dog with a bone. 'I can talk to her for you,' she said. 'She keeps trying to make me go on, like – dates! – with her. Shopping and nails and other things I fucking abhor. Her and Dad are both being really weird at the moment.'

Of course they were. Another round of treatment was imminent, Jenna was sure of it. The 'appointments' in the diary were getting so frequent it was hard to schedule around them, and Sasha was stressed and distracted, despite the fact that the Maple campaign needed her full attention. How was she even doing it though, when according to her emails to her friend Dr Rindell had said there was zero chance of success? It needed more research. She tuned back into Georgie, who was still droning on opposite her.

'I can just tell her she's not paying you a living wage when we're looking at some rip-off jumper she thinks I'll wear. The money she drops on clothes . . .'

'No, don't do that,' snapped Jenna. She both despised and envied Georgie's innocence; the girl truly believed that she just needed to tell Sasha she wasn't giving her assistant enough pocket money and gold coins would rain from the sky. Maybe she'd bypass her stepmother entirely and tap up the tooth fairy instead.

Georgie visibly flinched.

'I appreciate it, I really do,' qualified Jenna, 'but we're here to talk about you. Talk about Elevate! That meeting with the Maple execs that's coming up is going to be big.' Georgie started to puff up again. 'It's a huge campaign for Sasha.' No, appealing to her loyalty to Sasha was the wrong tack right now. 'And for me,' she added. 'I've been a big part of the creative, for the first time.'

'Really?'

'Yeah. I actually had your comments echoing in my head when we were working on it,' she said, watching how Georgie's cheeks flushed with silent pride.

'I just want people to wake up—'

'I know you do,' interrupted Jenna, before the younger girl could start banging on again. She thought for a second. It would be no bad thing for Sasha to register some improvement in the relationship thanks to Jenna's influence.

'Maybe you should go on one of those dates Sasha keeps inviting you on. Talk to her about global warming when you're in a different context, so she has the space to think about it. My mum always used to say – honey beats vinegar every time.'

She felt her heart beat a little faster – was it the caffeine she'd gulped down or the strange sensation of letting her mum live and breathe here in an Archway coffee shop? She had no idea if her mother had ever said that, but it felt like something that could've been true.

'No thanks – I don't want to go on a date with a capitalist oppressor. Leave Dad to do that. In fact, they're going away on some romantic break next weekend.' Georgie theatrically gagged. 'Can't even think about it.'

'Are they?' Jenna knew as soon as the words left her mouth that she sounded too interested, and she swiftly dialled it back. 'Yeah, I think I saw in the diary that she'd taken Friday off.'

'They're letting us stay in the house on our own. Dad's never done that before.' Georgie paused, muttering the next words. 'You could come over. Gimme a look at the campaign so I can do my homework beforehand.'

An invitation. An actual invitation to Sasha's house. It was hard to slow the pulse of excitement that was rippling up and down her spine.

'Don't you want to have some mates over?' she said, taking a casual sip from her almost-empty cup. 'Raid the wine fridge?'

Their house would definitely have a wine fridge; she'd had a sneaky look on Zoopla and found out it had cost over four million pounds. It was impossible to imagine what a house like that would look like inside, unless she saw it for herself.

'Not really,' said Georgie, her voice small. 'Don't worry about it, it was a dumb idea.'

'No,' Jenna said, holding Georgie's gaze. 'It's a really nice idea. Let's see how it works out.'

She already knew exactly how it was going to work out – there was no way she was turning down an opportunity this precious. She just needed to make sure that it stayed secret, along with her contract-busting second job.

A week already felt like too long to have to wait.

SASHA

It was the day of our very first – and what I was hoping was our very last – counselling session, the one that had been forced on us by Dr Rindell. I'd been careful to downplay my lack of enthusiasm to Steve, instead landing on our therapist Ruth's floral sofa with an eager smile plastered across my face.

'Tell me a bit about how you met,' she said, after we'd got over the initial niceties.

Her feathery ash-blonde hair looked as soft and unthreatening as the pastel furnishings of her comfortable Holland Park basement. But I noticed how watchful she was, how she peered out from beneath that nest of hair to scrutinize us both. Sixty-something, her face generously lined in a way that didn't rob her of a muted kind of beauty, she conveyed total command of the space.

Neither of us jumped in with a reply, so she offered us some gentle encouragement. 'First impressions, how it became something.'

I glanced over at Steve, the way his face was opening up at the question, revealing his essential goodness. He wrinkled his nose, his eyes twinkly. 'The internet. I mean, yuck. I never expected to find myself there. I would never have tried it without my kids pestering me. But then . . .' He turned to me. 'Look what I found, straight off the bat.'

Both of them looked over at me expectantly.

'I mean, I'd done it a bit,' I said. 'But I still hated it. I'd never met anyone I liked that way. Steve was completely different from the kind of arseholes who try and split the cost of a packet of salt-and-vinegar crisps.' I paused, took him in. 'He really listened to me.'

Ruth looked between us, her gaze mellowing at our visible warmth. It was probably a nice contrast to the couples coming here for marriage guidance, I thought smugly, with all of their snarking and bitching. Maybe my dread had been for nothing.

'And you were obviously at quite different stages of your lives,' she said. 'One of you coming into the relationship with a family in tow, one of you not.'

'Yes,' said Steve carefully.

'So, let's wind back. Talk about how you got to that point.' Ruth rested her hands in her lap, her sensible black slacks turned up at the ankles to reveal equally sensible lace-ups. 'You were married before?'

'I was,' Steve said, the light in his eyes extinguished. 'My wife – my first wife – wasn't a big fan of convention.' He gave a hollow laugh. 'She thought monogamy was for nerds, which was just about tolerable when we were students. I was naive enough to think she'd grow out of it once we'd had our family.' He paused. 'She never really did. I deeply regret the pain it caused our children, her upping sticks like that . . .'

'And there's your pain to acknowledge too,' said Ruth, simply.

'Yup,' he said, a single heavy syllable.

'How do you think it affected your view of marriage? Of long-term commitment? You've obviously managed to keep faith in the institution.'

'Sasha's very different from Lisa,' said Steve. He deliberated for a second, his next words delivered with quiet fury. 'I find it despicable that a person would take something as important as the commitment of marriage and treat it like shit to be scraped off a shoe. Integrity matters.'

My fervent wish had been that we could treat today's session like a parking ticket or a school detention – a minor inconvenience you just had to endure. But Steve – Steve was already all in. The walls, covered as they were in Colefax and Fowler lilies, were starting to close in on me.

'So, it increased your belief in marriage, rather than decreasing it?' observed Ruth.

'Yes, and I've been lucky,' said Steve, reaching for my hand. 'Unlike my children, I've been able to replace that relationship. Not that Sasha isn't a wonderful stepmother,' he added quickly. 'She very much tries to fill the void.'

Something flickered across my face.

'What's that you're reacting to, Sasha?' said Ruth, turning towards me as quick as a flash.

I looked at Steve, seeking his silent permission, then launched into the same spiel that had finally tipped the balance with him. That being a stepmother wasn't the same as being a mother, however much I loved his children. I was surprised how much my voice wobbled here, not with the first part – that was self-evident – but with the second. Mine and Jack's relationship was functional in a way that didn't overly trouble either of us, but Georgie was different. Much as she frustrated me, I did love her. I felt it viscerally as I said it, even though it was so often like pouring water onto parched earth. I waited and waited for a flower to peek out of the soil, and nothing ever materialized, until it became easier to nurture my exasperation with her. That bloomed effortlessly.

'And has having your own children always been something you've wanted, Sasha?' asked Ruth gently.

'Yes. I mean, I just always assumed I would. I think I'm naturally quite a maternal person. Steve's kids, my godchildren, even my assistant — they're all ways that I nurture younger people. I take real pride in it. But it's not the same thing, is it?'

'And how did you relate to the idea of motherhood throughout your twenties and early thirties?' Ruth continued. 'You two obviously met a little later on . . .'

I froze, the silence in the room deafening to my ears. I could tell Steve wanted to rescue me. Steve always wanted to rescue me. It's hard to convey just how much I miss that now.

'Sasha . . . she was very poorly treated in her late twenties. With the upset, she lost — well, the biological clock is a very unfair piece of kit, isn't it?'

I took a discreet gulp of air, commanded my cheeks not to flush.

Ruth subtly raised her hand. 'I'd like to encourage you both not to speak for each other.'

'First rule of therapy club?' I lamely quipped, but she was having none of it.

'You look unsettled, Sasha. Is there something here that we should unpack together?'

There absolutely was not, but there was no backing out. I needed to get this right. If I didn't, it could be catastrophic.

'I . . . I had a relationship that didn't work out. Bad timing. It took me a long time to get over it.'

I looked downwards, my hand edging back across the sofa, wrapping itself around my midriff. The silence didn't seem to want to break.

'Do you want to say a little more about that, Sasha?'

'Darling, you should . . .'

Now my words came out in a rush. 'He was a bit older than me. I looked up to him. Professionally and personally – we were colleagues. I'd only had one serious boyfriend at university; I was still pretty naive. I just assumed it would work out.' I ground to a halt here, casting around inside my panicked brain for a reason, trying to remember exactly what I'd told Steve. 'He'd never committed before, but I kidded myself he just hadn't met the right person.'

'And then he just turned around and married someone else!' Steve's outrage had clearly got the better of him. 'Barely even told her he was dumping her.' He turned to me, face suffused with love. 'No wonder it took her such a long time to trust someone again.'

I truly was a horrible person.

Ruth's hand gesture was fiercer this time, a traffic cop anticipating a crash. 'Steve . . .'

'No,' I protested. 'Steve's got it right. He just disappeared from my life. He was gone.' I heard my voice crack. 'Then it was just me, left behind again.'

'And did you still have to see him professionally?' asked Ruth.

My mouth was so arid, it was hard to drag a sentence out of it. 'He . . . he moved to San Francisco not long after that, so . . .'

'Probably didn't want to show his face,' Steve growled, reaching for my hand again and wrapping it up in a tight parcel. It was a funny thing – sometimes his moral certitude, his simplistic world view, drove me insane, but it also made me feel so safe. It was like a narrative from a children's book – all's well that ends well, with lashings of ginger beer.

The problem is, as I'm all too aware now, my swollen ankles propped up precariously on a kitchen chair in my lonely flat, that sense of safety was only a loan. He's taken it back, and it's never been a quality I've been able to self-generate.

Ruth was looking at me, waiting for me to continue. I took a deep breath, tried to keep my voice even. 'So, yeah, I wasted a chunk of time, and when I turned around, everyone else seemed to have it all sorted. Married. Engaged. Popping out babies – they made it look so fucking effortless. I just kept going on first dates.'

It repulsed me, the way my voice sharpened as I swore. I'd vowed to myself beforehand that I'd stay elegantly contained, toss up a nice word salad that didn't taste of much and get out of here, both of us left emotionally unscathed. But nothing was going according to plan. Ruth stayed silent, hands steepled under her chin, her eyes never leaving my face.

'Nothing's ever been effortless,' I added, sounding like a sulky teenager.

'Tell me about some of the other things that haven't been effortless,' she said softly.

'My family,' I said, almost surprising myself. I paused. 'I guess I wanted us to be like the Oxo adverts, or something – two point four kids. We were nothing like that. And now . . .'

'And now?'

'I . . .' I stared out of the window: a tree filled the frame, a crow taking flight into the murky autumn dusk as I tried to collect my thoughts. 'I suppose it's hard not to feel like I've failed.'

She didn't correct me, just pushed forward with her gentle questioning. 'So, if your family didn't look like the Oxo family, what did they look like?'

My hand withdrew again, wrapped itself around my still-empty belly. Steve's empathy felt like pity, and back then I was allergic to his pity. You don't know you're rich until you're broke.

'My dad . . .' It took a long time to get the sentence out. When I did it sounded formal, more like a police report than a precious confidence. 'He committed suicide when I was six years old. Then it was just me and my mother.'

Ruth nodded slowly, her face reflecting the gravity of what I'd told her. My eyes darted briefly to Steve, and then swivelled back to the window. Time seemed to have stilled, at least inside of me.

'I'm so sorry,' she said. 'That's a profound trauma to have lived through.'

'I mean, I don't really remember him,' I said. 'So, it's not like I miss him . . .' And then I started to cry, finally letting myself sink into Steve's ready embrace.

'We never talk about this, Sasha,' he said eventually. 'You never want to talk about it.'

'I'm fine,' I said, mascara running down my raw cheeks, my words more of a hiccup. I patently wasn't fine. I looked at Ruth accusingly. 'I just wasn't expecting to talk about it. I thought we were here to talk about the baby.'

'But all of this . . .' She opened up her hands like she was holding the world between them. 'All of it *is* about this baby, who may or may not be coming into your lives.'

I was already shaking my head. 'She's coming,' I said.

'The baby's a she, is she?' said Ruth. 'In your imagination? How about you, Steve? How do you relate to this etheric being?'

It was devastating how undeniable it was. His face was like a perfect freeze-frame – *ambivalent man*. The warmth and compassion that had been animating him had drained away, leaving a ghost in its place.

'Um, I don't know if I've got to that stage yet. We've been through a couple of miscarriages, so it's maybe hard to . . .'

He trailed off, the room thick with a bunch of words that were also yet to be born. Ruth let the silence settle, then piped up again.

'What do you imagine about this next phase you're moving towards? It doesn't matter if it's not as concrete as the picture Sasha painted for us.'

Steve's shoulders slumped. 'I can't – I can't quite imagine it, which is insane considering I'm the one who's been through it twice before.' He paused. 'Maybe there's an element of denial.' He turned to me. 'I'm sorry – I'm sorry to say that out loud.'

Just for a second, I hated Ruth so much that I could have strangled her, choked away those sneaky little questions that had laid us bare and left this devastation in their wake.

'This is a difficult place to end,' she said. *No shit, Ruth.* 'But we are going to have to wrap up this session soon.' She steepled her fingers under her chin again, fixing us each with her all-seeing eye. 'I think you've both been very brave, with what you've brought here today. But I would also urge you to consider taking some more time, even just an extra month, to untangle these threads before you embark on treatment.'

We spoke together, an imperfect chorus. 'I don't think we necessarily need—' I snapped, just as Steve said, 'I think that would be a very good idea.'

Ruth couldn't suppress the wry smile that wreathed her face. I looked over at Steve, trying to be a compassionate and mature wife, rather than a furious brat.

'We could start the treatment AND come back,' I said, pleading. 'I'm totally happy to carry on doing this if you want to?'

Steve's sadness was palpable. 'Let's just take a few days to talk about it before we decide,' he said.

'All the drugs have arrived, I'm psyched up to start it. It's not like it's easy, pumping myself full of hormones like a battery chicken . . .'

It was an apt analogy. No one else was speaking – it was just me, squawking away into the silence. Ruth's hands had reached her knees now, her powerful body language radiating the fact that it was time for us to leave. Her next couple of suckers were probably imminent; by now she'd be limbering up to tear their lives to shreds.

'If you want to be in touch to make another appointment, I'd be happy to see you, or I can recommend a colleague.'

Steve reached for my hand, but I wouldn't give it to him. He stood up alone. 'Thank you very much,' he said.

Unlike me, he meant it.

JENNA

Jenna had known that this plan had to be a slow burn. If visiting the family home had been a definite arrangement, it would have all been too delicious for Georgie. She wouldn't have been able to stop herself blurting out the news to Sasha, and as much as her boss had encouraged the friendship, she'd also kept an iron grip on how it developed. Having Jenna in her house would definitely have been a step too far.

Right now, Georgie was huffing and puffing her way up the steep hill, her round bottom encased in a pair of jeans so wide they made her legs look like a pair of circus tents. She turned backwards to look at Jenna, face red with effort.

'Sorry it's so fucking steep. I wish we lived somewhere normal.'

It wasn't normal, that was true. Once they'd walked a few minutes from the Tube, Highgate had started to feel more like a posh village in the countryside than part of the capital city. They'd made their way past a Dickensian-looking pub, and now they were winding their way up a tiny, narrow lane, higgledy-piggledy houses tucked in on either side.

'I like it. It's cool,' said Jenna.

Georgie's face wrinkled with the disgust of someone who'd never tried to rent a room in London. 'It's definitely not cool.'

She turned back again, the rest of the sentence thrown over her shoulder. 'Still can't believe you could be arsed to come all the way back from the Tate with me!'

That had been their date – a casual invitation from Jenna to see an installation in the late afternoon, supposedly the only available slot. Then an equally casual invitation from Georgie to come back to her house and watch *Strictly* with her. Jenna knew Georgie well enough by now to know that she'd quickly turned her face away after she'd spoken to hide how much it meant to her that Jenna *had* bothered to come. It was lucky she had turned away – if she'd been looking directly at Jenna, she might've picked up that it wasn't actually her first time at this particular rodeo. She'd tramped up and down the quaint high street in the sweltering heat on the morning of her interview at Bright, trying to imagine what it felt like to be looking in the window of the artisan bakery or the £30-a-throw candle shop when you were walking in Sasha Fulton's high heels. Or, as it turned out, an artfully scuffed pair of Golden Goose trainers. Either way, the field trip had definitely helped her to smash the competition.

Georgie ground to a sudden halt, swinging her tatty rucksack off her shoulder to retrieve her keys. 'Home sweet home,' she said sourly.

The house was set slightly back from the road, square and grand, with a navy-blue door and an impressive gold knocker. Grey stone steps led up to the entrance, shrubs in boxy pots sitting to the left and right. Sodium lights cut through the encroaching darkness as the house sensed their arrival.

A shudder ran straight through Jenna's body that could have been either nerves or excitement but was most likely a bit of both. Georgie unlocked the door with a complicated selection of keys, then shot through it to deal with the incessant, high-pitched beeps that were coming from the alarm system.

'Come on then,' she said, beckoning Jenna into the broad hallway. It was a million miles from the skanky passage in Penelope's houseshare, all peeling paint and mountains of takeaway leaflets. Here, the mushroom-coloured carpet was so soft and springy that Jenna immediately felt compelled to lean down and take her shoes off. An elegant contemporary chandelier cast a soft glow over the cavernous space; stairs stretched upwards, a huge living room visible through an open doorway. 'Let's go down to the kitchen and get a . . . a drink,' said Georgie, her nerves audible. 'Seriously, don't bother taking off your shoes. Make yourself at home!'

Jenna doubled back and thoroughly wiped her feet on the doormat like a horse shuffling its hooves after a muddy gallop. She couldn't risk treading dirt into her boss's pristine carpet. In fact, she couldn't risk leaving the slightest forensic trace of herself within these four walls.

Georgie was already clattering down another set of stairs to the basement kitchen, her head wedged in the fridge by the time Jenna arrived. The room was another jaw-dropper – cream and chrome, with a huge, wooden island in the centre and top-of-the-range appliances lining the walls, alongside an Aga. Everything she'd seen of the house so far managed to be both effortlessly chic and effortlessly cosy – it stank of money.

Georgie wiggled a half-full bottle of white wine at her, with a nervous giggle. Too soon.

'I'll just have sparkling water,' said Jenna, trying not to gawp. 'If you've got any.'

A flash of relief crossed Georgie's face. 'Yeah, of course,' she said. 'And I won't have wine if you're not. Although – LAME!'

There was an oval oak dining table next to the bay window, a built-in bookshelf in the alcove next to it. Jenna discreetly scanned the spines – history books she guessed wouldn't be

Sasha's, thick art books she was sure were, and a lot of novels. *The Time Traveller's Wife. One Day.* So, Sasha was a romantic, but it had taken her years to find true love. What had happened in between? Was it Fred, with his mean mouth and his messy jumble of compliments and put-downs?

'Here you go.' Georgie was suddenly right up in her business, thrusting a tumbler full of San Pellegrino at her, the bubbles spitting up into Jenna's face like pricy drizzle. 'I went for a beer. Let's go, it's starting in five minutes.'

Jenna couldn't help noticing the touted beer was a 0% alcohol job, a fact Georgie was trying to conceal by snaking her thumb around the label as she headed for the stairs. Jenna chose to follow more slowly, savouring the anticipation of getting to see another tantalizing sliver of Sasha's real life.

The lounge didn't disappoint – it was the length of two rooms, a corner sofa running around the fringes of the front portion, a massive, state-of-the-art TV fixed to the wall. She immediately spotted a cluster of pictures on the shelves that lined the other side of the room, almost having to physically restrain herself from swerving to examine them. There was a whole evening stretching out in front of them, after all. She'd need to leave before Jack appeared, but Georgie said her brother had gone to the kind of party that wouldn't end until the small hours.

Georgie flung herself down on one of the stretches of sofa, dirty trainers scuffing the oatmeal linen. It was hard not to wince. It was even harder not to feel a stab of loathing for her – the way she moaned about her terrible life when she lived in this palace felt like a hate crime. She grabbed for the remote, imperiously pointing it at the TV like a grungy princess.

'Who do you want to win?' she demanded.

Jenna's research skills had come in handy yet again. She

smoothly trotted out the name of a soap star who she hadn't heard of until her deep dive this week, and the female dancer he'd been matched with.

'She's *amazing*!' agreed Georgie, as the pair came out, the dancer exposing even more of her boobs in her sparkly outfit than Penelope's leopard pyjamas gifted Jenna on an average Saturday morning. 'But I'm Team Justin.' Justin was a rugby player with two left feet who'd come close to getting kicked off early on but had recently rallied. Georgie grinned happily, taking a theatrical guzzle from her beer bottle. 'Which is more fun because it means we're rivals.'

After a few minutes, Jenna felt like she could risk moving her attention from the TV, getting back up and heading over to the bookshelf. A box of tissues sat on a nearby occasional table, and she took one, casually turning towards the photos on the way back. She held up a school picture of Georgie – a front tooth missing, an unrecognizably joyful smile on her face – and angled it towards her.

'You were so cute!' she said, meaning it, but Georgie shook her head.

'I was a brat,' she said flatly.

There was something painful about the contrast between the teenager and her younger self, and Georgie obviously felt it too. Jenna put the photo down, zeroed in on another. The blue eyes, the clear gaze to the camera.

'Who's that?' she asked, although she was pretty sure she already knew.

Georgie barely looked up this time, grabbing another handful of crisps from the bowl she'd brought up from the kitchen, greasy crumbs spraying the linen. 'Sasha's mum,' she muttered through a full mouth. 'Why do you even care?'

Jenna stared at it a few seconds longer, committing the

clever, beady-eyed face to memory. It was lucky Georgie was too wrapped up in herself to even listen for an answer to her question. Jenna allowed herself an ogle of Sasha and Steve's wedding photo – a predictably elegant green column dress, a small gang of well-dressed people on the steps of a smart London registry office – and then crossed the room and sank back into the sofa.

'Can't believe they're going first,' she said, as the first pair of dummies started their pointless shimmy across the shiny floor. What she liked was proper reality TV – shows like *The Apprentice*, where contestants had to scrabble their way to victory by besting their rivals. This was a vanilla pudding of a programme. She whooped along in the right places, booed when Georgie's favourite scored high marks, then spotted her opportunity as the penultimate couple took to the floor.

'Where's the bathroom?' she asked.

'Oh my God, you can't go to the loo now,' said Georgie, predictably outraged. 'It's downstairs, but . . .'

'I think I'm coming on,' said Jenna, cueing Georgie to look frantically between the TV and her newly unhelpful guest. She was tracking the show on X with all the other moronic super fans – there was no way she was pausing it. 'Listen, don't worry,' said Jenna. 'Just tell me where I can find a tampon, and I'll sort myself out.'

'My bathroom's on the top floor, next to my bedroom. There's some in the cupboard under the sink.' Of course she'd have her own bathroom. It was a kind of poetic justice, that her rich girl privilege was gifting Jenna the keys to the kingdom. Or was it the queendom? She'd soon find out.

'Thanks, babes,' said Jenna, springing up. 'I'll be really fast.'

Her feet padded up the carpeted stairs like she was walking on air. It was unbelievable she'd managed to get herself this far, but there was no time for triumph – she really did need to be fast. She hit the landing, and took a look up another flight of stairs, which must've been the ones leading to Georgie's bedroom. Could she really be this brazen? Her heart was in her mouth as she pushed open the widest door on the first-floor landing – if Georgie challenged her, she'd have to tell her that she'd got confused or that the problem had got too urgent for any more looking around.

There it was – Sasha's bedroom. A massive antique wooden bed dominated the space, slate-grey linens and velvet throw pillows covering its surface. Jenna swiftly crossed to what she could see was Sasha's nightstand, the silky eye mask a dead giveaway. Homeopathic sleeping pills, a half-drunk glass of water, a pair of gold hoop earrings she'd been wearing in the office that week. Jenna couldn't help but run her fingers through the muddle of it, like it might transmit some secret intimacy between them. She took a brief glance at Steve's side next – earplugs and another boring-looking hardback, this time by some old white man with a punning title who thought he had the answer to social mobility. It probably sat on the nightstands of countless other four-million-pound houses in North London. Maybe it was that – the sheer unfairness of the fact that she'd never lie in a bed like this without committing a crime – that made Jenna throw herself backwards onto it like a starfish and sink into its soft embrace.

The double-fronted wardrobe was tempting, but it wasn't going to tell her anything she didn't already know; for example, that Sasha could drop a week of Jenna's wages on Net-A-Porter without breaking a sweat. The bathroom offered everything, including plausible deniability. It was, of course, en suite, and she quickly slipped inside. A shower with a large chrome head was trapped in a glass cubicle, a large bath built into the opposite corner. There was some expensive-looking oil in a heavy glass bottle, and Jenna couldn't resist tipping a little onto her wrist. Its musky scent was immediately familiar, another little fragment of Sasha.

She could hear the grating music coming from downstairs, the performance in full flow. She didn't have long. She swung open the doors of the mirrored medicine cabinet, quickly scanning the contents. Moisturisers and serums with complicated French names – she snapped a quick picture for no discernible reason. There were pill bottles and prescriptions for both halves of the couple, which also merited a snap. Her knee hit the handle on the cupboard door beneath the sink, and she dropped down to the floor, pulling it open. A cardboard box was shoved in here, a series of smaller boxes stacked inside it. The address label listed Sasha's name, the sender a drug dispensary. This immediately felt more promising. Jenna googled the complicated name that ran down one of the packets, finding it hard not to yelp with triumph when she got a hit. This was it – fertility drugs for another round of treatment.

She rocked back on her heels, the cupboard doors still gaping open, her mind whirring. Sasha *was* trying again, even though she'd been told there was no hope. So, what was it that was giving her hope? Maybe understanding what the drugs actually were would help to solve that mystery. She reached deeper into the box, taking more frantic close-ups, so absorbed in the task that she missed the sound of Georgie's footsteps coming up the stairs. She silently swore at herself for being so stupid – after all, the girl's tread was so heavy that it managed to make an elephant-style thud even on the soft stair carpet.

She was calling out now. 'Jenna, the show's nearly finished now!'

With only seconds to spare before she was discovered, Jenna

grabbed a decoy tampon from the top shelf of the medicine cabinet and roughly shoved the box of drugs back into the cupboard. She ran for the bedroom door and across the landing, jumping onto the bottom step of the second flight of stairs that she'd never bothered to climb. Georgie's head poked out onto the landing just a second later.

'There you are!' she said, churlish.

Jenna slapped a grin across her face. 'I bet you barely noticed I was gone.'

SASHA

Our table sat next to the mullioned French doors of the hotel restaurant, the floodlit lake just visible through the misty night. A couple of swans glided across the surface, perfectly in sync. *Lucky fucking swans*, I thought.

'My salmon tartare's delicious,' said Steve, as polite and solicitous as he would have been if this was a rerun of our first date. 'How's your burrata?'

No, that wasn't true. On our first date, he'd laid himself bare, in that particular, diffident way he had that always cracked my heart clean open. Now – now he was behaving as if we were a pair of strangers sitting next to each other at the Estate Agent of the Year awards.

'It's lovely,' I said, staring longingly at the waitress. I was dying to order another glass of Chablis but I was only allowing myself a single tiny one, and needless to say I'd already downed it. I didn't want to do anything – emotional or physical – to jeopardize my chances. Our chances. I decided to send him a tiny reminder. 'Yours looks even nicer, but I just think, raw fish, not worth it . . .'

His eyes moved downwards, as if said raw fish had just given him a stern reprimand. This was painful. We'd planned the trip last month as a final hurrah before the treatment, a chance to prepare ourselves emotionally and really connect. I'd kidded myself it'd be non-stop sex and laughter and maybe the happy kind of tears. Instead, it felt like pure misery.

'You've never liked fish that much though, have you?' he said.

It was my own fault my husband had turned into the world's dullest dining companion; since our awful session with Ruth, I'd refused the multiple gentle entreaties he'd proffered to sort through the emotional debris. I'd been hiding out at work – *this campaign's make or break* – and then collapsing into bed, my eye mask pulled over my face, and not in a sexy way. *I'm exhausted*, I'd claimed, which hadn't been entirely untrue, but then I'd spent the nights lying on my side, imprisoned by the dark silk shade, thoughts looping and circling until the wee small hours without offering me any kind of clarity. I ran my fingers up and down the stem of my cruelly empty glass. The truth was, the thing I most dreaded was too much clarity.

'I mean, I like cooked salmon . . .' I started.

My eyes finally caught his, both of us smiling in a relieved kind of disbelief at the exact same second. This wasn't us. Thank God this wasn't us. But then the dread began. Perhaps, just for now, this dull pair of imposters were preferable company to our real selves.

'Sasha . . .'

I reached across the table, grazed my hand against his stubble. 'Can't we just have a nice time?' I pleaded. 'That was what this was meant to be about.'

His hand reached back for my cheek, and he stroked it softly with a couple of fingers. 'We need to talk about this,' he murmured, so much sadness welling in his eyes that I had to look away. 'I'm sorry,' he said, while my head was still bowed, staring at the napkin that lay across my knees. I wanted to stare at it forever, never look up. I knew as soon as he said it, three syllables containing multitudes.

'Don't do this,' I said, my voice hoarse with emotion.

'Let's go upstairs,' he said, reaching for my hand and coming back with air. He was already nodding to the waitress, effortlessly taking command of the situation. He was so many steps ahead of me by now. 'Can you charge this to room thirty-two?' he asked, pushing his chair back from the table and coming around to my side.

The bedroom seemed like a cruel joke, the huge four-poster a stage for a second act that wouldn't be coming. I stood in the doorway, eventually allowing Steve to lead me towards the sofa area that took up the opposite corner, a laden brass drinks trolley strategically placed nearby. If only vodka was a viable option. I paced – I couldn't sit – while he slumped down onto the sofa. Every single action each of us took seemed like another brutal, silent reminder of how far apart we were.

'I've been begging you to talk about this, but you've been dodging it. I've been agonizing since that session – the things we said in there. We're not ready.' He looked away, guilty words escaping from him. 'And the truth is, I don't think I ever will be.'

'You can't . . .' I started, the end of the sentence lodging in my throat, choking me. If I acknowledged what I was witnessing, there would be no unseeing it. It would be me who had made it real.

'Sasha, I've tried so hard,' Steve said, his palms turned upwards in supplication. 'I've wanted to want this ever since you told Dr Rindell you were serious about it, but I don't. I want to make you happy, but I don't want us to have a child this way. It's not the same as IVF.'

'That's a lot of wants,' I said, numb with shock.

'I'm so sorry. You've got every right to hate me for going this far, but . . . it's only because I love you so much.' Nothing in his face said otherwise. It made it hard to hate him, however much I wanted to in that moment. 'I can't promise I won't resent it – resent you, resent the baby. And neither of you deserve that.'

I found my fire now – this was the fight of my life. Or at least, the fight of her life. 'You can't know that!' I said. 'You're just frightened. I'm frightened too – it's going to fuck up my body, my career. I'll be exhausted for the next five years. But it'll be worth it. It'll be worth it for you too. You'll love her – you're such a loving person, you can't not. It won't matter how she got here.'

I studied the map of his face – my words were landing on him, but not in the way I needed them to. It was a painful, humiliating kind of compassion that he was feeling, not any kind of softening in his resolve. I knew him too well to kid myself, but I wasn't ready to give up.

I crossed to him, grabbed the front of his shirt, my fingers slipping through the gaps between the buttons. 'Don't do this to us. Please don't do this,' I said, fists clenching around the striped fabric, tears streaming down my face.

I felt his chin surf the top of my head, his tears mingling with mine. 'I can't do anything but this,' he whispered. 'Because I can't lie to you. I can't lie to *myself* anymore.'

'Well then, let's give it more time,' I implored him. 'That's what Ruth said we should do.'

He gave a sorrowful shake of his head. 'I'd still be lying to you. This is the truth of how I feel. I can't just do it for you – it's not fair on either of us.'

I yanked my body away from him, a spiteful, dangerous energy rising up in me now. 'Do you know what, Steve, I could live with it,' I spat.

On and on it went, circle after circle. Steve is no saint, and after a while, his patience with me also started to fray.

'You can't make this whole situation my fault,' he exclaimed, after we'd gone a few rounds. 'Every time we talked about it, you only heard what you wanted to hear. My feelings were a minor inconvenience.'

There was truth to that, but by now I wasn't giving an inch. All of our deepest resentments were surging to the surface, weaponized and lethal.

'No,' I said, jabbing a finger in his face. 'The truth is, you never even wanted a baby! This is a convenient excuse. You've got your perfect little family. Me wanting to have the same thing — to be a flesh-and-blood parent — is something you've just been waiting for me to give up on. You must be thrilled — perfect get-out clause, right?'

Something flashed in his eyes, a partial recognition that he was never going to admit to now. Nuanced honesty had deserted us both, replaced by a vicious kind of self-preservation.

'That is so unfair!' he said. 'We went through all of that IVF together, the miscarriage . . . I was in it every step of the way.'

I slammed my way into the bathroom, splashed water on my ravaged face. The huge corner bath, so proud of its jacuzzi function, was the latest thing to add insult to injury. I stormed back into the room.

'Don't walk out on me when I'm trying to tell you how I feel,' he snarled. Unlike me, Steve never quite gets to shouting. 'I never said no to you, even when *you* never bothered to acknowledge how hard it might be on my kids . . .'

'*Your* kids?' I snapped back, full of self-righteous anger. 'Doesn't that just prove everything I've been saying to you?' I crossed to the wardrobe, yanked out my coat. 'I can't stay here. I'm going to go.'

'Sasha, you're in no state to drive,' he said. 'And I don't particularly want to be left here, either.'

'I'm not spending the night in this fucking knock-off honeymoon suite,' I screamed, grabbing the car keys out of my bag. 'You can come if you like, it's up to you, but I'm not sharing a bed with you at home either.'

Half an hour later we were speeding down the M1, Steve's foot pressed uncharacteristically hard on the accelerator. As I surreptitiously texted Maddi, too angry and grief-stricken to bear the idea of a night under the same roof as him, Steve asked Siri to call Georgie. 'Sasha's not feeling well,' he told her, giving me a silent side-eye that told me not to contradict the lie when we got home. I ignored him – I was well beyond making nice.

'You sure you want to come back, Dad?' said Georgie, her voice high-pitched and nervous as it boomed through the car speakers. 'Why don't the pair of you stay and have a fun time together?'

I should've known then that there was something off – when had Georgie ever been prone to playing Cupid? But I was too wrapped up in my own selfish agony to pay attention to the shifting sands.

Perhaps if I had given heed to what was right under my nose, I'd be somewhere very different now. Or perhaps Jenna's tightening grip on my life was already too firm for me to have any chance of escape.

JENNA

Jenna had dodged a few bullets during the course of the evening, but it was the last one which came closest to leaving her lying face down in a pool of blood.

First, she'd had to deal with her kamikaze escape from Sasha's bedroom. She'd tried to style it out, but Georgie had obviously sensed that something was up.

'You were ages,' she whined, looking up the stairs towards her own bedroom where Jenna had supposedly been. 'What were you *doing* up there?'

Jenna made a grab for her hand, sliding her fingers between Georgie's clammy digits. 'Are you seriously asking me what I did in the toilet?' she said teasingly.

They'd never made physical contact before, and the giddy shock of it immediately diverted the younger girl. Jenna tugged on her hand, pulling her towards the stairs that led downstairs.

'Come on super fan, we're gonna miss the judges' scores.'

Soon they were lying back down on the obscenely comfortable sofa, Jenna pretending she gave some kind of shit about which person in a tit-surfing diamanté leotard had performed the best foxtrot. It turned out the hulking rugby player Georgie liked had come out third on the leaderboard, and she wanted to toast his success with a real drink. Who was Jenna to crush her Saturday night dreams? She followed Georgie back down to the kitchen, marvelling anew at the fact that it was roughly the same size as her family's entire flat in Stoke.

Georgie waggled a bottle of the palest rosé she'd ever seen at her, and Jenna wondered how it was that every single thing in this house was so quietly tasteful. She hadn't actually been to the toilet yet, but she was starting to suspect that the paper would turn out to be sheets of woven cashmere.

'Sasha's favourite!' Georgie said, with a naughty grin. The bottle had a fancy plastic stopper pushed into the top. 'She normally gets stuck right in, but it looks she's only had a glass.'

'So, surely she's gonna notice if we drink more of it?'

Georgie wrinkled her nose dismissively. 'No. She's weird at the moment. It's like every time she wants to tell me off, she chokes on it.' She grabbed a couple of glasses from one of the tall cream kitchen cabinets. 'Do you think it's the Elevate thing?' She turned back towards Jenna, chinking the empty glasses together. 'Is she under my evil spell?' she said, barking out a theatrical cackle.

Jenna quickly scanned the bottle, noting the two pathetic centimetres that had been swigged from it before a conflicted person had shoved it straight back in the fridge. The boxes of drugs had looked unopened, but maybe the treatment had already begun. The thought of the drugs made her nervous – had she covered her tracks successfully enough? She needed to find a way to get back up there and do a clean-up.

'Maybe she is,' she said, watching Georgie splash out two generous pours. Fourteen-year-olds should not be swilling back Provence rosé like it was weak Ribena, but the drunker Georgie got, the easier it would be to solve the bathroom problem. Jenna grabbed a glass from the counter and raised it in a toast. 'Cheers!' she cried. 'You called it right. Justin IS a star.'

'I'm so glad you get it now,' said Georgie, smashing her glass against Jenna's before taking a massive gulp. 'Why he's the best.' She looked away. 'People thought he was a joke at the start of the season, but they'll be eating shit when he's in the final.'

'Yeah, well, you're always educating me,' said Jenna, taking a tiny sip from her own glass. For once it might be hard to control her intake – the rosé was every bit as delicious as it had looked in the bottle. 'Who do you normally watch it with?' she added lightly.

Georgie shrugged, slightly shamefaced. 'No one at school really likes it.' Or, more accurately, thought Jenna, they didn't really like her. 'But I think it's cool – the way no one really knows what you're capable of. They just ignore you or dismiss you, but in the end they have to recognize that you're more special than they ever knew."

That was clearly what she wanted more than anything, to be seen and recognized. Jenna looked sideways at her plump, pink face, flushed and sweaty from the combo of wine and excitement. She didn't look unlike one of her beloved pigs right now; her problem was she was always sticking her snout in the wrong trough in search of the validation she craved.

'Doesn't Sasha ever want to watch it with you?' Jenna asked, hopping up onto one of the stools that ran along the high breakfast bar and resting her elbows on the surface.

Georgie hopped up beside her, taking a big swallow of wine as she did so. She landed heavily, coughing and spluttering as it gurgled down her throat. 'We do movie nights,' she said, sullen. 'That's enough co-viewing for me and my brother.'

'Sounds fun,' said Jenna, pausing for a significant beat. 'Seriously, why do you reckon Sasha's making so much effort with you right now? I don't think it's just about Elevate.'

Georgie looked at her for an uneasy second. 'Don't know,' she said, uncertainly.

Jenna thought she herself did. And now she'd planted a seed of distrust that would grow into a mighty oak if she tended it the way she planned to.

She grabbed her glass, held it up. 'Come on, cheers again. To the best Saturday night – thanks for inviting me round. And for the delicious wine ...' She took a big swallow this time, watching Georgie mimic her.

'It's the fucking least I can do, when my stepmum's so badly exploiting you,' she said, the 'exploiting' turning mushy and slurred in her rosé-rinsed mouth.

Jenna was still stone-cold sober, but Georgie's drunken words resonated more powerfully than she expected. Zoopla had given her the brushstrokes of what Sasha had, but it was far more enraging now she'd witnessed the masterpiece in its full glory.

'She's not the only one I'm working with though,' said Jenna, giving her inebriated 'friend' a sideways look.

'What do you mean?'

'With Elevate. We're like an undercover unit, aren't we?'

Georgie's face glowed with pleasure. 'Are we?'

Jenna kept her expression serious. 'I think you're changing me, Georgie. Making me look at things a different way. We have to fight the fight, don't we? However hard it is. I want to be on the right side of history.' She paused for effect. 'With you.'

The statement was partly true – it wasn't like Jenna wanted the world to burn. It was just that there were other things that mattered more to her – situations that she actively wanted to raze to the ground.

The younger girl's eyes filled with tears. 'I'm ... You really believe in me!' She reached a hand across the breakfast bar, resting it on Jenna's. 'I know Sasha probably made you do this, first off. And I bet it was the last thing you wanted to do ...'

As if.

'But now, I ...' Georgie looked away, suddenly shy.

Jenna kept her voice deliberately soft. 'You can say it.'

Georgie's voice was choked with emotion. 'Now I feel closer to you than ... than anyone! You're, like, a proper ...' She tapped her heart through the thick fabric of her sweatshirt, her hand unsteady. 'Even though you're older than me, and you've got a job, and—'

'None of that matters though, does it?' Jenna shot back, searching inside for the perfect phrase. Sometimes she read horoscopes online, even though she didn't really believe in them. They pretended that fate was something you could believe in and worship at the altar of, while for Jenna the only thing worthy of that kind of worship was willpower. Still, it was horoscope language she needed to summon up. 'Not if you've got a soul connection.'

Now Georgie's tears started in earnest. 'Exactly,' she slurred. Before she could say more, the shrill ring of the house phone startled her. She held up a finger as she reached for the handset on the wall.

Her fingers tightened around the receiver as she heard the voice on the other end, her finger shooting out to press pause on the Sonos speaker that was blasting out Christina and the Queens.

'No, I'm just ...' She looked at Jenna guiltily. 'Here on my own. Solo *Strictly* par-tay!'

She let out a squeaky little laugh. Some people were so bad at lying, Jenna barely understood how they got through the day. As the conversation continued, Georgie's expression grew increasingly panicked.

'But if she's ill, doesn't she just want to stay in bed there? Driving's the worst thing you could do.'

She threw a desperate look at Jenna, passing her the baton of panic. How long did she have to clean up and get out of here? She'd thought she had a good couple of hours to play with. Time to plot and scheme with Georgie. A window to slip back upstairs and make sure Sasha's bathroom was pristine.

'Fifteen minutes?' said Georgie, widening her eyes at her. Jenna sprang down from the stool and headed for the sink, jetting water into the wine glasses from the brushed-gold taps.

'Okay!' squealed Georgie, slamming down the receiver and spinning around. 'They're just coming off the North Circular. Sasha's been sick.' Her hands flew through the air. 'Just . . . just put them in the dishwasher.'

Jenna shook her head. 'You've got to cover your tracks better than that.' She rinsed the froth off the two glasses, wiped a kitchen towel around the recesses and shoved them back into the cupboard. 'What else says two people?'

The pair of them raced upstairs and around the living room, scooping up the bowl of crisps and the empty beer bottle. Georgie was an amateur at the whole exercise – it was Jenna who had to demonstrate to her how to treat it like it was a crime scene. In many ways it *was* a crime scene.

She carefully plumped up the pillows until there was no imprint of a second body and wiped down the surface of the smoky glass coffee table so the two ghostly rings left by their drinks were smoothed away into oblivion. These were expensive minutes; back in the hallway, she took a longing look up the stairs that snaked their way to Sasha's bedroom. There was no lie good enough to get her back up there now.

Georgie stood there dumbly, traumatized and tipsy. 'I can't

believe ... I just wish you could stay. It's just another shitty kind of capitalism!'

'What are you talking about?' said Jenna, rifling through her bag to reassure herself she hadn't left any incriminating evidence behind.

'You're like, I dunno, some kind of serf,' said Georgie, launching into yet another one-woman TED talk on inequality. 'You cannot be seen in the master's house,' she proclaimed, spotlit by the chandelier that lit up the hallway. 'It's a Maya Angelou quote.'

There were so many things wrong with that sentence, but silencing her was more important than correcting her. Jenna hugged the girl tightly, feeling Georgie go slack in her arms, her hot breath stinking of wine. It was a worry.

'Don't say anything, okay? Just go to bed when they get back. You're ...' She stared into Georgie's eyes, lobbing a love bomb directly at her. 'You're too honest, I know that about you now. It'd be too easy for someone as smart as Sasha to catch you out.'

With that, she opened the front door and slipped down the path, cursing the bright floodlights that suddenly shone out, illuminating her exit. Rich people just couldn't help drawing attention to their every move, like they deserved a continuous round of applause for what they'd netted for themselves. As she slipped past the handsome privet hedge and onto the road, an equally bright pair of lights cut through the darkness and swerved into the driveway.

It was so dangerously close, and yet Jenna couldn't help herself. She flattened her body against the hedge, making herself invisible. A car door popped open, feet loudly hitting the gravel.

Sasha's voice rose out of the darkness. 'I'm not staying here.

I'm not playing happy families, however much you want to lie to the kids. Deny what you're putting me through.'

'We BOTH agreed not to tell them,' came Steve's reply.

'Well, there's nothing to tell now, is there?' hissed Sasha. Jenna had never heard her like this, all of her self-control crumbled to dust.

'Let's just get back in the car,' pleaded Steve. 'Give ourselves a few minutes to calm down.'

'Stop fucking managing me!' Sasha shouted, her tread heavy on the gravel as she raced for the front door. A second later Steve bolted after her.

Jenna's breath was caught tight in her windpipe as she inched her way towards the street, body still pressed tight against the tall hedge to avoid triggering the harsh glow of the floodlights. Finally, she was back on the pavement – back in her real life – her feet slapping against the paving stones as she ran towards the bus stop. Adrenaline coursed through her veins, making coherent thought impossible.

All she knew for sure was that nothing could stop her now.

SASHA

I just about stopped myself from slamming the door in Steve's face. It was tempting, but I didn't want a full-scale screaming match in front of the children any more than he did. It was a good call, as for some inexplicable reason, Georgie was marooned in the hallway when I stepped inside. I was too upset to ask her why.

'Hi, darling,' I said, aware the syllables were seesawing around as I tried to mimic some kind of calm. I tried for a relaxed laugh. 'Did you decide against a full-scale house party?'

I regretted it as soon as I'd said it; even in my state of inner turmoil I was alive to the fact that she only had about five friends. Not enough to fill a shed, let alone this ridiculous house. I thought she might crumple, but instead she gave a smile that looked distinctly smug.

'Nah, I just decided to catch up on my homework after *Strictly*. I'm going to bed soon.'

Something was definitely off with her, but I didn't have time to find out what. Steve had arrived in the hallway now, and I was currently finding him radioactive.

'Good for you!' I said, my feet already hitting the stairs. Steve picked up the thread, trotting out his lie about how sick I'd been to his clearly indifferent child. *Fuck all of them*, I thought, hurrying into the bedroom and throwing open the wardrobe doors. I pulled out a big cotton tote, started chucking in jeans and dresses and underwear. He wasn't far behind me.

'What are you doing?' he demanded.

'Unless your new cruel streak includes blindness as a side effect, I would've thought it was fairly obvious,' I said, pulling out a handful of bras. The hooks and eyes tangled themselves up together like they didn't want to leave this life behind.

'Sasha . . .' He sounded angry, not conciliatory.

I stayed buried in the wardrobe, refusing to look at him. It was easier to stay angry too. If I allowed the grief to start seeping in, I'd be liable to collapse. I quickly zipped up the tote, finding a grim satisfaction in the ripping noise the teeth made.

'Where are you even going to go?'

'Maddi's,' I said, turning around. It was hard to look at his face – every angle of it so familiar and beloved – and stay in this mode of relating. 'I texted her from the hotel.'

He took a step towards me across the carpet, pleading now. 'Please don't do that. Stay here and talk to me instead.'

His fingers were grazing my arm. It was dangerous. I jerked my body away. 'There's nothing to talk about,' I said. 'I offered to talk. To go back and chat shit to that woman who's destroyed my life. But you made it obvious there's no point.'

I was heading for the bathroom now. He took a step towards me, but I put a hand up. 'Stop following me around. Can't you see that I need space?'

He sat down heavily on the bed and carried on talking. 'Look, Sasha, if you need a few days, I get it. But please, don't just walk out on us.'

Us. He had an us. I had no *us* beyond him, not really.

'You're my . . .' His voice broke, but I wasn't there to see it. 'You're my wife.'

It didn't pierce me as deeply as it should have. I was distracted, and not just by my manic collecting of objects to stuff into my bag. I was on my knees, looking at the cupboard door below the sink. I was absolutely sure it had been firmly closed when I'd left that morning, but now it was slightly ajar. I swung it fully open, looking inside at the packets of drugs, the tiny, official letters that spelled out their names. They might as well have all said BABY in capitals, and the chaotic way they lay inside the bigger box made me suspect that someone else had seen them.

'Sasha?'

I pulled them all out, shoving them into my washbag. I couldn't leave them here, that much was clear. I thought about Georgie's odd half-smile. Was that the behaviour of someone who'd found out they might be in line for an unwanted sibling? I couldn't stop to analyse it.

I tried to zip the washbag up but it was too full, so I darted back out for the tote. Steve was still sitting on the bed, slumped forward with his hands on his knees, his face a picture of misery. I touched him lightly on his sloping right shoulder. Sometimes they're the hardest, those moments when life asks us to hold hate and love in one single handful.

'Let me take a few days, okay?' I said. 'I think if we're together we'll just keep having the same fight.' He looked up, his eyes wet with tears. 'It's better for both of us this way.'

He reached for me then, put his arms around my waist, buried his wet face in my stomach. It seemed like a cruel kind of irony.

'I love you,' he whispered, and I stroked his hair, despite myself. I bent down, whispered it back, and then pulled my body away from his.

It would've been hard enough to say goodbye to Georgie

anyway, but now I'd uncovered her betrayal of my trust it was completely impossible. I heard her climbing the stairs to her bedroom and slipped back down shortly after, manhandling my bags out of the house and into the cab I'd asked to wait a couple of doors down.

I wouldn't let Steve help me. He watched me instead from the bedroom window, a freeze-frame of sadness. His fingers rippled into a tiny wave as I slid into the cab, like he knew he didn't have the right to anything bolder than that. I sank backwards, looking at the wide, empty seat beside me. I guiltily travelled solo in these things all the time, too frazzled for the Tube, but it was a different feeling I had that night.

I turned backwards as the cab pulled away, but Steve was gone.

If I'd had a premonition in that moment of the future I was driving into, there is no doubt in my mind I'd have slammed on the brakes.

JENNA

If Sasha had been looking out of the window of her cab – watching London stream past her, instead of staring blankly at Instagram in a futile attempt to numb the pain of life as she knew it splintering apart – she might have spotted her assistant huddled inside the bus stop at the end of the road. The wind was like a knife blade, and Jenna pulled her coat more tightly around her as the cab sped past. The irony was, Sasha would shortly be driving past the end of Jenna's street, an easy drop-off en route to Maddi's family home in Hackney. But neither spotted the other, despite the fact that each were obsessing over the same bare facts.

Eventually the 134 appeared and Jenna got on. As it trundled its way down Archway Road she texted Georgie *All OK?*, her freezing fingers almost too cold to tap out the message. The rosé hadn't made her drunk, but there had certainly been something hypnotic about being cocooned inside that house. Now that she'd been ejected back into cold reality, she was starting to panic.

Sasha was on the edge. If she'd lost her shit with Georgie – spotted evidence of a bathroom break-in or decided to plough into the obviously half-drunk wine – there was no chance that Georgie would have been able to keep her motor-mouth shut.

But then the wobbly dots came, offering pure relief. *All quiet on the Western Front!* Georgie replied, sounding more like her posh dad than a London teenager. As the bus ground to a halt opposite Archway Tube station, Jenna sent her a thumbs-up, marvelling at how oblivious the girl was.

Both the upstairs and downstairs lights were blazing when she got home, giving the crappy old building the look of a low-rent dollhouse. Jenna tried not to think about the electricity bill – Penelope had threatened a spike in the kitty to cover winter costs, but then admitted she squirrelled cash in the summer to 'even things out'. The lack of control it gave Jenna made her teeth grind at night, but there were only so many fronts she could fight on at once. She pushed open the front door, and was greeted by a wail of music. Penelope stuck her head out of the door of the living room, a guilty half-grin on her face.

'Jenna!' she cried, flinging her arms around her. 'You're home.'

Jenna put down her bag, taking in the hum of people that seemed to be filling the house.

'Didn't know we were having a party,' she said.

'It's just a few mates for Laura's birthday.' Penelope's pupils were a pair of round black holes. 'Few of the other teachers. Good people, not like us!'

It seemed like there were about enough 'teachers' to educate an entire continent packed into the house. One lurched past them and raced up the stairs, looking like he was about to vomit through his splayed fingers.

'I reckon I am a good person,' said Jenna, smiling directly at her housemate. 'Don't you think I'm a good person, Penelope?' The black holes that had replaced Penelope's eyes widened even further, giving her the look of a panicked cartoon cat.

'Jo-king!' Jenna added, leaning in to hug Penelope back. The smell of her organic, rose-scented shower gel wafted up from her armpits, the sickly-sweet fragrance soured by a top note of rancid sweat.

'Of course I think you're a good person,' Penelope babbled. 'I think you're a *great* person! And I could've sworn I told you about the pa— ... gathering.'

'Good to know,' said Jenna. 'I think you're a great person too, obviously. Best landlady in the world. It'd make a good mug, wouldn't it? Maybe we should buy one from the kitty.'

Penelope smiled uncertainly.

'So, what are we drinking?' asked Jenna.

It wasn't like she wanted to join the party, but the noise was going to make getting any sleep impossible. And judging by the state of the guests she'd spotted so far, there was a pretty good chance one of the noble educators would be humping another one in her bed.

'Mainly fizzy water, to be honest,' said Penelope, smiling coyly, 'but there's loads of wine in the fridge.' She caught Jenna's dark look before she could disguise it. 'You knew it was a party house when you moved in – I thought that was what swung it for you?'

They both knew who had decided she would be living there, and it wasn't Jenna. She'd already suffered enough condescension in Highgate – it was time to find herself a drink.

'Sure you don't want anything?' she said, starting off towards the kitchen.

'I'm good with my water!' said Penelope, then grabbed her back with pinching fingers. 'I meant to say, that guy rang again. He said it was urgent.'

Jenna froze.

'Paul?' Penelope clarified. 'It's kind of retro the way he keeps doing it. I mean, no one calls the landline ever, apart from my family.'

'So, why do you even have one?' shot back Jenna, trying to control the fear that was threatening to engulf her.

Penelope looked taken aback, then obviously decided that her high was making her paranoid. 'You know – my aunt. She likes to keep it. Thinks it's cheaper.' Her pupils stretched even wider, pity beaming out of them. 'Is that why he rings on it?'

It was hard to speak through a clenched jaw. 'Yeah, no, we can afford mobiles in Stoke.'

Thank God Penelope was in no fit state to read Jenna's face. Paul must've gone to a lot of trouble to have got the number in the first place; the only way he'd have found it was from the rental guarantee she'd had to sign when she'd moved in. Now he'd found someone willing to take messages for him, there was no way he was going to give up.

She forced herself to sound grateful. 'Thanks for letting me know,' she said, then made a beeline for the crowded kitchen. She yanked open the fridge and grabbed a plastic cup to hold the white wine that she found open in the door. Knowing Penelope's Marie Antoinette attitude to the kitty, it was probably delicious, but it slipped down her throat far too quickly for her to have time to taste it.

Upstairs, her bedroom was mercifully empty, bar a couple of sticky cups, fag ends swimming in dregs of red wine. She tipped the murky ponds out of the window, then threw herself backwards onto the narrow bed, the duvet crumpled from the imprint of a stranger's arse. The thumping bass that resonated through the living room ceiling made it clear that sleep was a pipe dream.

Day-to-day life felt like an assault course right now. Jenna dug her nails into her palms, forcing herself to stay calm. An assault course demanded a strategy, otherwise there was no chance of a win. She'd sacrificed a double shift at the Falcon to capitalize on the incredible opportunity today had thrown her way and now she needed to make up for it.

She crossed to the thin metal rail that Penelope had provided in lieu of a wardrobe, whipping off the silky grey shirt Sasha had presented her with. She buried her face in it, still able to detect a faint trace of that French perfume in the stubby bottle that Sasha loved to spray into a heady cloud when she was leaving for a night out. There was another smell too, a whiff of her own sweaty anxiety, which took her back to the moment Sasha had humiliated her in front of that roomful of people. Still, she didn't want to get rid of it. If anything, it was a useful reminder of why she had to keep driving forward. She flung it back on the rail and ferreted around for the rest of the clothes Sasha had gifted her.

Soon they were laid out across the room, Jenna snapping pictures on her phone. There was the sharp black blazer with the rolled-up sleeves and a striped silk lining designed to be displayed. Two pairs of jeans, one far too small to fit over anything but Sasha's twig-like legs. Had she put them in there as a dig? A black, pleated dress in a heavy cotton, cut just above the knee, with a French label she didn't recognize. It should've looked like a school uniform, but instead it had a cheeky sexiness that made it hard to part with.

But part with it she must – all of it was on Depop by 2 am, with prices that should've made her balk, but which made perfect sense once she'd googled the brands. After that, she finally collapsed into bed, exhausted enough to be able to sleep through the monotonous beat that was still thumping from downstairs.

SASHA

The long cab journey was like a strange kind of trance, the Saturday night spillage of people through Holloway and Highbury nothing more than a blur that smeared the windows. I sat there, rigid, wishing I could cry. It was as if shock had sealed me tight inside my body, like any kind of leak would be as life-threatening as a haemorrhage.

I humped the jam-packed cotton tote I'd brought from home down the path and pushed the doorbell, listening for its discreet, melodious chime. Maddi and Richard's house was the kind of modern architectural miracle that got featured in newspaper supplements, the perfect bespoke design for their equally perfect family. Whereas our house – as tall and creaky as Steve himself – sometimes felt as if it only tolerated me.

Maddi flung open the door immediately, as though she'd been crouching on the other side.

'Darling,' she said, enveloping me in a hug and peeling the heavy bags off my shoulders.

I still couldn't cry. I tried to lean into her, to soak up the comfort she was offering, but my body felt as stiff as a tree trunk. I was a tree in desperate need of a forest.

'Thanks for having me,' I said mechanically.

'Don't be stupid,' she replied, holding me at arm's length

and assessing the damage. 'Come through. Do you need a drink?'

'Yeah, I think I probably do,' I said sadly. It wasn't like it mattered anymore.

Maddi dumped the bags in the hallway and hung my coat on the overloaded rack, a whole mess of clothing already weighing it down. I stared down at a pair of small yellow wellies, streaked with mud and abandoned on their sides, and felt myself starting to crack. I followed her through to the kitchen, a big glass extension that looked out onto the garden, and plonked myself down on the wooden bench that ran along the side of the oblong table. Soon we both had huge glasses of white wine in our hands.

'Tell me what happened,' she said, reaching across the table, but before I could start, her seven-year-old, Theo, appeared in the doorway, trailing a dog-eared teddy.

'You woke me up,' he whined, small hands clinging tightly to Maddi's legs, 'and now I need some chocolate.'

A long negotiation began, harder than the toughest client pitch, which centred around teeth and what hours the kitchen was operational for snacks. I crossed to the fridge in the middle of it, fishing out the open bottle of white for a top-up, and triggered a wail about 'Auntie Sasha' being allowed chocolate when Theo wasn't. I took a quick gulp from behind the fridge door, equally grateful for the alcohol hitting my bloodstream and the fact that it wasn't me having to reason with a small, wholly unreasonable person right now. The thought triggered a wave of shame – did Steve see a fundamental selfishness in me that I was too delusional to own and he was too kind to call out? Maybe his refusal to move forward was more about me than him. No – I loved Theo, but he wasn't mine. If he were my child, I'd also be kneeling on those hard kitchen tiles, crumbs sticking to the knees of my jeans, digging deep into an eternal supply of kindness and patience.

Maddi eventually withdrew to Theo's bedroom with a rice cake, leaving me to stare out at the garden. Lights were embedded in the flower beds, a fox illuminated in one of the beams as it snuffled around in the darkness in a desperate search for food. Everything seemed like a metaphor to my tired, sad brain.

'Sorry about that!' said Maddi, sailing back in. '*Goodnight Moon* was needed TWICE to prevent a full meltdown.' She crossed to the fridge, poured herself another glass of her own, and then sank down onto the bench opposite me. 'I love him so much, but sometimes he's such a little shit.' She paused. 'Sorry, was that insensitive?'

I squeezed her hand across the width of the table. 'No, it was a relief.'

'How so?' she said, cocking her head.

'It means I wouldn't have to be perfect either.' I paused, suddenly overwhelmed with emotion. 'If . . . if . . .'

Maddi jumped to her feet and came around the table to sit down next to me. She put an arm around my shaking shoulders and spoke into my hair. 'Tell me properly what actually happened.'

So I did. I described it all – the appointment with Ruth, who now felt like my arch-nemesis. The mute politeness between me and Steve in the days afterwards. The romantic getaway that was more of a romantic Armageddon. And, last of all, the bathroom cabinet. The secret drugs that Georgie had found, snooping in our bedroom, while we were gone. The rest of it made me desperately sad, but that part made me shudder. How much did she hate me to be spying on me like that? And if she did hate me that much, how much rage would she be venting at Steve about the very idea of an unwanted sibling? If there was any hope of him changing his mind, that would surely kill it stone dead.

Maddi stayed where she was, right next to me. Her hand held mine. 'Jesus, I'm so sorry, Sasha.'

I saw her eyes flick involuntarily around the warm chaos of the kitchen and read her expression immediately. I knew her so well – she was thinking about what she had, not in a mean way, but because it broke her heart that I yearned for it so much. She went on, '"Sorry" feels so fucking inadequate, but . . .'

It didn't. It felt like everything to know that someone who truly loved me was invested enough to feel it too.

'"Sorry" works,' I said.

'Do you really think he's definitely decided?' she asked. 'He worships the ground you walk on. Richard thinks I'm a dick half the time.'

She said it with the easy smile of the long-married. Richard was tucked away upstairs working, the two of them able to happily coexist without needing to be enmeshed.

'Maybe he hasn't,' I said, even though I wasn't even convincing myself. Steve was so honourable, so black and white. And he'd nailed his colours to the mast now.

'You could . . .' She paused, picking her words carefully. 'I mean, don't take this how it might sound. I love Steve, I was so happy when you found him. But you could do it on your own.' She squeezed my hand. 'We women have it so fucking hard, don't we?'

The tears started again, and I angrily scrubbed them away with my sleeve. 'I couldn't. I want to be married to him. And even if I didn't . . .' I shuddered all over again. 'The idea of some strange man being the father of my child. Their DNA stuck in my body . . .'

She was searching for the right words again. The people I

loved seemed to have to do this all the time now, walk on egg-shells like I was some kind of tempestuous fairytale queen. 'But the baby – you're doing egg donation anyway. So that's already someone else's DNA.'

I shook my head, my eyes trained on the grain of the wooden table. 'But I'll be pregnant with her. She'll be mine. And at least she'll have Steve as her dad.' I heard the alarm bell ringing in my own head. I was still talking in the present tense. 'And you couldn't do much better than him.'

I forced my voice to stay steady. My own father's absence felt more like a presence than it ever had recently.

'She's a she already?' said Maddi gently.

It was humiliating, the way people kept calling me out. I sat up straight, shook out my shoulders and took a swig of my wine. 'He, she,' I said airily, doing a terrible impression of not caring. 'The baby.'

Maddi was more generous than Ruth – she accepted the clumsy deflection like she was fooled. She took a mouthful of wine too, rubbed my back.

'I should go to bed,' I said, suddenly barely able to stay upright. 'I've just realized I'm absolutely fucking exhausted.'

'Course you are,' she said, standing up. 'Let's go and put your bags in your room.'

It was my third bedroom of the day, a small space that had been Theo's nursery when he'd been tiny. The bed was a pull-out job that took up most of the floor space and there was still a faint trace of luminous stars on the ceiling.

'Sorry it's a bit mouse-sized,' said Maddi, dumping down one of the two holdalls.

'Seriously, I'm really grateful,' I said, dropping the other, leaving only a few square feet of carpet exposed. It was true – I was grateful, but it also gave me a sinking feeling that it had really come to this. It was another, new kind of emotional vertigo, and I actually had to reach out a hand for the nearest wall to steady myself. It was like some hideous wormhole, as if the last two decades of my life had somehow evaporated, and I'd been dumped back into those hardscrabble London years after graduation. I'd lost Steve, Fred had my professional future in a chokehold and I was back in a bedroom in a shared house hoping there'd be room for my toothbrush on the bathroom sink.

'Let me get you a glass of water,' Maddi said, still fruitlessly searching for ways to make a shit situation less shit.

'Honestly, don't worry, I'm fine,' I said, even though it was patently obvious that I wasn't. 'Just . . .' Another wave of emotion hit me, a jagged kind of gratitude, and I heard how much my voice shook. 'Thank you,' I said.

Exhaustion plus darkness was a zero-sum game – it didn't add up to sleep. I lay there for what seemed like hours, my eyes wide open, my feverish brain pinballing around as I counted the ghostly stars above me.

Across the tiny room, I could see the outline of my two hastily packed holdalls, fat with the life I'd stuffed inside them. I stared at them for a second, thought about their contents.

I've never been someone who's good at taking no for an answer.

JENNA

'The early bird catches the worm!'

Lorna was officiously bustling past Jenna's desk on Monday morning, en route from the kitchen. Both of them looked across the empty office, a barren desert at 8.15 am.

'Yeah, well, I'm a lark,' said Jenna, flashing her a modest smile. 'And I want to get on top of this Maple data for Sasha. We've got a big catch-up this morning.'

Lorna took a noisy sip from her mug of tea, probably trying to disguise the pursing of her lips. The news that the Maple campaign was not, in fact, in the bag was still sending shock-waves through Bright's senior team three weeks later. Even the mention of Sasha's name made Lorna look as if the milk had curdled.

'Well, keep up the good work, Jenna,' she said, setting off purposefully in the direction of her office.

Jenna watched her retreating form, her badly fitting grey skirt suit pulled tight across her wide backside. She wasn't very Bright; perhaps Sasha was itching to give her a makeover too? One of the reasons Jenna was here so early was so that she could start dumping her boss's clothes in the post tray after a healthy weekend of sales. It had felt like poetic justice to wear the shirt that she'd given a stay of execution, and it was the very first thing Sasha noticed when she appeared at 9.45.

'The Theory blouse!' she exclaimed, her smile simultaneously exhausted and self-satisfied. Her blonde hair lacked the blow-dry bounce it usually had on a Monday morning; instead it hung in sad clumps, and the silk paisley maxi dress she was wearing had a jumble sale vibe, thanks to the crumpled scrunch of the bottom half. It was hard not to feel smug about the fact that for the first time ever, Jenna was the smarter dressed of the two.

'You know what, I couldn't live without it now,' she trilled. 'It's like, a cornerstone of my whole lewk.' She paused a beat. 'Good weekend?'

Georgie had been texting feverishly yesterday, distracting her from the equally feverish auctions that were going on for Sasha's outfits. Sasha had apparently disappeared into the night almost as soon as she'd arrived; the next day her dad had been sad and shifty, admitting she was staying with her best friend but refusing to reveal anything more. Hopefully Sasha had been too distracted to notice the disturbance in the bathroom cabinet and look for suspects. Georgie couldn't be trusted to keep her mouth shut if she was challenged.

Sasha's face fell. 'Lovely, thank you,' she said. 'I ...' she faltered. 'I went away with my husband.' She crossed abruptly to her desk, hiding her face behind the huge Apple monitor. 'Hope you had a good one too.'

Jenna couldn't resist. 'It was great,' she said. 'I've made myself a brand new friend, and let's face it, I really need a few more of those down here.'

'Good for you.'

'Yeah, I actually spent the whole of Saturday night with her,' added Jenna. 'Feels like we're getting closer and closer.'

Sasha smirked. 'So is she a friend, or a special friend?' she asked teasingly.

What a fucking cheek. 'Just a friend,' said Jenna, eyeballing her from behind the shit-brown cup of coffee she'd got from the machine in the kitchen. Frothy lattes were too much of a luxury when her boss wasn't picking up the tab. 'But, I dunno, I've just got this instinct that she's going to really mean a lot to me.'

* * *

Scarlett's long, glossy tresses almost seemed like part of a co-ordinated attack. They swung around her shoulders like a silky cloak as she 'fed back' to a bedraggled Sasha on the provisional set of additional shoutlines. The team had been in there for an hour, no one able to get behind anyone else's suggestions and choose a front runner.

'I don't know, "We've Got You" just seems kind of patronizing,' Scarlett said, balancing on her fingertips as she leant over the conference table. Her big brown eyes had the sad, pleading stare of a stray dog in an RSPCA Christmas appeal. 'I mean, no offence, but your generation hasn't *got us*. So much irreversible environmental damage has already been done.'

The ring of ten people around the table all looked to Sasha, standing by the monitor at the other end of the room. She was always so good at this, a virtuoso conductor leading an orchestra. The notes never clashed, instead each one built on the last until a symphony of a solution came out of the cacophony of different sounds. Not today. She pushed a hand through her messy mop of hair and scowled, not making any attempt to disguise her annoyance.

'Didn't you go skiing in Chamonix at Easter?' she said, her eyes narrowed.

'It was my grandmother's seventieth,' said Scarlett, bristling. 'We've got a chalet there. My family made absolutely sure we offset the carbon. And I took a *train* to Tuscany over the summer.'

Jenna remembered her banging on about it – she'd somehow managed to get Anna to give her an extra two days off because she was too much of a stuck-up bitch to fly EasyJet. Right now, Anna was nervously watching the escalating battle between her assistant and her friend, her bottom lip caught tight between her teeth. As the lead art director on the Maple campaign, she was stuck being the third point in a spiky triangle.

Sasha cocked her head, a dangerous look in her eye. 'So, you do enjoy travel,' she said. 'In fact, it sounds to me like it's a big part of your family's mythology.'

'I'm just giving you my gut reaction,' snapped Scarlett. 'You made a big song and dance about wanting to hear from us.' She flung out an angry hand towards Jenna and Pete.

'Yes, and this is us kicking the tyres,' said Sasha, fingers wrapped so tightly around the pen she was holding that her knuckles shone white. 'It doesn't sound to me like you'll never fly again. So, the idea of this shoutline is that we wrap two things up: you want to travel and you ALSO want to be part of the solution.' She brought the pen up and tapped the eco stats that ran underneath. 'Flying with Maple allows you to do both things. In fact, it sounds to me from all the trips you just took us through like you're their target audience.'

Scarlett swung backwards on her heels so that she was at her full, towering height. Jenna idly wondered to herself why posh people were all such giraffes – they obviously got the best, most nutritious leaves at the top of the tree. Scarlett's eyes were blazing, her whole body quivering with self-important fury.

'You're twisting my words! Making me complicit!' she cried, her hand clutching for her heart through her grey cashmere jumper. 'And like I said, you don't *have us*. We're the ones – us, and your children – who are going to live with the consequences of your generation ignoring what science was screaming in your faces.'

Sasha sank into her seat, wounded. *Your children.* That had to hurt. Jenna almost felt sorry for her, but not quite – she'd made herself immune to pity by now. Her boss stared down at the table for so long she wondered if her role meant she needed to go over and see if she was all right, but then Sasha's head abruptly snapped upwards.

'I'm afraid there's only so long you can have it both ways,' she snarled, her eyes narrow slits as she stared Scarlett down. 'You work for Bright, you work for me and right now we all work for Maple. You're being paid to be constructive. We could shut down the entire global economy and go and live in a swamp, but I doubt you'd survive all that long. So, we need to look for doable ways to become more environmentally re-sponsible.' Sasha paused, taking a deep breath. 'This is your actual job, Scarlett. Feel free to resign if it's unacceptable to you.'

The silence that blanketed the room was the noisy, danger-ous kind. Scarlett's bottom lip was trembling now, two spots of colour as red as her name splashing her high cheekbones. Tears threatened when she tried to speak.

'I can't believe . . .'

Anna sprang up from her seat, putting a hand on her elbow. 'Of course, we all feel very strongly about the climate emergency, but let's just try and bring the temperature down here . . .' She gave an awkward half-smile. 'Sorry, bad choice of phrase.'

Scarlett angrily shook her off. 'Jesus, you're all as bad as each other!' she spat. 'It's not a joke for us.' She bolted for the door, letting it swing closed with a thud behind her.

Everyone in the room froze for a few long seconds, like it was a children's birthday party and they were playing musical statues. Finally, Sasha broke the spell.

'I'd like to apologize to you all if that got a bit out of hand. I'm just trying to make sure we keep moving forward – campaigns are like sharks, and all that.'

Sasha's ability to blend authority and self-deprecating humour was another one of her Spidey skills, but today she was light years away from being any kind of superhero. No smiles returned to the nervous, pinched faces of her team; not even Anna felt obligated to offer her some silent reassurance.

She doggedly went on, 'I think we should leave it for today and get on with our other work. That way we'll come back to it tomorrow with a spring in our step!'

She was fooling no one. Energizing no one. Jenna could tell she knew it herself, which was why she was the first – no, the second – person to leave the pressure cooker of the boardroom. Jenna watched her boss's retreating back, the curved slope her shoulders made through the thin fabric of her dress. She needed to follow her. She stood up, leaving the room without making eye contact with anyone bar a tiny gaze-hold with Pete, who gave an almost imperceptible shake of his head.

This was bad, and everyone knew it. As she closed the door behind her, it was impossible to ignore the quiet muttering of voices that was starting to swell.

* * *

It had only been a couple of minutes, but there was no sign of Sasha on the office floor. Her coat had gone from the retro wooden rack, her handbag swiped off her desk. Jenna nervously fiddled with a document for an upmarket kitchen brand that they were due to pitch on, her eyes trained on the door of

the boardroom. It was almost ten minutes before anyone else
emerged, which meant that Sasha had been getting savaged in
there. She made a split-second decision, grabbing her own coat
and heading for the lift. This situation wouldn't be salvageable
between these four walls.

Luckily, she knew her boss's likely route; on a couple of
occasions when Sasha had been looking particularly sad, she'd
insisted on going out to get her own lunch and Jenna had
been powerless to resist the temptation to follow her. After
Sasha had grabbed a carton of some hot, healthy sludge from
Squirrel, she'd taken a circuitous route back to the office that
ran through a little grassy square, tucked away between the tall
buildings. Sometimes she'd sit on a bench and stare at the dirty
old fountain in the middle of it, almost as if it was a wishing
well in a fairytale that would grant her deepest desire. Surely
it had to be the first place she'd seek refuge after the fucked-up
forty-eight hours she'd just survived?

Bingo – Jenna spotted her there immediately. She was able
to slide onto the bench next to her – on this chilly November
day, the square was pretty much deserted. The only compan-
ions Sasha had were a couple of tramps sharing a can of beer
on the bench opposite.

'Nice weather we're having,' said Jenna. She knew it was
a risk.

Sasha's head jerked sideways. 'How did you find me?' she
asked, jumpy.

'I don't know. Instinct?'

Sasha's head turned away, her gaze trained back on the
fountain. It almost scared Jenna, how good she was at this.
It could be a lonely feeling, knowing people better than they
knew themselves.

'I knew I needed to find you,' she added. 'To say sorry again.'

Sasha darted a brief look in her assistant's direction.

'I know you feel like I didn't back you up properly during the Maple presentation, and now you're getting all that shit from Scarlett.' Jenna wrinkled her face like she'd smelled a pile of Saturday night pavement vomit, earning the smallest twitch of a smile from Sasha. 'And then you're dealing with Georgie's fucking rants every day.' Now her boss's gaze dropped down to the ground, one of her hands holding the other for comfort, fingers twiddling the bands on her ring finger. 'Jesus, you must hate every single person born after the millennium. But I want you to know I've got your back.' Sasha's gaze peeled upwards, her body turning towards Jenna. 'What Scarlett said to you wasn't true – you always hear me. You've been like that since day one. It's one of the many things that's brilliant about working for you.' Sasha's eyes were moist now, her face softening. 'One of the many fucking things. Sorry, I'll stop rabbiting on now.'

Sasha's smile was heartfelt. 'Rabbit away. You have no idea how much I need to hear a few compliments today. That meeting was—'

Jenna cut across her. 'Scarlett was being an arsehole. And I'm here for all the compliments you need.'

Sasha paused. 'I want to apologize too, if . . . if I was a bit harsh on you after that big meeting.' Her eyes brimmed with tears now. 'It wouldn't be appropriate for me to go into it, but there's been a lot going on for me personally. If it's splashed over the edges, I'm sorry.'

Jenna took another risk, reaching out to stroke Sasha's arm through the thick wool of her expensive camel coat. It felt electric, a crackle running through her cold fingers.

'Yeah, well, Fred's a total wanker, isn't he? It's not surprising he stresses you out so much.'

Sasha made a sound that wasn't quite a comprehensible word.

'And he's been in your life for so long,' added Jenna lightly. 'Feels like he knows just what buttons to press.' She affected a shudder. 'I'm glad it's not me who had him as a boss.'

Sasha stared at Jenna, weighing up her next sentence. 'Fred's a whole other story,' she said eventually. 'Let's not give him any more airtime.'

'You know you could tell me anything if you wanted,' Jenna said, miming zipping her mouth shut with her free hand. 'I don't want to boast, but secrets are my specialist subject.'

Sasha looked back towards the fountain, a confession floating like a thought bubble above her head. 'Thanks, Jenna,' she said, shaking her shoulders as the cold bit into her. 'But you deserve a few boundaries. It's hard though – sometimes it's like you're a cross between a friend and an assistant. A Frassistant?!'

'Sounds a bit too much like Frankenstein,' Jenna shot back, and they both laughed. 'I promise we'll get through the Maple clusterfuck,' she said. 'I'll keep the other assistants in line. And Georgie too.'

Sasha's expression darkened. 'I'd like you to leave Georgie to herself,' she said. 'I think just for now it's better you don't have more contact with her.' She stood up abruptly, avoiding any questions about that decree. 'We should get back,' she said, pulling up her big woollen collar to try and protect herself against the vicious wind. 'There's a lot to do.'

When Jenna rose to follow, Sasha unexpectedly looped her arm through hers, squeezing it tight against the flank of her own body for a second. Jenna could tell she felt too vulnerable to look at her when she spoke.

'I know I've said it before, but I honestly don't know what I'd do without you.'

It was true, Sasha had said a version of it before, but not like this. Her voice was low and guttural, soaked through with emotion she could no longer control.

Soon it would be time.

SASHA

Steve rang me every single day for three weeks. He sent red roses to the office before switching to pink peonies in case I thought they were a cliché. He wrote me a letter by hand, telling me how much he loved me. When he sent some spinach he'd grown in his greenhouse to Maddi's house, so they could keep me 'fighting fit', I knew it was time I softened my stance.

Ruth says I've got to get better at telling the whole truth, not just the half that suits my narrative. And yes, it wasn't just Steve's keen interest in my iron levels that propelled me home at that precise moment. There was careful timing involved. But it's also true that I missed my husband more than I could ever have anticipated – it was a physical ache that the strongest opioid could not have taken away. The tragedy is that both of those facts were true, and yet one would come to destroy the other.

Our first meeting after my midnight flit was back at the bar of Deia. I was deliberately late – ten minutes, nothing outrageously cruel – and I saw the back of Steve's head before he saw me. His tawny, brown hair was messy, ruffled over the collar of the shirt that poked out from beneath the black crew neck jumper I was always telling him made him look like he was wearing school uniform. He seemed so vulnerable to me right then, so lacking in guile. My love for him felt almost overwhelming, but I couldn't give in to it. This situation was more complicated than even he knew.

'Hi,' I said, tentatively touching his shoulder. He spun towards me, his face instinctively lighting up with pleasure before the reality of the situation drained away the joy.

'Hi,' he said, dropping down off his stool. He stood there for a second, rooted to the spot. 'Can I hug you?' he asked, tentative.

I didn't reply, just reached my arms up to give him the hug he'd asked for, weeks of tension draining out of me as I moulded myself against the familiar contours of his body. Then, just like he had been, I was sideswiped by the reality, my body stiffening against his.

I broke away, hopped up onto the stool next to his. 'It's lovely to see you,' I said.

It was odd, the way that he'd chosen the exact same pair of seats that I'd sat in with Jenna. Or maybe not so odd – they were the plum spot, right in the centre of the handsome marble bar, with a 360-degree view of the high-ceilinged room. It gave me a jolt, an unnerving reminder of how much had changed since that night. My relationship with her was almost the single bright spot. It was that night that we'd found the intimacy that had stood me in such good stead over these last few punishing weeks since I'd left home. She'd been a rock, unfailingly kind and supportive, never prying into why it was that I was such a sleep-deprived basket case or asking about the frequent, unexplained gaps that I was still insisting she carve out of my brutal workdays.

'I can't tell you how lovely it is to see you,' Steve replied, his dark eyes mapping my face as if he was committing it to memory. He gave a crumpled smile. 'Sorry, I'm a terrible date.

Let me get you a drink.' He paused, as nervous as he had been on our first one. 'I mean, should we just get a bottle?'

'I . . .' I paused, panic setting in. I definitely couldn't risk more than a few sips. 'I reckon we should just go by the glass.'

Steve's face immediately cratered, his hand shooting out to signal the barman like he was doing semaphore. 'Yes, of course. Sure.'

This was awful. Like with so many things in my life, I hadn't thought through what the inconvenient reality might feel like. I reached out my own hand, gently pulling down his arm.

'It's not like – a reflection of how much I want to be here with you.'

He was still looking for the barman, his eyes not meeting mine. 'It's fine, Sasha.'

I needed to be careful, not overplay my hand. 'I'll drink you under the table on the lime and sodas. It's just, there's all of this with us, and then work's unbelievably hard right now. Hardest it's ever been.' That at least was the whole truth, and he could hear it. He finally turned back towards me. 'It makes it really hard to sleep.'

His hand was touching my face now, his fingers hooking a strand of my hair and dragging it back behind my ear. 'I think you'd be able to sleep a lot better if you came back to your own bed.'

I reached my hand out for his cheek, letting my fingers graze the scrape of stubble. 'I think you're probably right,' I said.

The moment was broken by the barman sailing towards us, a wolfish grin of recognition on his face that didn't go unnoticed by Steve. 'So, what can I get for you guys?' he asked.

'I'll have a large glass of white Rioja,' I said, with forced enthusiasm. Dr Rindell would be horrified if he could see me now. Perhaps there'd be a plant pot I could surreptitiously pour it into when Steve went to the loo. 'And some of those delicious salty almonds. Actually, let's just get the food menu, shall we?'

Steve beamed at that news, ordering himself a carafe of something fancy and red in celebration. As he laid down the drinks menu, he risked covering my hand with his, catching my eye to check he wasn't being presumptuous. He wasn't – I loved the feel of his wedding ring nicking against my skin, the warmth that crept upwards and moved outwards until it filled my whole body. If only every moment of happiness didn't come with a silent postscript. I slid my hand away.

'What do you need me to do?' he asked, his eyes pleading.

This was the hardest pitch I'd ever had to win. If what I was hoping was actually true, the stakes were higher than they'd ever been.

'I can't just come back and plaster a smile on my face and pretend I'm not devastated.'

'And I'm not asking you to do that!' said Steve, frustrated. 'What kind of person do you think I am? We can go back to that therapist, work it through . . .'

People who loved therapy always thought it was some kind of magical elixir, it seemed to me. Talking to a schoolmarmish woman in sensible shoes about the situation was only going to make one of us feel better. I told him as much, the conversation growing increasingly heated, the wine in his carafe dwindling fast as he tried to take the edge off the stress that had poisoned our relationship to the point of near-death. Luckily, he was too agitated to notice the lake that still lapped the edges of my glass, despite my normal tendency to stress-swill.

'Okay, so you say that you're adamant you couldn't be a dad again.' My words continued in a flurry – I didn't need the knife wound of him confirming that fact again. 'But imagine if I just got pregnant. I know – the stats, the FSH levels, my sad old eggs – but imagine if I did.' Steve was watching for where I was going, wary. 'It's not like we'd have a termination.'

'Of course not,' he conceded.

The mess of the Maple campaign was a blip. Right from when I was a baby account executive, I've been a brilliant pitcher. It's all about finding the soft spot in the person you're persuading, twisting their warm heart in your hands. Making them feel like the best version of themselves, the person they fantasize they are every day inside their own head.

'Right! I know you – you'd get on board, you'd love that child. And the kids would love their sister, once she was staring up at them from her cot, asking them to hold her.'

A half-smile played across his lips. It was impossible not to imagine that baby now, and a person as loving as Steve couldn't help but experience a swirling fragment of that hypothetical feeling. 'Of course. But that's different from me actively wanting a child . . .'

I waved an airy hand. My work was done.

I dropped the shrillness out of my voice, held his gaze with a quiet intensity. 'I'll come home if you just acknowledge that; if we go back to Ruth and her awful floral curtains with the understanding that the situation's not black and white. It's not about the two of you persuading me I'm an idiot. We both have to examine our positions.'

'That's not really how I perceive therapy—' he began pompously, but I carried on talking.

'That's my offer,' I said, slipping my hand over his this time. 'You can take it or leave it.'

* * *

He took it. I knew he would take it – he loved me too much to do otherwise. And I loved him just as hard back. We stayed another couple of hours at Deia, increasingly affectionate and tactile. We'd found what was good about us again, each of us almost giddy with relief, a pair of addicts whose dealer was back from a long holiday. My relief was tinged with something way more complicated, but I'd managed to neutralize it for now. By the time we said goodnight with a long kiss on the pavement, I'd agreed I'd be home by the weekend.

The fears of walking back through the door were harder to neutralize, particularly once I was alone with my thoughts in a cab. Steve was obliviously optimistic, as always. He'd kept the reasons for our temporary separation hazy, made it seem like it would soon be over, but surely Georgie had to have her suspicions after she'd seen those drugs? Steve hadn't brought it up, which meant that she hadn't told him; maybe she was silently harbouring a resentment she'd unleash on me once we were back under the same roof. But that didn't wholly make sense to me either – why wouldn't she have thrown it in Steve's face? The cab drew up outside Maddi's house before I was able to come up with any logical explanation for it.

I couldn't spend too much time fretting. 'It's all going to be okay,' I told Maddi, once I'd finished recounting the whole evening to her. We were sat together on her sofa, the rest of her family already getting ready for bed. She didn't look so sure.

'But he didn't actually say he wanted a baby, Sasha. Or that he'd change his mind.'

I shook my head, drowning out her words. By now, any signs that pointed off the path I was marching down needed to be obliterated.

'Listen, you should be delighted! You get your study back. You don't have me moping around and leaving your straighteners on. I could've burned down this whole beautiful architectural vision.'

I flung my arms out into the space theatrically as I said it. I was so anxious about what it was I was about to do that, despite being stone-cold sober, I felt almost high.

'You can stay as long as you like,' she said, muted and serious. 'I'm just ... I just worry about you.'

I ignored her.

'Thanks for waiting up for me,' I said instead, reaching across the sofa to squeeze her knee. She was wearing a sleek pair of black trousers, the effect slightly ruined by the lump of bolognese she'd obviously dropped onto her thigh at dinnertime.

'Of course,' she said, barely stifling a yawn. She was such a good friend to me. I only hoped I could repay it over time. 'Are you going to do it now?'

'Yup.' I nodded as I said it, my breath suddenly tight in my throat, my heart pounding. I didn't know if I'd ever been this terrified.

'Good luck,' she called, as I stood up and headed for the bathroom.

Half an hour later I was back downstairs, tears streaming down my face. I held the two plastic sticks out towards Maddi as if they were a card trick.

'They're positive,' I gulped. 'Both of them.'

Maddi's eyes stretched wide, shock written across her face. 'You're pregnant?'

I nodded, barely able to believe it myself.

'I'm pregnant.'

JENNA

Jenna knocked so lightly on the toilet door that it was as if her knuckles were only kissing it. This was a big risk she was taking.

It was January now, and with the passage of time, some things had gone back to normal. Sasha's elegant maxi dresses were always pressed and pristine. She no longer twisted her rings like they were worry beads during meetings. But that wasn't to say that her boss was back to the person who had first hired her. Now, when Jenna was sent out for an oat latte, it was inevitably decaf. The mysterious appointments had got even more frequent. And Sasha also hadn't regained the soft power she'd wielded so effortlessly over her subjects in days gone by. All of this, combined with a key fact she'd wheedled out of Georgie – that Sasha had been on a 'health kick' the whole of Christmas and had barely touched a drop of rosé – had led Jenna to the conclusion that her boss was roughly two months pregnant. After all, she'd seen the way Sasha had knocked back the nine-quid white Rioja like it was water when she'd forced Jenna to spend a night out with her. Now all that was needed was the proof.

There was no response to the knock, although she could hear Sasha shifting around inside the cubicle. It was the disabled toilet she'd chosen, a deadly crime that Lorna was prone to sending shitty all-staff emails about. Maybe she thought it was Lorna herself who was knocking, performing some kind of spot inspection. Jenna whispered Sasha's name, but was met with silence. Just as she'd decided to pad away, go back to her desk and pretend she'd never been there, the door opened a crack. Sasha's face looked sticky, her mascara smeared around each eye. She was going to need to do a serious clean-up job before the lunch that was in her calendar.

'Hi, Jenna,' she said, her voice hoarse. There was no question that she'd been projectile vomiting in there – the over-powering smell was seeping out from the tiny crack that she'd opened. 'I'll be out in a sec.'

She went to shut the door, but Jenna knew how to connect their gazes by now, how to keep Sasha engaged by sending her silent waves of intimacy. The fact that she currently had no other allies in the office made her powerless to her assistant's easy warmth.

'Are you okay, Sasha?' Sasha's smudged eyes suddenly filled with tears. As she looked down at the tiled floor, Jenna inched her shoulder forward so that she was closer to the gap. 'You're not, are you?'

'I'm fine,' her boss muttered unconvincingly.

'You haven't got long before that lunch. I brought you some water. Let me help you get cleaned up . . .'

It worked. Sasha stepped backwards, sinking onto the closed toilet lid and letting the door swing open far enough to allow Jenna inside. The acrid smell of vomit hit the back of Jenna's nose, and she willed herself not to gag.

Sasha's head was bowed, but she swiftly forced it upwards, an empty smile now papering her clammy face. She reached out for the bottle of water that Jenna had brought. 'I just need a minute,' she said, in a too-bright voice. 'I think I must have some kind of stomach bug. But I can't give in to it, not today.'

No wonder she was dreading the lunch – it was a gruesome trio, Bridget and Martin and Fred – designed to soften Fred up before the heinously overdue presentation that was coming up. The man Jenna suspected was Sasha's one-time boyfriend, along with her disgruntled bosses, plus sushi.

'But if you're ill, you really need to go home. Let Steve look after you.'

Sasha looked even greener at that suggestion, shaking her head vigorously.

'No!' she snapped, then softened her tone. 'I mean, thanks for the thought. But I just need to get . . . get it done.'

Jenna observed her pinched, anxious face, a theory forming. These last few weeks, she'd had plenty of covert assignations with Georgie, who definitely didn't know Sasha was pregnant. Furious as she was that her stepmum had put the kibosh on their friendship behind her back, she'd have had no reason to keep that enormous secret for her. Now Jenna was starting to wonder if she wasn't the only one in the house who didn't know the truth – Sasha certainly didn't seem to want to go home to Steve. Maybe her own husband – the man she adored, and yet had left for some brief, inexplicable reason – was also in the dark. By Jenna's calculations she wasn't quite at the magic three months, but judging by Steve's loving ease with his kids at the Falcon she reckoned he'd struggle not to share such joyful news with them. And it would explain why Sasha was coming in earlier and earlier to take refuge in this grim, smelly box. She'd said to that friend of hers – the one who earned all the kisses and devotion in her emails – that he'd never really wanted a baby. Maybe he still didn't. But how could she have pulled off a pregnancy without his knowledge?

Jenna leaned backwards against the sink, cocking her head with fake concern. 'Me and Pete can fix it. We'll move it to next week. It's still a fortnight to the big Elevate session.'

The final presentation of the new, expanded Maple campaign had been postponed again and again, the creative never quite good enough for Sasha and her fearsome bosses to risk sharing with the client. Time had run out now, the finishing touches all that was left to add.

Sasha tried to stand up, then sat back down heavily. 'Nope. No cancelling. I . . .' Her words vibrated with emotion. 'I just need to get through this bit. Get to the other side.'

'Are you really okay?' asked Jenna softly. 'I don't want to overstep, but I . . . you know I care about you.' Sasha's face was suffused with a sad kind of gratitude, emboldening Jenna to keep creeping forward. 'I've watched you rush in here every single morning.' Their eyes met. 'Sasha, are you pregnant?'

Sasha's arms whipped across her chest, her eyes hitting the floor. 'It's a stomach bug.'

It was almost sad, looking at her now. The Sasha Jenna had first met could sell you anything, but the way she'd just uttered those words wouldn't even have convinced the toilet lid she was sitting on.

Jenna reached out the tips of her fingers to lightly graze Sasha's upper arm, feeling how it trembled at her touch. 'I promise you I won't tell anyone.'

The long silence was as pregnant as Sasha herself.

'There's nothing to tell,' she whispered finally, standing up abruptly and moving to the sink, forcing Jenna to step out of her way.

Sasha vigorously splashed cold water onto her ravaged face, almost as if she was committing an act of violence. Then she straightened up, her eyes meeting Jenna's in the dingy mirror.

When she spoke, her tone was firm, like she was grasping for her old authority.

'Please don't talk to anyone about this,' she said, betraying herself. A stomach bug was hardly breaking news, but a pregnancy . . .

'Of course,' said Jenna, formal.

'Like I said, I just need to get through this.'

The words felt like they wrapped around far more than just a business lunch.

'I'll help you, Sasha,' said Jenna, emphatic.

'I know you will,' said Sasha, gratitude vibrating through the four syllables. She nodded to the door. 'I just need a minute.'

Jenna slipped out through it. 'You can ask me for whatever you need,' she whispered, disappearing back into the office, into the fray.

SASHA

'You sure you don't want a splash?' Fred was grinning at me, the light in his eyes flashing their own secret code as he hovered the bottle over my glass. 'Half a glass won't kill you.'

I put a flat palm over it, shaking my head and forcing myself to smile in a way that wouldn't land as cold. 'Honestly, I'm fine. I'm saving myself until we can celebrate for real.'

It was hard not to feel guilty when I observed the smug curl his mouth made in response. The guilt boomeranged into a sudden rush of love for Steve, a man who would never sit across a table from another woman at a work meeting and stoke his own virility with this kind of meaningless flirtation. How could I ever have believed my torturous, addicted feelings for Fred were remotely akin to real love? And yet they'd still kept me stuck fast for three long years, not to mention the extended emotional aftermath.

I looked away, strengthening my internal resolve to confess everything to my husband that very night. I did have a logic beyond rancid dishonesty. I'd already been through the agony of losing a baby, knew how fragile our child's hold on life might be those first three months. I didn't want anger and recrimination to threaten her very existence, and I also wanted to buy us more bonding time before I dropped that bomb. At the moment, the relief of reunion had turned us into sappy teenagers, texting and touching each other in a way we hadn't done for years. Considering the latter, it was a wonder he hadn't worked it out. Maybe he was enjoying this strange kind of honeymoon too much, too – I wasn't the only one only seeing what they wanted to see.

'Fair enough,' said Fred, plonking the bottle of Pouilly-Fumé back in the ice bucket and looking around the table at Martin and Bridget. I clocked the glint of burnished gold on his left hand, wondered if he was feeling any of the same reflexive guilt that I did. He'd never seemed to feel it much back in the day, only approximating it when it suited his shameless manipulation of me. 'And we will be celebrating. It's not like I ever thought you guys would let me down.' He laughed, swigging from his own glass. 'It's just more fun to make it a bit spicy.'

'Nice of you to keep us on our toes,' Martin laughed back, taking a tiny sip from his own glass. Drinking on a midweek lunchtime was pretty retro for all of us bar Fred, even those diners who weren't liable to projectile vomit if they indulged. 'Sasha's kept the team suitably scared, anyway.' He turned to his wife. 'We think you'll be really impressed with the work that's been done, don't we?'

'Absolutely,' nodded Bridget enthusiastically. She summoned a waiter with an effortless flick of her right hand. No, what was truly effortless was the way she created a distraction. She was no fool – she knew full well how much we'd been struggling, the weeks of delay. 'We can't wait to share it.' She turned to the young Japanese guy, his pad held in his hand. 'Now do you think we should order à la carte or just go for the tasting menu?' She smiled at Fred. 'The chef here is off the scale. Everything's . . .' She shook her head in silent tribute, starting to order a few dishes for the table while we made our decision.

Edamame beans I could handle, but the very thought of plate after plate of raw fish arriving in front of me was already making the bile creep steadily up my throat.

'Gotta go with the chef, haven't we?' said Fred, ostentatiously tossing down the menu the waiter had handed him. He looked out from the dark velvet-lined booth that we were sitting in, drinking in the chic simplicity of the place, with its low lighting and impeccably dressed staff. Fred liked to feel special, and this kind of understated luxury, tucked away in a Farringdon back street, would make him feel like he'd been let into a secret. Bridget and Martin were always perfectly attuned to those tiny manipulations, creating a unique universe for each client like they were in their very own Truman Show. My automatic understanding of it was a reminder of how much I'd learned from them over the years, steeped in their techniques from the beginning of my career. It had always made me feel lucky, but on that particular day it felt more like corruption.

'You said it,' agreed Martin, slipping his liver-spotted hand over Bridget's and looking to the waiter. Before my fate was sealed, I knew I had to pipe up.

'I think I'm just going to order something simple,' I interjected, ignoring the subtle look of disapproval that Bridget was sending in my direction. I was scribbling on the perfect picture she was painting him. 'Can I just have the chicken katsu curry?'

Maddi had come with me to the first ultrasound earlier in the week, the two of us staring in wonder at the ten-week-old smudge on the screen. 'You have to tell him now,' she'd said, her mouth close to my ear, her face wet against mine, and I'd interlocked our fingers, tears cascading down my cheeks as I nodded my agreement. I knew how wrong it was, what I'd done. Leaving the consent forms we'd both signed for the treatment in place, never telling Dr Rindell that Steve had changed his mind. He'd been surprised not to see my husband at the appointments, but I'd told him that work was really busy for Steve right now, and he was far too busy and transactional to waste time digging into it.

Fred cocked his head as the waiter walked away with our orders, studying me. 'You're a bit of a ...' He paused, just about stopping himself from saying 'pussy'. 'Wuss in your old age, Sasha. I remember you as having a real pioneer spirit back in the day.'

I hated him, hated even more how much I still instinctively knew him. He was like a long-forgotten language that I'd recovered full fluency in after a head injury.

I stared back at him, keeping my eyes blank this time. 'It was a long time ago now, wasn't it?' I said coolly. 'And I just fancied something light today.'

He nodded, his eyes still raking my face as I forced myself not to blush. How obvious could he make it? Before the silence started shouting the truth, Martin broke it.

'I'm so glad you gave us the chance to go 360 degrees on the campaign, Fred.' He clenched his fists with faux passion. 'Get that environmental message out to the whole sweep of travellers, not just the ones who get to turn left.'

'Like us you mean?' laughed Fred. 'My kids howl if we go economy to France in the summer. Spoilt little shits. Archie's sixteen now, I can't believe it.'

His youngest child, the one I used to feel the most guilty about. Fred had his phone out by now, showing off pictures of his three glossy offspring to Bridget and Martin like they were a stable of prize racehorses. I took a cursory glance, forcing a smile. Everywhere I looked there were reminders of the relentless passage of time. I breathed in, felt my connection to the life inside me that was gaining strength with every day that passed.

'You should bring him along to Elevate,' said Bridget, looking admiringly at a shot of Archie on the balcony of an expensive hotel, a beer in front of him and what looked suspiciously like a joint burning away in an ashtray. I remembered Fred showing me photos of his son in footie pyjamas – real photos, that he kept tucked in his wallet – crying about how painful it was for him to love both me and his kids as much as he did. His 'anguish' made me love him all the more, just as he'd calculated it would. He knew I was stupid enough to think I was the first, would be the last.

'It's for disadvantaged youth, my love,' smirked Martin. 'And that boy is far from disadvantaged.'

My mouth went dry at that. I was sitting here judging them, but I was no better.

'Fair point,' conceded Bridget, giving a naughty grin as she took a sip of her wine. 'Aren't your stepkids about that age now, Sasha?'

I froze. 'No, they're a bit younger actually,' I stammered.

'Didn't know you were a stepmonster!' said Fred. 'Any pics?'

'You said it,' I shot back, forcing a laugh. 'I'm a stepmonster. Of course I don't have any pictures.'

Just then the waiter reappeared, carrying a tray that groaned with dish after dish of pungent fish. I'd never been more grateful for an interruption, but the smell was too overpowering for my sensitive nose. I took a long gulp of water and abruptly stood up, heading for the loo.

I sat on the closed seat for as long as I judged was socially acceptable, my two hands webbed over my belly. She felt like the person I was most intimate with now, which I knew was both dangerous and ridiculous. The cubicle, despite its relative luxury, was giving me flashbacks to earlier that morning.

I'd been trying to put out of my mind what I'd said to Jenna, kid myself that I hadn't given myself away the second I'd let her in. But she was no fool, and a world in which my assistant knew I was pregnant and my husband remained in the dark was not tenable. I played with the rings on my left hand, tried to control the anxiety that clamped my whole body tight when I imagined uttering the words. I knew how betrayed he'd feel, but surely there would be a postscript to that? I comforted myself with the memory of how he'd softened at the thought of our child, despite himself. I'd been trying to use our latest therapy sessions with Ruth to get him back to that place and over the line, but so far he'd remained entrenched. Surely the reality would feel different from the imagined, his anger eventually burning out to be replaced by something sweeter?

I was a good saleswoman; I sold myself the lie so well that I was soon ready to sail back to the table, determined to deliver what Martin and Bridget wanted from this lunch.

'So, what have I missed?' I trilled, slipping back into my seat.

'We were just talking about how the day should run,' said Bridget, casting me a little look. *Take care*, it said. *Don't go off script.*

'Yes,' I said, turning my body towards Fred and fixing a look of enthusiasm on my face. 'What exactly do you need from us? We were thinking we'd take you and the team through all three tiers of the campaign upstairs, then head down to Elevate to see it play out with the kids!'

Fred leaned back in his seat, taking a glug of his wine. 'Boring,' he said. 'Let's give it a bit more theatre. I know how much work you've put in. I want to create the opportunity for us to really savour it.'

The savouring was meant to be reserved for the absurdly

expensive sashimi, not for a presentation that millions of pounds of business was relying on. Even Bridget's smile faltered.

'So, tell us what savouring looks like,' she said, rallying. 'We're all ears.'

'Let's do the Maple overview and the specifics for Business and Premium upstairs,' he said, waving a dismissive hand. 'Looked great anyway, I'm not that bothered about it. Carbon emissions down, seat width up, blah blah blah.' A surge of anger shot through me, Georgie's flushed, indignant face almost projecting itself over his smugly self-satisfied one. He really didn't care at all. Life had been too easy to ever force him to care about anything – he hadn't worked the muscle hard enough for it to have any strength.

'And then?' asked Martin.

'Let's take it to the floor,' said Fred. 'Don't give us the Economy spiel up there – let's take it downstairs and hear it with the kids. Have you got that cockatoo girl coming? She's a riot.'

'Cockatoo girl?' asked Bridget, turning to me with a tinkling laugh.

It was hard to reply with my jaw clenched quite as tightly as it was. 'She's got like a, a pink streak, in her hair,' I said, as if I was wracking my brains, instead of remembering this morning's breakfast table. 'She had A LOT to say for herself in the meeting Fred came to.'

'Sasha had her under manners though,' said Fred, miming a couple of punches, his eyes sparkling at the memory. 'Bam, bam, bam!'

'Sounds dangerous,' said Martin, with a faux shudder.

He had no idea just how dangerous.

'I'm pretty sure she's on the list,' I said, my heart sinking as any last chance of excluding her from the meeting crumbled to dust. 'But are you sure you don't want time to digest it before you get swamped by their pushback? Like you say, they're pretty opinionated.'

Fred threw me a crocodile smile. 'No, you said that. You don't have to *manage* me, Sasha.' I recoiled at the snap, the sudden coldness in his eyes. 'I'm bringing the big guns for the show – might even have Michael with me.'

Michael Allpress, the chairman of Maple. Jesus.

Fred paused, looking between Martin and Bridget as if I'd ceased to exist. 'I want him to see why I chose you.' Fred had inherited Bright when he'd taken up his new post, but no one was going to correct him. 'Why I doubled down on the business.' Another untruth, as yet. 'I want Michael and all the head honchos to see how special Bright is. How you smash the boundaries. Not everyone has a cave full of teenagers in the building that they actually bother to listen to.'

'Aahh, thank you Fred!' said Bridget, her body angled away from me. 'We really appreciate the support, always.'

I sat there fuming, wishing that the entire lunch had sub-titles, lies exposed on a continuous loop. Right now, the ticker tape would be informing everyone that she'd done nothing but drop continuous F-bombs about his outrageous bait and switch with the account.

'We really do,' agreed Martin, discreetly signalling for the bill. 'It's been a long time we've been working together now.' He thumped his heart with his knuckles. 'Total trust.'

'Thank you, brother,' said Fred, bonhomie restored. He looked back at me. 'And thanks for keeping it all on track, Sasha.'

'My pleasure,' I told him, smiling as I took a decorous sip of water. It turned out I was no better at telling the truth than any of them. My hand went to my stomach and I left it there. I would tell Steve tonight; no more ticker tape.

Bridget glanced at Martin and then abruptly stood up. 'We have to dash I'm afraid, we've got a car outside. We've got to get over to Hammersmith for a meeting.'

I swallowed, my mouth going dry again.

Fred half stood, holding out his hand for Martin's. 'Shouldn't you be taking the Tube?!' he said, snorting with laughter at his own joke. 'Might have to fire you.'

Martin gave him a playful punch on the shoulder. 'The car's electric, scout's honour.' He shrugged on his jacket. 'Sasha can keep you entertained over dessert.' He threw me a smile that lacked any warmth as he headed for the door. 'See you back at the office.'

I stared after their retreating backs, wondering how quickly I could extricate myself without offending a man who currently had my professional fate cupped in his leathery old hands.

'Hello, you,' he said, sinking backwards into the velvet embrace of the deep booth, making it abundantly clear that he was in no rush. Those two little words were like nails down a blackboard – they'd so often been the first phrase I'd hear when I'd snatch up the phone after waiting days for him to call. So intimate, and yet so blocking of intimacy in the way that they denied me my rage. I just wanted to get through the rest of this impossible day and back to Steve. Try to somehow make it all okay.

'Hi,' I replied, stiff and prissy. 'Well actually, bye. I really should get back myself.' I forced a smile. 'I need to make sure your campaign's up to scratch this time.'

'Don't do that!' he said. We were opposite each other, and he leaned forward, almost as if he was considering grabbing for my hand. I stiffened even more. 'It's been weird, hasn't it? Seeing each other like this.'

'It was all a long time ago,' I said, my gaze roaming

the restaurant. I couldn't do this. 'It's not something I'm proud of.'

Fred's gaze burned into my skin until I was forced to turn back towards him. 'Proud of?'

'Being a ... whatever I was to you.' I performatively swivelled my rings back and forth on my finger. I spoke slowly, deliberately. 'It's not the way I'd choose to behave now I'm a grown-up.'

'Oh, you're a grown-up now, are you?' said Fred, playful.

'Don't do that,' I snapped before I could stop myself.

'Do what, Sasha?' he replied, all wounded innocence. I hated this. Hated him, the way he was still somehow wielding power over me. It made me feel the very opposite of a grown-up.

'Come on, you know what you're doing. I'm married. You've always been married.' He kept his face blank, like I was making no sense. I cursed myself for how flustered it was making me feel as I blundered on. 'It was always wrong, so don't do that – that flirty thing now. I felt like you were making it really obvious in front of Martin and Bridget too.'

As I watched his face turn to granite, I felt an unexpected rush of pity for my twenty-something self. It was hard enough now to deal with his hair-trigger mood changes, and I was a middle-aged woman with a baby in my belly. How had she, with all her love and guilt and emotional confusion, even begun to survive it? And for so many years?

'Thanks for the lecture, professor. I was actually trying to be respectful. Acknowledge the fact that we shared something, rather than behave like some corporate arsehole. If you'd prefer option two, I can arrange it for you.'

He splashed some more wine into his glass and took a petulant gulp, leaving only an inch in the bottle. My line of argument felt muzzy now, almost as if I'd downed that bottle

of wine with him. 'We did share something,' I said. 'It was . . .
I . . .' My tongue felt thick in my mouth. I certainly wasn't going
to tell him that I'd loved him; how the remnants of that love
had sealed my bruised heart shut against any other invader
for years afterwards. 'But it wasn't healthy. It wasn't good for
me. And right now, I just want to do a really good job on this
campaign.' I forced my voice to stay steady. 'Will you please
just let me do that?'

He shook his head in pantomime disbelief. 'Sure. I don't
know what your problem is. I've been trying to make this easier
for you. I was happy to see you again. And now it's all just . . .'
He flung angry fingers into the space between us. 'Drama.'
He gave a mean smile. 'Guess you were always a bit that way
inclined though, weren't you?'

A wave of fury surged through my body. 'When you're
giving me sex eyes in front of my bosses, yes, it makes me uncomfortable.' I grabbed my bag from under my feet, put it on
the table so he'd know I was serious about leaving. 'But please,
let's get through this campaign respectfully and deliver what's
needed to both of our employers.'

I tried to stand up, but the narrow semicircle of the booth
trapped my legs between the seat and the table. Fred seized his
moment.

'They always knew,' he said quietly.

'I'm sorry?'

'Bridget and Martin – *your bosses*. They always knew about
us. Might even have been why they promoted you.' His smile
was even nastier this time. 'You were a good, shall we say,
people person. The fact they've left us alone makes me think
they still think the same thing.'

Tears of humiliation were threatening just below the front of
fake calm. I knew, as he said it, that it was true; at least, it had

been back then. My twenty-something self hadn't known it, but my forty-something self had long since lost her innocence. I pretended he wouldn't see how deftly he'd landed the blow, even though his face was already registering his sense of triumph.

'Me and my team are really looking forward to delivering the campaign,' I said, forcing myself to look him in the eye with a steady gaze. 'I'll see you at the Bright offices on Wednesday the fifth.'

'Three months late!' he yelled after me, the booze clearly taking hold. 'Who do you think got you all of those fucking extensions?'

* * *

'Hi, darling,' said Steve, as I pushed open the door that night. He was waiting in the hallway, a glass of rosé held out for me in his right hand. I smelled the top note of it and tried not to gag. 'It's a peace offering,' he said, stepping forward, a rueful smile on his face. 'I've got a confession to make.'

I took the glass, creating a performance of unwrapping my big cashmere scarf to save myself from having to chink his and take a sip.

'What have you got to fess up to?' I said, hoping he wouldn't hear that my voice was already thick with tears that I knew I couldn't afford to shed. I let the scarf shield my face for a second.

'I went one ahead on *Slow Horses*,' he said. 'But I'll watch it again with you. I was going to do that anyway, but then I realized I couldn't pretend.'

I discarded my glass on the hall table, flinging my arms around his neck and burying my face in the soft hollow of his upper chest without saying a word.

'Wow, I should commit crimes against streaming apps more often,' he murmured, stroking my hair, his lips grazing my ear.

Did he feel me stiffen in his arms? My sense of shame felt like the rings inside a tree trunk, each layer of it denoting a different time. A different crime. Fred's words had felled me, left all of them exposed. Was every aspect of my life built on deceit? My professional success down to having been a solid seven out of ten when I was ripe enough to be mistress material? My one shot at motherhood coming at the expense of my sweet and gentle husband's trust in me? An entire career carved out of the ability to mould truth into a prettier shape?

I couldn't tell Steve the truth about the pregnancy, not yet. There was no way to make what I'd done to him any prettier. He'd stepped back now, looking into my face with a bemused expression on his face.

'Are you okay, Sasha?'

'Long day,' I said, reaching up to stroke his cheek. 'I need to eat. And I think there's a new episode of *Slow Horses* that's just dropped?'

He gave me his familiar hangdog smile, reaching out a hand to catch mine and lead me downstairs to the kitchen.

I wasn't ready to give it up. This version of happiness would break soon enough – didn't both of us deserve a little longer to sustain us in the coming winter?

How foolish I was, thinking that I'd be the one to decide how it would smash.

JENNA

Maybe London had changed her. Sitting here, her hand wrapped awkwardly around a fat crinkly cardboard cup, Jenna missed the quirky cool that Squirrel and the Humble Bean both had in spades. This was a chain coffee shop on Camden High Street, tourists streaming through the door to get directions from the staff or covertly use the disgusting toilet.

But there was method to the madness – she and Georgie had decided that meeting somewhere anonymous was the safest thing they could do. It wasn't so far from Highgate, but Sasha wouldn't be caught dead among the tightly packed market stalls that lined the street, laden with psychedelic bongs and 'I Heart London' T-shirts. It was oddly satisfying, this newfound feeling of superiority that Jenna had. A little bit more of Sasha had rubbed off on her than she'd realized. Sometimes it came in useful.

'Jenna? Earth to Jenna!'

Georgie was waving a moist palm in her face, breaking her trance-like gaze out of the window onto the chaos. Jenna refocused, galvanized by what she'd just noticed about herself.

'Sorry, I was just thinking about exactly how it plays out.' She gave the younger girl a knowing look, designed to flatter her maturity. 'You get why it's so important it doesn't seem like I'm part of it?'

'Yeah, 'course. You're the double agent, whereas I'm a . . . a provocateur.'

Now it was Georgie who had a faraway look in her eye, probably imagining herself in an industrial-chic Communist uniform pillaging the Winter Palace in the Russian Revolution. She'd been studying it at school and had already bored Jenna to death with its 'relevance to now'. She'd somehow managed to miss the fact that four-storey houses in Highgate would be right up there on the pillaging list come the next uprising, but this definitely wasn't the time to enlighten her.

'Exactly!' said Jenna. 'If Sasha fires me, I won't be able to work from the inside next time there's some shitbag corporation trying to greenwash their dirty business.'

'Do you really think she'd fire you?'

'Yeah, of course she would.'

Georgie's eyes widened, a certain doubtfulness crossing her face. Jenna had noticed this dangerous softening towards her stepmum over the last few weeks.

Jenna snapped her fingers for emphasis. 'In a heartbeat.'

Georgie took a sip from her wasteful synthetic cup, her eyes lowered. 'I think she really likes you though?'

It was hard to hide her frustration. Jenna could see that Sasha's disappearing act had scared her stepdaughter, made her appreciate the glue that she provided to their broken little family. They'd even been out for a couple of the brunches that Sasha had previously been left longing for. For all her talk of revolution, Georgie didn't like change. And that was the trump card that Jenna would need to play if all of this got shaky.

'I'm useful to her,' she said. 'I pick up her dry cleaning and get her lunch.' Sasha had never actually asked her to collect any dry cleaning, but she was always telling her she'd done it for Bridget as a none too subtle reminder of how much better

Jenna had it. 'I'm not too posh, so I make her look *woke* to the rest of the company.' She forced eye contact between them. 'And she really didn't like it when I tried to make her and the Maple execs understand why our generation are never going to accept flying around the world as a God-given right! She *silenced* me.'

Georgie preened a little at 'our generation'; she always became like the cat that got the cream when Jenna painted them as equals. 'Why the fuck won't they listen?' she said, scrunching up the wrapper from the vegan croissant they'd shared. Even if it hadn't tasted like greasy carpet, Jenna would still have let her have the lion's share. She was slimming her way into Sasha's Frame jeans, almost thin enough now to fasten the waist. 'It's like they don't care what kind of broken planet they leave us!'

'Exactly! And if she likes me so much, why do you think she's trying to stop us from being friends? Controlling, moi?'

Jenna could see the inner conflict streaking across Georgie's face as she laid out her half-hearted defence. 'It's shit, I know, but I think she probably just doesn't want you to know that she broke up with Dad for a bit. They're still totally gross together, not like parents, so she's definitely regretting it.'

'Do you think that's all it is?' asked Jenna, trying to lead her in the right direction.

Georgie wasn't in the mood to take the bait. 'It's also totally shit that she silenced you like that. But she was there in front of her bosses, so I suppose she was trying to keep the peace. That's what my dad said about ... when I opened my mouth in that first Elevate meeting. How hard it must've been for her.'

Jenna tried to quell her sense of panic. This was all getting too precarious – the affectionate chat about her 'parents', the newfound humility about her own behaviour. It was convenient

too. If you lived in a mansion on top of a hill, you benefit-
ted from the status quo. When the chips were down, would
Georgie really want to put her head above the parapet? Once
was careless, but twice meant real trouble for her. Jenna only
had a split second to strategize.

'It's really impressive how loyal you are to her,' she said.

Georgie shrugged, unwilling to articulate the affection for
Sasha that was coming off her like fumes out of a car exhaust.

'I mean, I thought you might be upset.'

Was she really doing this?

Georgie looked uncertain. 'Upset?'

Just then, a teenage boy in a cheap-looking burgundy
uniform – a nasty clash with his spiky carrot-coloured hair –
appeared next to them brandishing a dirty cloth. He wiped the
smears of frothy milk and crumbs from the table, aggressively
swerving around their cardboard cups without making eye
contact. It wasn't surprising they were enemy number one by
now – they'd been nursing those drinks for a good hour, the
coffee shop filling up with damp bodies sheltering from the
drizzle that had started outside. It created useful tension –
Georgie's face grew increasingly anxious as she tried to fill in
the blanks.

Jenna steeled herself, even though a shred of conscience was
threatening to derail her. After all, she reminded herself, Sasha
had everything now. A baby in her belly and a stepdaughter
who loved her. Plus, the adoring husband, the perfect home
and the glittering career – even if it was going through a rough
patch right now. Jenna didn't have any of it. More importantly,
her mum hadn't had any of it either. She looked away into the
crush of wet customers, the second thought bringing an unexpected stinging behind her eyeballs. Grief was a weird thing.
A dangerous thing.

She blinked, refocusing on the task at hand . 'It's going to be a massive change for you all isn't it?' She gave Georgie a conspiratorial smile. 'I know you've been discreet. Like I said . . .' She pointed a finger at her. 'Lo-yal.'

Georgie was panicking now. 'What . . . what do you mean?'

'What is she now, nearly three months? Hopefully the sickness will get a bit better for her in the second trimester.'

The colour drained from Georgie's ruddy cheeks. 'Sasha's pregnant?' Her eyes blinked with shock, her hand over her mouth like she herself was going to be sick. 'She can't be pregnant. She's like . . . she's old.' She started to recover herself. 'And anyway, my dad would have told me. He's a shit liar and he can't ever keep secrets from us.' She took a noisy slurp from her coffee, sucking it through the narrow gap in the cup's lid. 'No way is she pregnant. Besides, they've been together ages. Why would she get pregnant now?'

Jenna tried her best to keep her face neutral. Georgie's conviction about her dad felt right – it was what she'd suspected. There was something delicious about the fact that she knew more than either of them. She put a hand out, covered Georgie's free one.

'I'm so sorry. I never would've said a thing if I'd thought she was keeping it a secret.' Georgie shook her head in disbelief as Jenna carried on. 'She's definitely pregnant. She's been throwing up every day for weeks. She . . . she admitted it to me.'

Georgie's body swayed on the stool. 'Are you sure?' she croaked.

'I'm sure,' said Jenna, not yet withdrawing her hand. Georgie's skin felt cold to the touch, like the shock had frozen her solid. It was a good minute before she spoke.

'What the actual fucking fuck?!' she said. She grabbed between her feet for her ugly vinyl rucksack. 'I need to go and find my dad, right now.'

Jenna moved her hand, so that it trapped the younger girl's arm against the Formica table. 'Slow your roll. Let's just think it through together.' Georgie made to yank her arm away, but Jenna's steady stare made her submit. 'You're in shock. It's no wonder. I just want to help you work out the best way to handle this.'

Georgie slumped back onto the stool, her face a picture of misery. Jenna took advantage of the silence.

'If you blow this up now, Sasha won't let you anywhere near that meeting. You'll be stopped from doing something . . . something we've planned for ages. Something that's really important. I'm so fucking impressed by you, the way you never compromise.' Jenna stared at Georgie, manufacturing an adoring kind of intensity. 'We've all got a lot to learn from you, particularly those pricks from Maple. Honestly, you should hear what they say in the meetings when no one external can hear them, what Sasha says to that Fred guy – they don't give a shit. It's weird, it's like it makes them horny.'

Sure, she was winding Georgie up, but it wasn't wholly untrue. Fred had dropped in for an unscheduled meeting this week, Sasha as jumpy as a cat on hot bricks. Jenna had seen from the start how torturous it was for her, talking to him, and how much he in turn enjoyed it. Those two had a history that was more than professional, she was convinced of it by now.

Georgie's black-lined eyes were sooty and damp, her hands obsessively twisting a coffee-stained serviette. She was barely able to string a sentence together, the shock overwhelming her.

'I dunno, Jenna, I don't know if I can do it now . . .'

Jenna drove forward, cutting across Georgie as if the next thought had only just occurred to her.

'Hang on, no wonder Sasha didn't want us seeing each other. She didn't want me blowing her cover, telling you first.'

'But why would she tell *you* she was pregnant and not tell my dad?' wailed Georgie.

Jenna shook her head with mock outrage. 'Makes no sense. Not unless she's got something really bad she's trying to hide.'

'Do you think she's cheating on him?' Georgie was growing increasingly agitated. 'That would explain why she walked out on him like that – so she could go off with some dude. Then Dad takes her back, because he's such a fucking sap . . .'

'Maybe . . .' mused Jenna. 'I mean . . .' She paused, as if she was working something out. 'It could even be Fred.'

Jenna noticed how Georgie's shoulders sagged at the mere thought of her vulnerable father – a fierce, protective love that weighed heavy on her – and felt momentarily burdened by her own aloneness. It was funny how an absence could weigh so much.

'What if she is cheating and she tries to pretend the baby's his? She's . . .' Georgie slumped again, deep hurt etched across her face. 'I can't believe I've been going for avocado toast with her and getting her to help me with my fucking coursework.'

Particularly considering the outrageous amount of water it took to grow an avocado, thought Jenna. 'It sucks,' she said.

Georgie had gone back to scrabbling around for her rucksack on the dirty floor. 'He goes to his Italian course on Saturday mornings. I need to get to him before he goes home to her.'

'Georgie.' Jenna's tone was sharp – it needed to be to penetrate the whirling chaos inside the girl's teenage head. 'You're right, your dad's a softie. I saw how he looked at you that night in the pub. It's like – pure love.' Inevitably, Georgie melted at this, and Jenna pressed her advantage. 'Sasha's wily, she knows exactly what he's like. What if she just gets round him? Makes out you're the problem? He's not going to get a DNA test on that baby, is he?'

Georgie froze, the impossibility of her situation silencing her.

'If you just hold your nerve, do what we're planning, she'll have way less ability to fight. Work's everything to her, that humiliation's going to knock her flat. Then you can tell him.' Jenna spoke slowly and deliberately, making sure that the next words landed. 'If you really want revenge – not for you, for your dad – this is the way to get it. When she's on the floor, she won't be able to wriggle out of what she's done, the way she wriggles out of everything else. She'll have to tell him the truth.'

The silence between them felt like it stretched into infinity, the screeching hubbub of the café nothing more than white noise.

'Yeah, she does wriggle out of everything!' said Georgie eventually, her signature outrage starting to flood back in. As she started to rant, Jenna finally allowed herself to breathe out. 'You can't even afford your own fucking coffees, and it's not like she gives a shit about the planet – she's just taking money to help a corporation fake it.' She threw Jenna one of her awful, pitying smiles. 'I'll get these by the way, you don't need to worry about it.'

'Thanks, love,' said Jenna, with practised humility. Even she could afford a couple of these vile brews, coming in as they did at franchise store prices. 'She'll go nuts to your dad about what you've done – even though all that'll be is standing up for what's right – and then . . . then you land the killer blow.' She mimed a punch, a ripple of excitement spreading through her body as she did so. 'Ultimately, I think he'll be really proud of you!'

Georgie locked eyes with her, almost as if she was channelling Jenna's strength. 'Thank you,' she said, her voice quivering with emotion. 'I don't know what I'd do without you now.'

It seemed like no one did. Soon they would have to find out.

SASHA

Georgie was sitting at the kitchen table mechanically spooning granola into her mouth, a splash of oat milk and a handful of apple slices added to make it actually tasty.

'Good morning, early bird!' I said, looking in disbelief at the clock on the wall. It was only seven o'clock. I'd got so used to creeping out of the silent house under a blanket of darkness, trying my best not to wake anyone up, so finding her parked there was a shock. At least I hadn't stopped to casually vomit in the downstairs bathroom, opening the tiny window to make sure that the smell could diffuse before anyone else got out of bed.

She briefly twisted her head towards me. 'I've got to finish a history essay,' she said.

'Which one?' I asked, trying my hardest to remember them. 'Is it still German reparations?' It wasn't that I didn't care – far from it – it was just that it was Wednesday. THE Wednesday. The day of the Maple presentation. My teeth had ground so much in the night that by now I felt like I had lockjaw.

'No,' she snapped, and I felt stung. I'd sat up with her one night working on that one, dredging up my hazy memories of GCSE History and workshopping how she should set out her argument. I'd thought our relationship was making progress since I'd come home, but maybe it was wishful thinking. The sad fact was that I trusted myself less than I trusted anyone these days.

I shook on my red coat, which was hanging off the back of a chair. It was a loose bathrobe of a thing that conspired to hide my gradually expanding stomach. 'Okay.'

She sat up straight, giving me an unexpected smile. 'It's a different one, about the Hitler Youth. They were indoctrinated by the adults. I'd tell you about it, but I know you've got to get to work. Big day, right?'

The relief I felt was overwhelming. She didn't hate me; it was just that I didn't speak teenage as fluently as I thought I did. I needed to believe that our family was bonded enough to survive the news that it was about to swell. Once I'd got through today – escaped Fred – I was going to tell the truth. I'd booked lunch out for me and Steve at the weekend, ensuring that we'd be nowhere near the kids when I finally said it. Ensuring too – though I wouldn't admit it to myself – that his sense of decorum would mean he wouldn't completely lose his mind.

'You still on for it?' I said, grabbing the remaining apple from the fruit bowl. Both of my daughters needed vitamins, I told myself.

'Wouldn't miss it,' she shot back, spooning up another mouthful.

* * *

I was the first one in the office, which was not an unusual occurrence at this point in the pregnancy. Tube, vomit, work, repeat. Lorna was next on the floor, trilling something familiar about 'early birds' that made me realize I'd actually parroted her phrase back to Georgie that morning. Next to appear was Jenna, early as ever without me having to ask. I smiled my weary gratitude, handing her a big pile of glossy print-outs to check over for me.

I felt like so much was communicated silently between us now, the intimacy almost greater for the lack of words. I couldn't, I knew, confirm the pregnancy until I'd told Steve – there were only so many betrayals I could subject our relationship to. But knowing she'd likely guessed but also respected my privacy allowed me to endure the cold wind that blew through the rest of my working hours. Try as I might, I couldn't seem to regain that easy camaraderie I used to have with my team. Everyone – including me – seemed to blame me for the endless hours we'd ground out on the Maple campaign, bonuses lost and tempers frayed.

At least, I thought, by the end of today it would be over. Our fate would be sealed. And it felt to me that we were in good shape; after all, Fred had as good as admitted at that heinous lunch that the upper tiers of the campaign were already in the bag. I hadn't gone as far as coaching Georgie, but hopefully the newfound warmth between us would mean that 'Cockatoo Girl' would come through for me, delivering the kind of Gen Z input he was after without pushing her agenda too far.

As the rest of the team filtered in, I tried to rally them the way I used to, gratified to see that it seemed to be working. We were all too frenetic to waste time on snark, and everyone wanted to race over the finish line. Anna and I even chatted companionably in the kitchen as we brewed hot drinks, me making an excuse for my newfound taste for green tea over coffee.

'Scarlett never stoops to making me anything,' she said, pulling a pair of mugs out of the cupboard for us both, 'but I feel like Jenna always telepathically knows when you need watering.'

I smiled smugly – it was true. 'She's amazing like that, though I do return the favour sometimes.' I subtly leaned my aching body against the dishwasher. 'But Lorna's pulled her off somewhere just now.'

Anna made a 'Lorna' face.

'Think it's just some boring technical thing in her contract now she's been here quite a few months.' I took a risk, briefly squeezing Anna's upper arm. I'd hated the frostiness that had prevailed between us over the last few weeks. 'Anyway, I'm glad. Gives me ten seconds to catch up with you.'

The smile Anna gave me contained multitudes. 'Me too,' she said, squeezing back.

Another win, I thought, as I crossed back to my workstation, my hands wrapped tightly around my mug so I didn't spill it. I was definitely coming out of the woods, ready to face up to the rest of my life as soon as the first beam of light hit my face. It took a while for Jenna to come back, but my trust in her was so absolute that it didn't bother me. *She must have a good reason*, I told myself. She wasn't like some of the other assistants I'd had, who would've been scrolling through TikTok or squirrelled away somewhere applying for other, better jobs while failing at this one.

I wobbled briefly when Martin and Bridget picked up Fred from reception, leading him across the floor on the way back upstairs to their office. He ground to a halt as he passed my desk, a cold look on his face. A stab of shame pierced me at the visceral memory of what his parting shot had been at lunch, and I scrambled to centre myself. I was excellent at what I did. I surely hadn't been assigned this campaign because of – because of *that*.

'Looking forward to finding out exactly what it is you've got in store for me, Sasha,' he said, his eyes like flint.

Every phrase that began to form in my throat felt like it had a double meaning.

'It's not just me,' I eventually retorted. I gestured to the room, but my eyes landed on Jenna. 'It's a team effort.'

'Well, let's see how you did with your team then.' He quivered with scorn. 'This time around.'

Bridget and Martin didn't react, although there was no way they weren't picking up on the way the temperature had plummeted between us since our cosy little Japanese. Instead, they swiftly carried on across the floor, throwing out a few casual pleasantries to the team like crusts of bread flung at a pond full of ducks.

I could see Jenna solemnly reading my face, and I threw her a grateful look, even though I knew she couldn't – and shouldn't – know what it was that had momentarily felled me. Still, her silent concern helped me rally, and soon I was gathering the group for a final upbeat run-through, reassuring each and every one of them that their excellent work would speak for itself.

And it certainly seemed to. We assembled back in the boardroom an hour later, Fred joined by a phalanx of Maple execs, many of them senior to him this time. As soon as I realized that, I allowed myself to breathe out – this needed to work for him just as much as it needed to work for me.

The Business and Premium run-throughs were up first. As soon as the first board hit the easel, my words unpacking the message, my finger lightly highlighting the tiny changes we'd made in response to their 'excellent feedback', I knew we'd hit a home run. I'd actually pulled back some of the bigger creative swings after that lunch, aware that all Fred really needed was to be flattered into feeling he was a fire starter. Allowing his bosses to see how he'd flexed his muscles, creating an extra circuit for us to pant around, would be enough of a win for him. And now they were all smiling and nodding, turning to Fred to congratulate him on how well he'd guided the process.

I rattled through the rest of the boards, imbued with restored professional confidence. I barely glanced at Fred: if I could just get us through this afternoon's circus, he'd no longer be the ringmaster and we could get on with being the functional and happy team we once were. I'd forget about him all over again, forget what he'd said about Martin and Bridget and go back to the seamless dance I'd perfected with them over many years. One thing I knew about myself was that I was an excellent forgetter.

I cast a quick glance at Jenna, right in the middle of the room this time around, no longer lurking on the sidelines. I'd use my upcoming win to persuade them to let me promote her to junior account manager – it would be a quick rise, but she deserved it. There was no way I'd be standing up here today, authoritatively leading this room of people through a stellar presentation, if it wasn't for her dogged backup during these difficult months.

* * *

I sailed into that dark basement high on my own supply. The first portion of the day had ultimately received a standing ovation, the 'questions' no more than a shower of compliments.

I could see that Georgie had parked herself quite near the front, and I gave her a discreet smile, which she returned, making sure not to make any kind of extended eye contact. Fred and the Maple execs would be angled to the side of the podium so that they could see the presentation and also take in the reaction of the young audience. He'd have a good angle on 'Cockatoo Girl' from there. He was a few feet away now, laughing and joking with his happy cohort.

My breezy confidence was short-lived. As my eyes surfed the rapidly filling room, I felt that familiar lurch in my stomach, bile creeping up my throat. Today had been too good to be true, the nausea minimal. Not now though – I quickly glanced up at the huge digital clock that was projected onto the wall. If I dashed upstairs to the disabled loo, I could hopefully deal with this fast enough to be back by the time the room was getting settled. I slipped through the heavy doors, hoping the low lighting would mean that no one missed me.

I was an expert by this point, wet wipes stowed in my desk drawer along with spare mascara and a portable toothbrush. I timed myself: in and out in eight minutes, with perfect eye make-up and minty breath to boot. As I leaned down to shove my emergency kit back in my drawer, the phone on my desk rang next to my ear, my hand automatically reaching for it before my brain had time to engage. It was almost the unfamiliarity of it, a callback to a time before lockdown when people didn't automatically dial your mobile.

'Hello?' I said.

'Is that . . .' The woman hesitated, only her breathing audible. 'Are you Jenna's boss?'

It was another kind of callback, the cadence she had. Her voice had the same soft vowels that Jenna's did, but it was older. It took me back to sixth form, sitting there in A-level English sulking about the loss of my London life as Mrs Maxwell droned on about *Sense and Sensibility* with that Stoke burr.

'Yes,' I said warily. 'This is Sasha Fulton. She's not actually here right now, and I—'

The woman cut across me this time, her tone sharper now. 'I know she'll have said she doesn't want to speak to me, but . . .'

I took a panicky look at the clock, cursing myself for picking up the phone.

'I'm sorry, I don't mean to be rude, but I've just ducked out of a really important meeting. Jenna's actually in it too. If you give me a name and number, I'll make sure she calls you straight back.'

The sigh she gave somehow managed to convey anger and despair in a single puff. 'She won't need a number, it's her mother. But if you tell her that, there's no way she'll call me back. Paul's already tried a million times – he was gonna just come to London, but I said she'd go ballistic. This was my last hope, calling her boss.'

I froze, my hand a stiff claw around the handset. I couldn't dig for more, not now. 'I'll ... I'll ...' I was stammering. 'I'll be sure to have her ring you.'

I dropped the receiver back onto the cradle like it was radioactive. It could've been a figure of speech – the same as if I'd ever had the confidence to call myself Georgie and Jack's 'mum' – but there was something about the way she'd said it that had hooked itself into me, started a pulse of unease that I couldn't attend to just yet.

* * *

The room was humming by the time I got back down there, the tables all ringed with teens, the Bright gang lined up at the front. Chloe gave me a panicky look, rushing over with a tech guy to clip a microphone to the front of my dress.

'Are you all right?' she hissed.

'Yes, I'm fine,' I said, more curtly than I intended. I forced softness, the call I'd taken still ringing in my ears. 'Let's just get this show on the road.'

She discreetly tilted her head. 'Have you seen ...'

My heart lurched as I looked over and discovered that the Maple gang had expanded. Fred had delivered on his threat: Michael Allpress, the CEO, was sitting to his left. And was that ... I tried not to goggle at them, but the sight of a lanky blond teenager right next to him on the other side was hard to miss. Archie was no longer the adorable moppet who stalked my guilty memories, he was the entitled joint puffer that Fred had proudly bandied around on his phone at lunch.

I pulled a face at Chloe, briefly squeezing her hand. 'I'll take it from here.'

The walk to the podium felt like a mile, even though it was only a few short steps. The lights went down as I crossed the floor, breathing myself into the zone and clutching my iPad as tightly as if I were a child with a favourite teddy bear on my first day of school.

'Well, this is exciting, isn't it?' I was starting strong with my first lie of the day. Or was it my tenth? It had become worryingly hard to keep a tally recently. 'We're here to hear from you,' I continued, gesturing to the crush of bodies out there in the audience, 'because you are, as we always tell you, the future. These sessions are about us learning from you, not you learning from us. And today we want to understand more about your feelings about the future of air travel. How do we square the reality of the climate emergency – and make no mistake that everyone in this room knows that it is an emergency, including these fine people from Maple ...' I swung my arm around towards them, my gaze somehow locking with Fred's as I did so. His face was a slab of concrete – I tried not to falter. 'But we also know that both the need and the *desire* to see the world isn't ending any time soon.'

There were a few whoops and claps at that, which gave me a bit of comfort, and I carried on to explain how we'd take them through the campaign and then throw it open to the floor for feedback. I invited Chloe up to help introduce our key asset, which I was hoping would prove to be the trump card. After weeks of fruitlessly tweaking shoutlines and comping stupid visuals of beavers (beavers were Canadian and cute, right?), I'd finally decided we had to stop talking down to our intended audience. The Trellicker Whisky sales had gone through the roof since our campaign had started, consumers seduced by the smouldering magic of Callum McBride striding around a drizzly Scottish island or making 'come to bed' eyes at them over a wee dram from the other side of a Tube platform. Why couldn't we do the same for this younger audience? Using a celebrity to promote an airline was out of fashion – something reminiscent of a youthful Roger Moore or Michael Caine holding a gin and tonic in a pinstriped suit – but I'd decided the retro vibe could be part of the idea's charm. Chloe had backed me right from the start, offsetting any eye-rolling from the rest of the team. Next, she'd pulled some social strings to persuade a young actor who'd done his time as Doctor Who before achieving global fame via a string of movies to front a dummy campaign for us. We'd shot something quite guerrilla the week before, refining it in the edit right up to the wire. Now we'd see if his endorsement would move the needle for this age group in the way we hoped it would.

'Hello, you,' Nonso started, and a massive cheer went up at the very sight of him.

I risked a tiny look at Fred, praying that his narcissism would mean that hearing his own phrase in the mouth of a stone-cold leading man would charm him. Yes – he was finally smiling, nudging Archie and nodding with satisfaction as the film continued. Nonso was lounging in an airline seat, one that we'd mocked up to look as close to the livery of the Maple economy cabin as we could. 'You have to admit that green really is my colour,' he said, leaning forward towards the camera. 'And I think we know each other well enough for me to guess it's yours too.' The smile he gave as he threw a rice cracker into his mouth could've melted an iceberg, although that obviously wasn't the intention. On he went, reeling off statistics about the reduction in carbon emissions from Maple's new fleet, with their recycled fuel and lighter planes, plus the opportunities for travellers to plant guilt-reducing trees for every flight they took. From his perfect lips, Maple's environmental commitments felt like an uplifting story of hope rather than a dry collection of greenwashing platitudes.

Next up we had Nonso ambling down the length of the cabin, interfering with the entertainment systems of various other passengers because he couldn't wait to watch the latest must-see content. I slightly cringed at that section – with no budget for actors just yet, we were reduced to Scarlett's thespian skills, along with other even less talented members of the team – but our audience seemed to find it hilarious in just the right way. Then we watched him scoffing the plant-based food and donning the eye mask from his environmentally friendly goody bag, as if the amenities of economy were just as special as what you'd find once you'd graduated to the prestige cabins. We'd gone even further and added an idea for an enhanced loyalty scheme for those passengers, so they felt like part of the Maple family right from the get-go, rather than a herd of cattle, farting methane. With all of that information imparted, the filmed portion was over.

I gripped the podium, my whole body shaking as applause echoed around the room. Chloe and I exchanged smiles of pure relief. 'Do you want to do the next bit?' I whispered, letting her take the audience through the mocked-up stills for the rest of the campaign: a pyjama-clad Nonso in an eye mask, just the left side tipped up as if he was whispering precious secrets about Maple's ethical supremacy in the airline business; Nonso stowing his beautiful vegan luggage in the overhead bin, turning around to share more information as to why you'd be a fool to fly with anyone but Maple. On and on it went, every image managing to feel inclusive and exclusive all at once. Looking at the rapt faces of our audience, their excited chatter rising in volume, I let myself start to believe we'd pulled this off.

Chloe looked over at me, gave a discreet thumbs-up. 'Let's take a few minutes to digest and then come back for feedback and questions,' she called.

I turned to her with glee the minute she stepped down from the podium. 'Well done us!' I crowed.

'Thank fuck,' she replied, her face slackening as the tension leached out of it, reminding me yet again how much everyone had suffered to get us here.

'You've been amazing,' I shouted after her as she headed off to get a coffee. I looked out at the audience to see if I could spot Georgie, but there was no sign of her. It was probably for the best, I reasoned, assuming she'd just gone to the loo.

As I turned back, Jenna appeared at my elbow. I'd pushed away that phone call, but now it was front and centre again. This wasn't the place to mention it. It surely had to be some kind of mistake, and I didn't want to trigger her grief the way I had that night at Deia with my clumsy questions.

'Well done, boss,' she said, grinning at me. 'You aced it.'

'It was a team effort,' I said. 'You know that, you were there.'

'Still – you're our fearless leader,' she said.

It jarred – it wasn't a very Jenna phrase. The unease I'd felt earlier started to ripple back through my aching body. I grabbed a nearby metal chair and landed myself on the hard surface.

'Don't call me "boss",' I said, faking a lightness I didn't feel. 'It makes me feel like an old man.'

'You're definitely not an old man,' she replied, her gaze drifting towards Fred, a slight smile playing across her lips. I felt my skin prickle as I watched her profile. She couldn't know, could she? I shook the thought away. Now I really was being paranoid.

It was hard to be authoritative from my semi-prone position, but I gave it a try. 'There's something I need to talk to you about later,' I said, brisk. 'A call I got.'

Something shifted in her expression. 'Anything I need to worry about?'

'Let's just talk about it afterwards,' I said, standing up and moving towards Bridget and Martin, their faces already wreathed in delighted smiles as they spotted my approach. Martin went as far as hugging me.

'We knew you'd pull that rabbit out of the hat,' he said.

'Yes, but it was touch and go there for a minute,' added Bridget, giving me that headmistress look I remembered from the days when getting her blow-dry booked within a tiny window of time was my primary professional objective.

Martin gave a tiny shake of his head. 'Let's just celebrate the win, shall we, darling?'

Before I could start decoding the exchange, Fred had popped up.

'Hello, you,' he said, going in for a hug too.

My body stiffened as I forced a smile. 'Pleased?' I asked, a single syllable all I wanted to give him.

'Delighted,' he drawled.

'In that case, I should get back up there,' I said, pulling my body away from him, conscious of the life that was contained within it. I didn't want him so close to either of us. 'Give you a bit more magic.'

* * *

EVERYTHING YOU HAVE 307

Chloe and I kept going with our strange double act. We must have looked pretty odd up there – her in one of her signature denim boiler suits, me in a twee floral kaftan – but we juggled the plaudits and questions with aplomb. The campaign couldn't have been landing better.

'If he trusts you,' said one teen in the front row, pointing directly at the Maple CEO, 'then I've gotta trust you.'

'And what does trust mean to you?' I asked him, leaning forward towards him as if he was some kind of philosophical genius.

He chewed his knuckle, thinking for a second. He was small and intense, a yellow woolly hat pulled low over his brow. 'You want to do something different. It's not just about making money out of people and shitting on the planet.'

My eyes met Chloe's for a brief, triumphant second. He could have been a plant, but he wasn't.

'Thank you,' I said, moving on to the next waving hand. 'Let's hear from you in the third row.'

On and on it went, ideas and observations flying around, the whole room bubbling with a warm and excited energy. There were a handful of people who said they would never fly, but even they acknowledged that Maple was doing something worthwhile by committing to the airline reaching net zero and setting an example to the rest of the industry. I waited for Georgie to speak, almost hoping she would after all of Fred's excitement about her, but she didn't once raise her hand, staying hunched and insular in her seat. After an hour, it was time to wrap it up.

'We can't thank you enough for bringing so much to this,' I told the assembled crowd. 'Your feedback on the campaign is invaluable. We wanted to hear directly from you – the travellers of the future – so it's not just us in our boardroom or Maple in their fancy offices—'

And then there was Fred, bouncing up onto the stage in his lurid yellow trainers like he was some kind of prophet. He grabbed the mic that had been taken around the audience and yelled into it like he was headlining Glastonbury.

'You ARE the fucking future!' he yelled. I snuck a look at Archie, who was visibly cringing with embarrassment at the sight of his delusional dad, even though this whole performance was most likely designed solely to impress him. 'We hear you, we know our generation failed you and we WILL make amends.'

There was a smattering of slightly bemused applause before a voice cut across the noise.

'No, you don't!' shouted Georgie, leaping to her feet and starting to push her way towards the front. I watched her storming towards us, feeling like I was having an out of body experience. This couldn't be happening. 'You don't *hear* us. Don't lie to us. Stop patronizing us and talking down to us, when the world's on fire.'

I forced myself to look away from her angry purple face, so different from the smiley, diligent girl I'd chatted to at the kitchen table this morning. I couldn't allow the hurt right now, but the fact that she'd been faking all that warmth that I'd been obliviously basking in was absolutely devastating.

Fred gave an uncertain grin, unsure whether this was performance art or anarchy. 'Bit of healthy debate, that's why we're here. I remember you from last time . . .'

I urgently needed to extinguish this fire without anyone knowing I was the one who'd lit the touchpaper. I took a step towards Georgie.

'Why don't you just sit down, and we'll all listen to your feedback in the same way we've listened to everyone else's?'

The look of pure hatred on her face made me physically

recoil. 'You don't get to silence me anymore,' she hissed. 'Not me or anyone else.' She turned back towards the audience. 'Listen up, sheeple, they're making you their slaves. They're manipulating you with celebrities and pretty fucking pictures so you'll help them spread their lies. Airlines are the worst for fucking with the stats so they don't get held accountable, but the planet is dying because they're killing it. They're murdering cunts, and you're all falling for it!'

Bridget and Martin had stood up now. They were staring over at me, silently urging me to contain the situation. This didn't feel like healthy debate taken a little too far. Instead, there was a febrile energy rippling through the room, frenzied chatter swelling up from the teenage audience.

'Fuck you bitch, saying we're stupid,' someone shouted.

I reached out a hand, laid it on Georgie's shaking arm. 'Let's just talk about this calmly . . .'

She flung her arm out so violently that it grazed my face. My body lurched, and I just about stopped myself falling backwards, automatically wrapping a protective hand around my belly. I heard Chloe gasp behind me, looking around the room as if she was trying to get us some kind of physical backup. I was furious with Georgie, but I also didn't want it to get as bad for her as it might if this escalated. I could barely recognize her – this wasn't angsty teenage hurt funnelled into activism, it was a violent rage. How had she got to this place?

I leaned forward, close enough that she had to look at me. 'Georgie . . .' I said, very quietly.

'Now she's trying to silence me again,' she announced to the room, spinning away. 'No – she *needs* to silence me again. Because I know all her dirty little secrets. How they . . .' She pointed at Fred, and then gestured to the group of execs on the side of the stage. 'How they talk about us. They don't give

a fuck about climate change, they just want to rape the earth
and get rich. It's just a joke to them – they'll be dead before we
fry.' She turned back towards me, radiating pure venom. 'And
she's my stepmum even if she doesn't want anyone to know it,
so trust me, I know *exactly* what they say when we can't hear.'
She waved an angry finger between me and Fred, spittle erupting from her mouth. 'What you say to your fucking *boyfriend*.'

For a second, it was if the world had ceased to turn. There
was pure silence, only me in a bubble of stillness. Then the
shock broke, and I was plunged into pandemonium. The audience were shouting and catcalling, the whole Bright team
sat open-mouthed with shock. Martin and Bridget's faces
were two furious masks and Fred – he simply stared at me in
horrified disbelief.

'Georgie, stop this now,' I said, gripping her arm tightly this
time. 'You need to calm down and get a hold of yourself.'

Donovan and Pete were up from their seats and determinedly moving towards the stage now, obviously having
decided it was time to physically intervene. Georgie must've
spotted them at the same time I did. She yanked herself away
from me and bolted across the stage. And then, suddenly, the
room began to fill with smoke.

'I told you it was an emergency,' she shouted, as the fire
alarm began to wail, panicked bodies racing for the exit.

JENNA

Jenna sat stock-still in the midst of the smoky chaos, listening to the ridiculous shrieks coming from the crowd. People were starting to shove their way out, but she stayed frozen for a second, a still point in a storm. She was waiting for a sense of triumph to kick in, but so far it felt like a dud drug, one that never quite delivered the high it was designed for. Maybe it was the news about the phone call that was stealing her buzz.

'What are you doing?' hissed Chloe, looking down at her with that same sour-milk sneer she'd treated Jenna to when she'd first tipped up at Bright. 'They're evacuating the building.'

Jenna forced a look of shock onto her face. 'Fuck, sorry. I couldn't breathe. I felt like I might be having a panic attack.'

Chloe's face softened at that – mental health was a button you could push with reliable results around here. Jenna shoved back her chair and followed her as she raced towards the door.

She wanted to catch up with Sasha. Her face had been a picture.

SASHA

It's tempting to crown the night after the Elevate meeting as the worst one of my life, but that might not be true. Sometimes, sitting here alone in the semi-darkness, the room illuminated by the ugly sodium glow of the street lamps or the relentless churn of the Netflix dating shows I used to find funny and now find tragic, I start to think that it's only now I've hit the very worst.

Georgie used the smoky chaos she'd created to disappear from the building. Who knew that a box of indoor fireworks, bought with a single click on Amazon, could create so much panic? The fire alarm was set off by one of the traumatized Maple execs, and the entire building was evacuated. Their team disappeared without a word, Fred not even looking back at me, and then Lorna marched over to tell us that we were all being sent home for the day. Bridget and Martin had already summoned their chauffeured car; I tried to gabble an apology as they climbed in, but they barely acknowledged me.

As the firemen left, I tried to pull my team together for a brief huddle, telling them that I'd explain more when we were back in the office, but their wariness and mistrust was like a mushroom cloud by now. They barely spoke, all clearly desperate to escape. As I stood on the corner looking for a black cab,

Jenna walked past me, heading off for the Tube. She looked – was she almost cheerful?

'Do you want me to wait with you?' she asked.

I didn't have enough energy left to raise the weird phone call with her. Her 'mum' would have to wait a day.

'Don't worry,' I said, scanning the busy road. The wait was actually welcome; the second I was inside a cab I would have to call Steve and drop the bomb about what Georgie had done.

'What a shitshow!' she added, pulling her coat around her.

The anorak appeared to have gone, replaced by a beige trench that I might even have considered wearing myself. Her once pearly pink nails were painted a shade of matte grey that made them look like they'd been manicured in some hip salon in Old Street. And Jenna herself seemed relaxed and confident, free of the shell shock that had felled the rest of us. That prickling unease had started to creep its way back up my spine.

'I don't know if a shitshow is really the phrase I'd choose. It's a professional disaster, and Georgie's obviously in some profound distress.'

'Sorry, bad choice of words.' She gave a rueful smile. 'I guess I just wish I'd been able to keep helping you manage her.'

Now the sight of a cab was a cause for celebration, a tinny fakeness to her words jangling in my ears. I pulled open the door and cocooned myself inside, watching her determined stride towards the Tube out of the back window until she disappeared from view.

* * *

My phone had still been on silent when I'd got into the cab, so I'd missed the fact that Steve had beaten me to it. No, Georgie had beaten me to it. She'd been canny enough to go home and get to her dad before I could, which meant that he was already ringing me off the hook.

He appeared in the hallway at the sound of the front door closing behind me. As soon as I saw the look of fury and betrayal on his face, I knew I had to go on the offensive.

'Steve, what she did today was outrageous – I'll probably lose my job. She might have been arrested if she wasn't my stepdaughter. And if she's told you some crap about me having an affair, it's just bullshit.'

Where had she got that from? It was the shot of truth that ran through the lie that made it so chilling. Everything suddenly felt swathed in fog, like I could see the outline of things but not detect their full form.

Steve looked grave, his skin grey and pallid. 'Sasha, are you pregnant? Just tell me the truth. No more lies.'

I looked back at him, my face crumpling. Georgie must've been holding onto that suspicion for months now, ever since that night I'd walked out of the house after she'd found the drugs. I sank down onto the little velvet chaise longue that sat halfway down the hall. 'Yes,' I whispered.

The sound he made was somewhere between a howl and a scream. 'How could you do that to me? How could you go behind my back, and . . . and—'

I cut across him. 'You said! You said if it happened naturally, you'd want us to go through with it. That you'd love her. Why do I have to be punished just because my body refuses to fucking work like other people's?' I stared up at him, anger and guilt duking it out inside. 'I need this. It was my last chance. I just needed you to let me have this.'

I'd never heard Steve raise his voice the way he did then. 'I said no! What part of that did you fail to understand? I said NO! I didn't want to have this baby.'

Tears were streaming down my face by now, the full impact of what I'd done finally hitting me. This wasn't how it was meant to be. 'But you did at first. When we lost the first one. And you'll love her, I promise you you'll love her.' I crossed to where he stood on the opposite side of the hall and grabbed for his shirt. He pushed me away, refusing to look at me. 'You're such an amazing dad . . .'

He shook his head in disbelief. 'To the children I actually wanted. This isn't even your child. It's MY child, and it's not yours. You had no right to do this.'

Now I was the one shaking my head in disbelief; the idea that the little life stirring inside my body was somehow not my child was ridiculous to me by now. Before I could formulate a response, Georgie's head appeared, poking around from the stairs that led up from the kitchen.

'Georgie, just go away,' I shouted. 'I don't want to set eyes on you right now. What you did today was unforgivable.'

I saw the word land on each of them simultaneously, the painful irony of me throwing moral accusations. I was struck by something else too: how Steve's features were reincarnated in Georgie's – their hazel eyes widening in tandem, the jutting square that their chins made. In that sense, what he was saying was true. My baby would be part of their biological tribe, not mine. It winded me, that stark reminder, and I slumped downwards into my seat again.

'What *you* did to Dad was unforgivable,' Georgie shot back, jabbing a finger in my direction. 'You are pregnant, aren't you? And it's not even his! That Fred guy—'

'I'm not having an affair with Fred,' I said, feeling a blush creep up my face.

Steve's words layered over mine. 'It is my baby,' he said, without any pleasure. 'I just didn't know we were having it.' He took in my flushed cheeks, looking at me with a cold mistrust I'd never before felt from him. It felt far more dangerous than anger. 'And who the fuck is Fred?'

I batted away the question, focused instead on the words that had preceded it. 'Her,' I said quietly.

'Do you ... Do we know that?' asked Steve, with infinite weariness.

'We do,' I said, a hand on my stomach. Maddi had been there for the latest appointment too, just a few days earlier. Georgie stared at me, the reality of it beginning to hit her.

Steve leaned back against the wall next to the chaise. He was a few short inches away, touching distance, but the space between us was stretching into infinity. 'All those sessions with Ruth. You've sat there, knowing this, treating me like a fucking idiot.' He shook his head again. 'Me sitting there, begging you to be honest. To be vulnerable, when all you've been doing is trying to get me to sign up to a life you've already decided on. What a fucking joke.'

Tears streamed down my cheeks again. 'I wanted to tell you so much. I kept trying to find the words, but I just ... I just couldn't bear to break us apart again.'

Steve looked down at me with a kind of disgusted incomprehension that was entirely justified; I knew that my magical thinking sounded more like narcissistic delusion when I said it out loud. I scrabbled in my bag for a tissue, desperate for an excuse to turn away.

'Georgie, just go, will you?' I said. 'I'll speak to you later. Me and your dad need to talk in private.'

Steve turned to her, his tone immediately softer. 'You don't have to go if you don't want to,' he said. 'This concerns all of us.'

Now it was me who looked at him in disbelief. They were

closing ranks already. Their house, their family. I would soon be catapulted right out of it.

I was pleading now, increasingly desperate. 'I'm so sorry, Steve. You can't understand ...' I was hiccupping the words out through my tears. 'You've got them. You didn't even have to think about it. I need to be a mum. It can't just be me.' I thought I saw hurt sweep across Georgie's face before her features hardened again. 'Georgie, I'm sorry,' I sobbed. 'It's not like I don't love you and Jack. It's just ...'

Her response was predictable. 'I don't give a fuck.' This time, I'd lost her for good.

'I know how betrayed you feel,' I said to Steve, searching his face through the blur of my tears. 'How angry. I shouldn't have done it, I know that. But it was like I was on a train I couldn't get off. And I thought ... I thought ...' I petered out, my breath catching in my chest. 'I just thought it would be okay. That we'd be okay, because we love each other so much.'

His face was like a tombstone, the grave of our marriage. 'But if you loved me like you say you do, you'd never have done this. Love is a verb, not some meaningless noun you throw at some fucking campaign for vodka or petrol or whatever it is you're peddling this week. I'm not a client you need to get around. I was meant to be your partner.'

Was. One devastating syllable.

'I'm going to get myself a glass of water and then one of us needs to leave. I don't want to throw you out, but I can't be in your airspace and I doubt you and Georgie want to order pizza together.'

'Steve ...'

As he headed towards the stairs, I clawed at the back of his shirt, all dignity deserting me. His body was like a rigid column, a fortress against me. I could hardly blame him; in that moment my shame felt like a life sentence. Then it was just Georgie and I, marooned in the space.

'How long have you known?' I choked out quietly. 'I know you went through the bathroom cabinet that night we came back from the hotel. Why didn't you say anything to him then?'

'What?'

I'd lived with her long enough – loved her, in my own muddled way, long enough – to know that her look of confusion wasn't fake.

'My bathroom cabinet. The fertility drugs were in there. They'd been taken out – the doors were open.'

Something akin to shock crossed her face. It silenced her momentarily – she just stood there staring at me, like she was trying to work something out.

'I'm not angry about it anymore,' I added. 'You don't have to lie to me.'

She shook her head, like she was desperate to move on. 'I just guessed. You look like a stick insect normally, and now you're like . . . you're like a fat one.'

Something wasn't right here, but I was still groping my way through the fog, my own sense of shock making it thicker.

'And why did you say that stuff about Fred? I would never cheat on your dad.' Again, that look – furtive and almost frightened. 'Where did you get that idea from?'

When she replied, the words came tumbling out too fast to be convincing. 'I just wanted to make it worse for you. And for him and all his fucking corporate mates. The way you and Dad laugh at me – it's what you all think.'

'I'm sorry if it's ever felt like that. I do respect you for having principles. For – for not eating meat and wearing vegan trainers. I . . . I just haven't always known how to say that. How to talk to you.'

Georgie's eyes were round and wet as she looked at me. She looked so young right then, almost as if she were a Russian doll and I'd somehow reached inside and found a smaller version – the buck-toothed ten-year-old of our first tentative meeting. The sense of what I might be losing clutched at my heart, but I couldn't lose myself to sadness now. I had to force this conversation to its end and respect the fact that right now Steve couldn't stand for us to be under the same roof.

'Is that really why you said it? You were just making it up?' I paused, pushing my hair off my hot, damp face. 'I'm probably going to lose my job because of all of this . . .'

Her chin jutted out again, her jaw rigid, like the words were hard to get out. 'Yes,' she said, her voice little more than a whisper. 'That's why I did it.'

Something in her tone was discordant, like she was reading from a script that she'd only just been given. We looked at each other for a long, silent second before her eyes flicked down to the carpet, as if there was something fascinating to see there.

My focus was beginning to sharpen now. She wasn't telling me the whole truth, and the accusation about Fred was the part that made me most suspicious. She'd barely seen the two of us together, but Jenna was another story. She never stopped reading the room, and I feared Fred and I had given her plenty of material.

'Georgie, what's the deal with you and Jenna? Are you still seeing her?'

Her face was mutinous. 'You said she *couldn't* see me.'

I made my voice deliberately soft. 'I know, and I'm sorry about that. But that's not an answer to my question. It's important.'

That little girl was before me again. The one who used to push sticky fingers into my expensive moisturizer and swear blind she hadn't. 'I . . . I didn't . . .'

But before my interrogation could reach its conclusion, Steve's heavy tread came up the stairs.

'Sasha, please – I'll go if that's better, but I have to have space from you now.'

'Okay, okay,' I said, my palms raised in defeat, moving to the flight of stairs that reached up to our bedroom. His bedroom? Yet again, I shoved clothes and toiletries into a bag, my hands shaking uncontrollably. It was sad how much I'd learned from my last moonlight flit – I found a proper suitcase this time, filling it to the brim. When the cab arrived, Steve didn't come upstairs from the basement, but to my surprise Georgie appeared in the hall.

'You shouldn't carry that,' she said, grappling with the case.

Tears sprang into my eyes at the unexpected kindness as we wrestled it into the cab together. 'I love you, Georgie,' I said. 'As a verb, even if you didn't always realize it.'

'I did know that,' she said, so quietly I wondered if I'd mis-heard, before she scurried back towards the house.

Once I was inside the cab I couldn't stop staring out of the window, watching the door close on a life I'd loved and some-how seemed to have left for dead.

JENNA

'Double shot latte, please' said Jenna, when she finally reached the front of the queue. It always snaked out of the door at this time of the morning.

'Decaf, right?' said the bearded barista, giving her a harassed grin that conveyed pride in his excellent memory of her order history.

'Nah, caffeinated today,' said Jenna, grinning back. He was pretty hot. She'd been too distracted to notice things like that these last few months.

He hadn't stopped twinkling yet. 'You're full of surprises. What next – whole milk instead of oat?'

She took a second to think about that one.

'You know what, I'll have oat,' she said, getting out her debit card, ready to tap. She'd been paid on Monday, so she could at least guarantee it would work.

It was extravagant, but after all, today was the first day of the rest of her life.

SASHA

The first time I tapped my pass on the turnstile, I assumed I must've hit it at a weird angle. By the third attempt, I was starting to feel unnerved.

'Cherish, can you just let me through?' I said to the receptionist, immediately clocking the way she cringed at my request. 'Or call Jenna for me?'

'Yeah, just wait one minute,' she said, virtually ripping her phone off the cradle. 'Sasha's here,' she muttered into it.

It wasn't Jenna who appeared, but Lorna, dressed in an unpleasant mustard-coloured blazer. As soon as I set eyes on her, my heart begun to plummet as if it was in a broken elevator hurtling towards the basement.

'Good morning, Sasha,' she said, cocking her head to look down at me as if I was a naughty toddler who needed firm handling. 'Would you like to just come through with me?'

There was nothing I would've liked less, but her tone made it clear it was an instruction, not an invitation. As I followed her across the floor, my gaze trained forwards so I wouldn't make eye contact with any of my team, I couldn't help but flick a look towards my own desk, Jenna's adjacent to it. She was staring intently at her screen, a cup of coffee with that distinctive inky Squirrel stamp steaming at her elbow. I felt my skin prickle at the sight of her, the hairs on my arms standing up to attention.

When we reached Lorna's office, she gestured to the chair opposite her desk, then paused to eyeball the small sofa. 'Would you prefer something more comfortable?' she said, suddenly awkward.

'A chair's fine,' I snapped, sitting down ramrod straight as she picked her way around her desk to her own seat.

As she did so, I snuck a look at the couple of framed pictures she had turned towards her on the surface. I could see a corner of her wedding photo – a nasty-looking meringue outside a suburban church – as well as a picture of her ten-year-old twins in their school uniforms, metal train-track braces exposed by their obedient grins. How was it that I both emphatically didn't want her life and desperately envied it? She leaned forward, her face arranged into a serious expression.

'Sasha, I'm sorry that we had to suspend your access to the building today, but I'm afraid your status as an employee of Bright has changed.'

The room went dark for a second, my whole body contracting with shock.

'What ... they're firing me? They can't do that – I've been here more than twenty years!'

The number was shocking in itself; I'd lived virtually my entire adult life by Bright's unspoken rules, Bridget and Martin a strange pair of professional parents.

'I appreciate it's a shock,' said Lorna, deliberately holding eye contact. 'And if you need to take a few moments to process the news, I can leave the room before we talk further.'

Fury surged up inside me now. I couldn't let this happen. I couldn't let her do this to me.

'I appreciate that yesterday wasn't my finest hour, and the

fact that Georgie's my stepdaughter reflects very badly on me.
But there are some mitigating circumstances around it that
no one's aware of.' My voice was rising against my will. 'I'd
hoped to deal with this myself in a managerial context, but
I've uncovered some behaviour from Jenna Hall that has a real
bearing on what happened.'

Lorna wasn't impressed by my show of strength; instead, it
had the opposite effect. Her expression shifted to something
close to pity.

I tried to force myself to stay calm. 'Look, I know it sounds
pathetic, blame the assistant, but I think she's been worming
her way into my life to undermine me, and—'

Lorna's hand popped up like a stop sign. 'Let's just slow
down here, Sasha. You seem very emotional.' I gritted my teeth
to stop myself from shouting over her. 'Jenna's already made
us aware of the tensions within the professional relationship.'

'She's done what?' I paused, my brain whirring. 'Oh, so
after it kicked off, she came running to you to try and cover
her tracks and make sure her job was safe?'

Lorna's hand swung up again. 'No. She came to me earlier
in the day with her concerns.'

I wagged a finger back at her. 'Well, there's your smoking
gun right there. She knew exactly what was going to go down
because she'd been winding Georgie up and feeding her confidential information about the campaign. She'd definitely
thought through the timing of when to come to you.'

That infuriating, pitying smile was back. 'In fact, the first
time Jenna raised her concerns about the lack of professional
boundaries was over three months ago. This has clearly been
an ongoing problem.'

I sank back in my seat, pinioned by a profound sense of
betrayal. She'd been sneaking off to complain about me to HR

while she was sipping my wine and wearing my clothes. And, even worse, witnessing me heaving my guts up in the disabled toilets while my whole team turned their backs. How could I have been such an idiot?

But more than that – why did she hate me so much? My mind started spinning backwards, trying to audit our relationship in a few snatched seconds. I'd been good to her, hadn't I? I'd plucked her application out of the slush pile and anointed her over infinitely more qualified candidates. I'd encouraged her and listened to her. She'd told me again and again how much she liked working for me, how I'd changed her life. But if she'd been working to undermine me for months, the rot must have set in when she was barely through the door. It just didn't make sense. This wasn't climate rage or irritation about my weird coffee order – there was something fundamental here that I didn't understand yet. That I was going to need to figure out.

'The lack of professional boundaries?' I spat. 'All I've tried to do is be a mentor to her the way ...' The words were suddenly thick in my throat. 'The way Bridget and Martin were to me.'

Lorna left a significant pause before she continued. 'But, Sasha, you yourself are sitting here making accusations about your assistant's improper relationship with your stepdaughter when clearly the person who initiated the relationship between the two of them was you. The individual who held the power in the professional dynamic.'

Words were streaming out of me now, any semblance of calm long gone. 'She *asked* to meet with Georgie – I never suggested it. And I put a stop to the relationship weeks and weeks ago. But she's been continuing to see her behind my back – the bullshit Georgie was spouting yesterday came straight from

Jenna. She's set her up to tank the Maple campaign – that's gross misconduct right there!'

Lorna picked up a silver ballpoint pen, scribbling a couple of notes on the pad that lay on her desk, the faint rustle of the paper the only sound that penetrated the humid silence.

'But, of course, Georgina never should have been there in the first place,' she said eventually, that implacable smile once again fixed on her face. 'Elevate's sole purpose is to create access for underrepresented communities. The fact that you smuggled her onto the list is in itself professional misconduct, and a deeply disappointing swerve from Bright's ethical commitments from a senior member of staff.' Her eyes were like chinks of ice. 'Bridget and Martin only decided not to escalate the public order aspect of it because of their professional respect for you.'

My heart was thumping so hard it felt like it might leap out of my chest.

'Oh, come on, it was a couple of firecrackers from Amazon. The issue here is Jenna Hall. I can't believe you're taking the word of an . . . an *assistant* over the word of a creative director. I've delivered campaign after campaign, made so much money for them . . .'

'Bright is committed to a safe working environment for all,' Lorna intoned piously. 'Status is irrelevant. Bullying of any form is taken very seriously by our founders.'

The time Martin threw his phone receiver so hard at the assistant who followed my tenure that his temple was left with a blue-black bruise was obviously a piece of history that had been wiped from the records. It definitely violated item nine on the hallowed list of ethics – *Above all, be kind*. But then, I guess I hadn't resigned in solidarity. I'd helped to hold up the edifice.

'I never bullied her! If anything, I've been too nice to her.

She's the one casting aspersions about my relationship with a . . . with a client.'

I wasn't too keen to go there, particularly when I couldn't prove that Jenna was behind what Georgie had implied about Fred. Still, I couldn't help but notice how Lorna stiffened at the comment.

I pressed on. 'What is she actually accusing me of? Just spell out for me what it is I'm supposed to have done.'

'Jenna has stated that the working environment has felt unsafe for her for much of her time working for you.'

'Unsafe?!'

Lorna's fingers steepled the way Ruth's did when she was gearing up for a truth bomb.

'We've already discussed your encouragement of her relationship with your stepdaughter. You also insisted on a night out in a bar, even though she's virtually teetotal, and then went on to interrogate her about her sexual preferences.'

'That's bullshit, it – it was a conversation. She was asking how I met my husband—'

Lorna was on a roll by now. 'You undermined her peers – such as Scarlett Cummings – to her, effectively making her keep secrets. You then went on to undermine Jenna herself, criticizing her appearance and providing *your own clothes* for her to wear in a key meeting.'

'She's broke! I was trying to help her—'

'She found it extremely triggering. She felt as if she was being targeted for her socioeconomic background. Furthermore, she felt she was publicly humiliated in that Maple meeting in August as a punishment for previously expressing to you her ethical stance on air travel.'

'That's bullshit too. All I did was gently remind her that we were working on a campaign for an airline, so we needed to deliver on it. And in the meeting, I was trying to increase her visibility within the company. Mentoring her again.'

The more visibly distressed I became, the smugger Lorna looked. 'Other people corroborated her take on that incident.'

'What, Scarlett?'

'I can't expose confidential feedback. But I do need to tell you that Scarlett made a similar complaint about feeling humiliated by you in front of her colleagues.' She pulled herself a little taller in her seat. 'A pattern has emerged that we have a duty to address.'

My head dropped forward like my neck could no longer support its weight. 'I mean, that wasn't my finest professional hour. But I've been going ...' I knew I mustn't choke up. 'I've been going through a lot personally, and we were under unbearable pressure as a team. The last thing I needed was Scarlett shouting about the evils of air travel when we were trying to crack how to sell it.'

I knew by now that I was digging my own grave, and yet I couldn't seem to put down the shovel. Why had Martin and Bridget let it get this far? Of course, they'd be furious with me for yesterday's debacle, but even if their loyalty was scant, they cared about the bottom line. And it certainly mattered more to them than the welfare of an assistant they could barely pick out in a line-up.

Lorna picked up the silver pen again as if it was a prop, her face arranged into a sorrowful moue. 'Lastly, you mentioned the whispers around your relationship with Fred Williamson. Jenna did also cite an uncomfortably personal atmosphere between the two of you, which heightened her sense of your inability to hold appropriate boundaries. She says you obsessively discussed him with her in a way that felt unrelated to your professional relationship with him.'

She'd been all over that situation from the outset, sidling up to us whenever she could and slyly pushing me to spill my guts. Still, Lorna's sanctimonious twisting of facts was giving me pause.

Fred was part of this, I was sure of it, still poisoning my life all these years later. If he was in one of his titanic rages about what had been said in the Maple presentation in front of his son, he'd be asking Bridget and Martin for a head on a stick. Right now, that head was mine.

I dipped my face again, letting the tears I'd been locking so tightly inside finally fall. Then I jerked my wet cheeks upwards, looking straight into Lorna's eyes.

'I'd like to tell you what I've found triggering. Being forced to work on a campaign for a man who wielded his professional power over me in my twenties to coerce me into an extra-marital affair while we were working here at Bright. An affair that Martin and Bridget were well aware of at the time. Who knows, it might even be why they assigned this campaign to me.'

For the first time since we'd sat down, Lorna's self-assurance started to slip. 'That's . . . That's a very serious accusation.'

'That's exactly why I wouldn't make it lightly,' I said, my steel returning. 'Fred Williamson himself recently implied that it was the reason why I was put on this campaign. It's been extremely triggering. I've had to undertake extensive therapy to revisit the original trauma.' Finally I was finding a reason to appreciate Ruth. 'I certainly wouldn't want to have to reactivate it by recounting it in an employment tribunal.'

I took a sip from the glass of water that Lorna had thoughtfully left out for me before the meeting had even begun, watching her from over the rim.

'I did also wonder if you're aware that I'm pregnant – I can't see any other reason you'd have suggested sitting on the sofa when I came in. Jenna found out by ambushing me in the toilets, but I imagine she's implied that I volunteered the information. In fact, it was her who violated MY boundaries on that occasion.'

Lorna's game face was slipping: I'd obviously hit the bullseye with that one.

'Congratulations,' she said, in the least congratulatory tone imaginable.

'If you did know that – and I'm almost sure you did – it's not going to work in Bright's favour if you're trying to dismiss me without a mutually agreed settlement.'

We stared at each other as if it was a gun fight.

'We haven't even touched on the nature of the settlement yet, have we?' Lorna finally said, her voice brittle. 'Bright will certainly want to properly compensate you for your many years of service.'

'For my loyalty,' I added lightly.

'Absolutely,' she replied, dredging up a pleasant smile.

I'd won, but it was a single battle. There was a war I was yet to fight.

JENNA

At the sight of Sasha crossing the office for a second time, Lorna so close behind her that she looked like a skirt-suited prison guard, her assistant's heartbeat started to race. Jenna stared straight ahead at her screen, willing her boss (her ex-boss?) to disappear through the double doors, but instead Sasha swerved erratically towards her workstation. Her cheeks were flushed, her eyes glittering with a *fuck you* kind of fury. Reaching her desk, she yanked open the top drawer, piling perfume and vitamin bottles into her huge caramel-leather handbag. It was weirdly intimate, watching her scoop up the particles of her life like that. Jenna swallowed, suddenly shaken by the brutality of the goodbye that she herself had initiated.

Sasha's face turned sideways, words leaking from the side of her mouth. 'Your mum called,' she hissed. 'It seemed like she really wants to talk to you.'

Other staff were looking over by now, trying and failing to keep their glances subtle. Chloe and Anna were pale with shock, while Pete's mouth hung open. Sasha didn't even notice, wholly focused on Jenna.

Jenna froze. Her palms felt clammy, her heart pounding like a drum. She was safe now, right? Sasha's authority over her was finished. 'I don't know what you mean,' she said, forcing a cheeriness that was the exact opposite of how she felt. 'Are you okay, Sasha?'

Sasha risked turning her head to look directly at her assistant, her eyes narrowed with such hatred that Jenna drew back. 'I know exactly what you did to me,' she spat. 'Don't think this is the end of it.'

A nervous-looking Lorna stepped forward, so she was only a foot away.

'We can send on anything you can't pack up now,' she said to Sasha, looking like she might start shaking her drawers directly into her handbag to get the job done.

Sasha straightened up, her face a mask. Jenna had always admired that poise of hers, that natural authority that she could summon up at a moment's notice. She still admired it now.

'I'm ready to go,' she said, her voice clipped, and turned on her heel to stride out.

Jenna watched her boss's retreating back, waiting for her heart rate to slow to a normal pace. It took a while; even after Sasha was long gone, it was hard to drag her eyes away from the oblong of the door, to truly believe that Sasha wouldn't march straight back through it, chattering away through her snow-white AirPods, a beetroot juice clutched in her right hand. Jenna looked down at the smooth surface of her desk, worried that a rogue tear might splash down onto it like it had that night at Deia.

Sasha was wrong about one thing: she didn't know exactly what Jenna had done. Or at least, she didn't know *why*.

SASHA

The next couple of months were a strange kind of twilight zone. Nothing of my previous life existed anymore, all of it swept away and replaced by the new life that fluttered and kicked inside of me. I talked to her as I squeezed lemon juice into hot water or brushed my teeth, hoping she didn't feel the pressure of being a counterweight for so much.

These 'conversations' were one of the only strategies I had to stifle my incessant ranting. I'd taken to raging out loud against Jenna, stating my innocence and threatening vengeance, my words echoing off the blank walls of the tiny little flat. None of it did any good – it wasn't like Georgie was ready to talk, and I'd accepted the hefty payoff that Bright had offered on the back of my veiled threats, signing a non-disclosure agreement that I couldn't afford to break. I wasn't meant to have contact with anyone within the organization, but Anna and I had exchanged a few texts; it was a dark day when I heard that the Maple campaign was going full steam ahead, Jenna hailed as its lynchpin thanks to the 'continuity' she offered. When I offered a pithy bit of feedback on that decision, Anna declined to reply. Who could blame her – even I could see I was turning into some contemporary version of a madwoman in an attic, sustaining myself with lumps of cheese eaten directly from the fridge and talking into thin air. Considering the state I was in, it was extraordinary to think that I'd be allowed to take sole charge of another human being in three short months.

That wasn't entirely true. Steve was far too decent to abandon his unborn child, even if he currently wanted nothing to do with her mother. The two of us were back on Ruth's sofa, except now it was me, not him, who was desperate to be there, craving any kind of contact I could get. He was there to work out how we could successfully co-parent after such a massive betrayal, with a subcategory of exploring how it was possible to have a 'loving divorce'. I, meanwhile, attended with the sole purpose of trying to persuade him to take me back. The sessions would most likely only limp on until the baby was born, but by now the idea of losing this weekly window onto his emotions, however painful it often was, seemed like too much to bear. I could hardly blame him for his attitude to our marriage – I hated myself almost as much as he hated me.

On this particular Wednesday, I was feeling particularly bleak. I let myself be sucked down the escalator into the Tube at Camden Town (my black cab habit had ended – the Bright payout needed to last) and sat on the train as it chugged towards Holland Park. Huffing and puffing between lines at Euston, I spotted a short brunette in a beige raincoat, and quickened my lumbering pace. Of course, it wasn't Jenna, which I realized when I drew close – it was nothing more than another reminder of how dangerously obsessed I'd become.

I heaved myself onto the next train, suddenly struck by the painful irony that the last person I'd had such a toxic, twisted bond with was Fred himself. And before that – the echo reverberated all the way into my painful childhood ... It was a thought I was still wrestling with when I landed heavily on Ruth's awful floral cushions not long later. Steve wasn't there yet – it was his punctuality rather than mine that was question-able these days – and the sight of the empty space next to me made a lump rise up in my throat.

Ruth sat opposite me, beady-eyed as ever, but her gaze softened as she observed my expression.

'Would you like me to make you a cup of tea?' she asked.

Tears welled in earnest now; it had been so long since anyone had made me a cup of tea unless I'd paid them for the privilege. As the long afternoons stretched out, with no professional obligations to keep me busy, I'd been reduced to going to the horrible chain coffee shop opposite Camden Town and nursing a cardboard cup of the stuff just to glean some kind of human contact.

'The question seems to upset you, Sasha?'

'It's just . . .' I looked down at the water glass she always left on the occasional table at the end of the sofa. 'You've never offered before.'

She smiled briskly, standing up. 'There's a first time for everything, isn't there?' She looked down at me. 'And besides, there were plenty of times I'm sure you wouldn't have accepted.'

I was halfway through the mug when Steve finally arrived.

'Sorry,' he said unapologetically, sitting down without making any real eye contact.

The session set off on its predictable path: me throwing out my familiar whiny apologies, him reminding me that he thought he'd been betrayed in the most hurtful way possible by his first wife, only for me to figure out a way to stick a knife even deeper into his heart. On and on it went, until Ruth held up her palm, lollipop-lady-style, to call a halt.

'I think we can all agree we've been here before,' she said.

Steve looked at her, his eyes like stagnant ponds, and nodded. 'Maybe we should admit defeat.'

Panic rose up inside me. 'Defeat? We can't stop. We need to – to make decisions. Plan for the baby, and . . .'

Steve finally turned towards me properly. 'But we're not doing that. We're just having the same argument again and again, at great expense.' He turned back to Ruth, embarrassed. 'Sorry, Ruth, I hope you know that I think you're best in class.'

My heart mashed tight inside my chest as I watched his profile. That unfailing politeness of his almost broke me; in a nuclear apocalypse, he'd be the one holding the door of the bunker open for everyone else.

'Please don't do this,' I said, my voice tiny.

'I think we have to,' he said, almost as quietly.

Then all three of us sat there, frozen in our own individual moments, until words began streaming out of me like a gush of water.

'I get it – you don't want to sit here listening to excuses and apologies from me anymore – they're an insult to you. But my sorry *has* changed. It's not me trying to . . . to stick a plaster on a knife wound anymore.' Steve was watching me now, waiting to see where I would go with this. 'What you said to me when I left . . .' My breath caught in my throat, the trauma of that day still too raw to fully revisit. 'About me selling you fatherhood like you're a client, manipulating you – it's not just you, I've sold *myself* a version of reality my whole life. And it's taken me being on my own with no fucking distractions beyond my own screw-ups to see it.'

'What does that even mean, Sasha?' he asked, and I forced myself to keep talking, even though I was still desperately groping for the right words.

'My family never looked like other families. It wasn't just that my dad wasn't there, it was that where he'd gone was too sad and too shaming to tell anyone.'

'But why would you be ashamed of his – of his suicide?' asked Steve.

'I didn't know for a long time, but something always felt wrong. And then when I did find out – I think it felt like he'd left *me* by . . . by doing that to himself.'

I'd never said this out loud before. I'd never even really said it inside, and I knew why as I did so – the pain of it was almost too excruciating to survive.

'Like I wasn't enough to stay for. And I guess I just wanted to make sure that everything I could force to look perfect, looked perfect. That's exactly what my job's about. What *I've* been about.' I risked reaching a hand across the sofa and sliding it over his. Even now, my sand-coloured manicure was pristine, not a single nail chipped or bitten. 'I haven't told you the truth about so many things . . .'

Steve pulled his hand away, and I tried not to feel stung. 'Like what?'

'Like Fred, the guy on the campaign.' His eyes darkened. 'No, not that. I've never been unfaithful to you. But that man in my twenties – it was him. He didn't move countries away from me, he was never even *with* me really. Same as my dad, not sticking around to be a dad.'

I felt it again, just like I had on my way here: the undeniable connection between those two agonizing relationships.

'I couldn't tell you I'd wasted years of my life on an affair with a man twenty years older than me when your wife had left you for someone else. You'd have hated me.'

Steve slowly shook his head. 'No, I'd have hated *him*. You worked for him, correct? You were incredibly vulnerable.'

I sat with that for a second, wondering what the last fifteen years might have been like if I'd been able to extend the kind of compassion my husband had for me towards myself.

'I just felt like such a screw-up. I wanted to have it all in place, but I couldn't get my life together.'

Ruth spoke now. 'That patterning from our early life is very hard to overcome until we really look at it. It's almost inevitable it repeats – it's no failure on your part. It sounds like you and your mother never found a way to process the tragedy together?'

I shook my head, forced myself to confront the question. 'I don't think she ever processed it for herself. She buried herself in work. I always felt like her students were easier for her to be close to.' I gave a harsh laugh. 'Less of a reminder than I was, maybe.'

'It sounds like you both needed more support,' said Ruth.

I waved a dismissive hand, determined to return to what I was trying to make Steve understand. There was only so much pain around my father's loss that I could digest right then.

I turned towards him, willing him to look at me. 'I want this baby because I want a baby, but it's not the whole story.' I paused, feeling almost unbearably exposed. 'I guess I also couldn't bear to have failed at being a proper adult. And what I did to solve it was unforgivable – I don't blame you for the fact you can't. I did betray you – I have to own that.'

I watched him, to see how me finally admitting it – no excuses or sprinklings of fancy adjectives – would land. Something definitely shifted in the ether between us. I hoped that it was a softening in him, but the truth was that it felt like a hardening too. 'I'm so sorry, Sasha. I never really appreciated how hard losing your father was for you.'

'Neither did I,' I said. 'It's not like I gave you a chance to.'

Sadness crossed his face. 'I just wish we could've been enough for you,' he said. 'Helped it to heal.'

'You were! You are. You all are. I miss the kids so much . . .'

It was true – even Jack's manipulative charm was rose tinted now I didn't get woken up by his curfew-busting door slams anymore. And the loss of Georgie, particularly when I felt such a sense of foreboding about what I'd exposed her to, brought its own particular kind of pain.

'But we weren't enough for you, were we?' he said simply.

A sob dredged itself up from the depths inside me. 'I wish I'd been able to look all of this in the face. But the last thing – *the last thing* – I could risk doing was that. All I could do was keep working, keep trying to force my body to do what it was meant to do, and not look down. It's why I hated coming here so much. And now it's the best thing I do all week, but it's too late.'

I looked at him as I said it, and just for a second both of us laughed at the sheer absurdity of it. He was the one to reach for my hand this time, giving it a brief squeeze.

'You're right, I think it is too late,' he said. 'But I feel like we're going to do okay at parenting her. We can get through this.'

'Steve . . .'

He knew exactly where I was going and he gave the briefest shake of his head, so much more painful than the kind of angry admonishment I'd become used to. It said that we were in the aftermath, that that was where he existed now. Ruth looked between us both, leaning forward purposefully in the way that signalled it was her turn to speak.

'We're actually gone over our slot length now, but I want to congratulate you both on your honesty today. The work you've done here – particularly you, Sasha – is remarkable. You've lost a lot of the external components of your identity recently, but it feels like you've used that stripping down to go deep inside of yourself and own your actions.'

Despite the pastel soft furnishings and ruched blinds, there was nothing pastel about the way Ruth saw the world. She had no problem setting things out in black and white.

I couldn't help myself. 'I still fucking hate what she did to me. It's so unfair—'

Her hand was up again. 'Let's not return to your feelings about your assistant. Whether it's with me or with someone else, I'd encourage you to explore your grief for your father in individual therapy now. If you are going to continue to come as a . . . as a pair—' another knife to the heart – were we no longer even worthy of being called a couple? '—it would prohibit me from seeing you alone.'

'You should take her up on that.' Steve's loving smile as he delivered the news that he really wasn't coming back here almost broke me. 'Carrying on with someone who already knows your story would have a lot of value.'

The goodbye we said at the Tube that day was almost the saddest of the lot. It was lucky he insisted on hailing me a cab – the sight of a pregnant woman weeping as hard as I did all the way home was not one for public consumption.

* * *

I don't think I stopped crying for a full six hours. I started multiple texts to Steve and deleted every single one of them. I changed my searches on Spotify and listened to the kind of sad Nineties ballads that I'd slow danced to at school proms, as if I could somehow slip through the space–time continuum and right all the catastrophic mistakes I'd made in the intervening years. I ordered a katsu curry on Deliveroo and somehow forced myself to eat a few bites to make sure that the baby stayed nourished – it was bad enough I was turning her into a Michael Bolton fan without starving her too.

When the intercom buzzer went off, I assumed it was an error. I gingerly picked up the receiver.

'Hello?'

'Sasha, it's me.'

I held the handset away from my ear. I'd spent so much time alone recently that I'd started to doubt my own perception of reality.

'Georgie?'

'Please let me come up.'

I pushed the intercom button and leaned heavily against the wall in the corridor, waiting for her in nervous anticipation. When she emerged from the lift, I took an instinctive step towards her and then shrank back, embarrassed. To my surprise and delight, she rushed forward and hugged me, even though it was awkward over the bump. I clung on a bit too hard.

'It's so nice to see you,' I said into her pink-streaked hair. 'How did you find me?'

'All right, calm down,' she said, pulling back. 'I looked in Dad's phone.' She looked me up and down, but not unkindly. 'You're . . .'

'Not that long to go now,' I said, smiling apologetically. 'Do you want to come in?'

I saw her looking around the cramped kitchen–diner as she followed me in, trying to control her shock. I crossed to the fridge and pulled out some sparkling water, keen for a distraction. I waggled it at her and she gave a staccato nod.

'I'm going to look for something bigger before the baby comes,' I said. It was pathetic really, my hope embodied by these four close walls. I'd obviously been kidding myself – a speciality of mine – that this was temporary. Today had forced me to start accepting reality. It wasn't just about where I was living; I'd become more and more secretive, shame making me shrink away. Even Maddi and I were barely in touch, and I hadn't been able to bear telling my mum that Steve and I had separated, let alone why.

I handed Georgie a plastic tumbler full of water and she took a slug from it before thumping it down on the coffee table. 'I don't want you to!' she said. She never painted her nails – the couple of occasions when I'd suggested we go for a pedicure had been greeted with scorn – but I noticed today all the tips were purple. It looked cool on her.

'But we're going to need more space . . .'

'I know that!' she snapped. 'I'm not an idiot. I just think you should come home.'

I felt my shoulders slump, willing myself not to cry. I'd betrayed her too – she didn't deserve to be left looking after me. 'It's over, Georgie. Your dad can't forgive me. I don't blame him for it either. But this baby will be your sister, so I'll always be in your life.'

Georgie emitted a kind of low growl. 'But he's fucked! He's been sitting in the kitchen bawling like he's the actual baby ever since he came back from the shrink today.'

'Really?' I hated the upward lilt in my voice, the undeniable gratification. I really was a terrible person.

'He's been in a fucking RAGE for weeks, and now he's a . . .' She flung her arms around in the tiny space. 'A puddle. He's a mess without you. He didn't even ask me where I was going when I left.'

I could hear the hurt in her voice, the sense of abandonment. The butterfly effect of what I'd done fluttered out so far and wide.

'He seemed pretty adamant when we were there today,' I said. 'I think I have to start accepting it now.'

Georgie shook her head with frustration. 'He's so binary! Right is right and wrong is wrong . . . Brush your teeth till the timer goes off and pay your parking ticket the fucking second you get it!'

We spontaneously smiled at each other, each of us revelling in an affectionate kind of frustration. We loved him and we loved each other. We had always been a family; the tragedy was that it had taken shattering into a million pieces for us to see it. I stood up and crossed to the fridge before the sadness could overwhelm me again.

'I'm not saying what you did isn't really shitty, FYI,' she said to my retreating back. 'I'm still angry with you.'

I stood by the open door, thinking through my next move. I had to try, didn't I?

I crossed back to the tiny sofa and sat down, looking directly at her. 'It *was* completely shitty, you're right. But I tell you what else was completely shitty: me introducing you to Jenna.'

Georgie broke the silence after a tense few seconds. 'What do you mean?' she said, the words strangulated and unnatural.

'Come on, Georgie,' I said. 'I'm not an idiot either. Everyone thinks I'm paranoid, but I know she's the reason I lost my job, and I think she burned you too.'

Georgie's shoulders caved, a crimson blush creeping up her cheeks. It was shame that was overwhelming her, an unwarranted shame that made my murderous feelings towards Jenna surge and pulse.

'You didn't do anything wrong!' I told her. 'She's poisonous. She gets under your skin. She completely fooled me, and I'm nearly three times your age.'

'She doesn't even speak to me now,' Georgie muttered.

'What do you mean?'

She looked up, hurt blazing in her eyes. 'She's blocked me. Phone, WhatsApp, Instagram. I . . . She never gave a shit about me, did she?'

Fury – maternal fury – surged even more fiercely through me. It was only now that I saw how much Georgie's wounding mirrored my own, each of us believing we weren't good enough for a ghostly apparition of a parent. And I knew from the trail of destruction I'd just wrought how dangerous that was.

I covered her hand with my own, feeling the warmth of her skin. 'I don't think she gives a shit about anyone, Georgie. It's not about you. And I don't blame you at all for what you did. She told you the most heinous lies – she didn't think I was cheating with Fred for starters.'

Georgie looked at me balefully, not yet ready to speak.

'Did you have her round to the house when we were away?'

She gave a slow nod. 'I'm such a fucking moron,' she said, her free palm pounding on her forehead. 'She must've been laughing at me the whole time.'

'You and me both,' I said, thoughts racing. 'So, it was her, wasn't it? She went into my bathroom, found the drugs and worked out I was doing the fertility treatment.'

A shudder convulsed me, the true horror of it working its way through my body. She'd not just been in my home, she'd been in my bedroom. Where else had she been? A few months ago, I'd had some kind of fault with my personal emails, a handful of messages mysteriously marked as read. I feared the mystery was solved.

'Why did she hate me so much?' I demanded, fingernails biting into my own flesh as my fists balled up tight. 'I made her work late a few times, I got her to buy my coffee ...'

Georgie was too upset to engage with that, her body leaning into mine. 'I'm sorry I let her in. She's like a vampire. I've been such a bitch to you ... Maybe you and Dad wouldn't have even—'

I flung my arms around her, stroking her hair. 'It's not your fault. If anything, it's my fault for letting her anywhere near you. I'm so sorry.'

'I wasn't even going to do it . . .' she started, proceeding to tell me how she'd tried to pull out of the Maple protest, only to be told I'd got myself pregnant by Fred behind Steve's back and that this was her only way of avenging her dad.

I staggered to my feet, the fury almost impossible to contain by now. It was bad enough what Jenna had done to me, but she knew full well how vulnerable Georgie was. A string of curses exploded out of my mouth, my fists balled up like I was ready for a fight. The truth was, I was ready for a fight.

Georgie pawed at my leg. 'Sasha, calm down. Think about the baby!'

I looked down at her, my eyes blazing. 'You're my baby too,' I said. She wrinkled up her face in mock disgust, but I could see she liked it. 'Actually, did she say anything about *her* mum?'

'One time. She told me that she died of cancer.' Georgie paused. 'I feel like it was true. She actually cried.'

Was it true? I thought about Jenna's haunted expression when I'd told her that I'd spoken to her mum. It was more than just semantics around what that woman called herself; there was something there that Jenna was desperate to keep hidden.

I shook my head. 'I'm not going to let her get away with this.'

'What are you going to do?' asked Georgie nervously.

The words surprised me. 'I'm going round there.'

'To Bright? But you're not allowed.'

'Nope. To her house. I sent her flowers for her birthday,' I said, smiling grimly at the irony. 'I've got her address. I need to make her tell me why she did this to us.'

Georgie was looking increasingly stressed. 'Sasha, you're not being serious. You can't go round to her house!'

It was bad really, the way my brain could so easily handle

two simultaneous agendas. I dropped myself back down onto the sofa, pretending her wisdom had dissuaded me, and devoted another half hour to finding out anything and everything Jenna had confided about herself to Georgie. The information was predictably scant and neither of us could find her on Instagram, giving me the chilling thought that the account I'd combed through after our first meeting had been created especially for me.

It was a school night, and Georgie needed to get home. I called her a black cab, not an Uber, then hugged her tight on the threshold of my soulless temporary home, swearing blind that I wouldn't do anything stupid.

And I wouldn't. Stupid was far too mild a word for my next move.

JENNA

Thursday nights were often even busier than weekends at the Falcon, gangs of office workers blowing off steam or stressed-out North London parents grabbing a weekday date night in the restaurant.

'What are you having?' asked Sanjay, eyeing the busy bar as they pushed open the heavy doors. It was lucky he was volunteering to go up there – for now, Jenna needed the cover. 'I'm buying.'

'That's so nice of you!' she said. Asking for a lime and soda would make her suggestion they all go out for a celebratory drink seem shady. 'Um, gin and tonic?' It'd be a cool six quid, but Sanjay, like so many of Penelope's kin, seemed to have an endless waterfall of cash.

'You've got it.' He turned to the rest of the housemates, taking their orders. 'What you having, girls?'

Soon they were tucked away at a corner table, drinks in hand. The rest of them had a standing Thursday night date, but Jenna had rarely tagged along when Penelope had grudgingly invited her. This week was different. She had a plan.

'To Jenna!' said Penelope, raising her margarita glass in the air. Jenna snuck a look at a harassed Neil, who was battling his way through multiple orders behind the bar. Cocktails were one of the many things that made him prone to toddler-style meltdowns. 'Congrats on making it up another rung on the corporate ladder.'

'It's a creative job,' Jenna quickly reminded her. She knocked her glass against Claudia's, hearing the dull ping it made as the lawyer gave her a 'congratulatory smile' that barely qualified as such. 'It's not, like, *corporate* corporate.'

Penelope flashed her a tight grin. 'True, but you *do* go to an office every day,' she said, as if Jenna was stuck inside a maximum-security prison for murder. 'I'm just being silly. It's brilliant! And they're giving you a proper pay rise too.'

'Yeah, well bloody done,' said Sanjay, sincerity leaking from every pore. He was the one bright spot in Penelope's awful gang.

'I'm never going to make any money,' said Laura, taking a gloomy slurp of her white wine. 'Teaching pays fuck all.'

'Yeah, but the founders want their pound of flesh,' said Jenna, taking another sip of her gin and tonic. The problem with not drinking was that when she did, it went straight to her head. 'I'm virtually running this whole Maple campaign. It's worth millions of pounds to the business.'

'What happened to your boss?' asked Penelope. 'Do you just not have one anymore? I thought you really liked her.'

A cold sliver of unease ran down Jenna's back, her eyes darting around the pub. Sasha would be heavily pregnant by now, a midweek night out surely bottom of her agenda. Still, she sometimes felt as if she could feel her boss's icy gaze bouncing between her shoulder blades.

'She's gone on maternity leave,' she said. 'And 'cos we were so close, she backed me to step into her shoes.'

Not her *shoes* perhaps, but Jenna was wearing Sasha's silky trapeze shirt that night, the way she always did when she needed a shot of courage. She liked the way it rippled against her body, a strange kind of caress.

'Wowzers,' said Penelope, with a doubtful look.

She was right to doubt her. Jenna had been given more responsibility, but she'd also been gifted an annoying male account manager ten years younger than Sasha, whose fragile ego required that he put her back in her box every time he realized she knew far more about the Maple campaign than he did. There were no more jokes about oat milk or sly gossips about Scarlett to be had. Removing Sasha had made Bright less, well, bright, but it was a price that had needed to be paid.

The conversation drifted away from Jenna, moving instead to Penelope's frequent callbacks for jobs she ultimately didn't get – she was just *too much of a star*, according to Laura – and the villa Claudia's family were renting in Provence that summer, which she said they all HAD to come to while carefully avoiding making eye contact with Jenna. That was the moment she knew it was time for her to go and get a round.

As she approached the bar, sliding her way through the throng, Neil's dark, beady eyes began to focus.

His fat baby cheeks went purple at the sight of her. 'What the fuck . . .' he spluttered.

'Two gin and tonics, a Picpoul, a Merlot and a lime and soda, please.' She gestured to her flatmates with an airy little wave. 'I'll probably need a tray to get them over to the table.'

'I've called you ten fucking times. You knew you were rota'd tonight. How dare you waltz in here and—'

Jenna picked up the jug of tap water that stood on the bar, casually pouring herself a glass as Neil's face grew ever more bruise-like in colour. 'Oh yeah, sorry. Forgot to tell you. You can stuff your job, I don't need it anymore. You can shout and scream at some other mug who actually needs the cash. I've got

a real job with a real future. Whereas you – you've just got a
shortcut to liver disease and a shit credit rating.'

Neil was lunging across the bar by now, his face twisted
up with white-hot rage. At least she was spared buying that
round – it would have cost the best part of twenty-five quid by
her calculations. She eyed the door, wondering if she should
try to say goodbye to her flatmates, but decided a wave and
a made-up illness would suffice. After all, she'd be delivering
a speech similar to this one to Penelope as soon as she could
afford to. Plus, with Neil determinedly jostling his way past
the other staff behind the bar to square up to her, there simply
wasn't time.

SASHA

The siren is still wailing, high and insistent, as I shoulder my way into Jenna's kitchen, my racing heart keeping time with it. I need to be fast.

This grubby kitchen looks like it's been left untouched since an Ikea refurb sometime in the Nineties. In fact, this whole house already feels like a tasty morsel lying in wait for some greedy cash buyer to make the kind of offer that'll blast these poor tenants into the furthest reaches of Zone 4.

This isn't a time for reflecting on housing inequality. There's a festering pile of pans in the sink and a heap of post on the kitchen table – I flick quickly through the letters, scanning for anything addressed to Jenna. There's one envelope which I stuff into my coat pocket, justifying it as an analogue revenge for her hacking my personal emails.

The amount of other names on the mail makes me realize how many people must be stuffed into this house – it may not be easy to work out which room is hers. I rush down the narrow, dark hallway, a bunch of coats discarded over the banister, and heave my way up the long flight of stairs. Once I'm on the landing, I momentarily freeze. I'm basically a burglar. Me and my unborn child could face a night in a jail cell, a police conviction that will end my chances of ever getting another job. But I can't stop now.

I turn on the light, a bare bulb that hangs from the ceiling, and push open the door at the front of the house. I use the torch on my phone to take a look, surprised by how light and airy it is. The high ceiling has an elegant light fitting hanging down, and the king-sized bed is covered in so many pillows that I could almost sink into it and imagine all of this is a fever dream. But then I see the stylish khaki boiler suit hanging off the wardrobe door, the chunky leather boots that are lined up under the dressing table. None of this feels like Jenna. And in my guilt-tinged heart of hearts, I know that with the pathetic salary that we started her on at Bright she wouldn't have been remotely able to afford what's almost certainly the master bedroom. I scuttle my way into a couple more rooms, far smaller. One smells strongly of an acrid aftershave and one has a barrister's wig lying on a mannequin's head as if I've accidentally stumbled into a horror film.

The fourth door's the charm. Maybe charm is the wrong word – I can see a pair of my own Frame jeans neatly folded in two and draped over the back of a flimsy fold-up chair, leaving me blinded with rage. I snap on the main light – the risk seems worth taking, as the room's at the back of the house looking over the railway line – and obsessively scan the space. Jenna's bed is nothing like the pillow-laden haven across the hall: it's a sliver of a mattress, pushed tight against the wall. The floor space is nothing, a hanging rail running down the opposite wall and a small trestle table pushed under the window, perfectly placed to sit at and watch the noisy progress of the trains.

My breath is tight in my throat by now, my lower back aching with all of the effort it's taken to get to this point. I allow myself to sink down onto the bed, feeling how it sags its way down towards the floor. It's not just the extra weight I'm carrying; it feels like this mattress has been in service for years.

It's been a damp, cold spring and I automatically pull my thick coat tighter around me – the deep chill of this house tells me it hasn't been heated for days.

It's frustrating how all these little details catch on me, the guilt that began downstairs continuing to bloom. Bedroom's almost too flattering a word for this rabbit hutch that I'm sitting in. I shared a two-bed with Maddi within a couple of years of graduating, each of us in a room three times the size of this.

I can't waste more time – I need to galvanize myself with righteous fury and keep moving. First, I rifle through the post that she's tidily piled up on the table, with that quiet organization of hers that I came to rely on so much. There's nothing to find – just student loan bills for sums that will take years to pay off, and electricity bills in someone called Penelope's name covered in Jenna's scribbled calculations. There are a couple of plastic box files stacked under the table, and I pull out the papers inside. There's nothing useful – her Bright contract, old payslips from jobs in Stoke and bundles of receipts.

I'm hit by a wave of exhaustion now. I sink down onto the floor, not wanting to risk the chair, and lean my back against the bed. This is truly pathetic – what did I expect to find? How have I got myself to the point where I'm sitting on the musty carpet of a twenty-something's bedroom acting like I'm in the FBI? It's time to admit defeat on so many fronts – concentrate instead on making the best life possible for the poor soul who is currently urging me to get the hell out of here with a few well-placed kicks to the kidneys.

But just as I'm shifting my body around to heave myself up, I spot another box file. This one's marbled cardboard, and it's pushed deep into the recesses under the bed. I wriggle until my ungainly body lies flat against the floor so I can pull it out, grateful for the fact that Jenna clearly vacuums her carpet with a zeal for cleanliness that's entirely lacking in the rest of her housemates.

This box feels more personal as soon as I open it. There's a couple of handwritten letters in here, which I set aside to come back to. There's her degree certificate from the 'university' that my mum always sneers at. There's her passport, with a picture of a girl who looks more open-faced than the contained creature that I grew to know. There's her birth certificate, which gives me momentary pause. Her mum's surname is different from hers – not wholly surprising – but then her father isn't even named there. Where does 'Hall' come from? I don't have time to think it through – the room is covered in a blizzard of papers by now, and I have to get out of here. There are a few photos at the bottom, including a shot of an excited little Jenna at a kitchen birthday party, a caterpillar cake on the table with a waxy '6' burning down in the centre. I pause in the midst of the chaos I've created, staring at it for a second. It's almost impossible to hate a person when you see their chubby-cheeked younger self, all innocence. It's gross what I'm doing. I need to stop now. But before I do, I flick through the last two photos.

And now I'm frozen in place, my mouth arid and my heart racing. Because I'm not staring into Jenna's eyes anymore. I'm staring into the eyes of my own mother.

JENNA

Jenna swings open the front door and looks up the stairs, immediately noticing the band of light that glows like a promise from under her bedroom door. She should be frightened – she knows for certain that she'd left the room in darkness – but somehow she isn't.

Something indefinable is animating her. Something that stops her from considering the potential danger as she climbs up those creaky wooden stairs and approaches the door.

As she pushes on it, she's almost excited.

SASHA

Shock has shut me down so comprehensively that I don't even hear her until she's framed in the doorway. She steps into the room, standing above the chaos that I've created out of her life, papers strewn across the carpet and the photo still clamped tight between my fingers. What's most chilling is the fact that she doesn't even look especially surprised to find me there. I hold the photo out between my shaking fingers.

'What ... What is this? What are you doing with a picture of my mum?'

She doesn't reply immediately, pulling out the folding chair by the table and perching on it. She looks down at me, my back still leaning against the narrow bed. Every part of my body is aching by now, but the pain is numbed by the adrenaline that courses relentlessly through my veins.

'You should have the chair really, Sasha, shouldn't you? In your condition.'

'I don't care about the fucking furniture,' I spit. 'I knew it – I knew there had to be a reason you did this to me.' My shaking finger stabs at the picture in my hand. 'This must be like, twenty years ago. These are her students.' The freeze is starting to thaw, my mind beginning to work again. 'Is one of them *your* mum?' I stare at the image, at the girl with the heart-shaped face and the watchful dark eyes who used to inspire such hateful jealousy in me. I point at her. 'Was it her – was she the one who called me?'

Jenna's expression finally shifts, fury flashing across her features. I feel myself drawing back, the truth starting to come into focus. That flash in her dark eyes is like seeing a ghost of a girl I barely recall, but who is simultaneously burnt into the recesses of my memory. Beth was her name.

'It was her, wasn't it?' I say, hearing the quake in my voice. 'She's your mum, isn't she? You told me she was dead.'

'No, it fucking wasn't her,' she shouts, pain mangling her features in a way that tells me she's finally abandoned her manipulation. 'My mum *is* dead!'

My daughter is shifting inside me now, almost as if she can sense the emotional brutality taking place outside of the safety of my body. Although, are either of us really safe? I awkwardly struggle to my feet, shoving the photo towards Jenna as I do so.

'That's her though, isn't it? Beth.' I lean against the wall, furious and exhausted all at once. 'Just stop lying to me, okay? You did it. You won. At least you can do me the courtesy of telling me why.' I pause. 'I cared about you, Jenna.'

Something shrivels and diminishes in Jenna now. Her head drops downwards, her dark hair curtaining her face. Her voice is low when she finally speaks. 'She's my mum AND she's dead. Though she never got the chance to actually be my mum.' Her head snaps upwards, her face a picture of rage again. 'Thanks to *your* mum.'

'What are you talking about?'

'Your mum persuaded her not to keep me,' she says, eyes glistening with fury and hurt. 'She thought your mum was the fucking queen of Sheba, so when she was pregnant she asked her what to do. Your mum told her she was too fucking smart to just be *a mum*, so she gave me away.'

I take a gulp of air, putting out a hand to try to get Jenna to slow down and give me a minute to process what she's saying. I can only find quick flash cuts in my memory: Beth ensconced at our kitchen table with a steaming mug of tea, my mum waspishly sending me upstairs because they were 'talking'. For a while, it seemed like every weekend she'd appear on the doorstep, ushered in by my mum like it was a royal visit. And then, I can dimly remember a time when she stayed with us for a few days on the futon in the living room, me grumpily walking past her sleeping form as I left for school. Mum stubbornly refused to tell me why she'd washed up with us, insisting it was 'private'.

'Hang on – so you're saying my mum persuaded her to, what, to have you adopted?'

'Yes,' says Jenna, the story starting to erupt out of her now. 'She could've got rid of me, but she wanted to go through with the pregnancy. Then when she tells your mum about it, she starts persuading her to give me away.'

'You don't know that, Jenna, you weren't there . . .'

'Yes, I fucking do!' she screams. 'I've got her diaries! Your mum got in her ear, helped her talk to social services. Pick a hospital where I could be taken away after I was born.'

'I'm sorry, Jenna, but Beth can't have been sure. You can't possibly blame my mum. She cared about her. She would've been trying to help her think it through.'

My brain is frantically trying to compute what she's telling me, to hold it up to the light. There's no way this is my mum's fault, but I do know how overinvested she was in those students. I can imagine her stepping way over the line in a misguided attempt to take care of Beth. As I sit here, stranded like a beached whale in my one-time assistant's bedroom, it's hard not to cringe at the parallel. Said assistant isn't remotely listening to my pleas for reason; instead, her face is a mask of rage as she rants at me.

'So, then I get stuck with some family who have fuck-all money, fuck-all prospects. And then – ta da – they have two kids of their own, after years of trying, like I'm some kind of lucky charm.' She gives an angry shrug – lucky is clearly the last thing she feels. 'And then my dad – don't even want to call him that – gives even less of a shit about me. He left ages ago now, only bothers seeing my brothers. And my mum kept fostering kids, like she was Mother Teresa. It was fucking chaos.'

I look around us, taking in the sterile simplicity of her room, summarily trashed by my frantic investigation. She was like this the whole time she worked for me, methodical and diligent to the nth degree. I thought it worked in my favour, even though it was actually the absolute opposite – she took my life apart with that exact same superpower. The rage that was so strong that it fuelled me undertaking this whole mad enterprise is starting to crackle and spit again.

'I'm sorry my mum got involved. But it's not her fault and it's sure as hell not *my* fault that *your* mum made the decision to have you adopted. You've destroyed my life.' I splay a hand over my belly. 'Not just mine, you've destroyed her life, Georgie's life, my marriage. What the fuck is wrong with you, Jenna?' I shake my head in disbelief. 'It doesn't even make sense – why not go after my mum if you blame her so much?'

She throws me a nasty smile. 'If I'd got her fired, it'd just be an early retirement. But this – what stupid fucking phrase would you use, Sasha? It's a more of a . . .' She looks at me with total contempt. 'A *fleshed out narrative*. She hurt my mum. I hurt her daughter. An eye for a fucking eye.'

'You're a twisted little bitch,' I snarl, even though insulting her when I'm trapped in her space isn't the smartest move.

'And anyway, it's not *my* fault your husband threw you out,' she says. 'Your lies did that, didn't they? But it's nice to have me to blame, I bet. You love doing that – Georgie's the problem, Scarlett's the problem, *Fred's* the problem. Hate to break it to you, but you're no saint yourself, Sasha.'

It's lucky that I'm protecting a life inside this ungainly body of mine; if I wasn't, I'd be tempted to spring across the room and maul her. Her accusation has skewered me in a way that only something with a painful shard of truth can ever do.

'Are you an actual psychopath, Jenna?' I'm screaming at her by now. 'I gave you a job over people with ten times the CV you had! I spent two years picking up dry cleaning and dog shit before Martin and Bridget gave me the time of day, whereas you – I let you make creative suggestions from day one, and never once told you when they were naive.' I gesture angrily at the Frame jeans. 'I gave you the clothes off my back so you'd stop looking like you'd come up on the fucking Megabus for a day trip and get taken seriously. I was about to promote you. I was—'

Jenna's face twists into a sneer. 'Yeah, Sasha, you're so kind. So generous, with your jeans and your wine and your fucking lattes.' She picks the jeans up off the back of her chair with the tips of her fingers – still manicured, I notice – like they stink. 'None of it cost you anything. I was breaking my back for you, and you were throwing me crumbs so YOU could feel like a great boss. A great person. It'd be hilarious if it wasn't so shitty.'

That blow lands too – I was wrong about a lot of things, but I wasn't wrong about her being smart. I hate the whiny vulnerability I can hear in my tone when I hit back.

'I took you out for drinks because I wanted to know who you were. Because I *liked* you. And the whole time you're twisting everything to HR behind my back, trying to make sure me and my daughter end up on the streets!' Angry tears start pouring down my face, and I try to scrub them away with my sleeve. 'That's without even starting on what you did to Georgie – you know how vulnerable she is. Whatever you're blaming my mum for, it doesn't remotely justify what you did to us.'

Infuriatingly, Jenna's veneer of calm doesn't slip. 'People like you don't end up on the streets.' Her tone is molten scorn. 'People like *me* do. People working two jobs just to make rent on a shithole, knowing it'll never change. Oh yeah, the Falcon's where I go to work, not drink Rioja, unless I'm stuck listening to you whinging on till midnight about whether you're going to get cancelled.' She barks out a mirthless laugh. 'Forgot, that whole joy is over now.'

I feel myself swaying on my swollen feet, even though I'm leaning against a narrow strip of wall. I'm consumed with hatred, then sideswiped by a certain complicity that I can't yet deal with.

'I'm sorry you had to do that,' I say, keeping my voice deliberately level, like I'm still her boss delivering some useful feedback rather than a crazed intruder who's at her mercy. 'But none of it makes up for what you did to me. Did to my family. You invaded our life and poisoned it.' I look down at her, shaking my head. 'You're like a cancer.'

That's the moment. The one when she unexpectedly crumples at a blow from me, a sadness so deep you could drown in it washing across her face.

'Is that what she died of?' I ask.

'Yeah.'

Now I'm hit by my own wave of sadness, that must be

nowhere near as deep as hers, but still sweeps me off my feet. How can that girl – elfin-faced, watchful eyes roving Mum's kitchen from under a messy head of curls – be gone? I manoeuvre a couple of steps and perch on Jenna's bed, wondering if she'll snarl at me for the presumption. She stays quiet, the air in the tiny room thick with a murky kind of grief.

'When did it happen?'

Her face whips towards me, rage animating it again. 'Seven years.'

And yet it's still so raw. So dangerous.

'I'm sorry, Jenna.'

'No one fucking told me though, did they?' she spits. 'My mum,' she puts the words in angry quotation marks, 'gets a letter from my ACTUAL mum and decides it would be too upsetting to tell me. That she might be lying about having months to live because she hadn't written for years.' She's pure fury now. 'Because people do that, you know, just casually make up terminal cancer. So, when I finally decide to go looking for her a couple of years ago, it's too fucking late. She's in the ground.'

My own anger takes a sidestep – a polite dance partner – allowing compassion to sweep me up for a turn. 'That's heartbreaking. I can't imagine how that must've felt to you.'

My compassion doesn't move her – she's still staring at me with naked loathing. 'Yeah, and if your mum hadn't persuaded her to give me up in the first place, told her she was too smart to be living off handouts, I wouldn't have lost her in the first place.'

I reach out an instinctive hand to touch her, then pull it straight back. The depth of her pain is impossible to remain immune from, but to some extent I must.

'She moved to New York,' Jenna continues, 'became a professor. She tried to keep writing to me, but it was too painful.

Probably 'cos my useless fucking adoptive mum didn't ever bother to help me write back to her.'

'How do you even know all this? Where did you get her diary?'

'I tracked down her sister.' She gestures to the photo, lying abandoned on the carpet. 'Got some pictures too.' That cold stare again. 'She's writes a lot about you and your family in them. How lucky you are to have a mum like yours who's *so kind. So wise.* How she might not have had the strength to give me away without her mentor's belief in her.' She clenches and unclenches her hands, the pain needing to go somewhere. 'She nearly changed her mind when she held me, but, you know, she had your mum's voice in her head.'

The fight's drained out of me now, in a way I hope it will eventually drain out of her. There's no sign of that happening yet.

'I'm so sorry, Jenna. I know you might not be able to hear this, but I feel incredibly sad for you right now. She was lovely, your mum. I really liked her, even if I was a bit mean and jealous.'

I don't know why, but for some stupid reason I thought that me reminiscing about her mum might somehow make this all feel like less of a battle between the two of us. Instead it riles her even more.

'Even you fucking knew her,' she snaps. 'She goes on and on in her diary about your mum working on her – *don't give up on your dreams, Beth* – all that shit.' Her stare is pure hatred as she stands up from the chair. 'Your bitch of a mum was the one going round *really* ruining people's lives, not me. I've done nothing to you compared to what she did.'

I suddenly realize that Ruth's got under my skin, taught me more about the contradictory twists of human nature – my own most of all – than I ever used to comprehend. The last thing Jenna can afford to feel is the agonizing hurt of her mother's choice to abandon her. And she's weaponized that avoidance, turned it into rage, making herself as lethal as a suicide bomber in the process.

A shiver of fear runs through me at that realization. How unsafe am I? Are we? I need to get myself out of here, but I suspect it won't be as easy as strolling through the bedroom door that my eyes keep desperately flicking towards.

'But she didn't force your mum to do it,' I say. 'I know you need to tell yourself that, but it's not true.'

I immediately rue my bluntness as I see the flash of fury in her eyes. I try for something more conciliatory, subtly shifting my body towards the doorway.

'Your adoptive mum – she sounded like she really loves you, whatever mistakes she's made. And at least you've finally found Beth's family, some connection to her.'

She steps forward, screaming in my face, and I cower against the wall.

'I haven't *found* anyone. I haven't *got* anyone. I bet my mum wished she'd kept me once she knew she wouldn't even get the chance to see me again before she died. And you, you've got a fucking baby of your own now—'

'Jenna, you need to calm down . . .'

Should I make a break for it? Run at the door and heave myself down the stairs? But what if she chases after me and shoves me in the back, sends both of us tumbling? I curl in over my distended belly, willing this to be over. How could I have been this stupid?

'What the fuck is that?' says Jenna, abruptly breaking off from the foul-mouthed tirade she's returned to.

My panic was so great that I hadn't even heard it, but now

I do. There's banging on the door, Georgie's voice shouting through the letterbox.

'Sasha, we know you're in there! Open the door!'

And then, even sweeter, another familiar voice. 'Please Sasha, we're here to get you. I need to know you're okay.'

3 YEARS LATER

JENNA

Jenna's head is tipped back over the sink, the cold enamel biting into the exposed flesh of her neck.

'Are you okay there?' asks the shampoo girl anxiously. 'Tell me if the water's too hot.'

'You're fine,' says Jenna, vowing to give her a proper tip once this blow-dry's done.

She can feel the short puffs of breath the girl takes while she's working, the nervous pulse of her fingers as she works on her scalp. They're the tiniest tells of someone right at the bottom of the professional pile, fighting for her very survival.

Once she's back in the chair, a man who's all hairspray and attitude going to work on her, she allows herself to unlock her phone. It's an addiction that she tries to fight, but on a day like today, she feels like she's entitled to a hit. A starburst of anticipation explodes within her when she sees it: Georgie's got a new post.

'Just keep your head steady,' says the guy, pulling it away from the screen as he manhandles her cranium.

Jenna feels her face starting to mutate into a scowl, but she forces her lips upwards into a grin instead. 'Sorry, big day at work. I'm way too overexcited!'

His eyes meet hers in the mirror, his own smile more

lascivious than friendly. He'd be hot if it was possible to take a hairdresser with a man bun seriously. 'Nothing wrong with a bit of excitement on a Monday morning, is there?' he quips.

Now their smiles feel like a promise that they won't ever keep but are both enjoying making. Life's like that these days – people are drawn to her in a way they never were before. Sure, they like her stylish little outfits and her perfect nails – two signifiers she's got Sasha to thank for – but it's more than that. It's something indefinable. Perhaps it's that she never lets them close, but also allows them to feel like she might be within touching distance.

'There is not!' she replies, pushing an uptick into her voice, her greedy eyes already rolling downwards to her phone.

It's incredible really, after everything that happened, that Georgie still has an open Instagram account. Jenna – or rather Hetty Morris, an imaginary Classics student at Durham University who's her new alter ego – had high hopes for a new post today. After all, this last weekend had marked Georgie's sister's third birthday.

There it is. Excitement turns into something more jagged as Jenna stares at the picture. *Can't believe it's three years since you came into our lives!* the caption declares, Georgie holding the toddler in her arms, the frame filled by the rest of the family. Sasha looks older, lines starting to pull down the corners of her mouth and her hair cut short, like the glossy mane had become too much maintenance. It's true, as Jenna now knows first-hand, that regular blow-dries require a commitment. The sight of her former boss's fading looks should have been more satisfying than it was, but Sasha seemed to have netted something else in their place – a new kind of beatific peace radiates out of her, even through a screen. And even if she has lost some of her beauty, judging by the way Steve's beaming smile is spread across his face, he doesn't care much. Even Jack looked like he wasn't trying to wriggle away from his stepmum anymore. Jenna's eyes track down the rest of the caption. '*Happy Birthday Molly. We all love you so much. Biggest kisses from your big sister xoxo.*'

Her blood is like scalding water in her veins, the phone now hot in her grasp. Had she actually helped Sasha more than she'd ultimately hurt her? Georgie had been a sullen pain in her stepmother's arse when Jenna's campaign had begun, but putting the two of them under pressure had made them bond. It was Georgie who'd found her that fateful night, a luggage tracker discreetly slipped into Sasha's massive handbag after she'd threatened to hunt Jenna down. Georgie had actually shoved Jenna against the wall before Steve had pulled the two of them apart and told Jenna that they wouldn't take any of it any further if she kept quiet about Sasha's star turn as a fat cat burglar.

'Shut your eyes, I'm going to spray it now,' says Man Bun, a can held aloft in his right hand. 'You're going to look gorgeous for your big day.'

Jenna squeezes her eyes shut, unexpectedly grateful for the momentary darkness.

'What is it you do, anyway?' he says, once the hiss of the aerosol has stopped.

'I'm an account manager,' she replies. 'A *senior* account manager, as of today. At a big branding agency, Bright.'

The darkness had given her a much-needed second to get a hold of herself. These were nothing more than opening rounds in a game that was far from over. A long game. After all, it was only after the dust had settled that she'd really dug deep into how Sasha had managed to get pregnant, when she'd been so dried up that no doctor would treat her. Not even Dr Rindell, though as Jenna had discovered, his clinic didn't limit itself to straight IVF. He was also the go-to guy if you needed another woman's eggs. Was there anything Sasha's family didn't think they could take from someone else?

'What's a branding agency?' asks Man Bun gormlessly, as if she'd just said she was an ornithologist.

Jenna takes a beat before she replies, staring down at Molly's photo. She can see a ghost of Georgie's face in the set of her features, but maybe that's because the squirming little girl is about to cry; Jenna had endured enough whinging from her 'big sister' back then to know that look all too well. It's more than that, though. As the family huddle around their prize, there's no sign of Sasha's features in the toddler's dark brown eyes and sharp little chin. She's everywhere else in that photo apart from within her mum.

Slipping out of her reverie, Jenna points at the slim, gold canister of Elnett, with its retro line drawing of a woman sketched on the side. 'You don't know it, but you chose that hairspray because someone told you it was cool. Classic.' She cocks her head, looks into the hairdresser's eyes reflected in the mirror. 'My job is to know how to make you feel whatever it is I want you to feel.'

The faces of Molly's ramshackle family all looked more joyful than Sasha did – that told Jenna something too. She was an expert on egg donation now. Ethical protocol demanded transparency, but she couldn't help wondering if Sasha and Steve had ever got around to dropping the bomb about where their 'miracle baby' had come from to her siblings. After all, Sasha was almost as good a liar as Jenna was, and she'd always had her hapless husband's balls in a bag. If the older kids didn't know, how long would they delay telling poor old Molly?

Man Bun was so stupid that he thought that what she'd just

said to him was sexy. 'I'd love you to make me feel something,' he mutters, leaning so close to her ear that she can smell his Colgate breath.

Jenna scoops up her big handbag from the floor, drops her phone inside it. Someone will need to tell Molly the whole truth. Someone she might meet one day and get unexpectedly close to. A person who knows what a lying bitch her mother is. It'll be a while before the chance presents itself, but it will come – she'll make sure of it. After all, motherless girls need to stick together.

'I'll bear it in mind,' she says to Man Bun, although she's long since decided he's far too dumb to be fuckable.

Then Jenna taps her card effortlessly on the reader, paying the forty-pound fee. Perfect hair, cheap at the price. It's hard not to wonder if the consistent pay rises and promotions she's received are thanks to the fact that Martin and Bridget know that *she* knows where the bodies are buried, but who's complaining? She palms a fiver to the shampoo girl, knowing cash is always preferable when you have none, and swishes out of the door and onto the sunny London pavement.

She belongs here as much as anyone now.

Acknowledgements

Thanks are due as always to my unflappable, unstoppable agent Eugenie Furniss, who is always wise but also always a hoot. What more could an author ask for? Thanks also to Emily MacDonald for her unstinting support – we're all so happy to have you back.

Thanks to the team at Simon & Schuster – Clare Hey, Katherine Armstrong and, newest on the block, Georgie Leighton. I appreciate your painstaking editing through a heap of drafts. Thank you too to the whole publicity and marketing team, and in particular to Sabah Khan and Hannah Paget.

Thanks also to my film and TV agent Lucinda Prain, who is fierce in all the right ways. And massive thanks to Polly Williams and Stephanie Aspin who are working to make all of those shenanigans more than just an aspiration. It's been a joy.

Huge thanks to Mim Brent for juggling her towering script pile with my overheated manuscript – your notes were invaluable, as they are on everything you read. You remain my brain! Thanks to Naomi for multiple reads too. I promise I don't just love you for your level of *Strictly* nerdery! Huge thanks to Emma Booty for letting me bribe her with croissants to elicit her branding expertise. Apologies for the inevitable poetic license. And thanks to Kingsley, my favourite octopus.

With eternal love and respect to my Parliament of Owls –
I couldn't do it without you. Anne, Kate, Soph, Kay. And
Alison – a late addition, but an excellent one. We'll always
have Sicily . . .

Thanks to the sub-parliament who keep me intact enough
to keep juggling it all – Cabby, Bee and Foxey. Thanks also to
everyone at 42 who tolerated my grumbles as I multi-tasked,
particularly Rory. Thanks too to Ciara – I promise this isn't
personal!